PRASIE FOR HILARY  S

'Epic'   *Sunday Express*

'An unforgettable saga of love and loss in wartime'
                                          Good Book Guide

'Compelling'   *Publishing News*

'A delightful and heady mix of romantic ingredients
– spies, high-kicking dancers, forbidden love and
friendship in the face of death. Who could ask for
anything more?'   *Lancashire Evening Post*

'Leaves you holding your breath for the next instalment'
                                  Historical Novel Society

ALSO BY HILARY GREEN

We'll Meet Again
Never Say Goodbye

The Follies Series
Now is the Hour
They Also Serve
Theatre of War
The Final Act

ABOUT THE AUTHOR

Hilary Green is a trained actress and spent many years teaching drama and running a youth theatre company. She has also written scripts for BBC Radio and won the Kythira short story prize. Hilary is now a full-time writer.

HILARY GREEN

THEATRE OF WAR

HODDER

An Hachette Livre UK company

5

Copyright © Hilary Green 2008

The right of Hilary Green to be identified as the Author
of the Work has been asserted by her in accordance
with the Copyright, Designs and Patents Act 1988.

A Hodder Paperback

A CIP catalogue record for this title is available from the British Library

ISBN 978 0 340 93265 0

Typeset in Plantin Light by Hewer Text UK Ltd, Edinburgh
Printed and bound by Clays Ltd, St Ives plc

Hodder & Stoughton policy is to use papers that are natural,
renewable and recyclable products and made from wood grown in
sustainable forests. The logging and manufacturing processes are expected
to conform to the environmental regulations of the country of origin.

Hodder & Stoughton Ltd
338 Euston Road
London NW1 3BH

www.hodder.co.uk

This book is dedicated to the memory of the gallant men and women of the 'O'Leary Line', who risked their lives to send escaped POWs and downed airmen back to continue the fight against the Nazis, and to the Italian partisans, whose activities in harrying the enemy contributed in no small measure to the ultimate victory.

As always I am grateful for the help and encouragement of Vivien Green, my agent, and Alex Bonham, my editor at Hodder. I should also like to express my thanks to Silvano Valiensi, an ex-partisan who was kind enough to give up his time to make sure that my facts were correct and to provide me with many fascinating details. Thanks, also, to my husband David for proofreading.

I

'Manchester! Manchester!' The porter's voice echoed along the crowded platform.

Rose Taylor dragged her suitcase on to the platform and waited for the other four girls to follow. She was glad that they had all managed to get into the same compartment this time. It worried her when they were separated. Violet was such a flirt, always letting herself be picked up by passing soldiers or sailors, and pretty, flaxen-haired Alice lived in a dream and was quite likely to miss her station. And Peggy could be so spiteful when she was in a bad temper, which was most of the time, and took it out on poor, timid May. They were all talented dancers, but so young, none of them over twenty, and Rose was responsible for them. It was a role she had assumed less than a month ago and it was taking some getting used to.

A little farther up the platform she saw the squat figure of Monty Prince, the manager and resident comedian of the ENSA troupe, gathering the male members of the company around him. He bustled towards her through the crowd.

'All right, Rose? Cheer up, girls. Not far to go now. You're all staying with a Mrs Gibson, twenty-five Salford Street. Now, where's Miss F?'

Rose looked around the platform for the company pianist. 'I haven't seen her. She wasn't with us.' The guard blew his whistle and the train gave a series of shuddering snorts and began to move. 'Oh, don't tell me she's dozed off again and missed the stop!'

'There she is!' Violet said.

Rose was relieved to see a portly figure emerge from the ladies' waiting room, carrying in one hand a bulging suitcase and in the other a large cat basket. Miss Finnegan was, in Monty's words, 'a bit of a character'. A lady of indeterminate age, she kept aloof from the rest of the company and refused to allow anyone to use her Christian name. It was the firm belief of the four girls that she did not have one. The only creature to which she showed any attachment was her cat, which rejoiced in the name of Claude de Pussy, because he was, his mistress insisted, a very musical cat. He was a rebarbative animal who rewarded any attempt to stroke him with spitting and scratches.

'Here you are, Miss F,' Monty said. 'You're in the Laurels guest house. It's just down the road from the girls. Now, the rest of us have got digs on the other side of town, as far as I can see from the map, so I suggest we all have a quiet evening in and meet up again tomorrow morning. The first show's at Cox Brothers' factory, out on the Oldham road. Here you are, Rose. I've marked it on the map for you. We'll meet up there at eleven o'clock. OK? Now, get a good rest, all of you. We've got a pretty demanding schedule for the next week. See you in the morning.'

Rose picked up her case. 'Come on, girls. Let's see if we can find a taxi.'

There were no taxis, but they managed to find a bus going in the right direction. Rose gazed out of the window with an odd tremor in her stomach. Manchester was where Richard had gone to school. Didsbury, where his parents lived, was somewhere near here. Did he ever come to this part of town? Suppose she were to see him, walking along the street . . . She pulled herself together. That was a stupid train of thought. For one thing, Richard was away somewhere with his regiment. She had no idea where, but the chances of his being home on leave were so remote as to be not worth considering. And anyway, that was all over. She had seen him once in the past two and a half years, on that terrible New Year's Eve on the cusp between 1940 and 1941, and then only for a few minutes. It was all in the past and she must put it out of her mind.

She forced herself to concentrate on the passing scene. It was a depressing outlook. All the buildings were blackened with soot and there was a smell of smoke in the air. A cold rain was falling and the winter evening was drawing in. With no street lamps and every window close-curtained to prevent the escape of the slightest gleam of light, the whole area was shrouded in gloom. Rose found herself thinking nostalgically of the little village down in Dorset, where her mother and her sister Bet had taken refuge from the London Blitz. The blackout was as strictly enforced there as here but somehow it never seemed as dark as this. Never mind, she told herself, you'll feel better once you get a hot cup of tea inside you.

By the time the bus dropped them at the end of Salford Street night had fallen and the darkness was complete. Fortunately, in these times of blackout, it was second nature to carry a torch. Rose produced hers, holding it so that only a thin pencil of light escaped between her fingers, and they began to search along the pavement. It was a street of narrow terraced houses and few of them had numbers that were readily visible, and they had to stumble up several garden paths before they eventually found number 25.

The door was opened by a small woman with a belligerent expression. When Rose explained who they were her response was a sniff.

'Oh, you're here, then. You'd better come in, I suppose.'

They followed her up a narrow flight of stairs to a landing.

She opened a door. 'Two of you in here. Two more across the passage and one in the boxroom at the end. Bathroom's there and the lavvy's in the back yard.'

Rose looked around her. There seemed to be only the three rooms. 'Where do you sleep, Mrs Gibson?' she asked.

'Downstairs, these days. Nearer to the shelter if the Jerries start bombing again.'

Violet and Alice carried their cases into the room and Peggy marched into the one opposite, followed by a reluctant May. That left Rose with the boxroom, which suited her fine. They deposited their cases and returned expectantly to the landing, where Mrs Gibson was waiting, arms akimbo.

'Right. Let's get a few things straight. When the man from the council came and told me I'd have people billeted on me I didn't expect to have to take in *theatricals*.' She uttered the last word as if it left a bad taste in her mouth. 'So these are my conditions. Everyone in bed by ten, no noisy parties and absolutely no gentlemen callers. Understood?'

For a moment all five girls were too taken aback to reply. Then Rose saw that Peggy was about to go into the attack and interposed quickly.

'I don't think you've quite understood the situation, Mrs Gibson.' She indicated the badge on her uniform jacket. 'We belong to ENSA. We're here to entertain the workers in the factories. We'll be doing shows for the day shift and the night shift, so we very often won't be able to get back until well after ten. But I promise you we'll come in as quietly as we can. And as for parties and the rest of it, I think we shall all be much too tired for that. We're doing war work like everyone else, and we have to go where we're sent. I'm sorry if you find that an inconvenience.' She saw that she had taken the wind out of the little woman's sails and added, with her most charming smile, 'We'll try not to be a nuisance – and it's only for a week. Now, do you think we could possibly have a cup of tea?'

Mrs Gibson glowered at her for a moment, then turned to the stairs. 'No smoking in the bedrooms! And I'll need your ration books.' And then, when she was halfway down, 'Tea'll be five minutes.'

Peggy put out her tongue at the departing back. 'Miserable old cow!' she muttered under her breath.

'You told her where to get off, Rose,' Violet said. 'Well done!'

May sighed. 'I wonder what we'll get to eat. I'm starving!'

Rose forced a grin. 'Cheer up, kids! I think the old girl's bark is worse than her bite. I've met worse than her, in my time. Now, let's get settled in.'

She went into her room and started to unpack. What she had said was true. She was no stranger to the vagaries of provincial landladies. Some were warm-hearted creatures who took a maternal interest in the welfare of their clients, others were mean spirited and spiteful, providing the minimum of food and comfort and surrounding them with rules and prohibitions. You took the rough with the smooth, and Rose was prepared to do that now.

She went to the bathroom and had a quick wash. She felt chilled and grubby and longed for a soak in a deep, hot bath but the Plimsoll line painted round the tub reminded her that no one should use more than five inches of hot water. She sighed and reflected that at least there was a bath.

To their surprise, there was a good fire burning in the front room and Mrs Gibson brought in home-made scones with the tea. Her manner was still restrained but Rose guessed that she was regretting her earlier aggression and trying to make up for it.

It seemed she was right. The evening meal was as good as anyone could expect under the strict rationing of the day, and by bedtime Mrs Gibson had unbent so far as to ask about the show they were going to put on.

'What's this ENSA stand for, then?' she enquired.

Violet giggled. 'Every Night Something Awful.'

'Now then, Vi,' Rose reproved. 'It stands for Entertainments National Service Association, Mrs Gibson. The idea is to keep up civilian morale.'

'And what do you all do?'

'We're dancers,' Violet said.

'What sort of dancing do you do?'

'Oh, a bit of everything. You know, tap, can-can – even a bit of ballet sometimes.'

'You a dancer too?' She looked at Rose.

'No, not any more. Well, not at the moment. I hurt my ankle so I had to give up for a while. I arrange all the dances.' Rose had no intention of going into detail about her long struggle to get fit again and her disappointment when she failed to land a job. At least she was back in the theatre, even if it was only an ENSA tour. She knew that Monty Prince would never accept anything substandard. This might be just a small show, performed on improvised stages in factory canteens and church halls, but it was going to be as good as they could make it.

'Where are you all from, then?' Mrs Gibson enquired.

'I'm a Scot,' Violet said. 'And May's family live in Pinner. That's just north of London.'

'I'm a real Londoner,' Peggy put in. 'Born and bred in Hackney.'

'And I'm from just outside Liverpool,' Alice added softly.

'What about you, love?' Mrs Gibson looked at Rose.

'Oh, I'm a Londoner, too,' Rose said. 'A cockney from Lambeth.'

'You don't sound like one,' the landlady remarked.

'That's 'cos she's posher than us,' Peggy said.

'Oh, come off it, Peggy!' Rose exclaimed. 'My mum owns a small shoe shop in the Kennington Road. We live above the shop – or we did till we were evacuated. There's nothing posh about that.'

'What about your dad?' Mrs Gibson asked. 'What does he do?'

'He died when I was twelve. He was gassed in the first war and he never really got over it.'

'Oh, I am sorry.' The landlady shook her head in commiseration.

'Well, there are plenty of girls a few years older than me who never knew their dads at all,' Rose said. 'I have to count myself lucky, I suppose.'

'It's true, though, what Mrs Gibson said,' Alice remarked. 'You don't sound much like a cockney.'

'Oh well.' Rose shrugged, embarrassed. 'When you work in the theatre you mix with people from all sorts of backgrounds.' She thought of Felix, with his aristocratic family, and Merry, whose father was a colonel. 'Some of the chaps I worked with before the war were very well spoken. I suppose some of it rubs off.'

When they went upstairs, Mrs Gibson handed each of them a hot-water bottle. As she settled down to sleep Rose reflected that they could have fared a great deal worse. But sleep would not come and, as always when she had nothing else to occupy her mind, her thoughts turned to Richard. Where was he now?

She had written to tell him that she had broken off her
engagement to Matthew and begged him to get in touch,
but there had been only silence. She felt the tears starting and
turned her face into the pillow, willing herself to think of
something else.

When she woke the next morning the memory was still vivid.
She forced her thoughts back to the present. She had, somehow, to rouse four sleepy girls who would have preferred, like
most people in the theatre, to have a long lie-in in the
mornings, and get them to the factory in time to have a
warm-up and a quick rehearsal on an unfamiliar and probably
totally inadequate stage. She drew a long, slow breath and
dragged herself out of bed.

By mid-morning they had met up with the rest of the
company in the vast, echoing, cabbage-smelling canteen of
the factory. Here they began a familiar routine. While Rose
put the girls through a series of warm-up exercises Monty and
the men wrestled with setting up microphones and some
rudimentary lighting and Miss Finnegan ran disdainful fingers
over the keys of an untuned piano. She then slumped on the
piano stool, her old tweed coat, which she wore summer and
winter, wrapped closely around her, and fell asleep. Her
plump white cat slept too, on top of the piano. Rose was
constantly amazed by Miss Finnegan's ability to fall fast asleep
whenever there was a break in rehearsal, but then, on Rose's
'Thank you, Miss Finnegan', she would awake and start
playing from exactly the right point in the music.

They had just had time to run through the dance routines
and for the singers to try out a couple of verses to check the
sound system when the factory hooter sounded and the first
shift started to swarm into the canteen. Once they were all in

the manager announced, 'Ladies and gentlemen, it is our great privilege today to welcome Mr Monty Prince and company to present their show *Lighten Up!*', and they were on. It was not an easy audience to play to. Most of them were far too concerned with eating and catching up on the latest gossip to pay much attention. Monty's opening gags fell flat and vocalist Ronnie Cowley's rendition of 'You Are My Sunshine' was more or less drowned by the clatter of cutlery and the incessant chatter. Rose, waiting offstage with the girls, found herself thinking yet again of Richard and remembering how his powerful yet velvety tones would have filled the space without the need for a microphone.

It was the entrance of the dancers, high-kicking to Cole Porter's 'Anything Goes', which woke the audience up. There were wolf-whistles from the men but Rose noticed that the women in the audience were taking an interest, too. Perhaps it was partly because hunger had been appeased and the most urgent bits of gossip dealt with, but chairs were turned to face the stage, cigarettes were lit and the rest of the show went down very well. The next act was the Wilson brothers, who had a nice line in witty songs to their own piano accompaniment. Monty's second spot produced roars of laughter and then the girls were on again with a tap routine. Finally Ronnie came back to sing 'A Nightingale Sang in Berkeley Square' and they finished with the audience joining in old favourites like 'Pack Up Your Troubles', 'Tipperary' and 'There'll Always Be an England', with the four girls in scanty red, white and blue costumes doing a drum majorette routine. The concluding applause, augmented with whistles and stamping feet, left the cast in no doubt that their efforts had been appreciated.

In the evening the whole thing was repeated for the night shift, and it was obvious from the attitude of the audience that word had gone round that the show was worth watching. The girls arrived back at their digs weary but triumphant, to find flasks of hot cocoa and a plate of biscuits on the table and hot-water bottles in all the beds.

From then on the days settled into a similar routine, the only variation being the venue of each performance. On the Thursday, however, there was a change in the timetable. There was only one performance scheduled, in a local hall that evening for the benefit of voluntary organisations like the WVS, the ARP and the Home Guard. Rose was looking forward to a bit of a lie-in, followed by a chance to go into the centre of town and perhaps do some shopping – if there was anything worth buying, which was rare these days. Her hopes were dashed by a tap on her door and the appearance of a woebegone May.

'Rose, I'm sorry to wake you, but I've got awful toothache. I've hardly slept a wink. It's been getting worse all week. I can't dance like this.'

Rose hauled herself out of bed. 'Poor old you! Right, we'd better see if Mrs Gibson knows a good dentist.'

Their landlady directed them to a dental practice a few streets away, but when they reached it they found the waiting room chock-full of patients. After hours of tramping the streets, with May becoming tearful and Rose's temper stretched to the limits, they ended up, finally, in the dentistry department of the general hospital.

Rose picked up a magazine and flicked through the pages. A second later she felt as if the blood in her veins had ceased to circulate. She was staring at a photograph of a couple, the girl in evening dress, the man in army uniform. The girl was beautiful, with sleek raven-black hair drawn back in a chignon and huge dark eyes, but Rose's gaze was fixed on the man beside her. Tall and broad shouldered, with dark hair a fraction longer than strict army regulations required, well-marked brows and a strong, determined chin, he was a good match for his delicate partner. Underneath the picture the caption read, 'Miss Priscilla Vance, the niece of Sir Lionel and Lady Vance, with her fiancé, Captain Richard Stevens, arriving at the Gala Ball at Covent Garden in aid of the Spitfire Fund'.

May looked at her. 'Is there anything wrong? You look as if someone had walked over your grave.'

Rose caught her breath. 'No, no. I'm just a bit tired. And I recognised someone in the magazine.'

'Oh, really? Let's have a look.'

Rose passed her the picture. 'I used to know that girl. She was in the Follies with me before the war. She thought she could dance but she was hopeless really.' She tried to smile.

May looked at the photograph. 'Looks like she's done all right for herself. He's really dishy!'

Rose kept her eyes down. 'Not bad, I suppose.' So Richard was getting married – and to Priscilla Vance, of all people. How had that come about? But then, why should it surprise her? Priscilla moved in the rarefied atmosphere of the London arts scene. Her uncle was known as a patron of musicians and dancers and was friends with many influential people. And this was the arena to which Richard would inevitably gravitate, with his superb voice and his Italian operatic training. It was only natural that they should be drawn together. After all, she told herself, wasn't this exactly what you always knew would happen? Isn't this why, when he proposed to you, you turned him down?

Rose took a deep breath and swallowed the lump in her throat. It's best all round this way, she told herself. You always knew it had to be like this. Nothing's changed.

A nurse appeared in the doorway. 'May Turnbull?'

May got up quickly. 'That's me. Wish me luck!'

Rose dragged herself back to the present. 'Yes, of course. I hope it's just a filling.'

'Oh, I'll have the beastly thing out and get it over with.' She gave a crooked smile. 'Soon be back to normal.'

Soon be back to normal! The words echoed in Rose's head. That was the answer. Forget about Richard and get on with her life. If only she could have the memory extracted, like a rotten tooth, and be done with it!

2

R ichard Stevens got out of a taxi in front of his aunt's
house in Didsbury, the affluent suburb of Manchester
where he had grown up, and stood for a moment looking at the
building. It was a substantial, double-fronted Victorian house,
built of red brick and half hidden behind an overgrown laurel
hedge. He had known it well since his childhood, but it was
strange to think that it was now the nearest thing to a place he
could call home. The news that his parents' house had been
destroyed by a German bomb had reached him soon after his
return from France, but he had been too numb with shock and
exhaustion to take in the full meaning. He was only grateful
that his mother and father had both been out at the time. His
mother had written to tell him that they had moved in with his
aunt, his father's sister, and would probably remain there for
the duration. It was only now, standing on the pavement
outside, that he felt the sudden pang of loss at the realisation
that his first leave since his return would be spent as a guest
here, instead of at home.

This thought was not the only thing that made him hesitate.
He dreaded the inevitable inquisition into his own activities,
requiring the equally inevitable lies. And beyond that, he had
news to impart that might, or might not, be greeted with
approval. He took off his cap and ran a hand over the wavy
dark hair that no amount of Brylcreem could persuade to lie

flat, put the cap back on, straightened his shoulders inside his greatcoat and marched up to the front door.

His approach had obviously been observed from behind the net curtains because as he reached the front door it was thrown open and his aunt held out her arms to him.

'Richard! Come along in. It's grand to see you. How are you keeping?'

'Not too bad, Auntie Clara.' He had always sensed that his aunt, widowed when he was still a small boy, had a soft spot for him. He kissed her on the cheek. 'How's the rheumatism?'

'Oh, mustn't grumble. Don't like this cold weather but there's other folks in a much worse way.' She ushered him into the hall. 'Come in, come in. Your mother's waiting for you.'

As she spoke the door of the living room opened and his mother appeared. How typical of her, he thought, not to come rushing to the front door to meet him. He looked from her to his aunt. The contrast between them could not have been greater. Aunt Clara was like his father, stockily built and inclined to plumpness. His mother was a good four inches taller, slim and erect as a Greek column. He went to her and put his arms round her, feeling the corseted rigidity of her body. She lifted her face and gave him her cheek to kiss. Ada Stevens did not believe in 'letting yourself go', either physically or emotionally. Nevertheless, he detected the faintest tremor in the hands she laid on his shoulders and there was a hint of moisture in her eyes.

'Welcome home, son. It's good to have you back.'

'I expect you're ready for a cup of tea,' his aunt said. 'I'll tell the girl to make a pot.'

Richard shrugged off his greatcoat and she exclaimed, 'Ooh! Is that an extra pip I see? You've been promoted again! What are you now, a captain?'

'You never let us know,' his mother commented, her tone a mixture of pride and reproof.

'It only came through a week ago,' he replied. 'I was keeping it as a surprise.'

He saw the flicker of pleasure in her eyes and knew what she was thinking. Here was something to tell her friends – not that it did to brag, of course.

'Congratulations, son,' she said sedately. 'I'm sure it's not before time.'

'Hasn't he done well?' his aunt enthused. 'To think, when he joined up he was just a private.'

His mother sniffed. 'Well, that was a mistake, to start with.'

She led the way into the sitting room, where a small fire smouldered in the grate. Richard sat beside her on the horse-hair sofa.

'I was so sorry to hear about the bomb. But thank God neither you nor Dad were at home.'

'Yes,' she agreed, 'we've a lot to be grateful for. I was round at Mrs Murchison's with some other ladies, planning a concert to raise money for the WVS. Your father was doing his stint as an air-raid warden. He was only a few streets away when the bomb dropped and he realised at once it must have come down near our house. He rushed back but there was nothing he could do. It was a direct hit. I'm afraid we weren't able to save anything.'

'It must have been a terrible shock for both of you,' Richard said. He was genuinely concerned, but at the same time guiltily grateful for this absorbing topic of conversation. It delayed, at least, the moment when he must voice the matter that was uppermost in his own mind. 'When did you find out what had happened?'

'Your father came straight round to find me. We'd all taken shelter in the cellar. People were very good, everyone offered to help, to lend things and so on. We had nothing but the clothes we stood up in.'

For the first time the magnitude of the event struck Richard. 'Of course, how terrible!'

'Well, we're lucky. Your aunt offered us a home here for the duration. With your cousin Ben away in the navy there's room for us all.'

His aunt had come in and was poking ineffectually at the fire. 'We're glad to have you. Oh, this stuff won't burn! You can't get decent coal these days. And you, Richard, you must think of this as home, and treat it that way.'

'Thank you.' It crossed his mind to wonder how long the two women, so different in their attitude to life, would be able to get on under the same roof.

His mother said, 'I'm afraid all your things went up in smoke, too, Richard. And there were some letters I was keeping for you – personal letters, by the look of them. They came after you were posted away and I didn't know where to send them, so I thought it best to keep them until you got back. I hope it was nothing important.'

'I don't expect so,' he said. 'Don't worry about my things. As long as you're safe, that's all that matters.' Inwardly, he felt a pang of regret. Who could the letters have been from? He had lost touch with all his old school friends years ago, and he had never corresponded with the men he had served with in the first months of the war. It must be someone from the Follies company – Merry most likely. He regretted losing contact with him but he had probably missed his last chance now. He took a cigarette from his case and flicked on his lighter, but his hand shook so that he had difficulty bringing the flame to bear. He glanced covertly at the two women but to his relief neither of them appeared to have noticed. *Damn!* he thought irritably. *I ought to be over that by now.*

Fran, his aunt's maid-of-all-work, brought the tea and as she poured his aunt said, 'Now then. What about you? What did you think to America?'

Richard stubbed out his half-smoked cigarette. He had been preparing himself for this moment, but he hated the deceit involved. 'It's a fascinating country. But it's all a bit too brash and noisy for my taste.'

His mother nodded approval. 'So I've heard.'

'Where were you most of the time?' his aunt persisted. 'Those postcards you sent home didn't tell us much.'

'New York, mostly. And Washington.'

Victor, his conducting officer at SOE, had provided him with guidebooks to both cities and he had spent his spare moments over the last couple of weeks memorising the most important bits. He regurgitated some of them for his mother and his aunt now.

His mother listened for a while. Then she said, 'I do think you could have written a proper letter from time to time. We've no idea what you've been doing. When people ask me, I don't know what to say.'

Richard sighed apologetically. 'I'm sorry. But it's difficult, you know. So much of what I've been doing is confidential. I just felt that anything I put in a letter would probably be censored. Even telling you exactly where I was could have got me into trouble.'

'It's all very hush-hush, then?' his aunt said. 'What's the name of this outfit you work for again?'

'The Inter-Services Liaison Bureau.' It was the name by which the Special Operations Executive was known to the outside world.

He turned the conversation away from his activities by asking after his cousin, and then various other relations and friends. By then, tea was finished and he was able to slip away upstairs on the pretext of unpacking and changing into civvies. He stayed in his room – or Ben's room, to be accurate – until he heard his father come home from the factory.

Richard had always felt more at ease with his father than with his mother, though intellectually he had more in common with her. Although he owned the factory, Geoffrey Stevens liked to regard himself as an ordinary working man – bluff, straightforward and down to earth. His Lancashire accent was as broad as that of any of his employees and he regarded his wife's pretensions to gentility with amused tolerance. Yet he was a more cultivated man than at first appeared, widely read and passionately fond of music. It was while singing with the local choral society that he had met his wife and from him that Richard had inherited his fine baritone voice. Like Ada, and indeed like most of their acquaintance, he was not given to emotional display, but there was a warmth in his handshake and a depth of affection in his eyes as he greeted Richard that went some way to make up for his mother's cool reception.

Geoffrey had understood, more quickly than his wife, that Richard was not able to discuss his work, so the conversation remained general during dinner, centring mainly on the progress of the war. When they reached the dessert Richard braced himself and launched into the announcement that he had been rehearsing in his mind all day.

'There's something I have to tell you. Something important.'

They looked at him expectantly and his father said, 'Well, go on, lad. Don't keep us in suspense.'

'I'm engaged to be married.'

There was silence, except for a little gasp of delight from his aunt, hastily stifled. Everyone was looking at his mother.

'Married, Richard?' She pronounced the word as if it were some strange, foreign concept. 'Who to?'

'Her name is Priscilla. Priscilla Vance. Her uncle is Sir Lionel Vance. He's quite well known as a patron of the arts.'

He saw the colour come and go in his mother's face. 'Sir Lionel Vance? I know the name. Isn't he a patron of the Hallé orchestra?'

'Yes, I believe he is. He's very involved in the musical world. He's a friend of Malcolm Sargent and also of Ninette de Valois, who runs the Sadler's Wells ballet.'

'And Priscilla is his niece?'

'Also his ward – or she was until her twenty-first birthday. Her father was his younger brother. Priscilla's parents were both killed in a motor accident when she was thirteen.'

'Oh, poor girl!' This involuntary exclamation came from his aunt.

'Yes, it was hard. But Sir Lionel and Lady Vance have been very good to her. They have no children of their own, so they have always treated her like a daughter.'

'They'll be well off, then, I should imagine,' his father said.

'Oh yes. I believe the grandfather founded the family fortune as a merchant in India back in the 1880s. Priscilla's father made a second fortune in the City before he died and left it all in trust to her.'

Richard looked round the table. He saw the conflicting emotions chase each other across his mother's face. On the one hand, here was an obviously advantageous marriage. On the other, her only son was proposing to marry a girl who was not of her choosing, whom she had had no opportunity to vet.

His father gave him a shrewd look. 'Well, son, it sounds as if you've done very well for yourself. But I hope you've got better reasons than money for marrying the lass.'

Richard realised that in his concern to impress his mother he had sounded mercenary. He responded quickly. 'She's also very beautiful and talented, and wonderful company. We're very much in love.'

'Where did you meet her?' his mother asked.

This was tricky ground. 'Well, oddly enough I first met her when I was working in that summer show, just before war broke out. She was one of the dancers.'

'A dancer? On the stage? A girl from that background?' His mother's face expressed extreme scepticism.

Richard ground his teeth. His mother had managed to stifle her prejudice about 'going on the stage' in his case, since he had convinced her that the summer show was only a stepping stone towards his ultimate ambition of grand opera; but dancers were obviously beyond the pale, as he had known they would be.

He gave her a conciliatory smile. 'Yes, I know it's surprising. But you see, Priscilla was taken to the ballet as a small child and conceived a passionate ambition to be a ballerina. Her mother let her go to ballet lessons but her father would never hear of her taking it up professionally. Then, after her parents were killed so tragically, I suppose Sir Lionel and his wife spoilt her a bit – understandably. They let her start training seriously, but it was too late by then. She couldn't get into Sadler's Wells, so she ended up in the Follies, like me.'

'There, what did I tell you?' Aunt Clara was unable to restrain herself any longer. 'Didn't I say to you that summer, Ada, you mark my words, your Richard has found himself a young lady?'

'No!' Richard said quickly. 'No, it wasn't like that.' His aunt's words had brought a face flashing across his mental vision – heart shaped and dominated by a pair of violet-blue eyes and crowned with a drift of dark hair. But it was not Priscilla's face. He closed his mind to the memory. There was no way he was going to introduce Rose into the conversation. Anyway, Rose was safely married to her farmer down in Dorset. There was no point in opening old wounds. 'I didn't really get to know Priscilla then. She didn't stay with the company for long.' With a pang of sympathetic embarrassment he remembered Priscilla's humiliating exit, after a disastrous attempt to dance the role of Odette in an excerpt from *Swan Lake*, in front of a vociferously unappreciative audience. He pressed on. 'We happened to bump into each other again when I was posted to London last spring. She'd joined up, too, in the FANYs. I don't know if you've heard of them? The First Aid Nursing Yeomanry?'

'I know what you mean,' his mother said. 'I understand it's a very exclusive organisation.'

'Well, there are a lot of girls from very good families in it,' Richard agreed. He disliked himself for playing up to his mother's snobbery but it was a small price to pay to win her approval. 'Anyway, we started going out together while I was in London and then we took up again after I got back from . . . from America.'

There was a silence, broken by his father. 'So, when are we going to get to meet this young lady, then?'

'She's coming up the day after tomorrow. She's dying to meet you all.' He caught a look of dismay on his aunt's face and went on quickly, 'I knew you'd be a bit crowded here, Auntie Clara. So I've booked her a room at the George.'

'Oh well, that's probably best,' his aunt agreed. 'But you'll bring her to dinner, I hope.'

'Yes, of course.'

Once again there was a pause and once again all eyes turned to Richard's mother. She inclined her head. 'She sounds just the right sort of girl for you, Richard. I'm sure we'll get on very well.'

Richard sensed that he was not the only person at the table who breathed a sigh of relief.

Richard woke in the pre-dawn winter darkness and reached out for the warm body that usually lay beside him. When his hand encountered nothing but chill vacancy he could not immediately think where he was. Since his return from France Priscilla had shared his bed every night, apart from the first two, which he had spent in hospital. She had cradled and comforted him when he awoke from the nightmares that dogged his sleep, nightmares whose content he had never revealed to her. It was always the same scene. He was struggling along the riverbank in the darkness, searching, searching – and then finding her, half in, half out of the water. He could feel the weight of her sodden clothes as he dragged her on to the bank, see her poor, bleeding feet. Chantal! Chantal! Sometimes he was afraid that he had called her name aloud, but if he had Priscilla had never alluded to it. Now, lying alone in the unfamiliar room at his aunt's house, he felt an aching sense of loss. But whether it was Priscilla he longed for, or Chantal, or Rose, he could not tell.

He had started sleeping with Priscilla during the hiatus between finishing his training and leaving on his mission, and when he returned she had assumed that they would take up their relationship where they had left off. He had clung to her as a rock of sanity in the midst of the maelstrom of emotions that was battering him, and his proposal of marriage had been born from that turmoil. She had already made plans for both of them and he had allowed himself to be carried along by her excitement. And, after all, it made sense. They had so many interests in common, and if he was going to resume his career when the war was over – if he survived that long – her contacts would be invaluable. He remembered the sceptical glint in his father's eye and felt a shiver of doubt. Was that why he was marrying Priscilla? His feelings for Rose had been very different – but that was all in the past. And his relationship with Chantal had been based on sexual attraction and the shared camaraderie of danger. Now there was this new attachment to Priscilla. Not for the first time, he wondered whether there was some inherent flaw in his character which made him incapable of being faithful. But he had not chosen to end the earlier relationships. It was Rose who had given up on him, and Chantal had always made it clear that marriage was not on the agenda. And he did love Priscilla. So he told himself, lying in the dark and waiting for the sounds that would tell him the rest of the household was stirring.

Later that day he left the house on the pretext of looking up old friends, though the chances of finding any of them on leave were slim. After one or two fruitless calls, his feet turned automatically towards the street where he had lived all through his childhood. He found the place where the house had stood, but all that was left were a few jagged remains of walls, their peeling wallpaper reminding him of how the rooms had looked the last time he was there. He searched for some remaining vestige of his own bedroom, but there seemed to be not a scrap of paper or a stick of furniture that he could recognise. He thought of the books, the musical scores, the precious records of Gigli and Caruso and Jussi Björling and Boris Christoff that he had stored there. All his sheet music, all the notes he had made during his training in Italy, all had vanished, along with the toys and games he had kept from his childhood, the school books, the photographs of friends. He turned away and began to walk along the familiar street. Suddenly he found himself remembering a forest clearing, a small car out of petrol and a German soldier on a motorbike – and himself with a gun in his hand. The thought came to him that Richard Stevens, the boy who had lived in that shattered house, the young singer with such high hopes, no longer existed, and in his place had appeared this stranger, who passed under that name, or that of Ricardo Benedetti or Lucien Dufrais, and who was capable of shooting a man in cold blood.

Priscilla arrived the following day. Although he had prepared the ground so carefully, Richard was still on tenterhooks. No other girl had been good enough, in his mother's estimation, and she was just as likely to take against this one for being 'too full of herself' as she had against others because they were 'common'. In the event, he need not have worried. Richard watched with admiration as Priscilla charmed the household, deferring to his mother's opinions about the relative merits of Handel's *Messiah* and Mendlessohn's *Elijah*, singing snatches of Gilbert and Sullivan with his father, following his aunt into the kitchen to copy down her recipe for Yorkshire pudding. Before long it seemed to him that she got on better with his relations than he did.

One benefit of her presence was the fact that it distracted his mother from asking too many questions about where he had been and what he had been doing. Nevertheless, the sense of alienation that had gripped him when he visited the old house still haunted him. He was used to living a double life in France.

Now it seemed he must continue to do so at home. It was a relief when his leave came to an end and they returned to London.

As soon as he got back Richard went to the headquarters of SOE in Baker Street and reported to the office of Maurice Buckmaster, the head of F section.

After a few courteous enquiries about his health and his family Buckmaster said, 'Well, you did an excellent job in France. Congratulations.'

Richard frowned. 'It felt more like a complete disaster to me. You sent me to assist O'Leary's escape line and set up a new one through Brittany for our own people. Now they have both collapsed.'

Buckmaster pursed his lips. 'Don't be too hard on yourself. You made a lot of useful contacts and you managed to get one batch of escapers out via the sub that brought you home. The betrayal of O'Leary's *réseau* was regretable, of course, but nothing to do with you. I'm sorry about the girl.' He glanced at a file on his desk. 'Henriette Gautier.'

'Chantal,' Richard said, and added, almost under his breath, 'She preferred to be called Chantal.'

'Well, whatever we call her, her death was tragic,' Buckmaster said.

'Yes,' Richard agreed, woodenly. He did not intend to let Buckmaster probe that particular wound. He went on, 'Is there any information about O'Leary and the others? I know Garrow was arrested. Do we have any information about him?'

Buckmaster lifted his shoulders slightly. 'That's MI9's pigeon, not ours. They are responsible for escaping British servicemen. But I understand that O'Leary is still operational.'

'Thank God for that,' Richard murmured. He thought of the Rodocanachis and their friends, who had sheltered him when he was on the run, and wondered whether they were still free.

Buckmaster went on. 'This brings me to an important point. The fact that you were known to the members of O'Leary's *réseau* puts your other contacts in northern France in jeopardy.'

'No,' Richard said quickly. 'They only knew me as Lucien Dufrais. To O'Leary and his people I am Ricardo Benedetti.'

'Are you quite certain that no one could connect the two?'

'There were only two people who knew both,' Richard said. 'One is Jack Duval, my radio operator, and the other is dead.'

'Nevertheless,' Buckmaster continued, 'in future we must make sure that there is absolutely no connection between our people and any other organisation.'

'But that is the reason I volunteered for this kind of work,' Richard protested. 'I wanted to help the people who had helped me.'

'But, as I've told you, that is MI9's pigeon,' Buckmaster said.

'Then perhaps I should be working for MI9,' Richard retorted. His tone was less than respectful but his nerves were still raw.

'Perhaps,' Buckmaster agreed, equably. 'But the fact is, you are working for us. We trained you – and the work you can do, have already done, will still save lives. We need efficient networks to get our own agents out in cases of emergency, and the contacts you have made will be of great help there. Particularly the de Bernards. Their chateau in Brittany will make an ideal safe house for agents waiting to be collected by sea.'

'Am I going back there?' Richard asked.

Buckmaster shook his head. 'No, that would be far too risky. You're hopelessly compromised. The Gestapo will have a photograph of you. We'll send someone else to pick up where you left off.'

Richard tried to suppress a feeling of intense relief. He had quite expected to be dispatched to Brittany within days.

'So what do you want me to do?' he asked.

'I want you at Beaulieu, acting as a conducting officer to some of our new recruits. Your first-hand experience will be invaluable to them. We'll send you back into the field again when we see a good opportunity, but for now I think you deserve a bit of a rest.' He smiled, a rueful and ironic smile. 'If there was any justice you ought to be in line for a decoration of some sort but, as you know, we can't even officially admit that you exist. Perhaps after the war there will be an opportunity to rectify that. I'm afraid the promotion to captain is the best we can do for now.'

'That's all right, sir,' Richard responded. 'I don't expect anything.'

Buckmaster rose. 'Well, I think that's all. Report to Beaulieu tomorrow.'

Richard got up too and then hesitated. 'I think perhaps I ought to tell you that I'm getting married.'

Buckmaster cocked his head on one side. 'Ah! To the lovely Miss Vance?'

Richard swallowed. 'How did you know?'

'Victor told me that he thought you two had developed . . . a certain rapport. But, Richard, are you sure marriage is a good idea? You know that there will be a lot of absences that you can't explain.'

'That won't be a problem,' Richard assured him. 'Priscilla doesn't know what I'm doing, but she knows enough not to ask questions.'

'Well, it's your decision,' Buckmaster said. He held out his hand. 'I wish you both all the best.'

Richard shook hands and made his way down to the street. On the pavement he paused, assailed by a sudden feeling of anticlimax. So he was not going back to France. He could look forward to six months, at least, in the peace of the Hampshire countryside. And marriage to Priscilla.

3

'Coventry! All change! Coventry!'

For the sixth or seventh time Rose heaved her case on to the platform and waited for her small flock to gather round her. The different places were beginning to blur in her memory. But at least the days were longer now, so they did not have to hunt for their digs in the dark.

As usual, she collected the slip of paper with the address of the house where they had been billeted from Monty and they lugged their cases, bulging not with their personal things but with costumes for the show, out to a bus. As it ground along Rose was horrified by the view from the window. She had grown almost used to the bombed-out buildings and the rubble-strewn streets of London after the Blitz but she had never seen such devastation as that wreaked on Coventry by the Luftwaffe. Street after street had been reduced to nothing more than an infernal landscape of broken walls and piles of debris. Then they rounded a bend and saw for the first time the shattered shell of the cathedral, sticking up like broken bones from the surrounding rubble.

'Oh, look!' exclaimed May, who was sitting in the seat in front of her. 'How can they do that, to a church?'

'Well, they've had a taste of their own medicine now,' responded Violet triumphantly. 'It said on the news this morning that our boys have started bombing German cities.'

The bus dropped them some distance from the address Rose had been given and by the time they had carried their suitcases along the street they were all weary and footsore. Rose rang the bell and a large woman in a print crossover apron opened the door.

'Mrs Harrison?' Rose enquired. 'We're from the ENSA concert party. I think you're expecting us.'

'Oh, my dear lord!' exclaimed the woman. 'Didn't you get my telegram?'

'Telegram?' Rose asked, her heart sinking.

'I sent a telegram. I'm ever so sorry, my love, but I've had three engineers from the munitions factory in Daventry billeted on me. Just turned up out of the blue yesterday. I couldn't refuse. Well, you can't, can you? You've got to take what the government sends. I've only got the one room left.'

Rose lowered her case on to the doorstep. 'Well, is there anyone else you know who might have spare rooms?'

The woman shook her head despairingly. 'Things are that bad round here! So many people have been bombed out, and the neighbours have taken in everyone they can manage. There's whole families sleeping in one room as it is. I wouldn't know who to ask.'

'All right,' Rose said. She was too tired to think, too tired to go knocking on doors. 'If whole families can sleep in one room, so can we.'

'What, five of us, all in one room?' Peggy exlaimed. 'I'm not bloody well putting up with that!'

'Then you'll have to bloody well sleep on a park bench!' Rose snapped back. 'Come on, the rest of you. At least we can take the weight off our feet.'

Followed by a faintly protesting Mrs Harrison she marched up the stairs and, following the landlady's directions, flung open the door of a back room. There was just about room for two single beds. Rose looked around.

'Do you have a camp bed, Mrs Harrison?'

'Well, yes, there is one, but where would I put it? There's not enough room in here.'

'You can put it on the landing,' Rose said. 'People will just have to squeeze past.'

'You can't have a young woman sleeping on the landing, with three strange men in the house!' Mrs Harrison exclaimed.

'I'll sleep on the landing,' Rose said. 'I don't care. You girls will just have to double up. It's only for a week.'

'How can we sleep like that, with two of us in a single bed?' Peggy demanded indignantly. 'You can't expect us to dance if we haven't had any sleep.'

'Well, do you have a better idea?' Rose asked. Then she added more gently, 'Look, I'll go and find Monty in a little while. Maybe there's some more room in his digs. Let's make the best of this for the moment.'

Mrs Harrison looked from Rose to the other girls and sighed resignedly. 'Well, if that's the way of it, you'd better come downstairs. I'll put the kettle on.'

While they were drinking tea in the front sitting room they heard the front door open and cheerful male voices in the hall. A moment later three men in overalls came into the room. The first was a short, compactly built man with a very round head accentuated by his closely cropped dark hair. Rose guessed his age to be about thirty. Behind him came a large, bony youth with a face that looked as though it had been roughly hewn out of red sandstone and a shock of ginger hair. The third man was somewhat older, his hair greying and his shoulders slightly stooped inside overalls that seemed too big for him.

The leader surveyed them with a grin of delighted amusement. 'Hey-up, girls! What's this, then? A meeting of the local chapter of the Women's Institute?' The accent was unfamiliar but Rose thought it was probably from the north-east.

'No,' she returned frostily. 'As it happens we're members of an ENSA troupe. We're here to perform in local factories. We were actually booked in here before you arrived.'

'Booked in here?' The man looked genuinely alarmed. 'Where are you going to sleep? Oh . . .' He wiped his hand on the side of his overalls. 'I'm George, by the way. George Benton. This here,' indicating the younger man, 'is Will Prentice and that's Amos White.'

Rose reminded herself that the three men were not to blame for the situation and regretted her bad manners. She introduced herself and the other girls and there was no mistaking the appreciation in the men's eyes as they shook hands with five trim-figured, long-legged beauties.

'Look, I'm really sorry about the mix-up over the bookings,' George said. 'We were sent down from Sunderland – direction of labour, you know. We just go where we're told. How on earth are you going to manage?'

'We'll just have to cope somehow,' Rose said. 'The four girls can share the two beds in the back room and I'm going to sleep on a camp bed on the landing.'

'You are not!' George exclaimed. 'We can't have that, can we, lads?'

'I don't know how you're going to stop us,' Rose said pugnaciously.

'Well, for a start, you're going to move into my room. It's only a single, but I reckon we can squeeze a camp bed in there.'

'If you think I'm going to . . .' Rose began but he interrupted her and she saw that he was blushing.

'Nay, don't get me wrong! I'll shift in with the other two lads. I can sleep on the floor. It won't be the first time. Then you and one of the other girls can share my room.'

'Well, it's very kind of you . . . ' Rose murmured hesitantly.

'Don't give it another thought,' George exclaimed.

'Well, that's all right for two of you,' Peggy put in crossly. 'That still leaves three of us to share two beds.'

'I've been thinking about that,' Mrs Harrison said. 'If we take the cushions off the settee and the easy chairs, we can make a bed up in here for one of you.'

'There you are, you see!' George beamed at them. 'All sorted. Now, is there any tea in that pot, Ma?'

'I'll make fresh,' their hostess said. 'And you girls had better give me your ration books, if you're stopping, so I can get to the shops before they shut. Otherwise there'll be nothing for your supper.'

They had to eat in shifts because there was no way they could all sit round the dining table, and afterwards they took turns to use the only bathroom. Going downstairs after her turn Rose heard gales of laughter coming from the sitting room. It seemed that both George and Amos had a fund of shaggy dog stories, all told with a dry, tongue-in-cheek humour that made even the feeblest of them hilarious. In spite of her weariness, Rose found herself laughing too.

After a night on the hard camp bed, with Alice snuffling quietly beside her, Rose was woken by the noise of the three men getting up to go to work. She wanted to turn over and go back to sleep but she knew that she and the girls could not afford to lie in either. By mid-morning they were in yet another works canteen, preparing for yet another performance. They had learned the lesson of the first week and now the four

dancers opened the show with their can-can. It never failed to
get the audience's attention. To replace it in the middle of the
bill Rose had taken a risk and created a gentler number to a
waltz from Ivor Novello's *The Dancing Years*. She and the girls
had cobbled together some floaty dresses in pretty pastel
colours and she had put them in *pointe* shoes and introduced
some ballet steps. This was the first time they had tried it on an
audience and she was delighted to discover that it went down
very well. Afterwards, when Rose and the girls were snatching
a breather in the room they had been given as a dressing room,
there was a timid knock on the door. Three girls in their teens
stood outside.

'I hope you don't mind us bothering you,' one said shyly.
'It's just . . . well, we wanted to say how much we enjoyed the
show. Specially the dancing.'

As she spoke Rose could see that all three were peering over
her shoulder, wide eyed with fascination at the sight of the four
dancers, still in their costumes, with their feet up, smoking.
They might have been looking at creatures from another planet.

'That dance where you got up on the tips of your toes – that
was ballet, wasn't it?' the first girl asked.

'Yes, that's right.'

'I thought ballet was all girls in frilly dresses and nancy-boys
in tights,' her friend giggled.

'I'll tell you what it is,' Violet said, rubbing her toes. 'It's
bloomin' hard work.'

'That Sadler's Wells ballet are coming to the Hippodrome
in a week or two,' the second girl said. 'We didn't think we
fancied it, but now I'm not sure.'

'I never thought it was for people like us,' the leader said.
'Thought actors and dancers were . . . well, sort of different.
But you're just like us, really.'

'I'm not "just like them",' Peggy said after the three had left. She shuddered. 'Fancy spending all your life working in a place like this!'

'Well, just count your lucky stars, then,' Rose returned with some asperity. 'Actually, I think we've just been paid a big compliment.'

They were scheduled to perform again for the night shift but in between there was a chance to go back to the digs for a rest. Rose took the opportunity to slip out to the nearest phone box with a stack of small change. After some delay she succeeded in getting through to the home of Enid and Jack Willis, the couple who had taken her family in when the Blitz drove them out of their flat in Lambeth. Jack answered and immediately called her mother to the phone.

'Rose, love, is anything wrong?'

'No, Mum. Everything's fine. I just thought as I haven't been in touch for a week or two I'd better give you a call. How are you?'

'I'm fine, thanks. How about you?'

'I'm OK. A bit tired, but nothing to complain about. Is Bet well, and the two boys?'

'Yes, they're fine, too. The boys miss their Auntie Rose. They keep asking when you're coming back.'

'Tell them it won't be for a while yet. And give them my love.'

'I will. Oh, by the way, there's a letter here for you from Merry. He says he's fed up with the sight of sand. Oh, and some good news! He says Felix has been passed fit to fly again. Shall I forward it to the London flat?'

'Yes, you'd better. If you send it after me it'll probably never catch me up.'

Rose walked slowly back to the digs. It was a comfort to

know that her mother and sister were well and she was particularly glad to have news of Merry and Felix, old friends from the Follies concert party. There had never been any question of romance, with either man. But she was as fond of both as if they had been her brothers.

When she got back she found the four girls in the sitting room. Peggy was moaning because she wanted to wash her hair and there was no hot water, and blaming May for using more than her fair share. Violet was writing to one of her admirers and Alice was mending a hole in her last pair of stockings, her blonde head bent low over the work. Rose was just trying to summon the energy to intervene between Peggy and May when the front door slammed. A moment later the three Geordies came in and the room was filled with cheerful male voices.

'Hey-up, girls!' George greeted them. 'How's it going, then?'

Violet looked up from her letter with a smile and even Peggy's sulky face brightened. Very soon they were all swapping anecdotes about their day. Only Will remained silent, and Rose noticed his eyes straying repeatedly to Alice. Alice, however, seemed oblivious, her face hidden behind the sweep of her golden hair.

'What's this, then?' George enquired with a nod at Violet's writing pad. 'Keeping the boyfriend up to date?'

'One of them,' Peggy said. 'Vi changes her men as often as some people change their socks.'

Violet put out her tongue good-naturedly. 'Och, away! You're just jealous.'

'I am not . . .' Peggy began hotly but George interrupted her with a grin.

'I'll bet you've all got a string of young lads after you, lovely-looking girls like you.'

Will spoke for the first time. 'Have you got a feller, Alice?'

They all looked at him and Rose saw him turn scarlet.

Alice looked up, bemused. 'Me? No. Why?'

Will wriggled and looked as though he wanted to make a bolt for the door. 'Nothing, just . . . just . . . I wondered, that's all.'

Amos gave him an encouraging nudge. 'Nay, lad, there's nowt to be ashamed of. If you want to ask the girl out, ask her.'

'Me? No . . . no. That is . . . No, you're all right.' And Will succeeded in making his exit.

Violet looked across the room and winked. 'You've made a conquest there, lassie.'

Alice blushed and returned to her sewing. 'Don't be silly, Vi.'

From then on it was a constant source of amusement to the girls to watch the burning looks Will cast at Alice, which she pretended to ignore. The relationship never progressed further, but Rose was glad that he had chosen Alice rather than one of the others. At least she would not tease him, or let him think that she cared and then break his heart.

On the Wednesday afternoon, when they got back after the lunchtime show, Rose was surprised to find George sitting in the front room reading the newspaper.

'What's up, George?' she asked. 'Aren't you feeling well?'

He got up, smiling. 'Nay, it's nothing like that. It just suddenly crossed my mind how to make the sleeping arrangements a bit easier. I've asked the foreman to put me on the night shift. That way I get to sleep in a proper bed while the other two are out at work.'

'Oh, George!' Rose exclaimed. 'You needn't have done that. I feel really bad about it.'

'Nay, lass, dinna take on,' he responded, looking faintly embarrassed. 'It's no bother. I've worked nights often enough before.'

'Will you be able to change back after we've gone?' Rose asked.

'Happen.' He shrugged indifferently. 'It makes no difference.'

'I still feel guilty about turning you out of your room,' Rose said.

He smiled at her. 'Well, if you want to say thank you, that's easy. Let me take you out for a drink some time.'

She sighed. 'It's nice of you to offer, George, but it's not possible. I'm working dinner-times and evenings and the pubs aren't open when I'm free.'

'Well, it'll just have to be tea, then,' he said. 'You'll let me take you out for tea one day, won't you?'

Rose hesitated. She had not been out with a man, even for something as innocent as tea, since she broke off her engagement to Matthew – apart from one or two evenings in the local with Felix and Merry when they were all on sick leave at Wimborne, which didn't count. She liked George and did not want to hurt his feelings but at the same time she didn't want him to get the wrong idea.

'Come on,' he said. 'Say yes. I don't bite, you know.'

She smiled. He was so genuinely kind hearted that it would be churlish to refuse. 'All right. Thank you. Tea would be lovely.'

He grinned. 'No time like the present. Put your hat on.'

Rose protested that she must have a few minutes to powder her nose and hurried upstairs. She took off her uniform and changed into a dress. Strictly speaking she was not supposed to go out in mufti but she was darned if she was going out on a date – even just for tea – in the thick serge suit. She combed her hair and made use of the last tiny end of lipstick that she had saved for special occasions. Soon, she thought regretfully, it would be finished and she would be reduced, like many other girls, to reddening her lips with beetroot juice. She looked at her reflection in the mirror and sighed at the skimpy, knee-length skirt and the bare legs beneath it. Alice came in from the bathroom with a towel round her head.

'Going somewhere?'

'Yes, just popping out for a breath of air.' She wasn't quite sure why she was reluctant to tell the other girl that George was taking her out. She added, 'I just can't get used to these short skirts and no stockings.'

'Want me to draw seams up your legs?' Alice asked. 'Or you could see if Mrs Harrison's got any gravy browning. I heard that painting your legs with that looks like stockings.'

'No, thanks, love,' Rose said with a smile. '*Bare legs for patriotism!* Isn't that the slogan these days? It's quite warm out. I'll be OK without stockings.'

In the café, over weak tea and sawdust-dry buns, George said, 'I suppose you've got a young man out there somewhere, in one of the services.'

The image of Richard's face flickered in front of Rose's inward eye. 'No,' she said. 'There's no one.'

'A lovely girl like you?' he quizzed her. 'There must be someone.'

'No, really.' She could feel herself flushing.

'Oh, I'm sorry!' he exclaimed with sudden remorse. 'There I go, putting my great feet in it as usual. Was he . . . did you . . . lose someone?'

Rose managed to summon a half-smile. 'Yes, in a way, I suppose I did. But what about your family? Are you married?'

He shrugged. 'After a fashion, I suppose.'

'How can you be married "after a fashion"?' Rose asked.

'Well, I got wed at the age of nineteen, to a lass I'd known all my life. I guess we were too young to know our own minds – or we just hadn't seen enough of the world, or of other people. Anyway, the gloss soon wore off. We're still married, but I've always worked away from home a lot. It's easier that way. I'd have liked to join up, if they'd let me, but being an engineer I'm in a reserved occupation, see. The powers that be reckon I'm more use to the war effort in a munitions factory.'

'I'm sorry,' Rose murmured. 'That's very sad – I mean about your marriage.'

'Oh, don't go feeling sorry for me,' he said, with a return of his usual grin. 'I'm used to it by now, and I get by. The only time I really regret it is when . . .' He broke off.

'When what?'

'No, I shouldn't say it. You'd get the wrong impression.'

'Say what?'

'The only time I really regret not being single is when I meet a bonny lass like you. I made sure you'd be spoken for already – but since you're not . . .'

Rose looked down at her plate and felt herself blushing. She wasn't quite sure exactly how she was supposed to interpret that last remark.

George went on, 'But there it is. You may not be spoken for, but I am, and that's the end of it. Is there any more tea in that pot?'

For the rest of the week neither of them referred to their little tête-à-tête and George reverted to his usual humorous manner. He was in bed and asleep by the time Rose and the girls got up but he normally came and joined them when they got back to the digs after the lunchtime show. The other girls were usually around, however, and he did not make any further suggestion that he and Rose should go somewhere on their own. Rose wondered whether the original invitation had, after all, been no more than a casual, friendly gesture, or whether he felt that he had burned his boats with that last remark and saw no point in pursuing things further. In either case, she was relieved. She liked George and responded instinctively to his warm manner and his generosity, but she was in no mood for romance, or any form of emotional involvement.

The last show of the week was to be in the canteen of the factory where George and the other two men worked and George insisted that he was going to work a double shift so that he could be there. On the previous afternoon he found Rose sitting in the tiny back garden with a book, making the most of an unseasonably warm day.

'Mind if I join you?'

'Of course not.'

He sat down on the grass and rolled up his shirtsleeves. 'Oh, it's good to feel the sun! That's one benefit of being on nights. You miss the best of the day, stuck in that factory.' He was silent for a moment and Rose returned to her book. 'Not disturbing you, am I? I don't want to stop you reading.'

Rose put the book aside. She did want to go on reading. She could never afford to buy books, except second-hand, but she had been a member of Boots Lending Library since she was a child. The problem was, while she was touring she very rarely managed to finish a book before she had to return it and move on. She had almost got to the end of this one but it looked as though she was going to have to leave yet another heroine stranded in mid-story, almost at the point of being reunited with the hero but never quite making it.

She smiled at George. 'Will you go back on days when we're gone?'

'I don't know,' he said. 'I quite like nights.' He looked at her. 'I'll miss you when you're gone.'

'Like a sick headache!' she returned, laughing. 'Just think, you won't have to put up with our smalls drying over the bath, and everything smelling of Leichner Removing Cream.'

'Is that what it is?' he said. 'What's that for, then?'

'Taking off the greasepaint,' she told him. 'But the way things are going we shan't be able to buy any stage make-up soon, so we shan't need it.'

'Anyway,' he persisted, 'I shall miss you – all of you. You've brought a bit of life into the place.' He paused. 'But I shall miss you most of all, Rose. Where do you go next?'

'Burnley,' Rose told him.

'I was wondering . . . could I write to you? I'd like to keep in touch.'

Rose bit her lip. In a way it would be pleasant to hear from him, and to write back – and, after all, letters were harmless. A platonic friendship, conducted through the mail, could be quite enjoyable. But she knew instinctively that it would not end at that. Sooner or later he would want to meet – and then what? She said, 'Oh, it would be nice, George, but it's terribly difficult. I mean, I know where I shall be for the next couple of weeks, but after that . . . And you know how unreliable the post is these days.'

He dropped his eyes. 'Yes, you're right, of course. I don't want you to feel obliged, and I'll be off back to Sunderland soon.'

She looked at him. He was nice looking, in a sturdy, dogged sort of way, and she did like him. She hated to see him looking so downcast.

'Well, we could try, I suppose,' she said. 'I'll give you the address of my digs in Burnley and you can write if you like. If the letter doesn't get there before I move on, I can always drop you a line from the next place.'

He looked up at her and smiled, a grin of delight that transformed his face. 'I'll make sure it gets there! Tell you what, I'll write it before you go so you can take it with you! How about that?'

That night they had the first air raid for several days. Rose was woken by the siren and a moment later Amos banged on the door and shouted, 'Better get up, girls! Get down to the shelter at the end of the street.'

Groggy with sleep, Rose pulled on a dressing gown and shook Alice awake. By the time she had dragged the other girls out of bed and persuaded them to follow her out of the front door the first bombs were dropping. They could hear the low crump of explosions and the ground shook beneath their feet. Then there was a louder bang and the blast whipped their nightclothes against their bodies and made them stagger.

'Come on!' Rose urged them. 'That was pretty close!'

They had seen the urgency for themselves now and covered the last hundred yards to the door of the shelter at a run. At the entrance a warden in a tin hat was scanning the sky, where searchlights were performing their eerie aerial ballet. As Rose looked back a sudden gout of flame surged upwards from somewhere beyond the rooftops and the ground shook to a larger explosion. Will came running up.

'Something big gone up over there,' the warden commented.

'Looks like the direction of our place,' Will said. 'Hope to God they haven't hit the factory.'

It was three in the morning before the all-clear sounded and they were able to stagger stiffly back to their beds. All the time Rose had sat hunched in the blanket she had brought with her, thinking of George working the night shift in the factory. They would have shelters, of course. Probably the entire workforce would have gone straight down into them as soon as the siren sounded. And anyway, there were plenty of other factories in that area. There was no reason to suppose it was that particular one that had been hit.

It had been another hard day and she had come home from the last performance exhausted, only to be woken after an hour's sleep. By the time she got back to bed she was too tired to think and it was mid-morning before any of them woke up.

The five of them were snatching mouthfuls of tea and toast and trying to finish dressing at the same time when the front door opened and Amos came in, followed by Will. Their faces and clothes were black with grime and they looked shaken and weary.

Amos took in their frantic preparations at a glance and said, 'No need to hurry, girls. The factory's a wreck. There won't be any performance there today.'

Rose caught her breath. 'George? Is George all right?'

Slowly Amos shook his head. 'Direct hit on the tool shop where he was working. No survivors.'

4

In a curious way Richard found the return to the SOE 'finishing school' at Beaulieu quite soothing, at least to begin with. In such beautiful surroundings and with the country house atmosphere that seemed to pervade all the SOE training establishments, with the notable exception of Arisaig, it was almost possible to believe that the war was some kind of fantasy, an imaginary game they were all playing. But after a day or two the contrast between this easy existence and the reality of life in the field only added to his sense of dislocation. He found that he was expected to give lectures to the fledgling agents on how to conduct themselves in France so as not to arouse suspicion. He was also given personal responsibility for three men, who would be sent over as soon as their training was finished. He began to lie awake at night, going over and over in his mind every detail of the months he had spent in occupied territory, wondering whether there was some hint, some little nugget of information about regulations or procedures, that he had omitted to mention. Were there any mannerisms, any subtle differences of behaviour or speech, that might give his protégés away? Could something he had failed to notice mean the difference between life and an agonising death for one of them?

The news of the war brought no comfort. At the end of January the German forces captured the North African town of Benghazi and two weeks later the apparently impregnable island of Singapore fell to the Japanese. Meanwhile, the tiny island of Malta, so vital to Allied communications in the Mediterranean, continued to be besieged. The optimism that Richard had felt, in common with so many others, when the USA entered the conflict was rapidly dissipating.

In England, rationing grew ever tighter. The government banned the baking of white bread. The restrictions applied, of course, to Beaulieu as well as to the rest of the country, but the best of the available rations were always reserved for the men and women of the armed forces and Richard felt increasingly uneasy with his comparatively pampered existence.

The fact that he spent his free time in London with Priscilla made his problems worse. Priscilla had returned to duty with the FANY but she had a sleeping-out pass and so, whenever Richard was able to get away, they spent the night at her chic little flat in Mayfair. She was determined to continue with the project she had begun the previous summer of introducing Richard to people who might be useful in furthering his career when the war was over. Every available evening was filled with some activity. Often they dined with Sir Lionel and Lady Vance and always there would be an eminent conductor or a visiting soloist to impress. On other evenings they went out to a restaurant or to a party to celebrate the publication of a new book or the debut of a hitherto unrecognised talent. Increasingly, as the weeks went by, Richard began to feel that this world of art and music and ambitious jockeying for recognition was totally irrelevant to the life-and-death struggle in which he and so many others were engaged.

As the spring advanced Priscilla and her aunt immersed themselves in preparations for the wedding. Richard had assumed that, as it was wartime, the ceremony would be a fairly low-key affair for a small group of friends and relations. This was not in keeping with Priscilla's plans. Admittedly, the caterers would be limited in what they could provide while staying within the limits of rationing and the bride's dress would be remade from the one her aunt had worn for her own wedding. Nevertheless, Sir Lionel and his wife were determined that their niece's wedding should make as big a splash as possible in the circumstances. To his alarm, Richard discovered that it was to take place in St Margaret's, Westminster, with a reception for sixty people afterwards at the Savoy. What was more, among the guests were several titled personages and one Royal Highness.

When he and Priscilla were alone in her flat, on his next evening off, he raised the subject tentatively.

'Darling, do you really think it's suitable for us to have such an extravagant wedding at a time like this?'

'I can't see why not,' she returned, looking mildly surprised. 'After all, we're not spending anybody else's money.'

'No, but with rationing and everything . . .' He trailed off lamely and then tried again. 'I mean, when the government has introduced utility clothes and girls are having to shorten their skirts and do without stockings and men's suits are not allowed to have turn-ups, don't you think it just looks as if we're . . . well, flaunting ourselves?'

She laughed. 'Don't be silly, darling! After all, the material for my dress is second-hand and you'll be in uniform. Why should anyone object to that?'

Richard sighed. 'It's just that, in the middle of all this death and destruction, I feel it would be more appropriate to go for something a little less . . . well, flamboyant.'

Priscilla came over to him and put her hands on his shoulders. 'But don't you see, my sweet, that's exactly what people want these days, as an antidote to all this doom and gloom? People are just crying out for a bit of glamour. Why do you think they are all flocking to see *The Dancing Years*? Ivor Novello gives them exactly what they need, a chance to escape from the war for an hour or two. We shall be doing the same. I bet you there will be dozens of people waiting outside the church to see us come out!'

Richard sighed again. 'I suppose you're right.'

'Of course I'm right,' she said, kissing the tip of his nose. 'And anyway, her wedding is a very important day for any girl. It's the only chance I shall ever get to be the star of the show. You wouldn't want to deprive me of that, would you?'

'No,' he murmured, kissing her in return. 'Of course not.'

'Anyway,' she finished, turning back to her dressing table to put on her earrings, 'it's far too late to change anything now. Everything's organised for June the fifteenth.'

Towards the end of May Richard received instructions to present himself at Maurice Buckmaster's office in Baker Street. The head of F section greeted him in his usual genial manner but wasted no time in getting down to business.

'You recall our conversation regarding your involvement with the O'Leary escape line?'

Richard nodded. 'You told me to leave it to MI9.'

'Quite. As you know, I do not, in general, approve of any overlap between our networks and theirs. However, that does not mean we can't cooperate when the need arises. It so happens that I have received a request for assistance from them and I think you may be exactly the man they are looking for.'

'How so?' Richard queried.

'It seems they're having difficulty liaising with O'Leary and they wondered if we could help out. I wouldn't normally ask you to go back into the field so soon but in view of the fact that you've actually met a lot of the people concerned you seem to be the obvious choice. How do you feel about it?'

Richard suppressed a sudden queasiness in the pit of his stomach. The possibility of going back into France had been present at the back of his mind ever since the beginning of the year, but until now he had avoided confronting it directly, permitting it to surface only in the nightmares that disturbed his sleep two or three times a week. He knew that he owed his freedom to the man who went by the name of Pat O'Leary and those who worked with him, and he could not refuse his help if it was needed.

'I'll go as soon as you like,' he said. 'What do you want me to do, exactly?'

'That's up to the chaps at MI9,' Buckmaster said. 'Go along and see Jimmy Langley at the War Office. You'll find him in Room 900.'

Room 900 was scarcely larger than a good-sized broom cupboard, reflecting the low priority that the War Office gave to organising the escape of captured servicemen. It had just enough room for two desks and a couple of spare chairs. Richard was greeted by a small, moustached man in the uniform of a captain in the Coldstream Guards, whose empty left sleeve was neatly stitched to the front of his tunic.

'Richard, good to meet you! Come in – if you can get in. Do you know Airey Neave? He's just joined us after escaping from Colditz.'

'Colditz!' Richard exclaimed. 'That must have taken some doing! How did you manage it?'

Langley chuckled. 'You'll appreciate this, Richard. I'm told you're no stranger to the stage.'

Richard looked at Neave, who grinned back. 'There was a concert in the camp theatre. Under cover of that a Dutch chap and I managed to make an unauthorised exit through a trap under the stage. We'd succeeded in fabricating some reasonably accurate German uniforms and when the coast was clear we just walked out.'

'Fanstastic,' Richard said. 'Congratulations!'

'I think I was just lucky,' Neave said modestly. 'I was certainly lucky to be passed on to the O'Leary line.'

'You came out via Marseilles?' Richard said. 'So did I.'

'We know that,' Neave said. 'That's why we asked for you. There was a girl with you, who also worked for the line. What happened to her?'

'She was killed,' Richard said shortly. 'She was one of the people betrayed by Paul Cole last December.'

'Ah, Cole!' Langley cut in. 'That brings us to the business in hand. Sit down, Richard, and let me bring you up to date. Did you know Cole has been arrested by the Vichy police?'

'No!' Richard exclaimed. 'Bloody good thing too! But why would the Vichy police arrest him?'

'We think someone there is sympathetic to the Allied cause. They must have been tipped off about Cole's activities and decided to help out.'

'Well, good for them,' Richard commented.

'You are convinced that Cole is the traitor?' Langley enquired.

'Absolutely,' Richard agreed. 'I never took to the man, even though he was instrumental in getting me out the first time. O'Leary doesn't trust him either. He was far too fond of flaunting himself around with his mistresses in expensive nightclubs. It was too much of a coincidence that, only a few days after he was picked up by the Abwehr, the whole of the Lille end of the operation was betrayed and rounded up, including the Abbé Carpentier. By the way, is there any news of him?'

'He was executed by the Gestapo,' Langley said grimly. 'But not before he had smuggled out a note confirming that Cole was the traitor.'

'Dear God!' Richard murmured. 'That good, kind man!' He paused, profoundly shaken, and added after a moment, 'I got to know him quite well, you know, when I went back.'

'Yes,' Langley said quietly. 'We have had an account of your activities. I gather you were pretty lucky not to be picked up yourself.'

'Very lucky indeed,' Richard agreed, his mind still occupied with memories of that terrible night. He drew a deep breath and pulled himself together. 'So, what is it you want me to do?'

Langley settled himself behind his desk. 'I had a conference a few weeks back in Gibraltar with O'Leary and Donald Darling, our man out there. You've probably met him?'

Richard nodded assent. 'The man they call Sunday. Incidentally, talking of *noms de guerre* – who is O'Leary, really? He's obviously not an Irishman.'

Langley shook his head reprovingly. 'I can't tell you that. You should know better than to ask. You're quite right, of course, but I'm not going to reveal his true identity.'

'Sorry,' Richard said. 'You were saying?'

'I met O'Leary and Darling. We discussed other methods of getting men away from the south of France, instead of sending them over the Pyrenees, which is slow and laborious and runs the risk of them being interned by the Spanish.'

'I know!' Richard said with feeling.

'So, we are planning to set up a system of seaborne evacuations,' Langley went on. 'I believe you already have some experience there.'

'I was landed on the south coast when I went in last time, if that's what you mean,' Richard agreed.

'Well, it's a start,' Langley said. 'Our main problem is communication. Because of our low priority with the Air Ministry we've been unable to drop a radio operator to O'Leary. After our meeting we sent a bloke called Ferrière back with him. He'd volunteered and was a trained operator. He was carrying a set, but he has completely failed to come up on the air. Whether the Nazis captured him, or the set, or both, we've no way of knowing. What we need is someone to go in and find out what's going on, and then to liaise between O'Leary and Gibraltar when we set up the sea evacuations. What do you think? Are you game?'

'When do I leave?' Richard asked.

He waited until he was alone with Priscilla in her flat that evening and then said, 'Darling, I'm terribly sorry but I'm afraid you're going to have to cancel the arrangements for June the fifteenth.'

Guy Merryweather stared gloomily ahead of him at the undulating expanse of sand and rock shimmering under a pewter sky and swore under his breath as the wheels of the three-ton truck spun on a patch of loose ground. Gritting his teeth, he struggled with the controls and put the vehicle into four-wheel drive. The truck had been rattling around the desert for too long and was almost clapped out.

'Cheer up, duckie,' said his companion. 'It can't be much farther now.'

'We could drive right past them in this terrain, if they're well dug in, and never know they were there,' Merry pointed out.

'These tracks have got to lead somewhere,' the other man said. Merry looked at the faint tyre marks that they had been following for the last three or four hours. There were no roads here, but clearly someone – maybe several vehicles – had passed this way not too long ago. He looked at the compass on the dashboard and glanced down at the map on his knee. They were definitely heading in the right direction, but had they gone too far?

'We're probably following Rommel's staff car,' he pronounced heavily.

'Oh, goody! When we catch up with him we can put on the show. I'll do my act and end up sitting on his lap. Then I'll pop a grenade down his shirt front.'

In spite of himself Merry laughed. The mental picture of Corporal Clive Wood in full drag administering the *coup de grâce* while perched on the enemy general's knee was irresistible.

'Look out, love! There's a nasty pothole just ahead on the left,' Clive exclaimed.

Merry gave a passing thought, as he swerved to avoid the pothole, to the reactions of his fellow officers if they heard him being addressed in such intimate terms, but it did not worry him. His relations with the rest of the company had never been based on military discipline but rather on the discipline of the theatre, which demanded from everyone that whatever happened the show must go on. What was more, it must be the best show that could possibly be contrived in order to give men who had been living with the daily expectation of injury and death a few precious minutes of relief. He thought of the others, in the back of the truck, and those following in the second lorry. They were all tired, all heartily sick of the heat and the flies, fed up with being permanently coated with a mixture of sweat and sand, with inadequate washing facilities and monotonous food, and with jouncing around the desert in imminent danger of running into an enemy ambush or getting caught up in a skirmish. But, when they reached their destination – assuming that they ever did – they would perform with as much polish and enthusiasm as if they were fresh from the West End or from one of the more exclusive London nightclubs. This was in fact the milieu to which most of them had been accustomed, until the outbreak of war had seen them conscripted into the army and then seconded to the Central Pool of Artistes. Now they were members of Stars in Battledress, the elite corps of serving soldiers who could be sent to entertain the troops right up to the front line, in situations where the civilians of ENSA could not be allowed to go.

They had been on the move now for five months. At first, in January, they had been sent to perform for troops being rested in the Cairo area after the confused and costly battles around Sidi Rezegh – battles that had at one point turned into a pell-mell retreat now laughingly referred to as 'the November Handicap'. For a while it had seemed that Rommel's drive must carry him right to the gates of Cairo itself and the vital link of the Suez Canal, but somehow the tank battalions and their support systems had regrouped and the Germans had been driven back westward into Tripolitania. After that both armies, exhausted and low on supplies, had retired to lick their wounds.

The men in the rest camps had greeted 'The Merrymakers', as the group had insisted on naming themselves in tribute to their director, with boisterous enthusiasm. They had played to packed audiences who shouted and stamped and whistled and called for more. It was the performances in the hospitals which most of the company had found traumatic. There they had performed in front of serried lines of beds, fifty or a hundred to a ward, filled with men who had suffered horrendous injuries. Some had lost limbs, others had been blinded or terribly burned. How, some of the company demanded of Merry, could they crack jokes and play light music in the face of such suffering? But they soon learned that their visits were as therapeutic as anything the doctors could do. Men who had been lying gazing mutely at the ceiling for days pulled themselves into sitting positions to watch. Those who could not see turned their heads to listen. Some smiled for the first time since they were wounded. Those who had the use of their hands applauded, others called out for encores. And when the show was over the performers went from bed to bed, shaking hands, chatting, offering snippets of news or words of encouragement.

All this was not new to Merry. Alone among them, he had toured the hospital wards in England after the debacle of Dunkirk and all through the Battle of Britain. He knew what comfort music, in particular, could bring to lonely, frightened young men. Sometimes, when the show was over, he would stay on and sit down again at the piano and play Chopin and Beethoven and Mozart and often the nurses and orderlies and the hard-pressed doctors would congregate in the ward to listen as well.

From Cairo they had gone on to Alexandria and then from there they had been sent 'up the blue', in the current terminology. First along the made road to Mersa Matruh, then on over what was no better than a cart track, crowded with tanks and supply lorries and armoured cars, to Sidi Barrani, and finally to Tobruk. Everywhere they had met with the same rapturous reception. To men who had seen nothing but sand and heard nothing but gunfire for months the chance to laugh and sing and forget the war for a little while was guaranteed to boost morale.

Now they were heading out into the desert in search of the 4th Armoured Brigade, which was one of the units defending the Gazala Line. This was not a continuous defensive line, but a series of well-defended 'boxes' spaced out between Gazala on the coast and Bir Hacheim, which was held by the Free French. This was closer to the front than any of them had been so far, but the troops manning the boxes had been camped out in the desert for several months, waiting for the signal to go on the offensive, and some form of diversion was urgently needed.

'Hey-up! I think we've arrived,' Clive remarked suddenly, as they topped a small rise.

Ahead of them was a barbed-wire entanglement pierced by a gate, which was guarded by two armoured cars. Merry stopped and identified himself and his passengers and a corporal put through a call on his field telephone.

'Carry on straight ahead, sir,' he told Merry, 'and make sure you keep to the track. The ground on both sides of it is mined.'

Some minutes later they entered the main encampment. There were serried rows of camouflaged tents and several large marquees. At one side a football pitch had been marked out and two teams of men, apparently oblivious to the heat, were racing up and down on it.

'Gives a whole new meaning to the term "camping around", doesn't it?' Clive murmured in Merry's ear.

They were greeted by an officer who identified himself as Lieutenant Gordon Henshaw, the camp Entertainments Officer. 'Boy, am I glad to see you chaps! The lads here are going mad with boredom and I've just about run out of ideas.'

He conducted them to a clear area where a sloping dune formed a natural arena and informed them that their first performance was scheduled for 7.30 that evening. They settled into an accustomed routine. The two lorries were parked about twelve feet apart, forming the 'wings', with some wooden staging laid between them. The players would dress in the lorries and make their entrances from there. Merry's piano was offloaded and positioned in front of one of the lorries and a couple of spotlights were linked up to a generator provided by the camp. By the time the bugles sounded 'Come to the Cookhouse Door' they were ready.

As always the performance was an enormous success. Every soldier who was not on duty crowded on to the sand dune, while the top brass sat on benches in the front. Clive's appearance in full Carmen Miranda drag was greeted with rapturous wolf-whistles and his double entendres produced gales of laughter. The climax of his act was to pick out the most senior officer present and sit on his lap, pretending to flirt madly with him. Some officers received these unexpected attentions better than others, but on this occasion the colonel in charge entered into the spirit of the act with gusto, to the delight of his men. Equally popular were Long and Short, the comics. They had done their homework over supper and discovered which officers had particular habits or turns of phrase that the men found either amusing or irritating, and these were mercilessly lampooned, to the delight of the troops. Ronnie Davies changed the mood with 'I'll See You Again' and 'Smoke Gets in Your Eyes' and the men crooned along sentimentally. It was only during Tom Dyson's tap dance that Merry thought he detected an undercurrent of feeling that was not quite admiration in the wolf-whistles from some sections of the audience.

When the final bows had been taken and the audience was beginning reluctantly to drift back to their tents, the colonel came over and shook Merry's hand.

'Bloody good show, Merryweather! I have to confess, when I heard you lot were coming I wasn't sure what we were letting ourselves in for, but I must congratulate you. I would say that was a really professional performance.'

'That's probably because most of us are,' Merry returned dryly, but the significance of the remark seemed to be lost on the senior officer.

Merry excused himself at the earliest possible opportunity and made his way to the tent he had been allotted. The company were to perform again the following night, to enable those who had been on duty that evening to see the show, so he was looking forward to a brief respite in the punishing schedule of packing up and moving on, but he was not in the mood for company. It was not simply that he was tired. He was depressed by a nagging anxiety that had been with him ever since reading a letter that had finally caught up with him at Tobruk.

The letter came from Felix. And it had been posted in Malta. *Malta, of all places!*

Merry knew from what he had read in the newspapers, and from first-hand accounts, what a 'pasting' the island was getting. Positioned in the central Mediterranean, with its deep-water harbour and its airfields, Malta was essential to the Allied war effort, allowing the navy and the RAF to harass the convoys taking supplies to Rommel's Afrika Corps. Accordingly, Field Marshal von Kesselring had been given the job of neutralising it. For months the island had endured a blitz more intense than that visited on London and for months a small force of Hurricanes had attempted to drive off the much superior and more numerous Messerschmitt 109s of the Luftwaffe. Convoy after convoy bringing desperately needed supplies had been sunk or forced to turn back by enemy bombers or submarines and rumour had it that the people of the island were nearing starvation. In April the King had recognised their fortitude and awarded the whole island the George Cross for gallantry. Now the Hurricanes had been reinforced by Spitfires in a desperate attempt to clear the skies, and one of the pilots flying those Spits was Felix. Since receiving his letter, Merry had been beset, both waking and sleeping, by images of his plane crashing once again in flames.

Sitting in his tent, feeling the sweat dry on his body as the chill of the desert night took over from the sweltering heat of

Hilary Green

the day, he attempted to compose a reply. His efforts were interrupted by a voice from outside.

'Lieutenant Merryweather? Can I come in?'

Recognising the voice he called, 'Come in, Clive.'

The rather gangling figure of the female impersonator inserted itself between the tent flaps. Out of costume Clive Wood was an unremarkable-looking man with thin dark hair and a rather sallow complexion. It was the vivacious dark eyes and the mobile, humorous mouth which gave a hint of what he could become in a luxuriant wig and heavy make-up. He came to a stop in front of the folding table at which Merry was sitting.

'Sorry to bother you. It's young Tom. He's in a bit of a state.'

A frisson of nervous anticipation ran down Merry's spine. 'What about?'

'Some of the lads in the mess have been ribbing him. Asking him what he's doing dancing around instead of getting a gun in his hands and having a go at the enemy. Suggesting that he's . . . well, not as much of a man as he should be.'

Merry sighed deeply. 'What's new about that? He should be used to it by now.'

'This time it's gone beyond the odd snide remark. He's really taken it to heart. Can you have a word? I'm afraid he might go and do something stupid otherwise.'

Merry sighed again. The last thing he felt like coping with tonight was Tom Dyson's bruised ego. 'OK. Send him to me, will you, Clive? I'll see what I can do.'

When Clive had gone Merry put his head in his hands. He had not had a private conversation with Tom since last New Year's Eve. Since then, he had been careful to ensure that they were never alone together and Tom had apparently accepted the situation.

Clive put his head round the tent flap. 'Here he is,' he said, and withdrew. Tom came in and stood rigidly to attention just inside. Merry groaned inwardly. They had been through all this before.

'Relax, Tom. Come and sit down – please.'

Tom glanced quickly at him and hesitated. In the light of the hurricane lamp Merry could see that his face was flushed and his eyes unnaturally bright. He repeated gently, 'Come on, Tom.'

The boy relaxed his stance and dropped into the chair on the far side of the table, his eyes on the ground.

'Now, what's been going on?' Merry asked.

'I'm fed up with people taking the mickey out of me because I'm a dancer,' Tom said sulkily.

'Who's been doing that?'

'Some of the men in the mess. Ignorant sods!'

'Well, you said it yourself,' Merry remarked. 'Why should you care what ignorant sods like that say?'

''Cos they're calling me a fairy, a pooftah . . .'

Merry frowned. 'But why should you care about that, either? After all, it's something we both live with.' He laid the lightest of emphasis on the words 'we both'.

Tom shot him an angry look. 'You don't have to put up with it. You only mix with officers. You don't know what it's like.'

'Believe me, it isn't confined to the other ranks,' Merry said wearily. 'It may be a bit more subtle in the officers' mess, but it's there all right. I'm afraid there are certain people for whom three things are inextricably linked. If you're male and have any artistic or performing talent then you must be a) queer and b) a coward.'

'But it's not fair!' Tom exploded. 'Just because we're not like them it doesn't mean we're yellow!'

'No, quite,' Merry agreed. 'But let's try to separate these three strands. First of all, are you ashamed of what you do? Professionally, I mean.'

'As a dancer? No, I'm bloody not! They should try standing up in front of hundreds of blokes and dancing.'

'Exactly my point,' Merry said. 'So why don't you put that to them? Ask if they've got the bottle to get up and entertain an audience the way you did tonight.'

Tom looked away. 'But I'm not going to get shot at, am I? That's the point.'

'True,' Merry agreed. 'But neither are the boffins back home, or the medics in the hospitals, or, probably, the men who bring up the stores. It takes all sorts to run a war, and not everyone is in the front line. You are doing something very important, Tom. You're giving these men a chance to forget the war, forget the possibility of being killed tomorrow. They need that, as much as they need food from the cookhouse or medical care when they're wounded. Just remember the response you had from that audience tonight and weigh that against the gibes of two or three idiots.'

'More than two or three,' Tom protested.

'How many, then?'

'I dunno. Five, six.'

'Still only a tiny fraction compared to the rest of the audience.'

Tom was silent for a moment. Then he said, 'There's still the other thing.'

'Being called a poof?'

'Yes.'

'Tom, we are what we are. Society doesn't approve of it – but that's society's fault, not ours. There have been other civilisations that thought quite differently.' Merry paused, watching the boy's half-averted face. 'Did you know, for example, that in ancient Thebes under Epaminondas the crack regiment in the army was made up of pairs of lovers who were all sworn to win the battle or die together? They were called the Sacred Band and for a while they were invincible. Nobody called them cowards.'

Tom looked at him warily. 'So what am I supposed to say when they ask me if I'm queer? Tell them about Epamy-whatsit?'

Merry smiled. 'You could try that, I suppose. Or you could try saying, "Yes, I am. Come over here and I'll give you a big wet kiss."'

Tom stared at him in amazement. Then the humour of the idea got through to him and he grinned in spite of himself. 'Trouble is, I might get some takers.'

'That's a risk you would have to run,' Merry agreed gravely.

Tom glanced at him again, saw the corners of his lips twitch and could not suppress a snort of laughter.

'That's better,' Merry said. He waited for a moment. Tom said nothing but his face had relaxed. Merry leaned forward and folded his hands on the table. 'Tom, about last New Year's Eve . . .'

Tom looked up sharply. 'I don't want to talk about that. That was a mistake.' He got up, anger and hurt pride back in his face again. 'I thought it would be good, with you. I should have known better!'

He turned away and marched out of the tent, leaving Merry clasping his temples in frustration and despair.

6

The trawler *Tarana* slipped almost silently through the dark waters off the coast of southern France. To an observer she would have appeared indistinguishable from any other fishing boat. Only her crew knew that when she left Gibraltar a few days earlier she had been painted in naval grey and before returning she would again be repainted in that colour. But then her crew were members of the Royal Navy themselves and knew that *Tarana* was a naval 'Q' ship and was fitted out below decks with secret compartments and false bulkheads where men or equipment could be concealed from all but the most thorough search.

Richard stood in the bows, straining his eyes for the pinpoint of green light flashing the Morse letter V from the shore. It was three weeks since his interview with Langley and Neave in Room 900, three weeks into which had been crammed a series of briefings at Langley's flat in St James's Street, several discussions with Buckmaster – and his wedding to Priscilla. His original idea, when he accepted his current assignment, had been that they would postpone their marriage until his return – whenever that might be. Priscilla had had other ideas. On the whole, he reflected, she had taken the abandonment of the elaborate plans for a society wedding quite well, but she had insisted that they should be married before he left. So the ceremony had been carried out by special licence at Chelsea Register Office two days before his departure for Gibraltar.

He tensed suddenly, the thoughts of his marriage banished by a sharp pinprick of light ahead and slightly on the starboard bow. Three short flashes and a long one – the letter V.

'There!' he said softly to the man standing beside him, but the signal had already been seen and the *Tarana* altered course towards it. Shortly afterwards Richard let himself down the rope ladder and dropped silently into the rubber dinghy tied up alongside. Mindful of previous experience, he had taken off his trousers and knotted them round his neck. He had no intention of turning up in Marseilles salt-stained up to the thigh, as he had on his previous expedition. This time, however, the beach was sandy and the dinghy, rowed by two crew members from the *Tarana*, was able to run aground.

As Richard scrambled ashore a slight figure in black moved forward from the shadows and a voice whispered the password, '*Où est le chat noir?*'

Richard stood still, stunned. The voice was a woman's. The surprise was so great that he almost forgot to give the agreed reply.

'*Il est perdu dans la forêt!*' he hissed in return.

The woman came closer. 'Are you Artist?' It was the code name by which he was known to F section.

'*Oui.*'

A hand was extended and grasped his own in a firm clasp. '*Enchanté de vous connaître.*' There was something about the accent that puzzled Richard.

'*Moi aussi,*' he stammered, suddenly uncomfortably aware of his state of undress.

She handed him a package. 'This is for Jimmy.'

'Right.' Richard turned back to the dinghy and handed over the package with instructions that it should be forwarded to Room 900. There were whispers of 'Good luck' and the boat pushed off and disappeared into the moonless night. He turned back and began to unknot his trousers from round his neck. 'Just give me a minute, will you?'

He heard her chuckle softly. 'Thought you'd come ashore ready for a beach party!'

'You got the radio message all right, then?' he commented.

'Relayed from one of the other *réseaux*, yes. Lucky their operator is still working.'

'London didn't like involving someone else, but it was the only way to let you know I was coming.'

Once he was dressed she led him along a path that wound through the sand dunes to an isolated building that seemed too large to be an ordinary villa. She knocked on the front door, a rhythmic pattern of taps, and it was opened by a middle-aged woman in a black dress. Richard found himself in a large vestibule.

'Welcome to the Hôtel du Tennis,' said his companion. 'This is Madame Chouquette, the proprietress. She's been working with us from the beginning.'

Madame led them through to her private sitting room, where a meal of bread and sausage was laid out, and poured them both a large brandy.

'Cheers!' the girl said, raising her glass to him. 'I'm Ginny, by the way. What should we call you?'

'Ricardo,' he responded, and added, 'You're not French.'

'Only by marriage,' she answered.

'American?' he guessed.

'Wrong! Australian, born and bred. And I'd bet you're not Italian – but don't worry. I shan't ask questions.'

Now that they were in a lighted room he was able to see her properly for the first time. He guessed that she was about his own age, tall for a woman, with clear blue eyes and an open face bare of make-up but with a sprinkling of freckles across the nose. Her hair was fair, bleached into blonde streaks by the sun. Sitting across from him, sipping her brandy, she looked as confident and relaxed as if they were engaged on nothing more dangerous than a midnight feast. He would have liked to ask her about her husband and how she came to be involved with the line, but he had taken to heart the implied rebuke in her last remark and reminded himself that the less any of them knew about each other the better.

Before long Madame Chouquette showed him to a room, explaining that the hotel was closed to guests for the duration of the war so he had no need to worry about meeting anyone else. He pulled off his outer clothes, lay down and tried, with only limited success, to catch a few hours' sleep.

At first light, as soon as the curfew was lifted, Ginny produced two bicycles and they rode the thirteen kilometres into Perpignan, where they left the bikes with a friend of Madame Chouquette's and took the train to Marseilles. Richard was carrying the same papers that he had used on his previous venture into France, which identified him as Ricardo Benedetti, wounded and discharged as unfit from the Italian army. There had been considerable discussion between himself and Maurice Buckmaster, on the one hand, and Langley and Neave on the other, as to whether he should retain this name. In the end it had been agreed that the chances of the Gestapo in Lille having circulated his particulars to the Vichy authorities were remote and that, as O'Leary already knew him by that name, it would simplify matters all round. Besides, there simply was not enough time to construct a complete new identity for him.

Even so, he was thankful when the policeman at the exit from the platform passed him with scarcely a glance at his documents. He and Ginny had travelled together, since it was accepted that a couple were less likely to arouse suspicion than a man on his own, but at the station they parted and he made his way directly to the now familiar block of flats in the rue Roux de Brignolles. As before he avoided the lift and took the stairs to the second floor, where he rang the bell at number 21. Séraphine, the Rodocanachis' elderly maid, opened the door. Her face was impassive but Richard saw, from the merest flicker of an eye, that she had recognised him. He asked, as always, to see the doctor, but instead of showing him into the waiting room she led him directly to a room at the rear of the flat. O'Leary was already there. He rose to his feet with an exclamation of surprise. 'Ricardo! You! We were told to expect someone. I never imagined it would be you. I thought the Gestapo had got you in Lille!'

'Not quite,' Richard said, grimly. 'But it was a near thing.' He held out his hand. 'How are you, Pat?'

The slight, dark man who went by such an unlikely Irish name shook his hand and said, in his quiet, cultured French, 'I am well, *mon brave*. And you?'

'Quite fit, thank you,' Richard replied. O'Leary's presence, combined with the experience of being back in France, speaking French, slipping back into the identity of Ricardo Benedetti, had brought back so powerfully the memory of Chantal that he was almost overcome. He was aware of the other man's piercing dark eyes studying him, with compassion. He cleared his throat. 'Jimmy Langley sends you his best wishes – and Airey Neave.'

'Airey? So he got out all right. You have seen him?'

'Yes. He's working with Jimmy.'

'No, really? That's excellent news. Now we have two people who really understand what is going on working for us in England.'

'They're very concerned about you,' Richard said. 'What happened to the radio operator you brought back from Gibraltar?'

'Him? Pouf!' O'Leary shrugged contemptuously. 'He was too terrified ever to operate his set. Someone else had to bring it through the checkpoint at the station for him. And when the time for the first transmission came he was so frightened of the Germans picking it up that he set it up in such a way that London couldn't receive a thing.'

'What on earth made him volunteer for the job?'

'It seems he had a wife here, from whom he was separated when he was evacuated to England with the remainder of the French army after Dunkirk. His whole aim was to rejoin her.'

'The little swine!' Richard exclaimed. 'What happened to him?'

'I sent him back down the line, with his wife. He was too much of a liability to remain here. So I am still without a radio operator.'

'I know,' Richard said. 'Jimmy is looking for someone for you, but you know how it is. MI9 seems to be at the end of the line when it comes to trained radio operators and the means to get them here.'

The door opened to admit Dr Rodocanachi and his wife, Fanny. Richard was shocked to see how much older and more frail they looked than when he had been here a year ago, especially Fanny. It was clear that the strain of living with the constant danger of discovery was taking a heavy toll.

'Ricardo! *Bienvenue!*' Fanny took his hand and kissed his cheek. 'I'm so glad to see you well. Come and join us for lunch.'

Richard smiled and returned the greeting. Mrs Rodocanachi always behaved as if she were the hostess of a pre-war dinner party, and the table was laid, as he remembered, with spotless linen and sparkling glassware.

'We have some pâté,' Fanny said. 'Please help yourself.'

Richard took some and found it surprisingly tasty, though what gone into it he did not like to imagine.

'And to go with it we shall have this bottle of Sauternes, to celebrate your safe arrival,' the doctor said.

'Sauternes!' Pat exclaimed. 'I thought that was unobtainable now that the Nazis are in possession of Bordeaux.'

The doctor smiled ruefully. 'One of the last of a diminishing stock, I fear. But the occasion merits something special.'

Inevitably, as the meal progressed, the conversation turned to Richard's experiences of the previous winter.

'That damned man Cole,' Pat exclaimed. 'We lost half the *réseau* through his treachery.'

'I hear he's been arrested,' Richard said.

'Yes, thank God! But it's too late. We should have killed him when we had him here in this flat. Ian was in favour of giving him a massive injection of insulin, but Bruce was against it and while we dithered he escaped.'

'Do you have any news of Ian?' Richard asked. 'I know he was arrested.'

'He's still in the jail at Meauzeac, in the Dordogne,' O'Leary said. 'I want to mount a rescue attempt but London tells me not to take the risk. There seem to be other prisoners they are more interested in getting out.'

'Who, for example?' Richard asked.

'Have you ever heard of an American called Whitney Straight?'

'Wasn't he a famous racing driver before the war?'

'That's the man. When war broke out he volunteered for the Royal Air Force and apparently he's one of their star pilots. And the RAF are desperate to get him back. He was shot down over northern France in '41 but managed to evade capture and got himself across the demarcation line into the unoccupied zone. Then the idiot walked into a restaurant and tried to order a meal, without realising that you had to have a ration card! They put him in the Fort St Hippolyte but MI9 keeps nagging me to get him out.'

'Can you do it?' Richard asked.

'We got him out once. The doctor here is one of the medical officers for the fort. He helped Straight to fake an injury so that he could be certified as unfit for further service and repatriated.'

'He had an old wound in the back and damage to his eardrums from a previous incident,' the doctor said. 'I found that by mixing brick dust with soap it was possible to mimic a discharge of pus from the ear and I instructed him in how to present the symptoms of vertigo. It goes against all my medical training to encourage someone to fake a disability but I felt that in this case it was justified.'

'So what went wrong?' Richard asked. 'I assume something did.'

'We got him as far as Perpignan, with a group of others all due to be repatriated,' O'Leary said. 'By pure bad luck there happened to have been a big RAF raid on Paris the night before in which the Renault factory was almost destroyed. The Germans were very annoyed at having one of their main facilities for producing tanks knocked out, so in reprisal they persuaded their Vichy friends to halt the repatriation. Straight was transferred to a secure unit at the Pasteur Hospital near Nice.'

'What rotten luck!' Richard said. 'So now what?'

'We have a contact at the hospital. I won't go into the details. We should be able to get him out but the question is what to do with him then. He's not the easiest "guest" to accommodate. Too fond of having his own way! The first time we got him out, while he was waiting to be sent home, he went off to friends in Cannes and played tennis! Can you believe it? A man supposedly suffering from vertigo?'

Richard recalled the young airman who had given them so much trouble in Lille and said with feeling, 'As it happens, I can. But as to getting him back to Britain – that's really why I'm here. Jimmy wants to organise some seaborne rescue operations. He knows that you have far more men waiting to be sent home than you can cope with, and taking them over the Pyrenees is too time consuming and too risky. To say nothing of the danger of being picked up by the Spanish and ending up in Miranda del Ebro, which is a fate I wouldn't wish on my worst enemy. If we can get them out by sea we can take twenty or thirty at a time, but without radio contact it's very difficult to organise. I'm to tell you that, in the absence of further contact, *Tarana* will put in again on July the eighteenth. That gives us a month to get Straight out and assemble any others who are being sheltered locally.'

'Excellent!' said O'Leary. 'That is good news indeed. And what are you planning to do during that month?'

'I'm to place myself under your orders,' Richard told him. 'Tell me where I can be most help.'

O'Leary thought for a moment. 'We shall need someone in Perpignan to take care of getting the men to the right place when the time comes and to act as beach master for the evacuation. We also need couriers to escort them from other places along the coast. What will your cover be while you are here?'

'The same as last time,' Richard said with a smile. 'I intend to try to get work singing in hotels or clubs. If I can get engagements in several different places that will give me an excuse to travel backwards and forwards.'

'*Formidable!*' exclaimed O'Leary. 'I remember hearing you in Lille. You were very good. But are you sure it is safe? Someone might remember you from last time you sang here with Chantal and make the connection.'

'I thought I'd give Marseilles a miss, for that reason,' Richard said. 'There are plenty of other resorts I can try.'

'Very well,' O'Leary said. 'I suggest you make it a priority to establish yourself in Perpignan. After that, somewhere east of here would be useful. Cannes, Nice . . . or how about Monaco? Your Italian passport should get you in there without any trouble.'

'Good idea. I'll give it a try,' Richard said. Then he added, 'By the way, the girl who met me last night – Ginny?'

O'Leary smiled quietly. 'Ah yes, Virginia. A remarkable young woman, is she not?'

'She certainly took me by surprise,' Richard agreed. 'I was wondering – do you think she would be prepared to come with me, for part of the time anyway? I could do with an excuse for wanting to stay in France rather than going home to Italy. On a strictly platonic basis, of course.'

'Of course,' O'Leary agreed. 'She is, after all, a married woman. But perhaps that would give added colour to your story! You could say that you are trying to keep one step ahead of a jealous husband. She is a very dedicated helper. I think she would do as you ask. I shall enquire. Where are you going to stay?'

Richard named a small hotel near the harbour which he had heard was quiet and discreet and O'Leary promised to send him Ginny's reply by the next morning.

Richard left the flat after lunch and headed down towards the waterfront. He was tempted to go back to the hotel where he and Chantal had stayed two years previously but decided that it would be wiser to avoid any contact with places where he might be remembered. That place would arouse memories that were too sharp and too painful. Already, every street, every smell, the accents of the people he passed, transported him back to those few days when they had worked together at the Tour Blanche nightclub, days intensified by danger and made poignant by the expectation of imminent separation.

Abruptly he realised that he had been walking in a dream, exactly the kind of thing that he had warned his protégés against at Beaulieu, a warning that had been dinned into his own consciousness by Victor during his training. A few moments' inattention, something as simple as looking first right and then left before crossing a street instead of the other way around, could give an agent away to an alert observer. Richard paused and pretended to gaze into a shop window, studying the reflections of passers-by. There seemed to be nobody loitering in the vicinity in such a way as to arouse suspicion. To be on the safe side, however, he entered a large shop and left by a door giving on to a different street, then hopped on a moving bus and jumped off again when it slowed at a corner. By the time he reached the harbour and entered the hotel he was reasonably sure that he was not being followed.

He presented his papers at the desk, filled in the necessary form and went up to his room, from which he had a view of the shipping in the harbour. He unpacked the small suitcase of basic necessities that he had carried with him from the *Tarana* and sat down on the edge of the bed. Since waking that morning he had been running on the adrenalin of danger but now he was aware that he had had only three hours' sleep the previous night. More disturbingly, he was shaken by his recent lapse of attention and by the violence of the emotions that had been stirred up by remembering Chantal. It suddenly struck him that since landing in France she had been almost constantly in his mind, whereas thoughts of Priscilla, his wife of a few days, had hardly entered his head. He told himself that it was hardly surprising, under the circumstances, but the realisation brought into sharp focus a question that he had been trying to ignore for days, perhaps weeks. Was he really in love with Priscilla? He had convinced himself initially that the answer was yes and then shut his mind to any doubts. Now he was aware only of a great confusion of emotions. Had he been in love with Chantal? Perhaps. It was true he had wanted her to marry him, but that had been partly out of loneliness and a sense of obligation. Anyway, she had always refused on the grounds that one day he would return to England – to Rose. *Rose!* A dull, yearning ache stirred within him. It had all been so long ago. It was three years now since they had been together, and in all that time he had seen her once, on that unforgettable New Year's Eve when she had announced her engagement to another man. To say that he was in love with Rose was to say that he was in love with a dream, an illusion – a memory that grew fainter with every passing month. His relationship with Chantal had, at least, been real – wonderfully, agonisingly real – but that was over, ruled off with a terrible finality by death. Now he had to focus his mind on Priscilla. With a determined effort he recalled her elfin face with its sleek, dark hair; her dazzling, vivacious smile; her passionate kisses. He remembered how they had talked and talked, the plans they had made for the future. The plans *she* had made. The simple fact was that the whole world she represented had become unreal to him. Reality was this dangerous life of deception and risk in which the slightest error could mean imprisonment, torture and death. He drew a long breath and got up from the bed. That was his problem, this double life he had been forced to lead. There was nothing wrong with Priscilla, or her plans for the future, and when the war was over – if he survived – he would be able to go back and embrace them, and her, wholeheartedly. Meanwhile, he must concentrate on the job in hand.

7

Merry was woken on the morning after his interview with Tom by sounds of unusual activity. Motors fired, orders were shouted, running feet passed his tent. He rolled off the narrow camp bed and dragged on some clothes. Outside he discovered a scene of chaos. A convoy of lorries was grinding its way towards the main entrance. Squads of men, rifles on their shoulders, were running the opposite way, jeeps careering between the two. One skidded to a stop beside him and Lieutenant Henshaw, the officer who had greeted them the previous evening, jumped out.

'You'd better get your gear packed and get out as fast as you can,' he said crisply. 'Rommel's made a surprise attack. One of his divisions has hooked round Bir Hacheim to the south and turned our flank. Word is that there's a panzer column less than a mile away. If you hurry you can leave with the support trucks.'

Merry raced across the compound to where the rest of the company had been quartered. They were all up already and he yelled to them to follow him down to the arena where they had performed the previous evening. The stage and all their equipment had been left ready for the next performance and they began a feverish effort to dismantle it and load it into the trucks. In their haste Merry's piano, which was always the last thing to be loaded, got bogged down in the soft sand

and they were still heaving at it when an armoured car drew up alongside them and Henshaw got out.

'Leave that and come on!' he yelled. 'I've been given the job of escorting you back to the rear echelon. We haven't got a minute to lose.'

'Not on your life!' was Merry's response. 'Come on, lads, *heave!*'

With a last, superhuman effort they extricated the piano from the sand and shoved it up the ramp into the back of the second truck. A couple of minutes later the two vehicles were ploughing along the dusty track in the wake of Henshaw's armoured car. They passed through the gap in the barbed wire and then turned due east, crossing apparently trackless desert. Away to the south they could hear the sound of gunfire and then a formation of Stuka dive-bombers swept overhead. It was obvious, however, that they were after bigger game than two unarmed trucks and they passed over without incident. Seconds later Merry and his companions heard the crump of anti-aircraft fire and saw the white puffs of shells exploding in the southern sky. Then came the columns of dust rising from just over the hills that bounded the horizon and the truck juddered and swayed as the blast from the bombs hit it.

'Some poor bugger's getting it!' Clive muttered.

They ground on for a while and then the armoured car ahead of them topped a slight rise, came to an abrupt halt and reversed sharply. Merry stood on the brakes and the truck skidded to a standstill. Ahead of them Henshaw was crouching at the rear of his vehicle. Merry got out and went forward to join him. From beyond the sand dune he could hear the unmistakable sound of tanks in motion.

'Keep down!' Henshaw said. 'There's a whole column of panzers crossing our front in the wadi just beyond the hill.

That means the rear echelon has probably already been over-run. Fortunately, they didn't spot me. With any luck if we stay here and keep our heads down they'll just keep going.'

They crouched where they were until the noise of the tanks faded to a distant growl. Then Henshaw crawled forward to the top of the rise and scanned the ground ahead through his field glasses.

'I think we're OK,' he said, returning to Merry. 'Just pray that wasn't the advanced guard of a larger force!'

Merry returned to the truck and they forged on, over the hill and across a track running north to south, where the ground was churned into ruts by the passage of the tanks. The air was thick with dust and a rising wind blew curtains of sand across his vision and forced grit into his eyes and mouth.

'That's all we need, a bloody khamsin,' Clive grunted from beside him. The khamsin was the desert wind that could change the shape of the landscape by shifting whole sand dunes, clog up engines and make all movement virtually impossible.

The two trucks bounced and swayed onward in the wake of the armoured car, Merry straining his eyes to keep it in view through the murk. Suddenly he saw a lone figure materialise out of the blown sand just ahead of them. The car stopped, there was a brief conversation, then the figure scrambled in and the convoy moved on.

'Who the dickens was that?' Clive demanded.

'God knows!' Merry responded. 'One of our chaps, by the look of the uniform. But I can't imagine what he's doing out here on his own.'

Seconds later the truck was rocked by an explosion and a fountain of sand and rock spouted up a few yards ahead and to their right. Almost simultaneously there was a detonation somewhere behind them.

'Christ!' Clive yelled. 'We're being shelled!'

Ahead the armoured car was ploughing on. Another shell landed a short distance in front of it and Merry saw it swerve. He looked in his mirror and gave a yell of anguish.

'Oh God! The other truck's been hit!'

Behind them the second truck had keeled over on to its side and the canvas hood was on fire. Figures, indistinct in the whirling sand, were scrambling out of it. Merry stopped the engine and opened his door.

'Stay here,' he instructed Clive, 'and take over the driving if necessary.'

As he ran back towards the damaged vehicle another shell exploded near by and he felt a heavy impact somewhere beneath his ribs that knocked him off his feet. Gasping, he struggled up again and ran on. The men from the second truck were converging with him. Wally Long, who drove it, had blood streaming down his face and Ray Short was cradling a useless arm.

'Get in the other truck!' Merry shouted to them. He counted them as they streamed past him. Wally, Ray, Ronnie Davies, Chubby Hawkes, panting like a steam engine. There should be a fifth. With a sickening jolt Merry realised who it was.

'Where's Tom?' he yelled.

Chubby stopped and looked round. 'I thought he was ahead of me.'

Merry ran on. By the time he reached the rear of the truck the canvas cover was well ablaze. Peering inside he could make out a jumble of packing cases, spotlights and other impedimenta but he could see no sign of Tom. Henshaw appeared at his elbow.

'For Christ's sake, man! What are you doing? We can't stop here. Those gunners'll get our range any minute now.'

'One of my men is in here somewhere,' Merry panted. 'I can't leave him.'

He scrambled into the truck among the debris and heard a low moan. Tom was lying against the side of the vehicle, one leg trapped under the piano, which had broken loose from the ropes that restrained it. Merry saw that the front of his tunic was soaked with blood. Henshaw had climbed in after him.

'Help me shift this bloody piano,' Merry commanded.

Between them they managed to heave the piano up sufficiently to free Tom's leg. He cried out with pain as they half carried, half dragged him towards the tail of the truck. The heat from the burning awning was fierce and Merry could feel the hairs on his arms and the back of his neck scorching. He was becoming aware, too, of a vague, generalised pain in his belly but paid it little attention. Somehow they manoeuvred the wounded boy to the open air and lowered him into the waiting arms of Chubby and Ronnie. With shells bursting on both sides of them they scrambled back to the first truck and lifted Tom into it.

'Take care of him,' Merry instructed and climbed back into the cab. Henshaw had already reached the armoured car and in a moment they were grinding ahead. Two or three more shells landed close by but then the bombardment ceased as abruptly as it had started.

'What's happened? Are they out of ammo, or what?' Clive wondered.

'Maybe they just can't see us any more,' Merry said. 'There's something to be said for this khamsin after all.'

'Blimey! What have you done to yourself? You're bleeding,' Clive exclaimed.

Merry looked down. The lower part of his tunic and one trouser leg were dark with blood.

'No, it's not me,' he said. 'It's poor Tom's. He's in a bad way.'

Time seemed to have lost its meaning. Merry began to feel as if he had been jolting over the desert for days. He drove automatically, oblivious to everything except the outline of the armoured car in front. Then, as they crested another rise, he was jerked into full consciousness again as the car abruptly slewed to one side and came to a standstill. At the same instant he heard the unmistakable rattle of machine-gun fire and the whine of bullets as they ricocheted off the armoured skin of the vehicle.

He stopped the truck and stared ahead. The car remained stationary. Merry put the truck into reverse and eased it back away from the ridge.

'There must be a machine-gun nest just over the hill,' he said to Clive. 'They can't see us from here.'

'What's happened to the lieutenant and the others?' Clive asked.

'It looks as though they've been disabled,' Merry said. 'Or else the car's kaput. We're going to have to find out. There's no point in sitting here.' He turned back into the rear of the truck. 'Wally, come here and be ready to drive. Clive and I are going to see what's happened.'

He climbed out, aware of a sharp stab of pain in his side, and dropped to his hands and knees. Clive followed suit and, wriggling on their bellies, they gained the cover of the armoured car. Merry reached up cautiously and opened the driver's door. The driver's body tumbled out on top of him. There was a neat bullet hole in the centre of his forehead. Merry raised himself and climbed into the driving seat. Henshaw was slumped against the dashboard, his face unrecognisable from the impact of several bullets. Then, from the rear of the vehicle, Merry heard a groan. Looking round, he discovered the passenger who had been picked up earlier, a well-built man with iron-grey hair in the uniform of a colonel of the Royal Horse Artillery. He was clasping his shoulder and blood oozed between his fingers.

'Who are you?' he demanded gruffly.

'Merryweather, sir. What happened?'

'Machine-gun nest ahead at about ten o'clock. Caught us napping. Got us pinned down.'

Merry peered in the direction the colonel indicated. From somewhere in the middle distance he saw, through the sand-darkened air, the flashes as the gun fired again and heard the bullets ping off the armour plate. Just then a freak gust of wind parted the curtain of dust and he saw, down in the valley beyond the gun emplacement, a road and a convoy of lorries and armoured cars heading east. He leaned across to Henshaw and, suppressing a shudder of disgust, detached the field glasses from round his neck and studied the vehicles through them. From the insignia on their sides it was clear that they were British. All that stood between him and his company and some hope of safety was that machine-gun nest.

He looked at the colonel, but he was clearly in no condition to help. Rapidly he scanned the interior of the vehicle. Its only armament was a Vickers .303 machine gun mounted in the turret. He turned to Clive.

'Do you know how to fire one of these?'

'Me?' Clive responded, aghast. 'I've never fired anything bigger than a rifle.'

Merry looked at the gun. He dimly remembered having received some training on one like it, back in the early months of 1939 when he had been a 'proper', if unwilling, soldier. He looked at Clive again. 'Can you drive this thing?'

Clive looked doubtful. 'I dunno.'

'Well, you've got about thirty seconds to find out,' Merry told him crisply.

He climbed out of the car and, bent double, ran back to the truck, where Wally was sitting in the driving seat.

'When you see the car move, wait until we've gone about a hundred yards and then follow – and don't stop, whatever happens. There's a road ahead. If you can make that you're home and dry.'

He scrambled back to the car and got in. 'Right. When I give you the word drive straight ahead, and go like hell. OK?'

'OK,' said Clive, still doubtful.

Merry checked the gun. There was a new ammunition belt in place. He swung it round to the spot where he thought the firing had come from.

'Right, *go*!' he shouted.

The engine started and the car shot forward, bouncing and rocking over the uneven ground. Merry squeezed the trigger and clung to the bucking gun, swivelling it as far as possible to keep it trained on the flashes of answering fire. In a storm of dust and bullets the armoured car thundered down the hill and he kept firing until all the ammunition was used up. In the sudden silence he realised that the other gunner had ceased firing too. He opened the turret and peered behind him. The truck was following, swerving and skidding at a reckless pace, but miraculously there was no fire from the enemy guns.

'You've taken them out, lad!' the colonel growled triumphantly. 'Bloody good show!'

Seconds later they reached the road and set off in pursuit of the convoy. Merry suddenly realised that he was shaking all over and that his knees were about to give way. He lowered himself to the seat and closed his eyes for a moment. For the first time he took in the fact that he had fired a gun at live targets and had probably killed at least one man, probably more than one.

'Better have a look at that wound,' the colonel said. 'You're losing blood pretty rapidly. There's a field dressing pack in that box there.'

Merry looked down and saw that the blood that was soaking his trouser leg was, in fact, his own. He opened his tunic. There was a jagged hole about half the length of his finger in his abdomen, from which blood was welling. He looked at it in a kind of numb surprise. Then he opened the case containing the first aid dressings and examined the contents. There were some metal devices like small bulldog clips. There was surprisingly little pain as he drew the lips of the wound together and fastened them with two of the clips. Then he found a sterile dressing and with some difficulty taped it in place. Then he remembered the colonel, who was still clasping his shoulder.

'Can I do something for you, sir?'

The officer shook his head. 'Not much you can do. I think the shoulder blade's shattered.'

'I might be able to stop the bleeding,' Merry suggested.

He leaned over and carefully peeled back what was left of the tunic at the shoulder. There was a neat bullet hole at the front, but a far larger and messier exit hole at the back of the shoulder. He taped a pad over each of them and the flow of blood lessened, if it did not completely stop.

As he worked he said, 'If you don't mind me asking, Colonel, how did you come to be out there on your own?'

'I was at Seventh Armoured Division HQ. We were overrun about eight o'clock this morning. No warning at all. Complete bloody shambles. The tanks just came out of nowhere.

General Messervy's been captured, I'm afraid. We all scattered and I managed to slip out of camp without being spotted but I had no transport, of course. Just had to keep walking and hope I'd run into some of our chaps.'

'Lucky we came along,' Merry commented.

'What unit are you with?' the colonel asked.

'SIB,' Merry said.

'SIB? What the hell is that?'

'Stars in Battledress, sir.'

'You mean the concert party chappies? Good God, I thought you chaps were all conchies.'

'No, we're all trained soldiers, Colonel,' Merry said quietly.

'Well, you certainly proved that just now. It was you who went back for one of your men when the second truck got hit, wasn't it?'

'Yes, that's right.'

'How is he?'

'I don't know.' Merry pictured Tom Dyson, with his crushed leg and bloodstained tunic.

The car slowed and stopped. 'What's going on?' Merry asked.

'We've caught up with the convoy,' Clive responded. 'We're being challenged by the escort.'

Merry got out and limped over to the tank that had barred their way. After identifying themselves to the officer in charge they were waved on. Merry leaned into the armoured car.

'I'm going back to the truck to see how Tom is. I'll see you when we get to wherever it is we're going.'

In the back of the truck Tom was lying with his head in Chubby's lap. Merry leaned over him.

'How is he?'

'Not good, I'm afraid,' Chubby answered. 'He's caught a piece of shrapnel in the chest. I'm afraid it's damaged the lung.

We've done what we could to stop the bleeding and I gave him a shot of morphine, but he needs expert treatment.'

'Well, with any luck we should reach Tobruk soon,' Merry said. He looked down at Tom. His face was colourless and a small froth of blood flickered on his lips with every breath. 'Let me have him,' he said.

Carefully Chubby eased himself out of the way and allowed Merry to take over his position.

'You sure you're OK?' he asked. 'You don't look too good yourself.'

'I'll survive,' Merry replied. The dull ache in his guts was changing to a sharper, more urgent stabbing, but at least the bleeding seemed to have stopped.

Disturbed by the changeover, Tom stirred and mumbled and his eyes flickered open. He took in Merry's face and smiled faintly. 'Merry. Glad you're here.'

Merry murmured, 'Hello, Tom. Just try to relax. We'll get you to hospital soon.'

The boy was silent for a minute, then he whispered, 'New Year's Eve. I shouldn't have done it. I'm sorry.'

'No,' Merry answered softly. 'I'm the one who should say sorry. You . . . offered me something precious, and I took it and then . . . I behaved very badly, Tom. I'm sorry.'

What Chubby Hawkes, sitting close beside them, was making of this conversation Merry neither knew nor cared. Tom closed his eyes and Merry thought he had drifted back into unconsciousness but after a moment he opened them again.

'What I said . . . It wasn't true. You were good – really good.'

Merry swallowed. 'You too, Tom.'

After that Tom said nothing more and Merry allowed his own eyes to close. Time passed. The interminable rocking and swaying of the truck sent stabs of pain through his stomach and up into his chest. Finally, after what seemed like hours, the truck made a turn to the left and came to a standstill. Voices spoke outside and the company began to drag themselves to their feet and climb out. Merry was aware of hands gently removing Tom from his grasp. He tried to stand up, but his legs buckled underneath him. After that, there was just a confused impression of being laid on a stretcher and carried, faces bending over him, hands busy with his clothing, a bright light and then a sudden descent into unconsciousness.

Without any interval, it seemed, he was awake again. The pain in his guts had been replaced by a vague sense of nausea and a male nurse in a crisp white coat was bending over him and saying reassuringly, 'It's OK. You're in hospital. You've had an operation but you're going to be fine.'

Merry frowned up at him. He became aware that he was in bed, between clean sheets, in a long, echoing ward. 'What happened to me?' he asked.

'You copped some shrapnel in the stomach,' the nurse said. 'Don't ask me how. I wasn't there. But the doc took a piece of steel the size of a two-bob bit out of you. Lucky for you it wasn't a few inches higher or it might have hit something vital.'

Merry searched his mind. There was something he needed to know.

'There was a boy with me – hit in the chest. Do you know how he is?'

The nurse's lips tightened. 'Dead on arrival, I'm afraid. Massive internal haemorrhage. There was nothing you could have done. I'm sorry. Friend of yours, was he?'

'Sort of,' Merry mumbled.

8

On the day after his conversation with O'Leary Richard took the train back to Perpignan alone. Late the night before a note had been delivered to his hotel. '*I will meet you tomorrow in the bar of the Hôtel du Cheval Blanc at six o'clock. G.*' He passed unquestioned through the various checkpoints and found the Cheval Blanc without difficulty. It was well chosen – quiet and unobtrusive without appearing unduly seedy. The sort of hotel a respectable married woman might choose for an assignation with her lover.

At a few minutes before six Ginny arrived, looking very chic in a perfectly outrageous hat.

Richard rose and greeted her with a kiss on both cheeks. '*Chérie*, you look marvellous! Let me take your case.'

As soon as the formalities of checking in were finished he suggested they should go for a stroll before dinner. Ginny, well aware that once they were in the open air there was less danger of being overheard, agreed at once. Once they were outside, she looked at him, her eyes sparkling. 'Well? What's it all about?'

He explained briefly and added, 'But for tonight, we're going out on the town. Is there anywhere that provides entertainment – music of some sort?'

'There are a couple of rather sleazy nightclubs. I've never been into them. What are you looking for?'

'What about something a bit more sophisticated? Where do the *haute bourgeoisie* hang out?'

'There's a hotel called the Lion d'Or. They have a kind of gypsy band that plays during dinner.'

'OK. Let's try there.'

Here in the south, in the unoccupied zone, the French were trying to maintain the civilised life on which they prided themselves, in spite of rationing and the restrictions placed on them by the government in Vichy. The dining room at the Lion d'Or was almost full and they were lucky to get a table. A dark, saturnine man at the piano was strumming his way casually through a selection of light classics. Halfway through the evening he was joined by two more, a guitarist and an accordionist. As soon as they appeared the pianist's mood seemed to change and the three of them embarked on a medley of wild and haunting tunes that seemed to Richard to owe more to Spain than to France.

The evening ended early as there was a curfew in force here as elsewhere, but Richard noticed that the atmosphere was more relaxed and there were fewer uniforms on the street than there were in Marseilles. Nevertheless, he kept a sharp eye open for members of the Milice, the pro-Nazi secret police. Back at the hotel he escorted Ginny up to her room and said goodnight to her with a chaste kiss. As he made his way back to his own room it occurred to him that he had, in fact, in spite of the inherent dangers of his situation, enjoyed the evening.

The following day Richard returned to the Lion d'Or, asked to see the manager and launched into the story he had prepared. He was short of money and looking for work – and could provide a reference from the manager at the Tour Blanche in Marseilles. The manager agreed to try him out that night, with a view to a longer engagement if he proved popular with the clientele.

He went back to the hotel to fetch Ginny and explain the arrangement.

'You're actually going to sing for your supper?' she queried.

He grinned at the tone of disbelief. 'Quite literally, as it happens. A free meal is part of the deal.' Then, seeing the doubt in her eyes, he added, 'Don't worry. It's what I do.'

That evening he sang two numbers, which were so well received that the manager agreed to engage him for a two-week period. Afterwards he was free to join Ginny, who sat at a corner table watching him with a suitably adoring expression. She greeted him with a grin. 'Sorry about earlier. I didn't know what you were letting us in for but – hey – you really can sing!'

The next day they collected the two bicycles and set off to cycle back to Canet Plage, the beach where Richard had landed. He was anxious to check out the surroundings in preparation for the planned evacuation when *Tarana* returned. To his dismay, they found the beach crowded with holidaymakers.

'But of course!' Ginny said. 'It's a very popular spot. But there is no one here after dark – as you saw.'

'But we need to be able to assemble quite large groups of men without anyone knowing they are here,' Richard pointed out. 'They may have to wait twenty-four hours to be picked up – possibly longer if there's a hitch of any kind.'

'So? What's wrong with the hotel?' Ginny asked.

'OK. Let's check it out,' he agreed.

It was obvious at once that the hotel would not meet their needs. Although it was closed to residents, Mme Chouquette had kept the bar open and a number of people were drinking on the terrace. It would be impractical to attempt to hide a large group there for any length of time.

'We shall have to look for somewhere else,' Richard said. 'Let's try farther along the beach.'

They strolled along the sand, trying to blend in with the rest of the holidaymakers. Ginny slipped her hand into Richard's. 'We are supposed to be lovers, aren't we? Don't you think we ought to try to act like it?'

Richard looked at her. Her blue eyes met his with a mischievous sparkle. 'That suits me,' he said. 'I just didn't want you to think I was pushing my luck.'

She grinned. 'I'll tell you if you're overstepping the mark.'

He released her hand and put his arm instead round her shoulders. She was dressed in shorts and a sleeveless top with a plunging neckline, and a glance downwards showed him that she had nothing on underneath it. He felt a sudden stirring of excitement and removed his arm, reminding himself sternly that he was a married man with a job to do.

They had walked some distance when Ginny said, 'Look, over there.'

He looked and saw, just visible between two sand dunes, a red-tiled roof. 'Let's take a closer look.'

There were traces of a path leading between the dunes but it was obvious that no one had passed that way recently. Their own feet left deep imprints in the loose sand. On the far side of the dune they found themselves looking at a neat, white-walled villa. At some point someone had attempted to create a garden round it with some salt-tolerant shrubs, some of which were still struggling to survive, but the place had an uncared-for, abandoned look, and the track leading to it from the direction of the road showed neither footprints nor tyre marks. They went closer and peered in through the windows. There was furniture in the rooms but a thick layer of blown sand covered the floors and it was clear that no one had used the place for some time.

'This could be just what we're looking for,' Ginny said.

'Possibly,' Richard agreed. 'But if it's someone's holiday home they could turn up any day.'

'They could,' she pointed out, 'but the chances are that it either belongs to an English family who skedaddled off home when the war started, or else to some people from the north of France who aren't able to get across the demarcation line. Either way, there's no chance of anyone arriving to use it.'

'I wonder if there's any indication who it belongs to,' Richard said. 'Let's see if we can get in, shall we?'

The front door was locked, as they expected, but Richard had been taught house-breaking techniques by an expert – a burglar who had been offered a considerable reduction in his sentence on condition he imparted his expertise to the students at Beaulieu.

'Wait here for a minute,' he murmured to Ginny.

Leaving her by the front door, he set off on a tour of inspection. A very short time afterwards he opened the door from the inside and invited her to enter with a bow and sweeping gesture.

'That was quick!' she remarked. 'Had they left a window open?'

An inspection of the contents of cupboards and drawers left them no wiser as to the owners of the house but it was clear that in every other respect it was exactly what they were looking for. There were four rooms, plus two bathrooms and a kitchen. If the potential escapers could be brought here by night there was very little chance of anyone happening on them by accident and they would be handy for the beach where the *Tarana*'s boat would put in at the appointed time.

'What a pair of idiots we are!' Ginny suddenly exclaimed. 'Madame Chouquette will know who owns this place. She's bound to.'

'Of course!' Richard replied. 'OK. We'll go back to the hotel and ask, but first we need to remove all evidence that we've been here.'

At length Richard was satisfied that a casual observer looking through the windows would see nothing suspicious. Then they retraced their steps, brushing their footprints out behind them with branches pulled off a tamarisk growing in the neglected garden. At the hotel Mme Chouquette confirmed that the house did, as Ginny had suggested, belong to a Parisian family who had been unable to visit it since the outbreak of war.

'In that case,' Richard said, 'it would be a good idea if people actually got used to us coming and going. Can't we pretend that we've rented the villa for the summer?'

Ginny considered. 'It's certainly the sort of place a couple having a secret love affair might take. But how would we have contacted the owners?'

'No problem,' Madame said. 'I will tell anyone who asks that I am taking care of the place for the owners, who have asked me to let it if the opportunity arises.'

So Richard bought a new lock and key from a small locksmith's in a backstreet, let himself into the villa again through the rear window and set about replacing the lock. Meanwhile Ginny busied herself sweeping and dusting. Then they went to the nearest shops and stocked up with provisions, as far as their ration cards would permit, and carried them back openly along the track leading from the hotel to the villa.

Once they were unpacked and put away Ginny dusted her hands and remarked, 'Well, I guess we'd better check out of our hotel rooms.'

Richard stared at her, suddenly aware where his idea had led them. 'I didn't mean . . .' he began. 'I just meant that we should have a legitimate reason for being here . . . I never intended . . .'

She stopped him, laughing. 'I know what you intended, Ricardo. You're such a gentleman! But surely the whole point is for the place to be occupied at night.'

'Well, yes, I suppose so,' he said doubtfully. Then, 'No, it won't work. We'd never be able to cycle out here every evening after I finish singing at the hotel. We'd be breaking the curfew.'

'Yes, that's a snag,' she agreed. 'No, wait a minute. Suppose we do get stopped by the police. We tell them our story – we're two lovebirds heading back to our secret nest. We can't get here earlier because of your job. You know what the average French gendarme is like. He's a sucker for anything romantic. After that they won't think twice about it if they see us again.'

'As long as it is your average French gendarme,' Richard said dubiously, 'and not the Milice.'

'The Milice don't show up in out-of-the-way places like this very often,' Ginny said. 'Have you seen any around here?'

'No, it's true, I haven't,' Richard agreed. He looked at her and grinned suddenly. 'Ginny, you're a genius!'

'I have my moments,' she replied, laughing.

So the next day they checked out of their rooms and when Richard had finished his performance at the Lion d'Or they strapped their cases on to the luggage carriers of their bikes and set off for the villa. They rode without lights under a bright moon and saw no one at all, a circumstance that augured well for a future occasion when they might have 'parcels' of a more dangerous nature to deliver.

Once they were safely in the villa Richard began to feel slightly embarrassed again at the prospect of spending the ensuing nights alone with a woman who was not his wife.

'I don't know what your husband would say to all this,' he remarked uneasily.

Ginny handed him some neatly folded sheets, which she had unearthed from a cupboard. 'My husband is devoted to the cause,' she said. 'And anyway, he trusts me. What are you worrying about? There are three bedrooms to choose from. Which one do you want?'

Later, over a last cup of ersatz coffee, she said, 'Are you married, Ricardo?'

'Yes,' he said. 'Just.'

'How do you mean, just?'

'Two days before I left . . . Two days before I set out on this assignment.'

'You mean before you left England?' She smiled. 'OK, OK. I'm not prying. Your French is perfect. I'm sure your Italian is just as good. But I'd bet my bottom dollar you're English.' She put her hand on his. 'Poor old Ricardo! Fancy being torn away from your bride without even having a honeymoon!'

He squeezed her fingers. 'Well, it wasn't quite like that. I mean . . . we'd sort of already had the honeymoon.'

She chuckled. 'Good for you! Well, I'm off to bed. Sleep well.'

She paused beside him, one hand on his shoulder, and then bent and dropped a light kiss on the top of his head.

For the next few days they adopted a regular routine. In the mornings they continued their exploration of Perpignan and the surrounding countryside, since Richard knew that he might be required to assemble evaders from safe houses all round the area when the time came. In the afternoons they swam and sunned themselves on the beach, while keeping a careful eye on the path leading to the villa. It seemed that nobody ever went that way.

Then, in the evening, they changed their clothes and went to dine at the Lion d'Or and Richard sang.

It was, in many ways, a sybaritic existence and Richard frequently had to remind himself that he was not on holiday. He found, too, that he was enjoying Ginny's company more and more. She acted the adoring mistress in public very convincingly, leaning across the table to whisper sweet nothings and holding his hand at every opportunity. At first he found it disturbing, but then he saw the glint in her eyes and knew that it amused her to tease him. When they were alone she had a straightforward manner, neither flirtatious nor coy, that invited him to treat her on equal terms, as he might have done a friend of his own sex. It was an attitude he had not met before and he found it very refreshing.

One day they had cycled out into the vineyards in the foothills south of the city. It was very hot and by midday they had drunk all the water they were carrying with them. Seeing a small farmhouse sheltered under a clump of pine trees, Richard suggested that they knock and ask to be allowed to refill their water bottles. The door was opened by a tiny, wizened woman, who glowered at them suspiciously. Richard's polite request was met by a grudging gesture towards a pump that stood in the courtyard in front of the house.

As he pumped Richard murmured to Ginny, 'Charming old girl! What does she think we're going to do, rob the place?'

'She's certainly afraid of something,' Ginny agreed. 'I got the impression she couldn't get rid of us fast enough.'

Richard looked round. 'She's still watching us from behind the shutters. Come on, we'd better go before she sets the dogs on us.'

As they cycled on Richard wondered whether the old woman really did have something to hide and whether he should, perhaps, go back later and investigate. But he decided that her behaviour was probably nothing more than natural caution and his suspicions the product of paranoia induced by his own situation.

His unease was increased that evening at the hotel. He had been puzzled from the first by his three fellow musicians. They were an odd bunch who would have looked more at home, he thought, on a pirate ship than in a hotel. As they waited for their first appearance the pianist, Fernand, looked at him with hooded, suspicious eyes.

'Italian, eh?'

'Yes.'

'What brings you here, then?'

Richard produced his usual story, but he had the feeling that Fernand was not convinced.

'What part of Italy are you from, then?'

'Milan.'

'Got family there?'

'My mother, yes.'

'Got a girlfriend?' Xavier put in with a leer. He was a giant of a man with hands that looked too large for the accordion he played.

'I've just told you, my lady-friend is here. That's why I came.'

'Your people must be well off,' Fernand pursued.

'Not particularly.'

'What does your dad do?'

'He's dead. He died when I was twelve. He used to own a small restaurant.'

'So how come you learned to be a singer?'

The questions were all ones he had rehearsed over and over again with the men who had trained him at Beaulieu and the answers came pat, but it was exactly this which made him uncomfortable. They were the sort of apparently innocent enquiries that he might have used himself to check whether someone was genuine. He told himself that he was being unduly suspicious and must try to appear as natural and relaxed as possible. So when Fernand invited him, a night or two later, to join them for a drink, he agreed.

They took him to a bar in a backstreet a short distance from the hotel, on the grounds that the manager did not approve of them drinking with the guests and, anyway, the drinks were cheaper here. The conversation turned to the war and the progress, or lack of it, being made by the British and Americans. Richard was asked what he thought of Mussolini and how he felt about his country being allied to Germany. He shrugged and said that he had no interest in politics.

As soon as he decently could Richard excused himself, on the grounds that Ginny would be waiting for him at the villa. The others rose also, saying that they must be on their way if they were to be home before the curfew. Fernand paid for the drinks and they went out into the dark street. Richard said goodnight and turned away towards the main road, where there were still people hurrying homeward, but as he did so something cold and hard was pressed into his ribs and Xavier's voice growled in his ear, 'Turn left and keep walking. One squeak and you're finished!'

Richard contemplated the various moves he had been taught at Arisaig for dealing with an armed opponent but the gun was still tight against his side and he judged that it was too dangerous to try anything. He walked down the side street towards a parked car, cursing himself for his lack of vigilance and waiting for an opportunity when his captors were marginally off their guard. Old Alphonse, the guitarist, hurried ahead and opened the car door.

'Get in,' Xavier commanded.

Richard moved forward and bent as if to enter the car and in that moment he felt the gun lose contact with his side. He whipped round, striking at the arm holding the gun with the edge of his hand, and heard the weapon clatter to the cobbles. At the same instant, his other fist pounded into the big Frenchman's stomach and he doubled over with a grunt. Fernand plunged forward in time to receive a kick to the groin that collapsed him in a heap on the pavement. Richard jumped over the crouching Xavier to kick the pistol out of reach and simultaneously produced his own .32 Colt, which he always carried hanging from a loop inside his trouser leg, accessible through a false pocket. The elderly Alphonse had already backed up against the car and was flapping his hands in a gesture of surrender.

'Right!' Richard said, breathing hard. 'Don't move, any of you.' He stooped and picked up Xavier's pistol. 'Now, get into the car. Alphonse, you drive. Fernand, sit beside him.' He dragged Xavier upright and pressed the gun into his neck. 'One false move from anyone and Xavier gets it.' He pushed the big man towards the rear door of the car. 'In!'

They scrambled to do his bidding and he registered the thought that, whoever they were and whomever they were working for, it was unlikely to be the Gestapo or the Milice. Piling in next to Xavier he said, 'Drive, Alphonse. I'll tell you where to go.'

Following his instructions Alphonse drove them out towards the coast, along the route Richard normally cycled with Ginny. Before they reached the Hôtel du Tennis Richard instructed him to pull off the road under the shelter of a group of pines.

'Now,' he said, 'what is this all about? Who are you working for?'

'Who are *we* working for?' Alphonse squeaked. 'Who are *you* working for? That's what we want to know.'

After his recent display of aggression Richard realised that it was useless to continue the deception that he was simply a travelling entertainer. He said crisply, 'Never mind that. I'm asking the questions now. Who's behind all this?'

'No one!' exclaimed Fernand. 'We're not working for anyone.'

'So what are you afraid of?'

'Who are you? Gestapo? Milice? Look, all we're doing is a little bit of smuggling. It's nothing you need to concern yourself with.'

Richard's mind was racing. If they had put him down as Gestapo, what were they afraid of? He said quietly, 'Smuggling, is it? Smuggling what?'

'Cigarettes, mostly. Sometimes cognac. It's small stuff.'

'And people?' Richard suggested quietly.

'People? What people?' Fernand demanded, with an air of innocent surprise.

'No, no! Not people!' said Alphonse, rather too quickly.

'No?' Richard queried. 'That's a pity. Because if you were in that market I might be able to make it worth your while.'

There was a moment of electric silence in the car. Then Fernand repeated, '*Who are you?* Why were you sniffing round the farm the other day?'

'The farm?' Richard responded, taken by surprise. 'What farm?'

'My aunt's farm! You were there, pretending to want a drink of water. What were you after?'

'The question is,' Richard returned, 'what are you hiding?'

There was a pause. The three men looked at each other. Richard decided that the time had come, as it did in all these situations, when he had to take a gamble. He said, 'If you're hiding British airmen trying to escape, I can help you. I can even see that you are paid for your trouble.'

Alphonse twitched violently and turned round in his seat and he heard a sudden intake of breath from Xavier beside him.

Fernand said, 'Why should we trust you?'

'You don't have much choice, do you?' Richard pointed out. 'If I am with the police you've already said enough to get you into serious trouble. You'll just have to take my word for it that I'm not.'

Once again the three Frenchmen exchanged glances. Richard decided to risk another throw of the dice. He lowered the revolver, which he had until that moment kept pressed into Xavier's neck, and clicked on the safety catch.

'Pledge of good faith,' he said.

'If we're all on the same side,' Fernand challenged him, 'give me back my gun.'

For a tense moment Richard hesitated. Then he pulled the weapon from the waistband of his trousers and handed it over. Fernand checked the safety catch and, to Richard's great relief, put it in his coat pocket.

'There is someone you should meet,' he said. 'If he says you're all right, fine. If not, you won't catch us napping a second time.' He turned to Alphonse. 'Drive!'

The car was powered by gasogene, the substitute for petrol produced from a charcoal burner in the boot, which was about the only fuel available. Driving without lights, since it was now well after curfew, they skirted the suburbs of the city and reached the isolated farmhouse in the vineyards. Fernand led the way to the door, which opened directly into the large, tiled kitchen. The old woman was sitting at the long table, knitting, and at the far end sat a young man. He was dressed in the clothes of a French peasant but his large build and fair complexion proclaimed him a foreigner at a glance. As Richard entered the kitchen they both started to their feet, the boy with great difficulty, supporting himself on a crutch. His face, pale to begin with, had turned deathly white and there was panic in his eyes.

Fernand looked from him to Richard. 'He doesn't speak French. Can you talk to him in English?'

Richard moved over to the table and said reassuringly, in his own language, 'It's all right. I've come to get you out of here.'

The boy sank back on to his chair. 'You speak English? Oh, thank God! How did you know I was here?'

Richard said, 'What's your name?'

'Ben. Benedict Fry. Pilot Officer. And you are . . .?'

'You can call me Ricardo. I'm sorry, I'm not going to give you any more information than that. You'll just have to trust me. Now, I need to ask you some questions.'

'Name, rank and number,' the boy said. 'That's all you'll get out of me.'

'Quite right, too,' Richard agreed. 'Don't worry. I won't ask you anything about your unit or where you were stationed. But you'll appreciate I have to satisfy myself that you are genuine. I assume you were shot down, somewhere in the north. Is that correct?'

'The fuel tank was punctured and I ran out of juice. I managed to crash-land. Then I tried to set fire to the plane, like I'd been told, but with no fuel in the tank I couldn't get it to burn.' The boy was speaking quickly and Richard guessed that it was a relief to be able to pour out his story. 'So I gave up and set out across country. I walked most of the way. Sometimes I got a lift and a bed for the night. People were pretty good, really.'

'So, what happened to your leg?'

'I tried to get across the mountains but the weather turned foul – rain and thick mist. I slipped and fell into a sort of ravine. I realised very quickly that my leg was broken and I'd just about given myself up as a goner when I heard voices. It was these three.' He indicated Fernand, Xavier and Alphonse.

Richard turned to the three men. 'You found him?' he asked in French.

'Up there.' Fernand jerked his head in the direction of the Pyreneees. 'We were on our way back from a little . . . expedition, and we heard him shouting. He'd fallen off the path but he was lodged in a cleft in the rocks. Xavier managed to haul him up and we put him on the mule and brought him back here.'

'How's the leg now?' Richard asked the young pilot.

'They got a chap to set it,' he said. 'I think he was the local vet, not a doctor. It seems to be getting better but I can't put much weight on it yet.'

Richard turned to Fernand. 'Well? Satisfied?'

The Frenchman had sat opposite Richard, listening intently to the interrogation, obviously straining to pick up whatever words of English he recognised. Now he turned to Fry and gestured with his thumb at Richard. 'Him? English?'

'Oh yes,' the boy said, without hesitation. Richard clenched his jaw. His cover was blown, as far as these three were concerned, but that had been inevitable under the circumstances.

Fernand turned his gaze at him. 'You can get him out? He can't walk. There is no way we can take him over the mountains.'

'No, I can see that,' Richard agreed. 'Yes, I can get him out, but I can't tell you how. He will have to wait another week or two but I can promise you I will take him off your hands then.'

The relaxation of tension in the room was palpable. A bottle of brandy was produced and Fernand raised his glass. 'To Winston Churchill!'

The toast was drunk with alacrity.

Richard was anxious to get back to the villa, knowing that Ginny would have assumed the worst when he did not return, but it was senseless to ask Alphonse to take the car out again and risk being picked up for breaking the curfew, so he sat on talking and acting as interpreter between the young pilot and his hosts. He was curious to know how it happened that three apparently respectable musicians were involved in smuggling. The answer was given with a casual shrug. Everyone in the area did a bit of smuggling. It was part of the normal commerce of life. And these days, with shortages of everything and with a lot of the hotels and bars closing down through lack of trade, smuggling had become a lot more profitable than music. It was nearly dawn before Richard was offered a makeshift bed on a long settle and the household fell silent.

The next morning Alphonse drove him back to the city and he collected his bicycle and rode out to the villa. Ginny was sitting motionless at the kitchen table. When he walked in she rose and stared at him, without speaking.

He went to her and took both her hands. 'It's all right, Ginny. Everything's OK. I'm so sorry you've been worried, but there was no way I could let you know what was going on.'

She said, 'Tell me,' her voice dry and harsh. Her hands were trembling and he could tell from her eyes that she had not slept. He pressed her back into her chair and sat beside her, holding on to her hands while he told the story of the previous night's events.

When he had finished she said, 'Those three – smugglers?'

'I know,' he said. 'It's a pretty unlikely combination. But then, who am I to talk?'

She laughed then and said, 'I'll get some coffee,' but he got up and laid a hand on her shoulder. 'Sit still. I'll make it.'

She said nothing about how worried she had been, or what thoughts had gone through her mind during the night, but all that day they were very quiet and gentle with each other, as if both were recovering from a serious illness.

There was only one other incident before the end of Richard's two-week engagement at the Lion d'Or. One night, cycling back to the villa with Ginny, they were stopped by a police patrol. Fortunately one of the gendarmes had been in the hotel a few nights earlier and had heard Richard sing. So when Richard took him aside and murmured in man-to-man fashion that the young lady accompanying him was a married woman, which was why it had been necessary for them to find a secluded spot to set up home, they were dismissed with an understanding chuckle and a gallant salute.

At the end of the two weeks Richard felt he had done all that was necessary to prepare for the *Tarana*'s arrival and decided to return to Marseilles to report to O'Leary. They carefully closed up the villa, left the key with Mme Chouquette and headed for the station. As they cycled away Richard felt a twinge of nostalgia. It was almost certain that he would be back very soon, but he knew that there would be no repeat of the holiday mood that he and Ginny had shared for that brief time.

9

'Rose, love! Oh, it's good to see you after all this time. You look well! Doesn't she look well, Bet?'

Rose embraced her mother and then her sister and said, laughing, 'Well, it's easy to see country living suits you, Bet!'

'That'll be quite enough from you,' returned her sister without rancour. 'Just because you're thin as a rake again.'

'I don't know how you manage it, Bet,' Rose teased her. 'Specially now that sweets are rationed.'

'Beastly government!' Bet grumbled. 'Want to take all the pleasure out of life, they do.'

'Now then, Bet,' said Mrs Taylor. 'Don't start! What do you think of the cottage, Rose?'

'It looks lovely, like something out of a storybook,' Rose said. 'A real thatched cottage! And the garden's a picture. I can't wait to see inside.'

It was June, and more than eight months since she had left Wimborne to return to London, in an attempt to restart her career as a dancer. There had been a brief interlude at Christmas but for most of the time since then she had been either rehearsing or touring with Monty Prince and the company of *Lighten Up!*. During that time her mother and Bet had decided that they had imposed on the Willises long enough, so they had rented a cottage in the village. Mrs Taylor led Rose inside, and she sensed at once that her mother felt more at home there than in the flat in Lambeth.

'Look at all these lovely old oak beams,' she kept saying. 'And see how thick the walls are. Nothing jerry-built about this place.'

When Rose had been shown round every room her mother said, 'Well, what do you think?'

'It's lovely,' Rose said. 'Really cosy and homely!'

Over tea with toast and marge, liberally spread with Mrs Willis's home-made strawberry jam, they settled in for a good gossip.

'Have you heard from Reg lately, Bet?' Rose asked.

'He was home on leave about three weeks ago,' Bet said. 'I told you in my letter.'

'Yes, of course. How is he?'

'He's OK.'

Bet was never given to long speeches but Rose detected something more than her sister's normal reserve in the phrase.

'Army life suiting him, then?'

'Oh, he's having a whale of a time. Swanning around up there at Catterick. All beer and skittles you'd think, to listen to him.'

'I don't suppose it's as good as he makes out,' Rose said gently, wondering what was behind Bet's apparent resentment.

'How's Monty Prince?' her mother put in a little too quickly.

Rose sighed. 'Poor old Monty! He's really finding things hard at the moment. I mean, he's just like he always was when he's working. All the awful old jokes! And he goes down really well. The audiences love him. But offstage I can see he's not himself. I think he worries about Dolly back in London, coping with a house full of refugees. But it's more than that.

He told me something terrible the other day. I can't hardly believe it, but I suppose he's got it right. He says Jewish leaders in London have been getting reports of awful things happening under the Nazis. He says,' she paused, 'he *says* they've killed over a million Jews in France and Poland and Romania and other places they've occupied.'

'A million!' her mother exclaimed. 'Oh, that can't be true, surely! They'd never get away with it. Anyway, why would they want to do that?'

'Monty says they hate the Jews and blame them for the depression and unemployment and everything else that's gone wrong in recent times.'

'But to kill them, and so many of them!' her mother said. 'No, I can't believe that. That must be wrong.'

They were interrupted by the arrival of Billy and Sam, Bet's two sons, and the next half-hour was filled with eager questions and answers. When the boys had finished their tea and gone outside to meet their friends Rose said, 'They look so well, Bet! And so full of beans!'

'Yes,' Bet said contentedly. 'They've really settled in here. Billy's doing ever so well at school and they're both much healthier than they were in London. Some of the refugee kids couldn't wait to get back to town but Billy and Sam don't want to leave.'

'Well, it must help that you're here,' Rose pointed out. 'Some of the other poor kids must have been missing their mums.'

'Yeah, I suppose so,' Bet agreed, 'but I'm not sure they'd want to go back even if I wasn't here. They've really taken to the country life.'

'And so have you, by the look of it,' her sister remarked.

'Yeah, that's just it,' Bet said, with a note of sadness.

Their mother was in the kitchen, making a fresh pot of tea. Rose leaned across to Bet and said quietly, 'What's up, Bet? There's something wrong, I can tell.'

'Oh, it's nothing really,' Bet said with a shrug. 'I expect it'll all come out in the wash, as they say.'

'What will?' Rose insisted.

'It's just that when Reg was here he kept going on about what we were going to do after the war, and it was all about getting back to Lambeth and getting another flat and going back to his old job in the garage. And I don't want that, Rose! I love it here. I love the countryside, and the people and . . . well, everything.'

'Did you tell him?'

'Yes, but he didn't want to listen. He just kept saying I'd feel differently when everything was back to normal. We had quite a row about it, as a matter of fact.' She paused and added, 'We had quite a few rows during his last leave.'

'I suppose it must be hard, for both of you, when you don't see each other for so long,' Rose murmured. 'It'll be all right when you're back together permanently.'

'Maybe,' Bet said. 'But it's not just about going back to London. There's other things as well.'

'Such as?'

'There's always trouble with the boys when he comes home. He reckons they're being spoilt, living with two women and no dad to keep them in order. So he comes down a bit hard on them. He says they need to learn discipline. I try to tell him they're as good as gold when he's not here. They just play up when he comes home. But he doesn't like to hear that, of course.'

'I suppose that's understandable,' Rose commented.

'The thing is,' her sister went on, 'Billy's growing up. He'll be twelve next birthday. And he feels like he's the man of the house when his dad's away. When Reg comes back and starts ordering him around he doesn't like it. I caught Reg about to take his belt to him one evening.'

'Why?' Rose exclaimed.

'He reckoned Billy had cheeked him somehow.'

'What happened?'

'I wouldn't let him do it. I stood between them and said if he wanted to belt Billy he'd have to belt me first!' Bet's voice shook at the recollection.

'What did he do?'

'I thought he was going to hit me for a minute. Then he threw the belt down and stormed off out to the pub. Didn't come back till closing time.' Bet gave a sudden, half-suppressed giggle. 'Funny thing was – as he went down the path I could see his trousers were falling down. He had to keep stopping to hitch them up!'

Both girls collapsed in helpless laughter, so that Mrs Taylor, coming in with the teapot, asked them cheerfully what the joke was.

It was not until they were washing up after supper that they had a chance to continue the conversation.

'There's something I ought to tell you,' Bet said. 'I've got a part-time job.'

'Good for you! What are you doing?'

Bet paused, apparently intent on rubbing an invisible spot on a plate. 'Well, I kept feeling I ought to do something. I mean, I used to help Jack Willis in the market garden when we were living there, just to pay for my keep, like. I mean, we always paid for our food, of course, but they'd never take anything in the way of rent so I felt it was the least I could do. But when we moved out, he didn't really need me. I mean, there wasn't enough work to make it worthwhile paying me.

And I wanted a bit of pocket money. You know, money of my own.'

'So what are you doing?'

'It's only part time. Just mornings, while the boys are at school.'

'What is, Bet?' Rose repeated, exasperated.

Her sister hesitated again, her head bent over the dishes. 'You're not going to like this.'

'What do you mean?'

'I'm working up at the farm, for Matthew Armitage.'

Rose stared at her in silence. Then she managed to say, 'For Matt? You mean, helping with the farm work?'

'No. He's got a Land Girl to do that. But she won't touch anything inside the house. So I go up every morning and wash up the breakfast things and clean round and cook them some lunch.'

Rose stood still, the tea towel idle in her hands. She was remembering early mornings at the farm – the smell of bacon, the taste of porridge with fresh cream straight from the cow, the warmth of the big range on her back. She remembered the way she and Matthew used to wash up together before going back out to clean up the milking parlour.

She said quietly, 'How is he?'

'Matt? He's OK. He's lonely.' Bet looked round at her. 'He'd have you back like a shot, Rose, if you only gave him the word. Why don't you go up and see him?'

Rose shook her head. 'I couldn't, Bet. It wouldn't be fair. Besides, why would he want me now? He'd always think he was second best.'

'He'd settle for that,' Bet said. 'He'd have you on any terms you'd like to make. And after all, it's not as if . . .' She trailed into silence.

'Not as if what?' Rose prompted.

Bet looked at her. Then she turned away and opened a drawer in the dresser. 'We weren't sure if you'd have seen this. You haven't mentioned it and we didn't know whether to bring it up or not.'

She held out a sheet of newspaper. Rose unfolded it and found herself looking at a photograph of a girl in a wedding dress and a man in army uniform. The caption read 'Vance Heiress Marries'.

She took a deep breath and handed the paper back to her sister. 'I knew they were engaged. I hadn't seen that they were actually married.'

'What a rotter! He must have been carrying on with her behind your back all the time you were in the Follies.'

'I'm sure it wasn't like that,' Rose said quickly, surprising herself with a flash of anger that was directed, not at Richard, but at her sister. 'They must have met up again after . . . after he got back from France.'

Bet gave her a sceptical look and sniffed. 'Well, he obviously knows which side his bread is buttered.'

'I don't think he would have married her for her money.' *Why am I defending him?* Rose asked herself. The answer came at once. 'He went off because he thought I was engaged to Matt. You can't blame him for finding someone else. And she'll be a big help to him in his career. More than I could ever have been.'

'If he really cared for you he'd have stuck around and given you the chance to choose,' Bet said. 'Anyway, the point is, it's not as if you're ever likely to hear from him again. Is it?'

'No,' Rose answered, very quietly. 'I'm not likely to hear from him again.'

'So?' Bet went on. 'Why not give Matthew another chance?'

'I can't, Bet,' Rose protested. 'It wouldn't be fair – on either of us.'

'It's got to be better than what you've got now, hasn't it?' Bet persisted doggedly.

'No!' Anger flared in Rose again. 'No, it hasn't. I like what I'm doing now. I've got a career, Bet, and I'm enjoying it. I don't want to give it up.'

'What about kids, then?' Bet demanded. 'You want kids, don't you?'

Rose was silent for a moment. Then she took a breath and lifted her chin. 'Who wants to bring kids into a world like this?'

The next morning Rose went to say hello to the Willises and received their usual warm welcome.

'Doesn't she look smart, Jack?' Mrs Willis exclaimed. 'I didn't know ENSA had a uniform.'

'It only came in this year,' Rose told her. 'I think it's a bit silly really. After all, we're not one of the armed services.'

'Well, nor are the Land Girls,' Jack pointed out. 'But you had a uniform when you were one of them.'

'Oh, don't remind me!' Rose exclaimed with a laugh. 'That dreadful hat! And those ghastly breeches!'

Mrs Willis laughed too. 'I'll never forget you standing in our kitchen the night it all arrived. Talk about laugh!'

'Well, this is certainly a big improvement on that,' Jack said. 'And I guess it makes it clear that you're doing your bit. After all, now all you young women have been called up, it means you don't have to answer questions about what you're doing.'

'That's true, I suppose,' Rose agreed. 'But I think it's mostly for the companies that are sent overseas – so they don't get shot as spies, or something.'

'Oh, Lord!' Mrs Willis exclaimed. 'They won't send you overseas, will they, Rose?'

'There's no telling,' Rose said. 'It's like the song – "We Won't Know Where We're Going Until We Get There!" They never tell us in advance. It's all frightfully hush-hush. They give Monty a sealed envelope and he's not supposed to open it until we're on our way.'

'But how do you know where to get on your way to, if you don't know where you're supposed to be going?' Jack asked, mystified.

'That's just it,' Rose said with a grin. 'It's daft, isn't it? Apparently there was one group, in the early days when our boys were still in France, who were halfway to Calais before they opened their sealed orders and found out they were supposed to be going to Catterick!'

When the laughter had died down Rose went on, 'How's Babe? Have you heard from her lately?'

'Oh, Barbara's getting married,' Enid Willis said.

'Married! How lovely! Who to?' A glance at Enid's face told Rose that she was less than happy about the news.

'He's a Canadian,' Jack said. 'One of the boys who volunteered to come over right at the start. He's in the Fleet Air Arm.'

'What's he like?' Rose asked.

'Oh, he's a nice enough chap,' Enid said grudgingly. 'But a Canadian! Of course, when the war's over he wants Barbara to go and live in Canada with him.'

'Oh, of course.' Rose reached out and squeezed her arm. 'Well, just think. You'll be able to go and visit. Which part of Canada is he from?'

'Vancouver,' said Enid. 'I looked it up in Barbara's old school atlas. It's right on the other side of the country, about as far away as you can get. I can't see us going all that way.

I'll never be able to watch my grandchildren growing up, will I?'

'You never know,' Rose said. 'He might like it so much over here that he'll decide to settle.'

'Some hopes,' sniffed Enid Willis.

Two days later Rose was sitting in the garden of the cottage, reading, when a movement, seen out of the corner of her eye, caught her attention. She looked up and saw Matthew Armitage coming across the grass towards her. Shocked, she scrambled up from her deckchair, uncomfortably aware that her face was unmade up and her hair in need of combing. He stopped a few paces off and she saw that he had changed little in the past eighteen months, but perhaps his face was more weather-beaten, the fine lines around his blue eyes a fraction deeper.

He said, 'Hello, Rose. How are you?'

'I'm fine,' she answered. 'And you?'

'Fine, fine.'

She put out her hand and he shook it formally, and she felt the sudden shock of recognition at his touch.

He said, 'Bet told me you were home on leave. I hope you don't mind me calling round.'

'No, of course not,' she replied. What else could she say?

He went on, 'I hear you're back dancing again.'

'No, not actually dancing,' she said. 'I just do the choreography and look after the girls.'

'But you're enjoying it?'

'Yes, it's good fun – most of the time. Sometimes we have to perform in places that are a bit . . . well, a bit grim. And the travelling gets you down. But yes, I enjoy it.'

'That's good.'

They looked at each other in silence. Rose said, 'Come inside and have a cup of tea. I'm sure Mum would like to see you.'

'No, no thanks,' he replied. 'I mustn't stop long. I just wanted to say hello.'

There was another pause. Then she said, 'Well, sit down for a minute, at least.'

'Thanks.' He sat on a low wooden bench and she sank back into her deckchair.

She said, 'How's the farm?'

'Doing well, thank you. I've increased the dairy herd. Got six more milkers than I had when you were with me.'

'Oh, that's good.'

'You remember that old Dotty? The one that was so contrary always?'

'Oh yes! I remember her all right!'

'I had to get rid of her. The new girl couldn't manage her at all. Got so she wouldn't go near her in the end. She's never had the knack with the animals that you had.'

'I only did what you taught me,' Rose protested.

'Well, I tried to teach the new girl the same things, but it's no good. Oh, she knows what she's doing all right – been trained at one of those special dairy farming centres they've got. But she's got no feeling for the cows. She doesn't really like them, and they know it.'

'I'm sorry to hear that,' Rose murmured. She had the feeling that he wanted her to feel guilty.

'Oh, we manage,' he said. 'And Bet's a big help. It's nice to have someone to look after the house a bit. And she's a good cook, your sister.'

'Oh, I know,' Rose said with a smile. 'She's always been fond of her food, has Bet.'

They were silent again for a few minutes, while she searched her mind for something to say.

In the end he got up. 'Well, I'd best be getting along. Lord knows there's plenty to do at this time of year.'

She walked to the gate with him and when they reached it he said, 'If you feel like coming up to the farm one day, you'd be welcome. Come up with Bet, why don't you?'

'I . . . I'll see,' she said, and he nodded and murmured, 'Right, then,' and walked away down the lane.

Rose wandered back to her seat, but she did not take up her book. She had forgotten, until that moment, how attractive Matthew was. Not conventionally handsome. Not a head-turner, like Richard. But pleasant and lean and warm, like a beautifully weathered piece of wood. For a moment she allowed herself to dwell on what might have been. Now, in the summertime, the living in the farm would have been pleasant; rising with the dawn to fetch the cattle in, the milking parlour smelling of fresh hay; working in the dairy, emptying the pails of rich, creamy milk into the spotless vats; later riding out into the fields on the back of the big shire horse, with the sun warm on her back. Then, in the evening, sitting on the bench by the front step, watching the sky pale to duck-egg blue and Venus hanging brilliant in the western sky and then . . . bed. She got up abruptly. She liked Matthew. She had been very fond of him. In a way she still was. But even when she agreed to be his wife, she had somehow pushed the idea of going to bed with him to the back of her mind.

The thought came to her that she had never slept with a man, never experienced anything more passionate than a few kisses. It was the way she had been brought up. Her father had warned her constantly about men who would try to 'take advantage of her'. Her mother was convinced that beyond a certain point men were unable to control their impulses. If you didn't want to get into trouble the only way was to keep them at arm's length. So whenever she had felt desire welling up within her she had broken off, forcing the need down, closing herself to the possibility of surrender. Now she would probably never know what it was like to give way to that feeling. You're going to die a virgin, she told herself. A crabbed old spinster! Then she rejected the thought. A virgin, perhaps, but that didn't have to mean bitter and joyless. She would make sure of that!

10

In the days after he was wounded Merry was moved repeatedly, first to Sidi Barrani then to Mersa Matruh and finally back to Alexandria as the British army retreated before Rommel's relentless drive towards the Egyptian border. In the confusion he lost touch with the rest of the company, in spite of frequent enquiries as to their whereabouts, until Clive and Chubby appeared at his bedside in Alexandria. Apart from Tom, they told him, no one had suffered serious injury, though Ray Short had a broken arm. Their big news was that they were all being sent back to Britain for some leave on the next available troopship, which was due to sail in three days' time. Merry made an urgent request to the medical officer in charge of his ward, asking to be allowed to sail with them, but was told that he was in no condition to leave hospital at present.

On the day before they sailed the entire company appeared in the ward and gave an impromptu performance by way of farewell. It went down very well with the rest of the patients but Merry, still weak from loss of blood, had to struggle to restrain his tears. There was a terrible poignancy in watching the familiar acts but not being part of them, and he was aware, as the rest of the audience was not, of the gaps in the programme. Over the last nine months the members of the company had become close friends, almost the extended family that Merry had never known, and now they were leaving him and he had no way of knowing when, or if, he would ever catch up with them again.

As soon as he felt strong enough Merry wrote to Felix, giving him a brief outline of what had happened and apologising for the long delay in answering his last letter. He also wrote to Tom Dyson's parents. It was one of the hardest tasks he had ever undertaken. He could speak, quite genuinely, of Tom's talent as a performer and his great potential, and he could tell them that he had been a popular member of the company. But these glib clichés left so much unsaid. He could not even tell them that death had been quick and painless. He could say only that everything possible had been done to ease his last moments and that he had died peacefully in the arms of a friend.

It was during this period of convalescence that Merry happened to be thumbing through a newspaper that had arrived from England, weeks out of date as always. His casually roving eye was caught by a photograph of a man in the uniform of an army captain with a beautiful girl in bridal white on his arm. For a moment he studied the picture and the accompanying text. Then he laid it aside with a deep sigh and said aloud, 'Oh, Richard, you stupid bastard! Poor, poor Rose!'

By the time Merry was discharged from hospital and sent to recuperate at a rest camp outside Cairo there was something approaching panic in the city. But somehow the battered British 7th Armoured Division managed to regroup and to hold the advancing Germans at El Alamein, the dusty little town named after the twin cairns on the hill above it.

He had been at the camp for a week when he was sent for by the commanding officer.

'Got some news for you, Merryweather. Two bits of news, actually.'

'Good news, I hope, sir.'

'Well, I think you'll be pleased. This arrived for you today.'

The CO handed over an official-looking envelope with a crest on it. Merry opened it and read: '*On the recommendation of the GOC Middle East, His Majesty the King has been graciously pleased to grant the award of the Distinguished Service Order to Lieutenant Guy Stephen Merryweather for courage and initiative under fire.*'

Merry felt the blood rush to his face and then recede again. 'I don't understand. What have I done to deserve this? I went back to get poor Tom Dyson out of the second truck, but any human being would have done that. Anyway, I thought there had to be an officer present to witness the action.'

'You picked up Colonel Walton later, didn't you? I heard you cleared out an enemy machine-gun nest single handed and got your people through to the main road. Bloody good show, old chap. Well-deserved recognition.'

'It wasn't courage. It was pure bloody desperation!' Merry said.

The CO laughed. 'I dare say that could be said of a good many acts of bravery. Now, to my other bit of good news. You're going home.'

'Home?' Merry queried in surprise. 'How? When?'

'Tomorrow. There's a Blenheim flying out to Gibraltar and they've got room for a passenger. I thought it would be better for you than hanging around here waiting for a ship. From Gib you'll either be able to get on a ship or possibly cadge another flight back to Blighty. OK?'

'Wonderful!' Merry agreed. 'Thanks very much.'

*　　*　　*

Merry had never flown before, but he thought he had a fairly clear impression of what it was like from Felix's ecstatic descriptions. The reality turned out to be rather different. The rear compartment of the Blenheim bomber was noisy, cold and dark. There were no portholes to look out of and the only seating was on top of some anonymous bales that comprised the aircraft's cargo. The crew did their best to make him welcome and to make conversation but they all had their own jobs to do and for most of the journey Merry was left to pass the time with his own thoughts, as best he could.

After a boring and uncomfortable couple of hours he was just beginning to wish he had waited for a ship home when matters suddenly took a violent turn for the worse. The plane abruptly banked hard to the right, throwing Merry painfully against a bulkhead, and then began to dive. A few seconds later he was thrown in the opposite direction as the pilot executed another sudden turn, and at the same moment there was a series of thudding impacts along the fuselage, starting from the direction of the tail and moving rapidly towards the engines. It did not need the appearance of a line of bright pinholes to convince him that they were under attack.

He scrambled forward and put his head round the door to the cockpit. 'What's going on?'

The co-pilot shouted back, ''Fraid we've attracted the attentions of a couple of 109s. We're radioing for back-up from any Spits that happen to be in the area, but things may be a bit uncomfortable for a while.'

As if to emphasise his point, the plane executed another violent banking turn and then went into another dive. The angle of the floor, together with the discomfort in his ears from the changing pressure, assured Merry that they were losing height fast and he began to wonder how long it would be before they hit the deck. He stumbled back to his seat and hung on to a strut. He had no way of knowing whether they were over land or sea, but he assumed that they were somewhere over the Mediterranean. He looked around, trying to work out how to open the hatch and wondering how long it would take for the compartment to fill with water. Curiously, he did not feel any panic but rather a sense of sad inevitability. It was ironic to have come through the cauldron of the retreat from Gazala to meet his end when he least expected it. He wondered briefly how long it would take for the news to reach Felix.

At that moment the plane levelled out and began to climb again, but even as Merry drew a breath of relief, one of the engines spluttered, died, fired again and then fell silent. The co-pilot appeared and yelled, 'Luckily for us there were some Spits quite close by and they've seen off the Huns, but we're going to have to make an emergency landing. Should be a piece of cake, but hang on to your hat!'

Minutes passed. The plane was listing to port and Merry could sense that the pilot was struggling to keep it on an even keel on its remaining engine. He heard a grinding noise from beneath his feet, which he realised later was the sound of the undercarriage being lowered. The plane rocked, touched the ground, bounced and then settled again and ran to a standstill. After a moment someone from outside opened the hatch and Merry clambered out, blinking in the fierce light and heat. He looked around him. They had come to rest on a broad, dusty plateau, pockmarked with bomb craters. At some distance in one direction there was a series of sandbagged enclosures, within which he could make out the outlines of planes that he thought were Spitfires. In the other direction was a collection of low huts and nearer at hand a single, low, stone-built building with a ramshackle veranda.

The aircrew were climbing out of the plane, one of them nursing what looked like a broken arm. A jeep came bouncing towards them over the uneven surface and a man in the tropical uniform of an RAF flight lieutenant jumped out.

'Hello, chaps! I'm John Holmes, the IO for this squadron. Welcome to Malta!'

Malta! Merry's mind had been racing ever since he got out of the plane and now his best hopes were confirmed. The intelligence officer, however, was occupied with the reports of the pilot and his crew. After a brief consultation they were packed into the jeep, which headed away towards a hut with a Red Cross painted on its roof, and Holmes turned to Merry.

'Sorry about that. Gather you've had a bit of a rough ride. Let's get out of this sun, shall we?' He pointed to the stone building and they began to walk towards it. 'Sorry. You are . . .?'

Merry introduced himself and added, 'You did say Malta?'

' 'Fraid so. Out of the frying pan into the fire, you might say. Things have been pretty hot round here, in every sense, for the last few months.'

'So I've heard,' Merry said. 'Which airfield is this?'

'Takali,' his companion told him. 'I'll get your kit transferred up to the mess as soon as there's a vehicle free. It's up there in M'dina. Bit of a trek, I'm afraid.'

Merry looked up and saw the ramparts of an ancient city crowning a sharp hill above them. He remembered Felix waxing lyrical in his letters about the place and its history, and the throb of excitement that had begun deep inside him when he first heard the name of the island grew more intense. As they reached the shade of the veranda they heard the sound of low-flying aircraft and turned to see three Spitfires sweep in to land in rapid succession and then taxi away towards the protective pens on the far side of the airfield.

Merry said, 'Which squadron is based here?'

'There are three, all sharing this airfield,' Holmes told him. '126, 603 and 249. I'm with 249.'

'In that case,' Merry went on, almost unable to breathe for the pounding of his heart, 'I think you have an old friend of mine on the strength. Flight Lieutenant Mountjoy?'

'Ned Mountjoy? Yes, of course. He's in charge of A flight. Great chap! Brilliant pilot. Friend of yours, is he?'

'From before the war,' Merry told him. He took a deep breath. 'Is he likely to be around anywhere?'

'Well, unless I'm very much mistaken that was him landing just now. He'll be over in a minute to make his report.'

Merry strained his eyes in the direction of the aircraft pens. Three figures were heading towards the hut, talking together animatedly. They were too far off for him to see their faces but the lithe upright walk of the central one and the gleam of blond hair were as familiar to Merry as his own reflection.

'Look,' Holmes was saying, 'I'll have to go and sort things out with the chaps who flew you in here as soon as I've got Ned's report. If you don't mind, I'll leave you with him, since you're old chums. He'll take you up to the mess and see that you get some lunch and I'll get someone to sort out a room for you. You obviously won't be going anywhere in a hurry in that crate!'

He moved away towards the three young airmen and Merry drew back into the shadow of the veranda. His heart was beating so violently that it made his ears sing, and suddenly he was unsure how to greet Felix. He watched as Holmes reached the men and saw them exchange words but Felix did not look towards the hut, so Merry assumed that the intelligence officer had not mentioned his presence. After a brief conversation the three pilots came on towards him and, suddenly overcome with diffidence, Merry withdrew into the room behind the veranda. Felix came in, followed by the other two, both of them very young – hardly more than schoolboys, Merry thought. They were laughing together at some story Felix was telling. Felix was wearing battledress, his Mae West still draped casually around his shoulders, his bright hair slicked down to his scalp with sweat. Their eyes unaccustomed to the gloom of the hut, none of them noticed the silent figure of the stranger who stood at the back of the room. Felix hung his Mae West on a hook, his back turned towards Merry, still finishing his anecdote.

Merry waited for him to pause and stepped forward and said quietly, 'Hello, Felix.'

The two young pilots spun round in surprise but Felix seemed momentarily frozen. Then he turned, slowly, as if afraid that a sudden movement might break the spell.

'Merry?' His eyes took in Merry's face and lit up. '*Merry!* Where on earth have you sprung from?'

'Just dropped in,' Merry said, trying to sound casual.

For a moment they stared at each other, poised like two divers on the edge of a high board. Then Felix exclaimed, 'Oh, what the hell!' and launched himself into Merry's embrace.

Merry held him for a few seconds, closing his eyes and drinking in the smell of him, the mixture of soap and sweat and the bay rum he used on his hair, and a sharper tang that he did not recognise – aviation fuel, perhaps – and beneath it all the familiar, unmistakable scent that was uniquely Felix. Then he let him go and smiled into his eyes.

'How are you, Felix?'

'Fine! Never better!' But already Merry was taking in how

lean and spare he looked, as if the constant pressure of the situation had fined away everything superfluous, both physical and mental. 'How about you?' Felix went on.

'I'm OK.'

'How the devil did you get here?'

'Courtesy of the Luftwaffe. They shot up the plane I was in and we had to make an emergency landing.'

Felix glanced towards the bright oblong of the airfield framed by the doorway. 'You were in that Blenheim?'

'Yes.'

He laughed suddenly. 'I don't believe it! We were the chaps who saw off the 109s and escorted you back here!'

'It was you, in the Spits that rescued us? That's incredible!'

'Somebody's guardian angel was doing his job,' Felix commented enigmatically.

Merry looked at the other two pilots. 'Well, in that case, I'm sincerely grateful to you – all of you.'

His look recalled Felix to the presence of his two colleagues, who were standing by, smiling but slightly embarrassed by this ecstatic reunion.

'Let me introduce you. This is Rusty Rogers and this character is Mitch Mitchison, one of our colonial cousins.'

'Thanks, Skipper. That'll be enough of the colonial bit, if you don't mind,' remarked Mitchison affably, in an accent that placed him somewhere in the Antipodes.

'Gentlemen,' Felix continued unabashed, 'I want you to meet Guy Merryweather – a very good friend of mine and, incidentally, the best bloody MD in the business.'

Merry shook hands with the two boys and Rogers, whose auburn hair presented an immediate explanation of his sobriquet, said politely, 'How do you do, Doctor.'

Merry blinked and Felix gave one of his characteristic yelps of laughter. 'Not MD as in Medical Doctor! MD as in Musical Director.'

'Oh,' said Rogers, looking bemused. 'Sorry, sir.'

'Are you with one of the military bands, sir?' Mitchison enquired.

Merry shook his head. 'No. I'm with an outfit called Stars in Battledress. Roughly the equivalent of your Ralph Reader's Gang Show, I believe.'

'Really? That sounds like fun,' Mitchison said, but already Merry had seen that slight glazing of the eyes which he was used to encountering in fighting men when they realised that they were speaking to someone who had no experience of the front line.

Felix had seen it too. He flicked the back of his fingertips playfully across the breast of Merry's tunic, where the ribbon of the DSO still showed its colours, undimmed by age. 'How about this, then? You dark horse! Come on, I want the full story!'

'I say, sir!' exclaimed Rogers. 'The DSO! Bloody good show!'

Felix, having drawn attention to where he felt it was needed, turned away and began to strip off his battledress jacket and trousers, revealing khaki shirt and shorts underneath. 'Look, I'm absolutely parched. You must be too. We're off duty now. B flight will be here any minute to take over. Shall we walk up to the mess? It's a bit of a long drag, I'm afraid, but it's the only way.'

As they walked Felix returned to the subject of Merry's medal. 'Come on, Merry. I'm itching to hear the full story. What happened?'

But Merry shook his head. 'No, really, Felix. It's a long story and my throat's as dry as dust. Can we save it till later?'

'Excuse me, sir,' Mitchison put in. 'Why do you keep calling him Felix?'

Merry interrogated his friend with a glance. Although he was well aware that in the RAF he was known by his real name, and was even used to addressing him by it in letters, he was never able to bring himself to call him anything but Felix to his face.

Somewhat to his surprise Felix said, 'It was my stage name. Merry and I worked together before the war.'

'Stage name?' queried Rogers. 'You were on the stage, Skip?'

Merry, given leave by Felix's admission, cut in with, 'Gentlemen, this is my chance to return the compliment. You don't realise it, but you are in the presence of Felix Lamont, alias Mr Mysterioso, illusionist extraordinaire – and the best bloody magician in the business.'

'Magician?' asked Mitchison. 'You mean, like a conjuror?'

'Oh, much more than that! An illusionist. Vanishing objects, ladies sawn in half . . .'

'You're kidding! You've never mentioned it, Skip.'

'Oh, I don't make you youngsters privy to the details of my misspent youth,' Felix said flippantly. 'It might give you ideas.'

'Can you show us some tricks?' Rogers begged. 'The other chaps would be fascinated, I know.'

Felix shook his head and held up his right hand, the fingers still slightly hooked and misshapen from the cockpit fire that had almost destroyed his face and seemed for a while to have ended his career as a pilot. 'Sorry. I'm afraid my days of prestidigitation are over.'

'We could always try the sawing-the-lady-in-half trick,' Merry suggested. 'I'm sure one of these lads would volunteer if there are no girls available.'

'Hmm,' mused Felix. 'I never did get that trick quite right.'

'Which accounts for the number of one-legged women hobbling around Fairbourne-on-Sea,' Merry agreed solemnly.

The two young pilots laughed uncertainly. They passed under the gateway in the walls and into the cool, shadowy streets of the town and came to the front entrance of an ancient and beautiful mansion.

'Here we are,' Felix announced, leading Merry into the foyer. 'The Xara Palace. Built in the fifteenth and early sixteenth centuries. Belongs to a Baron Chappelle but at present requisitioned for our use.'

'Nice spot!' Merry commented.

Felix turned to the other two. 'Look, I want to freshen up before lunch, so I'm going straight upstairs. Come up with me, Merry?'

'Of course.' Merry's heart was thudding again, and not just from the climb.

'Hey, you promised to buy us both a drink,' Mitchison objected.

'Buy your own drinks for once,' Felix told him affably, adding with a grin, 'I'll make it up to you later. Come on, Merry.'

He led the way upstairs and along a corridor and opened a door, standing aside for Merry to enter. He scarcely had time to push the door shut before Merry's arms were round him. For a long moment they clasped each other in silence, absorbing the unlooked-for joy of being together again, recognising the familiar contours of each other's body. Then they drew back and studied each other's face.

Merry said, 'I take it back. You're the second-greatest magician in the business.'

Felix smiled. 'The first being Archie McIndoe?'

'It's amazing,' Merry said. 'I would never have believed it possible, in those first awful weeks.'

It was true. Although he had watched the slow, painful reconstruction of the right side of Felix's face during the early months of the previous year, Merry had never imagined that the final result would be so good. Underneath the tan the faint lines of the scars were still visible, and the contours of the cheek and mouth would never quite match the symmetrical perfection of the left side, but by contrast with the grotesque, mask-like face he had worn when they first became lovers Felix looked almost like his old self.

Merry traced the scars with delicate fingertips. 'How does it feel?'

'Pretty good. I don't have as much sensation there as on the other side of my face, but I'm used to that now.'

'God, but you're thin!' Merry added. 'I can feel every bone in your body.'

'We're all underweight,' Felix admitted. 'The whole island's been on starvation rations for months. They tried to get a convoy through to us about a month ago but only two ships finally made it. We've got enough food to last for another two or three months, but only if we tighten our belts even further.'

'That's terrible,' Merry said. 'How can you fight under those conditions?'

'Oh, you'd be surprised.' Felix smiled. 'I suspect that we all used to eat too much. But how about you? You were wounded.'

'I'm fine,' Merry assured him. 'It was just a flesh wound. Didn't hit anything critical.'

They looked at each other for a moment in silence and then kissed for the first time, at first tentatively, as if they had half forgotten how it was done, and then with rapidly mounting passion, until Felix drew back.

'We'll have to stop this.'

For the first time Merry realised, to his consternation, that there were three beds in the room, though the other occupants were absent. He looked at Felix. 'I suppose there's no chance . . .?'

'Not a hope!' Felix told him. 'People are in and out of here at all hours. There's absolutely no privacy.'

'When, then?' Merry asked.

Felix lifted his shoulders helplessly. 'I don't know. Have they given you a room?'

'Not yet.'

'Well, maybe we'll strike lucky there. But I don't hold out much hope. Everywhere's bursting at the seams already.'

They gazed at each other woefully. Then Merry reached out and gripped Felix's shoulder. 'Never mind. We're together for a bit, when we didn't expect to see each other for months. That's what matters.'

Felix kissed him again, briefly, and then turned away. 'I must have a wash. I must smell terrible. Water's strictly rationed and we only get a bath every other day. In this climate that's no joke.'

'You smell wonderful to me,' Merry assured him.

He waited while Felix pulled off his shirt and splashed himself with water from the washstand in the corner and then changed into clean clothes.

'We'd better go down, if we want any lunch,' he said. 'There's little enough to be had. God knows we can't afford to miss out on anything.'

In the mess Merry was introduced to the rest of Felix's flight and some of the officers serving with the other two squadrons.

The food, as Felix had predicted, was meagre and the quality poor. There were two slices of bully beef each, accompanied by black, bitter bread spread with what the airmen termed 'gharrie grease' and a few vegetables. For young, healthy men working under extreme conditions at constant risk of their lives it was a totally inadequate diet. There were no complaints, however, and the atmosphere in the mess was unrelentingly cheerful.

When the meal was over, they all adjourned to the terrace, which looked out over the plain below and gave a good view over the airfield. In the heat of the afternoon conversation became desultory, until Felix suddenly started out of his chair and went to the balcony rail.

'Heads up, fellers! There's a flap on.'

At the same moment they all heard the distant sound of aero engines starting up and the other men also rose to their feet. Joining Felix at the rail, Merry could see the small figures of men running from the hut where they had met towards the pens that housed the Spitfires, and within a couple of minutes the first plane had taxied out on to the runway. Three others followed, and one by one they sped across the uneven surface and took to the air, circling to gain height. Immediately they were followed by four more.

'Both sections up,' Felix commented. 'It must be a big one.'

As he spoke the air-raid warning began to wail and somebody said grimly, 'Hang on to your hats, boys. We're about to get another pasting.'

The Spitfires had disappeared, climbing away to the south, but very soon they heard a different sound, the low throbbing drone of German bombers – a sound no one who had lived through the Blitz would ever fail to identify.

'There they are,' someone said, and Merry saw three planes, coming in low from the east, and above them the smaller shapes of the accompanying fighters.

'Junkers 88s,' Felix said helpfully, but Merry had seen enough of them in the desert to recognise them.

Watching the planes draw closer, from their grandstand position on the battlements, Merry had a strange feeling of unreality. His instincts told him to take cover but none of the others seemed to be in the least concerned for their own safety. Instead, all eyes were scanning the sky.

'Here come our boys!' somebody shouted, and suddenly the four leading Spitfires appeared, diving straight through the formation of fighters to attack the bombers below.

'Classic!' Felix exclaimed. 'Straight out of the sun. They'll never know what hit them.'

Merry saw the four little planes close with the bombers and, when they were apparently only yards away, saw spurts of flame appear along the leading edges of their wings. One of the bombers abruptly turned over and spun out of sight beyond a hill, from which point a second later a column of black smoke arose. The cheers of the watchers were still ringing out when a second was seen to be trailing white vapour from one engine and turned for home. By now the Me 109s had recovered from their surprise and a number of individual dogfights were developing above the airfield. Meanwhile, the lone remaining bomber, determined to succeed where his companions had failed, came on to sweep low over the airfield. With a deafening cacophony of sound the anti-aircraft batteries around the field opened up and puffs of white smoke appeared all around the plane. But it flew on as if bearing a charmed life and the balcony beneath their feet shook to three successive concussions, while the blast sent a glass crashing on to the tiles. Three columns of smoke rose from the airfield below them.

'Bastards!' muttered Felix. 'That's going to make it hard for our chaps to get down safely.'

At that moment there was a second cheer as the remaining section of four Spitfires came diving out of the sun to join the mêlée. The Messerschmitts, seeing that they were getting the worst of the fight, wisely turned and headed for home, pursued by the Spits. As soon as the all-clear had sounded two lorries were to be seen heading out on to the airfield and within minutes groups of men, stripped to the waist, were working in the blazing heat to fill the bomb craters.

Once the excitement of the raid was over men began to drift away, some to sleep, others to read or write letters, four to a game of bridge, but Merry noticed that Felix did not leave his vantage point until all eight aircraft were safely back on the ground. Then he said, 'Fancy a stroll round the town?'

Merry assented and for the next couple of hours Felix entertained him to a guided tour of the ancient and picturesque walled city, accompanied by a potted history of the island from the shipwreck of St Paul in the first century AD to the first siege of Malta by the Turks in 1565.

On their return to the Xara Palace Merry found a message waiting for him to say that a billet had been found for him in a house a short distance away. He and Felix walked down there but found that they were no nearer to solving the problem that had been nagging at them both all afternoon. Merry was to share the room with two officers from the artillery battalion that provided the anti-aircraft cover for Takali.

'You'll dine in the mess with us, at any rate,' Felix said, 'as my guest.' And it seemed that with that they would have to be content.

By evening the mess was buzzing with the full company of officers from three squadrons, darkness having put an end to flying for the day. Merry was surprised to find that the rooms were lit only by oil lamps and candles, until Felix explained that the use of electric light had been banned to conserve resources. There seemed, however, to be no shortage of alcohol. Felix handed him a pink gin and took him round to introduce him to his fellow officers, including his squadron leader, a Canadian by the name of Grant, and the station commander, who was affectionately known as 'Jumbo' Gracie.

'I hear you're a musician,' Gracie said genially. 'There's a piano in the next room. Care to tinkle the ivories for us after dinner? The lads could do with a bit of light entertainment.'

When the spartan meal had been consumed Felix led him to the piano, on which had been placed one of the few oil lamps. 'I've no idea what sort of condition this thing is in,' he said dubiously.

Merry lifted the lid and ran his fingers over the keys. It was an excellent instrument, as one might expect in such a setting, and amazingly it was still pretty well in tune.

'It's fine,' he said. 'What do you want me to play?'

'That's up to you,' Felix told him.

Merry looked round the room, which was almost in darkness except for his lamp and a few strategically placed candles. The pilots had sunk into the available armchairs and some were even sitting on the floor. In the gloom the pale blurs of faces were turned expectantly towards him.

'Any requests?' he asked.

There were plenty of suggestions and soon men gathered round the piano and began to sing along. When they ran out of steam and drifted back to their seats a tall, lean young man came over to the piano and fixed him with intense dark eyes.

'Can you play Chopin's *Grande Polonaise?*'

'Whew!' Merry responded. 'That's a tall order. I used to, but I haven't touched the classics for months. I'll have a go, if you like, but don't be disappointed if I break down in the middle.'

He did not break down and the piece ended to a storm of applause. The station commander appeared at his side.

'I think I sold you a bit short in my introduction. I understood you were just one of these ENSA-type entertainers. I didn't realise we had a concert pianist in our midst.'

Merry gave him one of his grave, self-deprecating smiles. 'It's all right. I do both.'

Soon after that men began to drift off to bed. Felix said, 'Fancy a nightcap?'

He bought them both a brandy from the bar and they took them out on to the terrace. In the distance searchlights crisscrossed the sky above Valletta and they could hear the noise of planes taking off.

'American Beaufighters,' Felix said. 'They operate at night from Luqa.' He took a sip of his drink and yawned. 'Look, I'm terribly sorry, but I have to come to readiness at dawn. I'm going to have to get to bed.'

'Of course,' Merry responded, heavy hearted. 'You must get your sleep.'

'Can you find your way back to your billet OK?'

'Yes, don't worry about me.'

They finished their drinks and Felix said, 'I'll see you out.'

In the dark portico of the palace they paused. Merry said, 'When shall I see you?'

'You can come down to the dispersal hut and keep me company, if you like,' Felix replied. 'Even if we are scrambled we're not usually away for long.'

'I'll see you in the morning, then,' Merry said.

Felix reached up and gripped his shoulder. 'Goodnight. Sleep well.'

'And you.'

He went down the steps and paused to look back. Felix raised a hand in farewell and went inside and Merry trudged off down the dark street to his room.

II

Richard paused at the corner of the rue Roux de Brignolles and looked casually around. There was no unusual activity in the street, no black Citroën, the car favoured by the Gestapo, parked outside the apartment block. He turned to look into a shop window. The reflection showed no sign of anyone following him. He waited a few minutes longer, making sure. After a week in the relaxed atmosphere of Monte Carlo it would be easy to become overconfident.

At the Rodocanachis' flat Pat O'Leary was waiting for him, and with him was a dark young man with a patch over one eye and a restless, fidgety manner. Richard assumed that this was another 'parcel' waiting to be transferred down the line but O'Leary said, 'Ricardo, I want you to meet our new radio operator, Jean. We call him Jean le Nerveux, because he can never keep still.'

Richard shook hands with the new arrival and said, 'Well, you're a welcome sight! So Jimmy managed to find someone at last.'

'I was glad to volunteer,' Jean said. 'I owe a lot to the good doctor and the other members of the line.'

'Jean passed through here in '41,' O'Leary said. 'He lost part of an eye when he was shot down and we had to take care of him until he was fit enough to make the trip across the mountains. We've been in touch with London, and they confirm that the pick-up by the *Tarana* is still on for the eighteenth.'

'Excellent!' Richard exclaimed. 'What about Straight? Have you managed to get him out?'

'Yes. One of our people knew a nurse at the hospital. She gave him sleeping pills to put in the guards' lunchtime wine and when they were dozing he and another prisoner were able to slip out. We had someone waiting for them on the outside and they are now at a safe house in the city.'

'Things are going well, then,' Richard commented.

'What about you?' O'Leary asked. 'How were things in Monte Carlo?'

'No problems. I got myself a job singing in one of the plush cafés near the casino and found a room above a hairdresser's shop. I told them I had another engagement in Perpignan next week but said I'd be back after that. Now, what do you want me to do?'

'I need you to escort Straight and his friend to the safe house on the beach and keep them out of sight until the ship is due. You'll have your hands full, I'm afraid. Straight doesn't take kindly to having his liberty circumscribed. Ginny will come with you again, to back up your cover story. Other couriers will be bringing men from various locations and, of course, there are several already in safe houses in the Perpignan region. They have been told to rendezvous at the Hôtel du Tennis. It will be up to you to collect them from there and take them to the beach house and you and Ginny will have to see that they are fed during the time they are waiting. There could be upwards of thirty by the night of the eighteenth. I shall join you with the last batch, to be on hand for the actual evacuation. Can you cope till then?'

'We'll have to,' Richard responded. 'It will be pretty cramped, but I suppose we shall only have the full number for a short time. Food could be a problem. Ginny and I laid in what stores we could while we were there. It helped that we were able to eat at the hotel most evenings. But I'll have to rely on the black market to top up the rations.'

'Speak to Mme Chouquette,' O'Leary said. 'She has useful contacts. And don't worry about costs. I'll give you back some of the cash Jimmy sent out with you to cover expenses.'

'Right,' Richard agreed. 'Where do I pick up Straight and his friend?'

'Be at the railway station at six a.m. tomorrow. Wait by the tobacconist's kiosk and carry this book.' He handed Richard a copy of Alexandre Dumas' *Les Trois Musquetaires*. 'Someone will contact you. The password is "*Est-ce que le train pour Avignon est parti?*" And the answer, "*Il ne part pas d'ici.*" Straight speaks good French, so you shouldn't have a problem there. I don't know about the other man.'

The first person to meet Richard at the appointed place was Ginny, wearing another of her amazing hats. She caught his hands and breathed, 'Ricardo, darling! It's so good to see you again!'

'And you, sweetheart,' he responded, kissing her on both cheeks.

A few moments later a small, grey-haired woman appeared with two young men at her side. They stood casually together a little way off and Richard made sure that his copy of *The Three Musketeers* was clearly visible. After a short wait the two men kissed their companion goodbye and came over.

'*Est-ce que le train pour Avignon est parti?*' the leader of the two enquired. He was a good-looking, dark young man with a brooding expression and a mouth that seemed to be set in a permanent expression of dogged defiance.

Richard gave the required reply and added, 'But we can go to Perpignan instead. This way.'

He had already purchased the tickets and they passed through the barrier and boarded the train with only a cursory glance from the ticket collector. The journey was slow and tedious, with frequent stops, and at one point they found themselves sharing a carriage with two uniformed German officers, apparently on leave. It was clear from the start that Straight's companion spoke no French at all but the American pilot chattered away confidently – too confidently for Richard's peace of mind.

When their papers were being checked at the end of the journey Straight grinned cheerily at one of the gendarmes.

'*Dis donc, mon brave*, caught any spies lately?'

The man looked at him glumly. 'What the hell would a spy be doing here?'

'Ah, but would you recognise one if you saw him?' Straight asked.

With a grunt the gendarme handed back the papers and gestured to Straight to move on. Richard, waiting for him with sweat trickling down his spine, had to admit that the man had nerve.

They had left the bicycles with the concierge at the hotel and Straight and his companion waited on a park bench while they fetched them. Then they took it turns to ride and walk the thirteen kilometres out to the coast. They reached the villa hot and tired. Straight looked out of the window. 'Is that the beach, just the other side of those dunes?'

'Yes,' Richard told him. 'It's only about a hundred yards.'

'Great!' said the American. 'Whose for a swim?'

'Nobody!' Richard returned sharply. 'You have to stay hidden until the ship comes.'

'Why?' the other man asked, the downturn at the corner of his lips becoming more pronounced. 'What's wrong with a swim?'

'There are dozens of people down there on the beach,' Richard pointed out.

'So? What's one more or less?'

'Look, people are used to seeing me and Ginny going backwards and forwards. We're supposed to be conducting a secret romance. It's going to look funny if suddenly all sorts of other blokes are seen going in and out.'

'Why should anyone notice?' Straight demanded.

'You never know who's watching,' Richard said, growing exasperated. 'I'm sorry, but this is my show. I'm in charge and I'm responsible to Pat for what happens. You're not going to jeopardise the success of the whole operation just because you fancy a swim.'

'Oh yeah? And who's going to stop me? You?'

'If necessary,' Richard said.

Straight turned away with a shrug. 'OK. Keep your hair on.'

At bedtime the two escapees found themselves required to share a double bed.

'There are three bedrooms, aren't there?' Straight asked. 'What's wrong with the third one?'

'I'm in it,' Richard said. 'You can share with me, if you prefer.'

'I thought you and Ginny were . . .?' The American looked at him with raised eyebrows.

'Only for the purposes of maintaining our cover,' Richard replied icily.

Straight looked at him with pursed lips and shook his head amusedly. 'Oh dear, dear! Such a perfect gentleman! Well, it's your loss, chum.'

They had three days to wait until the *Tarana* was due – three days in which to collect together the men who were waiting for the ship that would take them to freedom. So the next morning Richard left Ginny to look after their two 'guests' and went back into the city. He had to find a source of extra provisions for the men who would shortly begin to arrive, and also he needed to make contact with Fernand and the others and make arrangements to collect Ben Fry from the farm. On his return he found Ginny fuming in the kitchen.

'That bloody man has disobeyed your orders and gone swimming! And he's taken his pal with him.'

'Oh Christ!' Richard groaned. 'Well, there's no point in me going and making a scene on the beach. We'll just have to wait and hope for the best.'

The two miscreants returned an hour later, looking as blithe as two kids on a seaside holiday.

'What the hell do you think you're playing at?' Richard demanded.

'No one took any notice of us,' Straight said with a shrug.

'How do you know? You don't know who might have been watching from the dunes.'

'We just went for a swim, like anyone else.'

'Did you take precautions to see you weren't followed?'

Straight looked uncomfortable for the first time. 'Not particularly. Why should anyone follow us?'

'Because you're strangers – and because by now the Gestapo will be looking for you and your description will have been circulated. You idiots! For all you know the Gestapo could be outside the house now. It'll be no thanks to you if we're not all in custody by tonight.' Richard could hear his own voice rising in volume and made an effort to stay calm. 'Wait here. I'll have a look round outside.'

He went out and strolled to the top of the nearest dune, trying to look as though he were just enjoying the breeze off the sea. There was no sign of anyone on the path, and he caught no glint of reflected light from binoculars on the nearby dunes. It seemed that his fears had been groundless.

When he got back to the house the atmosphere was still tense. 'Well,' he said, 'we seem to have got away with it this time. But that's it! No more swimming.'

'I don't know who the hell you think you are to give orders!' Straight growled.

'I'm the bloody idiot who's risking his neck to get you back to the RAF,' Richard responded furiously. 'Though I'm buggered if I can see why they're so keen to have you. And I'm not the only one at risk. If you don't care about me, think of Pat and all the others who have helped you. Think of Ginny!'

Straight glared at him for a moment, then he turned away with a shrug. 'OK. Have it your way. I didn't realise paranoia was a requisite for the job.'

Later, Richard returned to the Lion d'Or, where he found the trio of musicians waiting for him. Fernand led him into the small cubbyhole of a room where they kept their instruments and said, 'Well? When will you be taking our friend away?'

'Very soon,' Richard told him. 'How is he?'

'Improving, but he still can't walk far and then only with the help of a crutch,' was the reply.

It was agreed that they would meet Richard the following night at the clump of pines where they had talked on that earlier occasion, and bring Fry with them.

During the course of the next day several couriers arrived at the Hôtel du Tennis with their 'parcels', strolling in casually and ordering drinks from the bar. Ginny was there, doubling as a waitress, and when each group identified itself by an agreed formula she signalled Richard by shaking a blue duster from a window. Richard then collected them and led them along the track to the villa. With ten of them packed into the four rooms there was no longer a question of who should share which bed. For the moment Ginny's room remained sacrosanct. The rest of them dossed down wherever they could find space.

As soon as he had finished his performance that evening Richard made his way to the rendezvous. After a tense wait he heard the noise of the old car's engine, hideously loud in the still night. Alphonse was driving, with Xavier beside him, and Ben Fry was in the back, his damaged leg stretched out along the seat.

'My God, am I glad to see you again!' he exclaimed fervently, as Richard leaned into the car to greet him. 'I've no idea what's going on.'

'Don't worry. You'll soon be in safe hands,' Richard assured him.

With some difficulty they manoeuvred the injured man out of the car and propped him on the seat of Richard's bicycle.

'Here!' Xavier said, and thrust a package into Richard's hands.

'What's this?' Richard asked.

'Cigarettes,' Xavier said. 'From our last little trip over the mountains. Give them to your friends – or use them to bribe the police.'

Richard thanked him and they set off, Ben pedalling with his good leg and 'rowing' with his crutch to keep his balance, while Richard held on to the back of the saddle. In this way they made good progress until they were within a few hundred yards of the coast, when Richard suddenly stopped and gripped Ben's arm.

'Ssh! I think I heard voices.'

Ahead the road bent between two sand dunes and from beyond the corner came the sound of men talking. For a moment Richard thought it might be another party of escapers heading for the hotel, but the voices were too loud and too confident for that. The only people who might be chatting so casually on the road at that time of night were the police. Richard wheeled the bike, with Ben on it, off the road and whispered, 'I think there's a police roadblock ahead.'

'Is there any way round?'

'Not for someone in your condition. You'd never make it over the dunes.'

'I could try.'

Richard shook his head, his mind racing. 'Listen. They're used to seeing me coming back late at night. I'll have to talk our way through. Pretend to be dead drunk – absolutely incapable. We'll have to get rid of the crutch. Give it to me.'

He scrabbled a shallow trench in the loose sand and buried the crutch, then gripped the back of the bicycle saddle again.

'Keep your head down and for God's sake don't speak!'

They set off again, Ben slumped over the handlebars and Richard steering an erratic course and admonishing him in French. 'Sit up, you idiot! What do you want to get yourself in this state for? I don't know what your sister-in-law's going to say.'

They rounded the corner and saw the two gendarmes standing beside their parked car ahead of them. One of them called to them to halt and shone a torch into Richard's face.

'Oh, it's you! You're back, then?'

Richard grinned cheerfully. 'Yes, I'm back, *mon ami*. The lady's husband has gone away on business again, so here we are.'

'Are you singing at the hotel again?'

'Oh yes, for a week.'

'Good. I must bring the wife to hear you.' The gendarme turned the torch on to Ben's drooping figure. 'Who's this, then?'

Richard lowered his voice. 'This is Madame's brother-in-law. I think the husband sent him to spy on us but he's got a bit of a drink problem. My guess is Monsieur gave him money to pay for his keep while he was here and he's blown the lot on a real bender. Look at him! I found him staggering around without a clue where he is or where he's going. Pathetic, isn't it?'

'So where are you taking him?'

'Home, with me. Madame's got a soft spot for him. God knows why! She'd never forgive me if I left him to fend for himself.'

At this point Ben, presumably feeling he ought to make some contribution to the deception, gave a high-pitched giggle and belched convincingly. Richard said, 'Oh God! You're not going to be sick, are you?' He looked at the gendarmes. 'I'd better get him home, before he pukes up all over the bike.'

'Can you manage?' the first policeman asked. 'Do you want a hand?'

'Oh no!' Richard said hastily. 'Thanks all the same. I've got him this far. I'll manage the rest. I wouldn't want him puking all over your uniform.'

'On your way, then.' The gendarme turned to his colleague and laughed. 'What some of us do for women, eh?'

'Ah, but it's worth it in the end, isn't it?' Richard responded, as he pushed the bike with its slouching cargo past them.

He was about to breathe a sigh of relief when one of the gendarmes called after him. 'Hold on a minute!'

Richard stopped, feeling Ben tense beside him. 'Is something wrong?'

'What have you got there, on the carrier?'

Richard looked round. He had forgotten about the carton of cigarettes that Xavier had given him. He thought fast and then grinned sheepishly. '*Merde!* Caught in the act, I'm afraid. It's cigarettes.'

'Cigarettes? Where did you come by a whole carton of cigarettes?'

The second gendarme laughed. 'He's been working with Fernand and Xavier. They're up to their old tricks again.'

His companion laughed too. 'Of course, I should have guessed. But what are you going to do with all these?'

Richard allowed his voice to assume what he hoped was a tone of amused resignation. 'Well, I was thinking of selling them in Marseilles when I get back. But naturally, I'd be happy to give some away to friends. Why don't you help yourselves?'

The two policemen took a couple of packs each, then had second thoughts and took two more. After which they wished Richard an amiable goodnight and let him go on his way.

Ben kept his head down until they had covered several hundred yards. Then he whispered, 'Are we OK?'

'Yes, I think so,' Richard whispered back. 'But stay quiet. We're nearly there.'

At the villa he eased Ben off the bike and helped him to hop inside. Willing hands took the burden from him and soon the bewildered young man was seated at the kitchen table.

'Who are all these people?' he demanded, staring round at the crowded room.

'Chris Parker, Flight Lieutenant,' said the man who had helped him in, extending a hand.

'You're RAF! Good Lord!' The relief and amazement on the boy's face were almost comic. Smiling, Richard left him to introduce himself and occupied himself with handing round what remained of Xavier's cigarettes. Ben, however, had not got over recent events.

'This man is incredible!' he declared, indicating Richard. In dramatic terms he related their encounter with the gendarmes and added, 'I'd never have had the nerve to do what he did. I don't know who the hell he is, but he deserves a bloody medal!'

Richard, murmuring a self-deprecating disclaimer, looked up and caught Whitney Straight's eye. The American gave him a small smile and bent his head in half-mocking salute.

The next day dragged. The weather was very hot and the atmosphere in the house became increasingly fetid but this time nobody suggested a bathe. Late in the day O'Leary arrived with three more refugees.

At 1 a.m. Richard led the first group of men down the track between the sand dunes to the beach. There was no moon and the sea was flat calm. Conditions were perfect. He left the men there and went back for a second batch, and within half an hour all thirty-five, plus O'Leary and Ginny, were crouched at the edge of the dunes waiting for the ship. Just before 2 a.m. Richard and O'Leary went down to the edge of the water and Richard began to flash the agreed Morse letter into the darkness. For what seemed a long time there was no response, then O'Leary touched his arm and whispered. 'There!' From a short distance to their right came the answering flash of red light and a few minutes later the dark shape of an inflatable materialised on the quiet water.

'*Avez-vous trouvé le poisson rouge?*' Richard whispered hoarsely.

'*Non, mais j'ai attrappé beaucoup de crabes,*' came the expected reply.

The boat grounded with a soft hiss and two black-clothed men clambered out. O'Leary had already brought the first group of escapers down to the water's edge and with the minimum of conversation they were loaded into the boat, which quickly pulled away from the shore. It seemed a very long time before it returned, during which Richard crouched on the sand, straining his ears for the sound of approaching vehicles or a challenge from seaward. It took three journeys to transport all the escapers out to the *Tarana*. Whitney Straight insisted on waiting for the last boat and just before scrambling on board he turned to Richard and held out his hand.

'Thanks for everything.' He spoke in English, although up to now they had always conversed in French. 'Sorry I gave you a bit of a hard time. I just didn't take kindly to being ordered about by a Wop crooner. I see what my mistake was now.'

Richard grinned and took the proffered hand. 'Think nothing of it,' he said, in the same language. 'Give my regards to Jimmy Langley when you get back.'

The American held his gaze for a moment. Then he winked and briefly tightened his grip. 'I'll do that.'

12

By the time Merry had eaten breakfast the next morning Felix and his flight had been at readiness for a couple of hours. He found them sprawled in broken-down chairs on the veranda of the dispersal hut, some of them reading, most chatting quietly or absorbed in their own thoughts. Although it was still early, the day was already hot and flies buzzed around with infuriating persistence. The cloudless sky was empty and quiet. Felix looked up with a smile.

'Morning. Sleep well?'

'Pretty well, thanks.' It was a lie. He had lain awake for hours, plotting how he and Felix could steal some time alone together – plots that had come to nothing.

He greeted the others and realised that there was one whom he had not met before. He was a short, wiry man, with ginger hair and a wispy moustache, his fair skin reddened and blistered by the Mediterranean sun. Felix introduced him. 'This is Len Harrison, my wingman.'

'How do?' The accent was unmistakably Yorkshire.

Merry shook the proffered hand and queried, 'Wingman?'

'It's the way we fly nowadays,' Felix explained. 'No more of those tight V formations with some poor sod acting as tail-end Charlie and weaving about trying to watch everyone else's backs. These days we fly in open twos, with each pilot looking in towards his partner and scanning the sky from twelve o'clock to six o'clock.' He indicated with a gesture a sweep of vision from directly in front to directly behind him. 'That way no one can creep up on either of you unaware. Everyone becomes very reliant on his wingman and I'm very lucky to have Len. I know he'll never let me down.'

The Yorkshireman's face became redder than ever. 'It's mutual.'

'Why didn't we meet yesterday?' Merry asked.

'I wasn't flying,' Harrison told him. 'Off sick with the "Malta dog" – gippy tummy, in other words.'

'Anyway,' Felix put in, 'Len's a sergeant pilot so he can't come into the officers' mess. It's ridiculous that we have these antiquated social distinctions. We've got several non-com pilots who should have been commissioned months ago. We keep pushing for it but so far the powers that be haven't got the message.'

'It's no matter,' Harrison mumbled, and Merry saw him look at Felix. It was a look of pure hero worship and Merry had a sudden ignoble twinge of jealousy, coupled with gratitude for the other man's lack of physical attractiveness.

He found himself welcomed by the rest of the flight. After months cooped up on the island they were glad to have any news from outside, or simply to encounter someone who had different stories to recount or jokes to tell. In return they told him the harrowing tale of the desperate defence of Malta.

'Some of the fellows have been out here since February,' Felix said. 'God knows how they survived. We were so short of aircraft sometimes the maximum number of planes we could put into the air to meet an attack was five. I came out with the first wave of reinforcements in March, flying off the carrier *Eagle*. We brought in thirty-one Spits but by the beginning of April we'd only got a handful left. The Huns were at us non-stop. Valletta was taking a hell of a pounding – worse than the London Blitz.'

'That was when the King awarded the island the George Cross?' Merry put in. 'I read about that.'

'Bloody well deserved, too,' Felix said. 'Then, on April the twentieth 601 and 603 Squadrons flew in forty-six Spits and within forty-eight hours the Huns had destroyed all but seven.'

'Good God!' Merry exclaimed. 'How did that happen?'

'We weren't sufficiently prepared. Most of them were destroyed on the ground before the crews could turn them around and refuel them. We got it right next time. When they sent out some more in May we had blast pens ready to receive each plane as it touched down and the ground crews were able to have them ready to take off again within minutes. And we had experienced pilots waiting to take them up. Since then things have been a lot easier.'

'What's it like, flying off a carrier?' Merry asked.

'Scary!' said Felix, and several voices concurred.

Before he could elaborate, the telephone rang inside the hut and immediately the men around Merry became alert. Felix rose and gave him a small, tight grin. ''Scuse me a minute.'

Inside they heard him say 'Hello?', then, after a pause, 'OK, Woody. I've got that. I'll let you know when we're in position.'

He came out again, carrying battledress jacket and trousers and his Mae West.

'Control says there's something building up over Sicily,' he said. 'Probably bombers preparing to attack a convoy out to the west. He wants four of us to go and have a look-see. Mitch and Rusty, you're with me and Len. OK. Let's go.'

The four of them climbed into battledress and flying boots and pulled on silk gloves. Felix grimaced at Merry. 'Trouble with this climate is, it's hot as hell on the ground but freezing up above, so you stew while you're waiting to take off.' He slung his life jacket round his shoulders and glanced at the others. 'Ready, chaps?'

'Ready, Skip.'

Felix met Merry's eyes for a minute. 'See you soon,' he said lightly and headed away towards the blast pens, where the Spitfires were already being warmed up.

Merry watched them go with a terrible feeling of helplessness. It seemed that John Holmes, the intelligence officer, who had been sitting with them, had noticed his distress.

'If we go over to the control room we can follow what's happening on the radio,' he suggested. 'Shall we?'

In the control room a wireless operator crouched over his apparatus and another airman plotted the position of aircraft on a large tabletop map. Jumbo Gracie stood by the window, looking out at the sky. After a word or two with the operator Holmes handed Merry a headset. To begin with he could hear nothing but static in the earphones but then Felix's voice came over the air.

'Gondar, this is Red Leader. Do you read me? Over.'

A deep bass voice responded. 'Red Leader, this is Gondar. Reading you loud and clear.'

'I'm in position,' Felix's voice came back. 'Can't see anything at the moment.'

'Red Leader, there are four big jobs at angels fifteen. You should see them below you at about nine o'clock.'

'Big jobs?' Merry queried.

'Bombers,' Holmes elucidated.

'Any little jobs about?' Felix enquired.

'Fighters,' put in Holmes.

'Not so far, but they won't be far away. Watch your tails.'

A pause, filled with static. Then, 'This is Red Leader. I see them, Woody. Eighty-eights, heading west. OK, fellers. Mitch and Rusty, you take the starboard pair. Len, take the outer port and I'll take the other one. Acknowledge, please.'

One by one the acknowledgements came in. 'Red Two, roger.' 'Red Three, roger.' 'Red Four, OK, Skip.'

'Right!' Felix's voice was cool, precise. 'Turning hard to port now and going in.'

Another silence, then the unmistakable rattle of gunfire and a triumphant exclamation from Mitch.

'Got the bastard!'

Felix's voice again. 'Red Leader to Control. One enemy aircraft down in flames. A definite kill. A second heading for home trailing smoke. Red Flight, break off and re-form.'

Then, suddenly, Rusty's voice, urgent and excited. 'Red Leader, bandits at two o'clock, angels twenty-five! Coming in fast!'

Felix. 'OK, fellers. Make as much height as you can – and try to stay in pairs!'

There followed a confused cacophony of imprecations, shouts of triumph or warning, then clearly out of the chaos the voice of Len Harrison.

'Look out, Skip! On your tail! Break now!' Then came the sound of gunfire and Harrison's voice again. 'Oh Christ! They've got him. Skip! Skip, are you OK?'

Merry felt the ground sway under his feet. There was no response from Felix but Mitch's voice cut in.

'No you don't, you bugger! You don't get away with that!' A pause, then, 'Got the swine! Me 109 down in flames.'

Harrison's voice again. 'Skip, can you hear me?'

At last Felix spoke, his voice unsteady. 'OK, Len. He's

winged me, but it's not serious. The old kite's in a bad way, though.'

The deep tones of the controller came through Merry's earphones, calm and reassuring. 'What is your situation, Red Leader?'

'Under control, Woody, but losing height. Heading for home, but I may have to jump.'

'What is your position, Ned?' Control asked. 'I'll alert the air-sea rescue boys.'

Clearly and methodically Felix relayed the map references and height. Harrison's voice came over again.

'I'm just above you, Skip. I'll give you cover, but you're trailing glycol. It doesn't look good.'

'Glycol?' Merry asked.

'Engine coolant,' Holmes told him. 'It means his engine will eventually overheat and cut out.'

'Red Leader, this is Control. If you're losing height don't wait too long before you hop out, Ned. You can't afford to hang on much longer.'

'Thanks, Woody. I'm watching it. I'll try to bring her in for an emergency landing. We can't afford to lose any more planes.'

'We can't afford to lose pilots of your calibre, either,' the deep voice countered.

There was a long, agonising silence. Then Felix came on again. 'I can see the island now. I think I can make it.' Then, despairingly, 'Shit! The engine's cut!'

Merry turned to Holmes. 'Will he do it?' he asked desperately.

'If he's got enough height to clear Dingli Cliffs he should be OK. Here, see?' Holmes indicated the map, which showed a line of low cliffs to the west of the island. 'If we go outside we should be able to see him any minute.'

As they went out on to the airfield two trucks roared past them, heading for the runway. One was an ambulance, the second a fire engine. *Oh God!* Merry begged silently. *Not the fire again! Not that, Lord!*

All around the field men were standing, straining their eyes to the west. Merry jumped as there was a series of small explosions and red Very lights shot into the air.

'What's that for?' he demanded.

'To warn off any other aircraft. Let them know there's an emergency landing about to take place.'

There was another tense hiatus and then Holmes said, 'There he is!'

Merry saw the small shape of the Spitfire appear over some high ground, so low that it seemed its belly must brush the top of one of the stone walls that divided the tiny fields. Holmes said, 'If he can get his undercarriage down he stands a good chance. Yes! There it goes. Well done, Ned! Keep her nose up. Attaboy!'

In an eerie, whistling silence the plane swept over their heads, touched down and ran to a standstill. A cheer went up all round the ground and Holmes exclaimed, 'Bloody marvellous! Only Ned could bring a plane in on a dead stick and make a perfect three-point landing!'

Merry was straining his eyes towards the aircraft, waiting for the cockpit cover to be pushed back. There was no sign of movement. The ambulance was racing towards the spot but the ground crew who looked after the plane were there first. A fitter climbed up on the wing and pushed the cockpit cover open. Merry watched numbly as he leaned in, his hands busy with something, then reached farther down, braced himself and hauled an inert figure into view.

'Oh God!' Merry said, and it came out as a sob. Then, 'No, he's all right! Look!'

Felix had sat up and swung his legs over the edge of the wing, allowing himself to be lowered into the arms of the waiting airmen. A minute later he was in the ambulance and being bounced across the potholes towards the dressing station.

By the time Merry reached the building there was no one in the outer office except a clerk, who came to attention and enquired, 'Can I help you, sir?'

'I've come to find out how Flight Lieutenant Mountjoy is,' Merry replied breathlessly.

'The doctor's with him now, sir,' the man replied. 'If you wouldn't mind waiting . . .'

From an inner room a voice called, 'Is that Lieutenant Merryweather out there?' and Merry called back, 'Yes! Are you OK, Felix?'

The inner door opened and an orderly appeared, grinning.

'The flight lieutenant says you'd better come in, sir, otherwise you won't believe anything he tells you.'

Felix was sitting up on the couch, stripped to the waist, while a doctor bent over a long gash in his left upper arm. Beneath the tan he was as pale as the sheet but he grinned cheerfully at Merry. 'See? Nothing to worry about.'

The doctor glanced up. 'A flesh wound only, but he's lost quite a lot of blood. A few stitches and it'll be fine, but I'm afraid you won't be flying again for a while.'

Merry realised with a jolt of delight that out of the near-disaster might come the opportunity he had been longing for.

Felix said, 'How long?'

'Five days at least. Probably a week.'

There was a stir outside and the door opened to admit the station commander.

'Thank heaven, Ned! For a bit back there you had us all worried.'

'Sorry about that, sir,' Felix responded with a smile.

'Well, you saved your aircraft. Well done!'

Gracie went on to ask a few questions of the doctor, who repeated his decision that Felix should not fly for at least five days. Gracie nodded, apparently satisfied, and then turned to Merry.

'Care to walk up to the mess with me? They'll bring Ned up in the ambulance when the doc's finished with him. I'd like a word.'

'Of course, sir,' Merry agreed. Behind Gracie's back he exchanged an interrogative look with Felix, who shrugged and shook his head.

'Set me up a double brandy, will you, Merry? I feel I could do with it.'

'I bet!' Merry agreed. 'See you in a bit.'

He followed Gracie out of the building and as they started to walk up the hill the squadron leader said, 'You and Ned are pretty close, eh?'

The hairs on the back of Merry's neck prickled. Had he, in that last desperate half-hour, betrayed himself? Was he about to be warned off, or worse still accused of a crime that could result in both himself and Felix being cashiered from their respective services? Gracie's easygoing manner did not suggest anything of the sort but nevertheless he answered cautiously, 'I suppose you could say that.'

'I'm glad,' Gracie said unexpectedly. 'The fact is, most of the chaps here have formed some pretty close friendships but Ned – Felix, you call him, don't you? – has always been a bit of a loner. He's a thoroughly nice chap, a brilliant pilot and an excellent officer – friends with everyone, but no one seems to have really got close to him. That's why I'm glad you've turned up. You may have more influence over him than anyone here.'

'Influence in what way?' Merry was beginning to breathe more easily.

'He needs to ease up. He's been out here since March and he must have flown more operations than anyone. The trouble is, even when he's not on the slate – not down to fly that day – he will insist on hanging around the dispersal hut. He watches them all go off and counts them all back in again. It's very creditable, of course, but he needs to take a break sometimes. Even when I've insisted that he take some leave he won't go away. We've got a very pleasant rest station up at St Paul's Bay – beautiful spot, plenty of opportunity to swim or play tennis or just relax – but whenever I've managed to persuade him to go up there he's back within a day or two. He can't keep going at this pressure much longer. Today was a case in point. If he'd really been up to his usual standard he'd never have let himself get caught out like that.'

'So what do you want me to do?' Merry asked.

'Take him away somewhere, up to St Paul's probably. Keep him occupied. Try to take his mind off what's going on here.'

Oh, I'll do that all right! Merry's racing pulse beat out the words. *But I don't know if you'd approve of my methods.* Aloud he said unwillingly, 'The only trouble is, I'm not really supposed to be here. I'm not sure if it's on for me to hang around.'

'Oh, you don't need to worry about that,' Gracie said with a wink. 'It's going to be at least a week before we get round to repairing that Blenheim.'

The ambulance passed them as they reached the top of the hill and when Merry entered the Palace he was met by an orderly who told him that Felix had gone straight up to his room. Merry bought a double brandy for each of them at the bar and carried them upstairs. Felix was sitting on his bed, leaning back against the headboard, dressed only in his under-pants. His arm was in a sling and his face, before he sum-moned his customary grin, looked haggard. Merry handed him the brandy and he took a large swallow. They looked at each other, suddenly unable, after the tension of the last hour, to behave naturally.

Felix said, 'Give me a cigarette, will you? Oh no, I forgot, you've given up. There are some over there, in my pocket.' He indicated his tunic, which was draped over the back of a chair.

Merry took out the cigarette case and a lighter. He took a cigarette, put it in his own mouth and lit it, then placed it between Felix's lips. It was a small gesture of intimacy that they had evolved in the days when Felix had so little use in his right hand that manipulating such things presented difficul-ties, and which they had retained as a secret symbol of their relationship. Felix drew deeply on the cigarette and Merry sat down on the edge of the bed, feeling suddenly weak at the knees.

'Christ, Felix, I never want to go through another half-hour like that!'

Felix took the cigarette out of his mouth and contemplated it. 'No. Can't say I enjoyed it much either.'

'I was in the control room all the time, you know,' Merry told him. 'I heard it all on the wireless.'

'You were?' Felix's eyes widened. 'I didn't realise. That must have been pretty grim.'

'It was,' Merry agreed. Then he added, 'You know, all the time I was sort of shouting inside myself. I don't know who I was talking to, but I kept saying over and over again, *You can't do this! You can't let this happen! We've been apart for so long, and we only met again yesterday and we haven't even been able to . . .*'

He left the sentence unfinished and Felix cut in with, 'And I was talking to the plane. I kept saying, *Come on, old thing! You can't let me down now, not today! I've got to get back today. Merry's waiting for me.*'

Their eyes met and abruptly Felix reached out with his good arm and hooked it around the back of Merry's neck, pulling himself into his embrace.

'Hold me tight a minute, Merry,' he mumbled, his voice muffled against Merry's neck. 'I really thought I was a goner for a bit up there.'

Merry folded his arms round him and rubbed his face against his hair. His own eyes were wet. He could feel that Felix was shaking, the delicate, electric tremor that he remembered from those terrible days in the hospital after his first crash. It occurred to him that he was probably the only person in the world who knew what it cost Felix to present that calm, cheerful exterior in the face of danger. He was not fearless, far from it, but he would never let his own fears be transmitted to those serving with him. Little by little he felt the trembling ease and the tense muscles relax, but they clung together in silence until Merry became aware of a cigarette smouldering dangerously close to his ear. He disentangled himself gently, took it from Felix's hand and inhaled a long breath of the smoke.

'I thought you'd given up,' Felix said.

'I have,' Merry replied, 'but there are times when nicotine becomes a medical necessity.'

'How true,' Felix agreed, repossessing his cigarette.

They smoked turn and turn about until it was reduced to a small butt. As Merry stubbed it out Felix said, 'What did Jumbo want?'

'Ah,' Merry said, smiling. 'He wants me to take you away from all this.'

'What?' Felix looked incredulous.

Merry became serious again. 'He says you've been overdoing it. Apparently you've been flying too many missions and you refuse to take leave when it's offered.' Felix looked away, a mutinous expression on his face. Merry went on despairingly, 'Oh, Felix! What did I say to you back in England? You don't have to prove anything! You've done more than your bit. You can't fight the war single handed.'

'I'm not trying to,' Felix protested. 'But I do have responsibilities to these fellows under me. How can I go off and enjoy myself and leave the likes of young Rusty Rogers to fend for themselves?'

'You can't do anything for them once they're in the air,' Merry pointed out.

'I can if I'm flying with them,' Felix insisted. 'I can watch out for them, warn them . . .'

'Like your wingman warned you today,' Merry said. 'No one's invulnerable, Felix. What good will it be to them if you get shot down and killed?' Felix did not reply and Merry pressed on. 'Take today. Would that have happened if you'd been really at the top of your form?'

Felix was silent for a moment. Then he said, 'Well, it looks as if I'm out of it for a few days, anyway.'

'Exactly!' Merry said. 'A few days we can spend together. What about this St Paul's Bay place?'

'God, no!' Felix exclaimed. 'It's full of kids playing gramophone records and horsing around.'

Merry smiled inwardly at the way in which the boys Felix was so keen to protect in the air had suddenly transmuted into irritating kids. Aloud he said, 'Where, then?'

'I don't know,' Felix said. Then his face suddenly lit up. 'Yes I do! There's a family here in M'dina – very rich, very old established family by the name of Gonzago. They've been very hospitable to some of us since we arrived. I remember once old Signor Gonzago told me that they have a villa somewhere on the west coast. They don't use it at present because they feel safer here in M'dina but he actually offered it to any of us who wanted somewhere to go for a spot of leave. I've never taken him up on it but as far as I know the offer still stands.'

'When can we go?' Merry asked, almost unable to credit the turn of events.

'I'm not sure. We can't call on the family until later on. It's not done to arrive in the middle of siesta. But we could pop round about teatime and ask if we can use the villa.'

'Brilliant!' Merry exclaimed. He looked at his watch. 'Are you coming for lunch?'

Felix shook his head. 'I don't feel like eating. I think I'll just have forty winks.'

'Good idea,' Merry agreed. He tucked the mosquito netting carefully round the bed and left the room.

By four o'clock that afternoon Felix, looking rested and spruce in a clean uniform, was leading Merry through the narrow streets to another ancient house much like the Xara Palace, though on a smaller scale. Here they were received with great courtesy by Signor Gonzago and his beautiful wife, who, in spite of the privations the whole island was suffering, looked as if she had just left the salon of a Paris couturier. They were offered wine and fruit in a shady courtyard and when Felix mentioned the possibility of using the seaside villa for a few days the response was immediate.

'But of course. You are welcome to stay there as long as you like. I shall drive you there myself, this evening if that suits you.

And Maria, who lives in the village, will come and cook for you.'

All offers of payment were brushed aside. Nothing, the old gentleman declared, could possibly wipe out the debt he and his people owed to the gallant British airmen who were risking their lives to defend the island.

By sunset they were installed in a spacious white villa perched on a low cliff at the head of a narrow inlet. Below the terrace honey-coloured rocks plunged into sea with the colour and clarity of sapphire. As soon as they had waved goodbye to their generous host they turned by mutual, silent consent and headed up the staircase to the master bedroom. Here long windows gave on to a balcony with a view of the ocean. The first faint breeze of evening was stirring the white curtains and the misty mosquito net over the big double bed. Still without speaking Felix began to unbutton his shirt. Merry went to assist him, easing his arm out of the sling and carefully sliding the shirtsleeve over the bandages. It was an accustomed routine, developed when Felix could only use one hand and needed help with dressing and undressing. Unhurriedly, with a luxurious sense of living in a world where time no longer had any significance, they shed the rest of their clothes and moved over to the bed.

'I don't want to hurt you,' Merry murmured, touching the bandaged arm lightly.

'You never hurt me,' Felix said, reaching out to him.

They had made love many times before, passionately or with languorous delicacy, but never with a deeper tenderness than that afternoon. After such long abstinence it might have all been over in a few minutes but somehow they managed to retain that sense of timelessness, so that for both of them the climax, when it came, had an intensity that obliterated almost a year of separation.

Afterwards, when they lay sprawled in a drowsy tangle of limbs, Felix stirred and murmured, 'See? Four arms, four legs, two heads – one person. We're complete again.'

'The miracle is,' Merry responded, smiling at the recollection of the Platonic conceit, 'that we survived so long as two separate halves.'

They were roused eventually by the smell of frying fish wafting up through the open window. Felix raised himself with a jerk on to one elbow.

'God! That must be the woman from the village. I wonder what she imagines we've been doing up here.'

'Sleeping, I hope,' Merry returned. 'Let's go and find out what she's cooking.'

They ate on the terrace by the light of candles, a meal of freshly caught fish and goat's cheese, washed down with a bottle of the local wine. Even the bitter 'half-caste' bread that was the island's staple diet tasted better that evening. Maria turned out to be a motherly character who was deeply concerned for the welfare of these two gallant young fighters, who had obviously arrived exhausted from the fray. Signor Gonzago had insisted that they make free with the contents of the cocktail cabinet in the sitting room, so after the meal they sat on over glasses of brandy and watched the searchlights and explosions over Valletta as if it were a fireworks display laid on for their entertainment. Then, yawning, they retired to bed again.

As they undressed Felix exclaimed, 'Hang on. Come here a minute.' He took hold of Merry's arm and turned him so that he could examine the deep scar beneath his ribs. 'You told me it was a minor flesh wound,' he said reproachfully.

'So it is, compared with some of the wounds I've seen in the last month or two,' Merry returned.

'Another inch or two up or to the left and it certainly wouldn't have been minor,' Felix commented.

'No,' Merry agreed. 'I was lucky.'

'We both were,' Felix agreed, pressing his arm.

But the exchange had brought to the surface of Merry's consciousness another, deeper wound that had been festering at the back of his mind for the last forty-eight hours. In bed, he realised that the time had come to lance it.

'Felix, there's something I have to tell you.'

Felix studied him thoughtfully for a moment, reading his face with his usual intuitive ease. Then he said, 'There's been someone else, hasn't there?'

'Is it so obvious?' Merry exclaimed, aghast.

'No,' Felix replied, 'except that I can't think of any other reason for that hangdog expression.'

Merry dropped his eyes. 'I'm sorry,' he murmured. 'I really am! I never intended it to happen. It was a sort of accident.'

'Tell me about it,' Felix invited.

In disjointed sentences Merry explained about the unwelcome attentions of Tom Dyson on the voyage out to Egypt and the boy's clumsy attempt at seduction; and about his response and the final denouement in his tent on New Year's Eve. 'I can't even give the excuse that I was drunk,' he finished. 'I'd hardly touched a drop all evening.'

Felix said, 'He was the one you went back to rescue, wasn't he?'

Merry nodded. 'But it wasn't because . . . because I cared . . . well, yes, of course, I did care, in a way. I mean it wasn't because I was in love with him. I just felt guilty.'

'Guilty?'

'Yes. I mean, he came to me basically because he was lonely and frightened and in need of a bit of comfort and I sent him away feeling . . . unwanted, rejected. I could have handled the situation so much better! I felt I owed him something.'

'And you nearly paid the debt with your life,' Felix commented.

Merry looked at him for the first time since beginning his story. His eyes were grave but not angry and as Merry met them a smile grew in them. Felix put out a hand and ran his fingers through Merry's hair.

'Don't look so woebegone, poor old Eeyore! It's not the end of the world.'

'You don't mind? You're not angry or . . . or hurt?'

Felix considered for a moment. 'I should have been bloody angry if you'd got yourself killed trying to save him – with him and with you.'

'But as things are . . .?'

'As things are – I'm not going to let a one-off incident like that upset me. It would be different if he was still around, if you wanted to keep up some kind of relationship with him. I couldn't bear to share you, Merry. But after all, we hadn't seen each other for such a long time. Something like this was almost bound to happen to one of us, sooner or later. It would be daft to let it come between us.'

'Thank you, Felix,' Merry said humbly. 'I can't tell you what a relief that is. I wasn't going to say anything originally. I thought it would be better if you never knew. But then I found I had to get it off my chest.'

'So now you have,' Felix answered, putting an arm round him. 'And now we can both forget it.'

* * *

The next five days developed a regular routine. In the morning they would make their way down a flight of steps cut into the cliff to the tiny, sandy beach at the head of the inlet. Felix was unable to swim because of his wounded arm, but he found a convenient flat-topped rock where he could sit up to his armpits in water and rest his bandaged arm on a rocky shelf. Merry, asthmatic as child, had never been a great swimmer, but he was happy to float near by or to haul himself out, seal-like, on to the rocks to bask in the sun. When they tired of this they retired to the beach to play chess or read until it was time to climb back to the house to see what Maria had prepared for lunch. It was usually fish, but after the unvarying diet of bully beef and Maconochies stew which the mess provided it was a welcome relief.

After lunch they retired to the bedroom for what they euphemistically termed a siesta and usually they did, eventually, sleep for a while. Then, when the hottest part of the day was over, they went for a stroll along the cliffs, returning in time for a cocktail before dinner. Drinks on the terrace accompanied by the nightly 'fireworks display' brought the day to an end, and neither of them had any desire to stay up late.

All through this time they talked, filling in the gaps in their knowledge of what had happened to each of them, reminiscing about old times with the Follies, occasionally speculating about the progress of the war. The most important thing, as far as Merry was concerned, was that Felix was beginning to relax, to forsake just for an hour or two the constant mental and emotional vigil that he kept over the welfare of the pilots in his squadron. His face grew less gaunt, the fine lines around the eyes smoothed out, his body seemed to physically elongate.

'By the way,' Felix said one evening, 'have you heard anything from Richard lately?'

'Not a word,' Merry said. 'But I saw in the papers that he's married.'

'Yes. I saw that too. I suppose we know he's still alive, at least.'

'I'm amazed at him marrying Priscilla Vance,' Merry commented. 'I always thought of her as a spoilt little rich girl.'

'Well, let's face it,' Felix returned, 'he's obviously on to a very good thing. With her money and Sir Lionel's connections his career ought to take off like a lift when the war's over.'

'You think he's married her with an eye to that?'

Felix shrugged. 'I don't know. But you have to admit it's a possibility.'

'I can't see Richard behaving like that,' Merry said. 'It just doesn't seem in character.'

'Maybe not. But then he never replied to Rose. That doesn't sound like the Richard we used to know, does it?'

Merry sighed. 'No, true. Poor Rose!'

'Poor Rose, indeed.'

On the last afternoon, as they were dressing to return to the base, Merry voiced the question that had been at the back of his mind all day. 'How much longer do you think you will be based out here?'

Felix lifted his shoulders. 'Who knows? A few weeks, a month? It will all depend on the penguins at HQ.'

'Penguins?' Merry queried.

Felix grinned. 'Penguins are supposed to be birds. They flap, but they can't fly.'

'Oh, I get it.' Merry smiled in return but then pursued the theme. 'Surely your tour must be almost over?'

'It should be,' Felix agreed. 'The trouble is, they need a few old hands like me to teach the new boys the ropes. But it can't be much longer. My guess is I'll be home by the middle of August, latest.'

'And then what?'

'I should think I'm due for a spell flying a desk – and for once I shan't mind, for a bit.'

'Well, thank God for that,' Merry said. 'I might get a few months' peace of mind.'

The day after their return Gracie found him as he was eating breakfast. Felix had already left for the airfield and he was alone.

'Got you fixed up with transport home,' the squadron leader said. 'There's a Hudson heading for Gib at first light tomorrow. You'll find it a good deal more comfortable than that Blenheim. I've arranged for a car to pick you up at five thirty.'

Merry and Felix spent their last night in an olive grove on the hillside above Takali. They did not make love but Felix spread a borrowed groundsheet and they lay, with his head pillowed on Merry's shoulder, and watched the stars move across the cloudless sky. They talked little, since they had already said all there was to say.

When his watch showed five o'clock Merry stirred and murmured, 'I'll have to go.'

Felix started up. 'I'll come with you.'

Merry pressed him back against the groundsheet. 'No, don't. I'd really rather you didn't. I hate trying to say goodbye in front of other people.'

Felix relaxed. 'Yes, you're right.' He reached up and drew Merry's head down and they exchanged a long kiss.

Merry said, 'I know it's no use telling you to take care. Just try to remember you're more use to me and everyone else alive than dead!'

'Don't worry,' Felix said. 'Only a few more weeks and I'll be home. I'll be due for some leave. We'll go to Shoreham.'

Merry rose slowly to his feet. 'Yes, that'll be good. I'll see you soon, then.'

'Yes,' Felix replied. 'See you soon.'

Merry turned and made his way along the hillside towards the road. When he looked back Felix was already out of sight among the trees.

13

Richard finished his week's engagement at the Lion d'Or and then returned to Marseilles, where he headed at once for Dr Rodocanachi's flat. It had been agreed that if anyone queried his frequent visits he should say that he was receiving treatment for incipient arthritis in his damaged leg. That, and the fact that his hypothetical mistress lived in Marseilles, gave him sufficient reason for returning there on a regular basis.

As usual, Pat O'Leary was waiting for him, on this occasion with an open bottle of red wine to hand.

'Congratulations, *mon ami*!' he said, pouring out two glasses. 'We heard from London about an hour ago. Apparently they have received a message from "Sunday" in Gibraltar. Our friends were transferred to a British destroyer somewhere off the Balearics and landed safely on the Rock this morning. Room 900 are delighted.'

'Well, that's good news,' Richard said. 'Did they say anything about another pick-up by sea?'

'They're waiting to hear from us. There's another man they are very anxious to get out.'

'Who is it this time?'

'A Squadron Leader Higginson.'

Richard made a grimace. 'Another Brylcreem Boy!'

O'Leary smiled his quiet smile. 'Don't worry. You won't have any trouble with Taffy.'

'Taffy?' Richard queried.

'Actually, we are old friends. Cole brought him down the line back in 1941. By the way, he is convinced that Cole is not a traitor and won't have a word said against him. I had just arrived at that time and we both stayed here. Then Taffy was moved on to Perpignan but something went wrong and the guide refused to take him. He was picked up by the police and rearrested. He eventually fetched up in Fort de la Revère above Monte Carlo, along with quite a few other POWs. That's why I wanted you to establish a base in Monaco.'

'So what's the plan?' Richard asked.

'While you were in Monte did you come across the local basketball team?'

'No,' Richard replied, puzzled.

'They are coached by a man named Vladimir Bouryschkine – London knows him as Val Williams. He's a White Russian émigré who has been working for us for some time. He found out that the prisoners at the fort were not getting enough exercise to comply with the rules laid down by the Geneva Convention, so he persuaded the Vichy authorities to let him go in a couple of times a week as a PT instructor. We also have another contact – Father Myrda, the priest who ministers to the prisoners' spiritual welfare. I'm waiting to hear from them what the best method might be for getting Taffy out – and some others with him, we hope. That's where you come in at the moment. I want you to act as liaison between them and me, since you seem to be able to travel backwards and forwards reasonably easily.'

'OK,' Richard agreed. 'How do I contact this Vladimir character?'

'Have you come across the Scottish Tearooms in Monte Carlo?'

'Yes. I've been in a couple of times.'

'It's run by the Misses Trenchard. They work for us.'

'Those two little grey-haired spinsters!'

O'Leary smiled. 'Never underestimate the British spinster, *mon cher*. Those ladies are indomitable. They perform an invaluable function as a meeting point for couriers and escapers. Make a point of going in there for tea every afternoon and when he is ready Val will contact you with a message for me.'

A week later Richard was back in Marseilles.

'Val says there is a sewage pipe from the fort that comes out on the bank of a small stream at La Turbie. There is a coal chute that goes down from the room where Higginson is kept to a kitchen. From there, there is a window overlooking the moat. If they can let themselves down into the moat they can get into the sewer, but they'll need a hacksaw to cut the bars on the window and also the grid over the pipe at the far end.'

'Well, it's worth a try, I suppose,' O'Leary said. 'Can Val smuggle in a hacksaw blade?'

'Yes, he says that's not a problem. But they need to move fast. There's a rumour going round that all the officers are to be transferred to a prison camp in Italy soon.'

'OK. Let me know when they plan the breakout and I'll make sure there is a reception committee waiting to pick them up at La Turbie.'

Richard returned to Monte Carlo, where he had become a popular feature at the Café Pique Dame. Monaco, being a neutral, independent state, stood on the sidelines of the conflict that had engulfed the rest of Europe, and he was constantly amazed at the number of wealthy people, including English expatriates, who were still apparently enjoying life there.

A few days later he was sitting at his usual table in the Scottish Tearooms when Val, the big, powerfully built Russian, came and joined him.

'It's all set for the night of August the sixth. Taffy says they've managed to make a rope out of the string from Red Cross parcels to let themselves down into the moat. But they need some kind of diversion to keep the guards occupied and cover any noise. They're trying to organise a concert or something similar but it's short notice and they're not sure they can get together enough acts to keep the thing going long enough.'

'Do you think they'd appreciate a guest artist?' Richard asked.

The big man raised an eyebrow. 'An Italian singer? I'm not sure what sort of reception you'd get.'

Richard had to think quickly. For a moment he had forgotten that the prisoners in the fort would naturally regard him as an enemy. He said, 'Do they need to know my nationality? I could just be introduced as a singer from Monaco.'

Val considered for a moment. 'I don't see why not. I'll have to have a word with the governor but I think I can probably convince him that a little entertainment will be good for morale – and take the prisoners' minds off escaping! But what about an accompanist? Will the chap who plays for you at the café do it?'

'I doubt it,' Richard said. 'He thinks the Nazis are going to win the war and is terrified of doing anything to upset them.'

'I'll ask at the fort,' Val said. 'Whoever is organising the concert may be able to come up with a pianist.'

On the evening of the 6th Richard presented himself at the gates of the forbidding medieval building on the hill and, after a cursory search, was conducted by a guard into a large, echoing hall, which was already filling up with men in various uniforms. He was introduced to a thin man in worn army uniform with a major's badges of rank, who glanced at the sheet music Richard handed him and nodded briefly.

'Yes, I can manage that.'

Richard had to remind himself that he was not supposed to speak English. 'Is OK, yes?' he queried, in what he hoped was a convincingly broken accent.

The major raised his voice. 'Yes, OK. OK.'

'*Bene!*' responded Richard with a broad smile.

The inmates of the fort had organised the opening items of the concert for themselves as agreed. Some of the acts were excellent, others suggested that the organisers were really scraping the bottom of the barrel. The reception for all of them, however, was vociferous, and Richard wondered how much of it was simply a reaction to anything that relieved the tedium of prison existence and how much was because some of them, at least, knew the reason for that night's performance.

When his turn came, the compère announced him as a singer who had achieved great success with the patrons of a very exclusive café in Monte Carlo and he was received in a rustling, uneasy silence. He nodded to the accompanist, who struck up the opening chords of the Toreador's song from *Carmen*. That had always gone down well with audiences at Fairbourne, and he judged that this one could not be so different. He followed up with 'Funiculi, Funicula' and heard, with amusement, voices joining in the chorus with a particularly ribald English version. Grinning broadly and apparently unaware of the meaning of the words, he conducted the audience, encouraging them to sing up.

'So!' he said, when the number was finished. 'You like to sing? Here is a song you all know.'

Reverting to his cabaret style, he sang 'Lilli Marlene', first in the original German and then in the English version. Hearing the voices of a hundred men raised in evocation of the yearning nostalgia of the tune brought a lump to his throat. Scanning the faces in front of him, he experienced a sudden shock of recognition. Surely that was a face he knew? He focused on the shoulder flash on the man's uniform. It was his own old regiment, the South Lancs! His stomach clenched and only his professional training prevented the song from dying in his throat. He could not remember the man's name and he had seen no answering sign of recognition – but it needed only an unguarded exclamation to blow his cover. He presumed that this man, too, must have been left behind on the retreat to Dunkirk and had made his way south, only to be arrested and interned by the Vichy authorities.

When the song ended the applause was enthusiastic. He beamed and thickened his accent. 'So, now we all sing – yes? What you want to sing?'

They sang 'Tipperary' and 'Roll Out the Barrel' and 'If You Were the Only Girl in the World' and 'Keep the Home Fires Burning', as if their lungs would burst, and the concert ended only when the prison guards insisted that it was time for the men to return to their cells.

As Richard left the stage and was escorted towards the door he suddenly found himself face to face with the man he thought he knew. For an instant, recognition flickered in the other man's eyes and then they went blank.

'Thanks, mate!' the man said. 'Enjoyed it.'

Richard gave him a vague smile, as if he only partly understood the words, and passed on. The prison governor wanted to entertain him to drinks but he made the excuse that someone was waiting for him – a lady, he let it be understood – and escaped. Once outside the gates he found that he was sweating.

He was halfway down the mountain road, heading back towards Monte Carlo in the car he had borrowed for the evening, when the fort was suddenly revealed in his rear-view mirror, starkly illuminated in the glare of floodlights. He caught his breath and stopped the car. With the engine off he could clearly hear the sound of sirens from the hilltop above him. The escape had been discovered. But were Higginson and his companions already out, or had they been discovered before they managed to find their way into the sewer pipe? He knew that Val, together with Jean le Nerveux and another member of the *réseau*, would be waiting by the outlet of the pipe to conduct them to a safe house for the night, but he recognised that within minutes the whole area would be swarming with police. It was not only the escapees who were in danger.

There was nothing he could do to help. He started the car and drove on down the winding road. After a mile or so he was not surprised to see a police car blocking the road ahead. Sweat prickled again in his armpits. You could never tell how the French police would behave. Some of them had not forgotten that France and Britain were, theoretically, allies and were prepared to turn a blind eye to any infringements of regulations laid down by the renegade government in Vichy. Others were too rigid, or too intimidated by the Milice or the German secret police, to cooperate. There was no reason why they should connect him with the escape, but on the other hand his presence must look suspicious. He opted for a touch of bombast.

'What is it? Why have you stopped me?'

'Get out of the car, please, monsieur.' The gendarme looked like one of the officious types.

Richard complied, with an irritated shrug.

'Your papers, please. What have you been doing up at the chateau?'

Richard produced his papers, together with a letter signed by the governor of the prison.

'What's going on?' he asked.

'There's been an attempted escape.'

'What, tonight? I, Ricardo Benedetti, give up my one free evening to try to bring a little bit of culture into those blighted lives, and this is what they do!'

'Well, what do you expect?' the gendarme asked. 'They're only stupid English soldiers. You can't expect them to appreciate culture.'

'I shall not make the same mistake again,' Richard vowed.

The policeman gazed at him for a moment, then shrugged and handed back the papers. 'You'd better be on your way, Signor Benedetti. And if you see anybody on the road, don't stop. These men are desperate.'

Richard slept little that night. He imagined the escaping airmen crouching in the stinking sewer pipe while the search went on over their heads, or scrambling around on the mountainside in the dark. Had they managed to make contact with Val and the others, or had they all been arrested?

In the morning he made his way to the Scottish Tearooms. He ordered coffee and a scone and sat pretending to read the paper. Shortly afterwards the door opened and Pat O'Leary came in. Richard knew at once that something must be amiss. O'Leary sat down at a table near the window, ordered coffee and began to do the crossword. Time passed. Other customers came and went and one of the Misses Trenchard brought Richard a second cup and exchanged a worried look with him. Then Richard saw O'Leary lean forward and peer down the street. A moment later a man in blue overalls several sizes too big for him, tousle headed and unshaven, came in and paused, looking about him. O'Leary beckoned him over and they spoke softly together for a minute. Then O'Leary called for his bill and exchanged a few quiet words with the other Miss Trenchard. After that he and the other man left the café together.

Miss Eva, the elder of the two sisters, came over to Richard and murmured to him, 'Pat says you are to go to your flat and wait. He will deliver some parcels to you later. The password will be *J'ai laissé mon parapluie*. Take this with you.'

'This' was a large basket covered with a napkin. Inside Richard found freshly baked rolls, some cheese, a dish of pâté and a bag of tomatoes.

Richard returned to his apartment above the hairdresser's shop and stationed himself by the window looking out on to the street. The hairdresser, who normally lived in the flat, had returned to England at the outbreak of war, so the shop below was empty. Richard had formed the habit from the outset of keeping the shutters almost closed, in common with most of his neighbours in the heat of the Mediterranean summer, so once they were inside it was unlikely that anyone would be aware that he had visitors. It was important, however, that they should be admitted rapidly and with a minimum of fuss. From his position by the window he could watch the street through the small gap between the shutters without being seen himself.

It was afternoon before he saw a man approaching. Few people were about as yet, since the shops were still shut for the afternoon siesta. The man paused, glanced around him casually and then turned into the alleyway that led to the entrance to the flat. By the time he rang the bell Richard was already halfway down the stairs.

The password was given, in a strong English accent, and Richard closed the door behind his visitor.

'Ricardo,' he said, extending his hand.

'*Je m'appelle* Taffy,' the other responded, adding, in laboured French, '*Je ne parle pas français.*'

Unable to resist the temptation, Richard grinned. 'Good to meet you, Squadron Leader.'

Higginson blinked. 'You're English!'

Richard met his eyes squarely. 'My name is Ricardo and I'm Italian. That's really all you need to know.'

Higginson hesitated and then nodded. 'Fair enough.'

Richard led the airman upstairs and offered him some of the provisions Miss Trenchard had given him.

Higginson turned to him apologetically. 'What I'd really like first is a good wash. Is that possible?'

By the time Higginson had finished a second man had strolled up to the door of the flat and given the password. Richard recognised him as the one who had come into the teashop that morning. He gave his name as Hawkins and his rank as flying officer. He was followed by three others – a flight lieutenant and two flight sergeants. A good haul, Richard reflected! He hoped the RAF would appreciate it.

He found himself in a quandary in dealing with these fellow Englishmen. None of them spoke French, so he was unable to maintain his cover by talking to them in that language, as he had with Whitney Straight. To have maintained a phoney Italian accent all the time would have been a strain and would, he felt, be an insult to them. So he decided to stick to the position he had taken with Higginson. Understandably, the five men found it confusing. It was not long before the youngest of them, a New Zealander called Jackson, remarked, 'You speak very good English, for an Italian.'

Higginson intervened. 'Don't ask questions. His name's Ricardo and he's on our side. That's all we need to know.'

Over the picnic provided by Miss Trenchard and a bottle of red wine they told Richard what had happened the previous night. It seemed that they had had difficulty breaking through a grille at the far end of the sewer pipe and had only just succeeded in dislodging it when the alarm went up. In the confusion they had failed to make contact with the reception committee and had simply headed downhill as fast as possible. By dawn they were hiding in bushes above Cap d'Ail. Hawkins was the only one with reasonable forged papers, so he had volunteered to walk into Monte Carlo and go to the tearooms. The overalls had been purloined from a washing line near by. O'Leary had then gone back with him, collecting fresh clothes for them all on the way, and had directed them to Richard's flat.

Richard was uneasy about leaving the men alone while he went to do his usual performance at the café but he knew that suspicions might be aroused if he failed to turn up. He explained the situation.

'I suggest you organise a rota to keep watch from the window. Don't imagine, just because Monaco is supposed to be neutral, that you're safe here. The German secret police are all over the place and they will be hunting for you. Don't answer the door to anyone. In an emergency, there is a fire escape from the back bedroom. That just might give you a chance, in the case of a routine search. I'll be back as early as I can manage.'

As he dressed he was pondering the problem of feeding five hungry men without drawing attention to the fact that his grocery requirements had suddenly mushroomed. He need not have worried. Hawkins, who was stationed at the window, suddenly called softly, 'Two little old ladies heading for the door.'

It was the Misses Trenchard, each bearing a basket. In one were two freshly baked meat pies, in the other a selection of delectable-looking cakes. Richard took the provisions and handed back the baskets and the two ladies continued primly on their way, promising to drop by in the morning with coffee and fresh croissants. The ration problem, at least, was solved.

Next afternoon Richard kept his usual rendezvous at the teashop and was delighted to see Val Williams come through the door. He explained that a series of minor mishaps had delayed their arrival at the designated meeting place the previous night. He went on to relay a message from O'Leary. Richard should expect a call from a M. Guiton, a barber, who would cut the hair of his five guests, and also from Father Myrda, the Polish priest who acted as spiritual adviser to the inmates of the fort.

The barber duly arrived the next day and made use of the vacant facilities in the shop below and then, when his charges were all looking spruce and clean shaven, Richard took them, one by one, to a photographer who was known to be reliable. The photographs were delivered to the teashop and, the next day, Richard received from Miss Eva a set of immaculately forged documents for each man.

Meanwhile, from the invaluable information service provided by the two ladies, he had learned of further developments. Forty-eight hours after the escape all the remaining officers in the fort had been transferred to a prison camp in Italy. They were now beyond the reach of the O'Leary line.

On the afternoon of the third day Father Myrda arrived, carrying a Gladstone bag containing a spare cassock, and half an hour later Taffy Higginson, convincingly disguised, accompanied him out of the flat. Later, Richard took the other two officers to the teashop and left them there to be collected by another courier. Finally, the following morning, he set off with the two flight sergeants, now with new identities as traders in fresh flowers, which were such an important commodity along the whole of the coast. They reached Marseilles without incident and met O'Leary at the Rodoconachis' flat.

'Have a glass of champagne,' he said, speaking in English for the benefit of the two airmen. 'I'm celebrating.'

'What is it, your birthday?' Richard asked.

'No. I've just heard some good news view Jean's radio. Apparently I've just been awarded the DSO.'

'Well, no one ever deserved it more!' Richard exclaimed. 'Congratulations!'

'Have you heard the latest?' O'Leary asked.

'No, what?'

'Last night all the non-coms in Fort de la Revère staged a mass breakout. Apparently sixty of them got away.'

'My God! Can we cope with that many?'

'No. But the chances are they won't make contact with us. The likelihood is that most of them will be recaptured within hours, but keep your eyes skinned in Monte. Some of them may very well head for there.'

'I will,' Richard promised. 'Any news from London about the *Tarana*?'

'Not so far. We may have to wait a few weeks, I'm afraid.'

'Tough on this lot,' Richard said, nodding at the airmen.

'Not as tough as walking to Spain,' O'Leary remarked dryly.

*   *   *

The following evening Richard was leaving the café after his performance. As he passed a doorway he was aware of a figure lurking in the shadows. Before he could react a voice hissed, 'Hey, Caruso!'

Richard stopped in his tracks. It was the nickname by which he had been known during his time as a private soldier, before Dunkirk. There was no doubt in his mind that the speaker was the man from the South Lancashire Regiment whom he had spotted at the fort. So he had recognised him – and had had the sense to keep his mouth shut. He drifted casually over to a shop window close to the door and gazed into it.

'Follow me at twenty paces,' he said, without looking round. 'Stop if I stop – and for God's sake don't speak!'

He set off again, strolling easily towards his flat. After a short distance he glanced behind him. Not one but three men were following him. He felt a stab of alarm. Could he be mistaken? But only one of his old comrades would have known that nickname. Was it possible that the other two men were Milice agents who had spotted the escaper and were now trailing him? He glanced round again. No, the three were definitely together. Three escapers, then.

He walked on until he reached the hairdresser's shop and paused to make sure that they saw him turn down the alley at the side. A moment later he was letting them into the flat. In the hallway he turned and faced the man who had hailed him.

'I were right!' the man said, grinning broadly. 'It is you. I knew as soon as I heard that voice that it had to be. What the 'eck art tha doing here, lad?'

Suddenly the man's name came back to Richard. 'It's Wilf, isn't it? Wilf Cook.'

'Aye, that's right. And tha's Dick Stevens. *Private* Dick Stevens, as I recall. And it's Sarge, not Wilf.'

Richard smiled inwardly at the thought of the captain's pips on the shoulder of the uniform he had left hanging in his wardrobe back in England. But he said, 'OK, Sarge. And who are these?'

'This here is Sergeant Pete Cowley and this is Corporal Dave Williams.'

Richard shook hands with the two men and said, 'Come upstairs. I should think you could do with something to eat, couldn't you?'

Upstairs, Wilf looked around the living room of the flat and remarked, 'Nice little place you've got here.'

From the tone of his voice it was obvious that he had come to the conclusion that Richard had somehow found himself a cushy spot and had avoided returning to England to continue the fight.

'It serves, for the time being,' Richard replied, shortly.

He rifled the kitchen cupboards and found some tinned sardines and a loaf of black bread. 'I'm sorry I can't offer you something better,' he said, 'but it'll keep body and soul together until morning and I'll do better for breakfast.'

The way the three men fell upon the food was proof enough that they had eaten little since the breakout. Richard said, 'How did you end up in the fort, Sarge?'

'I got left behind on the retreat to Dunkirk,' Wilf said, through a mouthful. 'You remember how we marched for days on end, never getting more than a couple of hours' sleep?'

'Vividly,' Richard agreed.

'One time, when we stopped in some village, I lay down behind a wall. I just meant to rest my legs for a bit. Next thing I knew, it was getting dark and there was no sign of any of you. You'd marched on and left me behind, bugger you!'

'You weren't the only one,' Richard commented. 'By the end no one knew who was with us and who wasn't.'

'Well, anyway,' Wilf went on, 'I kipped where I was that night, then next day I started out towards the coast, near as I could tell. I walked for two days – or three mebbe – but there was nowt to eat and the country was swarming with Germans by that time. So in the end I knocked on the door of a farmhouse where the people hadn't run off and they took me in. I stayed there for a while but then the Jerries started looking for us, so I thought I'd better move on. I'd heard by then that the Frogs had thrown in the towel and that the southern half of the country was still free, so I started heading south. I met up with these two on the way and we just kept walking. Sometimes we hid in barns, sometimes people took us in and gave us food or clothes. We got across the demarcation line, or whatever they call it, hidden under a farmer's load of hay. We were doing all right, weren't we, lads, until we got within sight of the sea. Then I reckon somebody must have shopped us, because the police suddenly turned up at the house where we were sheltering and arrested us. We were moved round a bit, from one prison to another, and then ended up in the fort about a year ago.'

'That was rotten luck, when you were so close,' Richard sympathised.

'You'll have heard about the breakout two nights ago?' Wilf enquired.

'I'd heard rumours,' Richard agreed.

'So what happened to you?' Wilf asked. 'Did they leave you behind too?'

'Yes,' Richard agreed. 'I was wounded and couldn't walk. I spent some time in a German POW hospital.'

'Ay, I saw you were limping,' Wilf said. 'So then what? You escaped?'

'Yes, and headed south, like you.'

'And you've been here ever since,' Wilf said.

'Not quite,' Richard told him, but did not elaborate. Instead he said, 'What are your plans now?'

'Well . . .' Wilf looked at his two companions, who seemed to be happy to concentrate on the food and leave the talking to him. '. . . we're all determined to have another go at the Jerries, aren't we, lads?' They mumbled agreement. 'We were thinking we'd stow away on one of the boats in the harbour here. If we can get across to North Africa, happen we can join up with our boys over there. The thing is, we need somewhere to hide up until we can find a ship going to the right place. Can we stay here? It'll only be for a few days, with any luck.'

All three of them were gazing at Richard, and he saw in their eyes, not the cocky confidence Wilf was trying to transmit, but the fear of recapture and reprisals. He said quietly, 'I think I can do better for you than that. I can't go into details. You'll have to trust me. But it's highly probable that I can get you on a Royal Navy ship that will take you to Gibraltar and from there you'll be sent back to Britain. How does that sound?'

They stared at him for a long moment in silence. Then Wilf said, 'By 'eck, lad, you always were one of them still waters that run deep!' He looked at his two friends. 'We used to call him "the professor", you know. Always knew he was a cut above the rest of us – in the brain department, anyway.'

Richard allowed himself a moment to enjoy the irony of the sergeant's sudden change of attitude and then said, 'OK. That's the deal, then. But you may have to be patient for a few weeks. And there are certain house rules you'll have to agree to while you're here.'

'Such as?'

'You must not leave the flat – any of you – unless you're with me. I'll see that food is brought in and I'll do my best to entertain you, but I'm afraid it will be tedious. Also, you must keep the shutters closed and stay away from the windows. If anyone comes to the door you must hide in the back bedroom until I give you the all-clear. And when the time comes to move, you must obey my instructions exactly – or those given you by anyone else I may pass you on to. Understood?'

The three exchanged glances and then Wilf said, 'What's going on here, then? Are you involved in some kind of secret outfit?'

'Let's just say I'm not here for the good of my health,' Richard said. 'And, as a matter of interest, it's not *Private* Stevens any more.'

'No,' said Wilf slowly, 'I can see that. OK. You're in charge. We'll do what you say.'

The next day Richard paid another call on the Misses Trenchard and before long more baskets of provisions were arriving at the door, followed by M. Guiton the barber. Then came the obligatory visit to the photographer and a few days later the appearance of three sets of forged documents. The three soldiers docilely accepted Richard's instructions and seemed quite content to lounge around the flat, playing poker or sleeping.

At length he got word via the Misses Trenchard that it was time to move his three guests to Marseilles. He briefed them carefully about the journey and rehearsed them in a few brief words, such as '*Bonjour*' and '*Merci*', then led them to the railway station. Their amazement and admiration had grown daily and they followed him like lambs. He found their trust touching.

They met Pat O'Leary by the Vieux Port, but when Richard suggested that he might see them later O'Leary told him that they were to be accommodated elsewhere, since 'the place you are thinking of is bursting at the seams'.

Richard shook hands with all three and said, 'We'll meet again before you leave. Don't worry about anything. I promise you you're in safe hands.'

Later, at the Rodocanachis' flat, he found not only the four airmen but two more soldiers who had managed to find their way there from the fort.

'How many of the non-coms from the fort have reached us?' Richard asked O'Leary.

'Thirty-four altogether.'

'That's wonderful!'

O'Leary sighed. 'For them, perhaps. For us it presents difficulties. Every safe house between here and Perpignan is bursting at the seams. These men are clogging up the line. It's airmen we really need to get back. The sooner we can get rid of this lot the better.'

'Any news on that front?'

'Yes. *Tarana* will arrive on September the thirteenth. They are calling it "Operation Bluebottle".'

Richard looked more closely at the fine-boned, sensitive face of the man in front of him. 'Something's wrong, Pat. What is it?'

'A setback. I almost said a disaster. Jean was arrested three days ago. He was collecting equipment from a parachute drop with Gaston. Someone must have given them away. The police were already there, hiding. Mario managed to get away and told me.'

'Oh God!' Richard groaned. 'You're right. It is a disaster.'

'We'll get over it,' O'Leary said, straightening his shoulders. 'But meanwhile I am without a radio operator again.'

'So how will that affect the *Tarana* pick-up?'

'Luckily it was arranged before Jean was taken, but I shall need to confirm it nearer the time. I shall have to contact one of your circuits. I know they don't like us to use SOE channels, but this is a case of necessity.'

'Of course,' Richard agreed.

'There is more bad news, too,' O'Leary said. 'The Germans are slowly but surely taking over more and more functions in the so-called free zone. You know Laval has allowed them to come in to search for unauthorised transmitters?'

'Yes, I'd heard that.'

'Now he has agreed to send a hundred and fifty thousand workers to Germany in exchange for fifty thousand French POWs. It will mean virtual slave labour for thousands of young men. And there are rumours that Jews are being arrested and deported, too.'

'I don't understand,' Richard said. 'Why should Laval agree to such things?'

'Because he will do anything to avoid the Nazis taking over the whole country. But it won't do him any good. My bet is that they will be in control before the end of the year.'

'How will that affect us?' Richard asked, with a sudden chill of fear. 'Will you still be able to operate?'

'We must, for as long as we can,' O'Leary responded. 'But I wonder sometimes how long it can go on.'

By the week of the thirteenth Richard was again installed in the villa on the beach at Canet Plage. He had made two journeys, escorting three escapees on each occasion, and over the next few days more and more arrived until every available space was occupied. He made a point of seeking out his old comrade from the South Lancs, who greeted him warmly.

'By 'eck, lad! You've got some organisation going here!'

'It's not mine,' Richard told him. 'I'm just helping out. It's Pat who's responsible. Listen, there's something I want you to promise me.'

'What's that, lad?'

'When you get back, you mustn't say anything to anyone about meeting me. As far as the rest of the regiment knows I'm doing a desk job at the War Office. You mustn't tell them any different.'

Wilf nodded. 'OK, lad. You can trust me.' He half turned away and then turned back again. 'By the by, I think you're doing a grand job. A grand job!'

14

On his return to London, Merry surprised his CO,
George Black, by refusing the offer of some leave, on
the grounds that he had just spent several weeks lounging
around in Alexandria convalescing.

'But,' he said, 'I might take you up on the offer in a few
weeks' time. Felix should be back from Malta quite soon.'

'Ah,' said Black with a smile, 'all right, then. Let me know
when the time comes.'

Merry nodded and thanked him. They had never discussed
his relationship with Felix, but he had a pretty shrewd idea that
George Black understood it.

'In that case,' Black went on, 'you can make yourself useful.
I'd like you to go and visit some of the units that are putting on
their own concert parties and see if you can pick up some new
talent for SIB.'

'You don't want me to start work on a new show, then?'
Merry asked.

'Soon, soon,' Black assured him. 'But most of your people
have been redeployed to other companies. We've got so many
demands on us now that we're really short of top-class acts.
That's why I want you to act as a talent scout for a few weeks.
OK?'

Merry agreed quite contentedly and spent most of the next
month travelling around the country, attending shows in

garrison theatres and mess tents and NAAFI canteens. In between trips he found time to telephone Jack and Enid Willis and to ask after the Taylor family. They were all well, he was told, and Rose had been home on leave but was now back in London, staying at the flat in Lambeth while she and Monty rehearsed a new show. On his first free evening he went round to the flat. Rose came to the door with a towel round her head.

'Merry! Oh, how lovely to see you! Oh, look at me! I was in the middle of shampooing my hair. I wasn't expecting visitors.'

'I could go and wait in the pub till you've finished,' he offered.

'Don't be silly. Come on up. We can talk while I dry my hair. It's not like we were strangers, is it? You're one of the family.'

He followed her upstairs and produced the half-bottle of gin he had managed to wangle from the mess sergeant at the last army barracks he had visited. Rose had a bottle of orange squash and he fixed the drinks while she combed out her hair. She left the bedroom door open and he watched her in the mirror, at the same time answering a barrage of questions about his time in North Africa. He was relieved to find that she seemed to be in good spirits and that the news of Richard's marriage had not been the crushing blow he had feared.

'So, what have you been up to?' he asked, when her questions dried up.

'Oh, you know. Touring with *Lighten Up!*. I've lost count of how many factory canteens and ack-ack batteries we've played to. Nothing as exciting as what you've been doing.'

'But you're enjoying it?'

'I'm working. That's what matters. It's always been like that for people like us, hasn't it? But after last year I'm more grateful than ever to have a job, doing something I really love.'

He contemplated asking whether she had found a new
boyfriend but decided against it. Instead he said, 'Do you
fancy taking in a show? There's just about time, if we leave
now.'

She turned to look at him. 'It's sweet of you, but it would be
a bit of a busman's holiday for both of us, wouldn't it? Let's
just stay here and have a really good gossip.'

Towards the end of August he received the letter he had been
waiting for. Felix was coming home as soon as his replacement
arrived in Malta – and to crown it all, he had been promoted to
squadron leader.

*'I'll let you know as soon as I can exactly when I expect to
arrive,'* he wrote, *'and I shall be due for some leave. Can you
arrange to be free as well? We could spend the time at Shoreham.'*

Merry had a word with George Black and was told to take a
week's leave whenever he wanted it. A few days later a
telegram arrived.

*'Should reach England Monday stop Meet you Shoreham
sometime that evening stop Felix.'*

Merry took his leave from the Sunday and travelled down to
Shoreham to get the house in which he had spent his childhood ready. He had called in once since his return and found
everything intact, though the overgrown garden and the
furniture shrouded in dust sheets made it look like the Sleeping
Beauty's castle. This time he telephoned in advance and asked
Mrs Pierce, the woman who came in from the village to cook
when he was at home, to go in and clean up. He arrived to find
the floors swept, the dust sheets removed and the boiler alight.
He had made the most of his contacts with NAAFI sergeants
and now unloaded in the kitchen a bottle of champagne, one of
gin, a jar of Gentleman's Relish and a packet of Bath Oliver

biscuits. Then he wandered into the sitting room and stood still in the doorway, absorbed in recollection.

Almost exactly a year ago he had stood here and seen for the first time the baby grand piano that had been Felix's birthday present to him. He went over to the instrument and ran his fingers experimentally over the keys. It needed tuning, that was only to be expected, but the tone was still beautiful. He made a mental note to contact the piano tuner the next morning. He also remembered that Tuesday would be his birthday, and he would be thirty. What wonderful luck it was, he thought, that Felix and he would be together.

The next day he started the Lagonda, which Felix had left in the garage when he was sent to Malta, and drove to the farm where he had done odd jobs as a boy. The farmer's wife was delighted to see him and would have detained him but he was anxious to get back for the telephone call that would tell him Felix had arrived back in England. He returned armed with fresh butter, a chicken and a dozen eggs.

He put the champagne in the fridge and then set to work on the neglected garden. He was not by nature a keen gardener but he knew that Felix loved it and had spent hours there the previous summer when he was stationed only a short distance away, and he did not want him to come back and find it totally overgrown. Besides, it was a way of keeping himself occupied while he waited for the phone to ring. When it had not rung by six o'clock he lifted the receiver and found that the line was dead – a not uncommon occurrence these days. That explained why he had not heard. He decided to cook the chicken so they could eat it cold, whatever time Felix finally arrived.

When ten o'clock came, with no sign of Felix, he reluctantly made himself a sandwich and by 11.30 he knew that the last train had arrived some time ago and that Felix would not be coming that night. He went upstairs and stood in the bedroom they always shared. When he had first arrived he had almost taken his suitcase into the monastic single room where he had slept since his childhood but then had turned away and gone into what had always been known as the 'spare room'. It was here he had accommodated Felix on his first visit, and here that they had spent that first delirious night together while the German bombers droned overhead. Unpacking, he had discovered some of Felix's civilian clothes in the wardrobe and now he went to it and took out a cashmere sweater that had been one of his favourites. He held it up to his face and found that it still smelled faintly of Felix. He was tempted to take it to bed with him, like a child's comfort blanket, then pulled himself together and put it back in the cupboard.

The next morning, his birthday, he went out into the garden and set to work again. Felix must have been delayed somewhere, he concluded, but since there had been no message he must be on his way. When he saw the telegraph boy coming up the path he greeted him with a smile. This would be the explanation for the delay. He tipped the boy and slit open the envelope.

'*Signal received this morning from Gracie, Station Commander, Malta. Reads as follows: Regret to inform you Ned Mountjoy missing in action, believed killed. Letter follows. Deepest sympathy. George.*'

Merry was never quite sure how he passed the next hours. He realised afterwards that he must have continued mowing the lawn, his body following the habitual actions while his mind was as blank as if he were under anaesthesia. When he returned to any consciousness of his surroundings he was sitting on a chair in the living room. The telegram was on the table beside him, and the angle of the sun across the polished surface of his piano told him it was mid-afternoon. He got up, stiffly, and went over to the instrument, but instead of opening the lid he spread his arms across it and laid his head on the top.

It was thirst which roused him. Not a normal thirst but a raging need for water. He went into the kitchen and filled a tumbler. He had forgotten to run the tap and the water was lukewarm but he drank it off anyway and refilled the glass. He had not eaten since breakfast but he had no sense of hunger. What he felt, suddenly, was a desperate need for company. He must talk to someone, must somehow unpack the pain and confusion he was experiencing. He reviewed in a muddled fashion the possibilities. He could go back to London and rout out one of his old companions from the show. He knew Chubby Hayes was in town. They could go out and get drunk together. Or he could go and find George Black. George would understand – after a fashion. Or perhaps he should go down to Dorset and stay with the Willises, who had always been so kind to him. But the thought of sleeping alone in the big double bed he had so often shared with Felix was unbearable – as unbearable as the thought of another night alone in their room upstairs. Then he thought of Rose. Rose, of all people, knew how much Felix meant to him. In a daze, he changed into his uniform, threw a few clothes into a bag and called a taxi to take him to the station.

He had not stopped to check the times of the trains, so he had to wait for nearly an hour on the platform. He sat in a trance, numb and unthinking. By the time he reached London and made his way to the familiar street it was late evening and almost dark. Rose opened the door of the flat and gave a cry of delight, which immediately turned to an exclamation of distress at the sight of his face.

'Oh, my God, Merry! It's Felix, isn't it?'

He tried to speak but his throat felt as though a hand were clamped around it. Rose caught his arm.

'Come in. Come on upstairs.'

She led him up to the kitchen and sat him down at the table. Then she drew a chair close and took both his hands in hers.

'What's happened, Merry?'

He cleared his throat and managed a husky whisper. 'Missing, believed killed.'

'When? How?'

Keeping his eyes on their clasped hands he told her brokenly about the telegram.

'Missing?' she repeated. 'It only said missing.'

'Believed killed,' he repeated.

'But they don't know for certain?' She laid her hand on his cheek and pulled his head up so that he met her eyes. 'It means he could still be alive, Merry. Maybe he baled out. Maybe he's a POW by now. Or perhaps he's just trying to find his way back. It isn't definite.'

He shook his head. 'If he'd baled out one of the others would have seen the parachute open. They always fly in pairs. His wingman would have watched to see what happened.'

'But if he'd crashed, he would have seen that too, wouldn't he?' she pointed out.

'They must have looked for him and not found him,' Merry said. 'They wouldn't send a telegram like that unless they were pretty certain.'

She sighed and put her arms round him. 'Oh, Merry, I'm so sorry. So sorry! I wish there was something I could do. You loved him so much, didn't you?'

He wept then, his face buried in her shoulder, and she held him in her arms and rocked him like a child.

At length, when he had grown quiet from exhaustion, she said, 'When did you last eat?'

He shrugged and shook his head. 'I don't know. Breakfast, I suppose.'

She detached herself from him and straightened up. 'I'll put the kettle on. You look as if you need a stiff drink as well. Wait there. I shan't be a minute.'

He heard her go out of the front door. Very soon she was back, with a miniature bottle in her hand.

'They've run out of brandy and whisky in the pub. This was the best I could do.'

It was crème de menthe. He grimaced at the taste but the alcohol warmed his stomach and stilled the shivering that had gripped him. Rose put a cup of tea in front of him and a Spam sandwich. He still had no desire for food but he ate automatically. Then Rose led him to the bedroom he had used in the early months of the war, when he first joined SIB, and persuaded him to go to bed. He slept at once.

Merry woke the next morning to the purest and most acute pain he had ever experienced. It was so vivid, so present, that for a moment he thought it was a physical wound. Then he remembered the cause. For a long time he lay still, hoping that it might ease, wondering what he could do to dull it, but there were no drugs, no treatment, for this. He wondered how long it would be before it became something he could live with, a dull quotidian ache that would allow him to function more or less normally. At length he got up and found a note from Rose. She had had to leave for rehearsal, but she would try to be back early and he should help himself to anything he wanted to eat.

He remembered the chicken and the champagne in the fridge at home and almost gave way to tears again.

He spent the morning alternately pacing the flat and sunk, immobile, in a chair. Once or twice he thought of putting on the wireless. There might be news, or some decent music. But the idea of doing anything so mundane seemed like a violation of Felix's memory. He was dead, and there was nothing left for Merry to do but mourn. But out of that thought came a new resolution.

Rose returned soon after midday. 'I told Monty what had happened and he insisted I should come back and look after you. He sent his deepest sympathy and said to tell you that if you want to go and stay with him and Dolly you'd be most welcome.'

'I didn't think he knew – about me and Felix,' Merry said.

'Oh, Monty knows more than he lets on,' Rose responded. 'Would you like to go and see them?'

Merry shook his head. 'I've been thinking. I'm going back to work. I can't sit around doing nothing. Anyway, the letter Gracie referred to will come to our HQ in Grosvenor Street. It's the only address he has. I want to be there when it arrives.'

Rose tried to persuade him to stay another night but, as suddenly as he had felt the need for company, he now felt the necessity of being alone – or at least only in the presence of people who did not know what he was suffering. Sympathy and gentleness would only reduce him again to tears. He packed his things and moved back to the room in the small hotel that he always used as his base when he was in London.

The next day he presented himself at the headquarters of the Central Pool of Artistes and told George Black that he had decided not to take the rest of his leave.

'Are you sure?' George asked. 'You don't look up to work.'

'I've got to occupy my mind somehow,' Merry said. 'I'll go mad if I don't.'

His CO looked at him shrewdly for a moment. Then he nodded. 'OK. There's some paperwork in your office that needs seeing to. I'll let you get on with that.'

Merry retired to his desk and went through the motions, dealing with correspondence and drawing up lists without being fully aware of what he was doing. He was about to leave when Chubby Hawkes appeared at the door.

'Heard you had a bit of bad news, old boy. Fancy a drink?'

Merry tried to refuse but Chubby would not take no for an answer. Over the next few days not only Chubby but various other members of the 'Merrymakers' cast arrived, all insisting that he join them in the pub. As a result, Merry went to bed each night drunk enough to lose consciousness before the real agony could kick in.

The promised letter from 'Jumbo' Gracie arrived on the fifth day.

My dear Merry,

I hope you will forgive the informality, but that is what we all learned to call you during your recent spell with us and the way he – Ned/Felix – always referred to you.

I can't tell you how desolate we all are at his loss. He was a brilliant pilot and a wonderful leader who was an inspiration to all those who served with him. He was also a valued friend and companion, whose unfailing courage and humour helped many of us through the dark days of the last few months. It is a bitter irony that he should be lost just as things seem at last to be getting a little easier and within days of completing his tour.

As far as I am able to piece together the events, what happened was this. Ned had led his flight on a sortie towards the Italian coast. They got into a scrap with some ME 109s and in the confusion Ned's wingman lost sight of him. It seems his radio must have been damaged, as neither his fellow pilots nor Ground Control were able to raise him. However, all the men flying with him are adamant that he did not go down during that scrap. When they were unable to contact him they all made their way back to base, assuming that he was on his way there too. It was only when they had all landed and there was no sign of Ned that we realised something was wrong. B flight took off immediately to search for him and we alerted the air-sea rescue boys, but although they hunted over every yard of the distance between the island and the spot where the fight took place there was no sign of anyone in the water, or of any wreckage. Later on all the chaps in Ned's own flight insisted on going up again to have another look, and spread the net farther, but by dark there was still no sign of him and we had to give up the search. We are forced to the conclusion that, either during the scrap, or later on the way home, he must have been shot down. It is possible that he baled out and his 'chute failed to open and the plane then crashed and went straight to the bottom, or perhaps he was shot at the controls and went down with the plane. Several sorties have been flown over the surrounding area since then, but there has been no sign of any wreckage.

There is, of course, one other possibility and that is that somehow he came down over enemy territory, but this would have to mean that he had gone a long way off track – an unlikely explanation for someone as experienced as Ned. If this is what happened, he could have been picked up by the Italians and be a POW by now. In which case, we should eventually hear something from the Red Cross. Of course, if that happens I will immediately let you know, but I have to say that I think it is a most unlikely contingency.

I know that you were probably closer to Ned – Felix, I suppose I should say – than anyone else and I saw for myself what a beneficial effect a few days of your company had on him. I wish there were something I could say to lessen the pain of his loss but all I can do is to repeat that he is mourned and deeply missed by all of us here, as I know he will be by everyone who knew him.

Merry sat for a long time at his desk with the letter in his hands but it told him nothing that he had not imagined for himself a dozen times in the last five days. He saw the cockpit once again in flames and Felix desperately fighting to get out; imagined the terror of baling out, pulling the ripcord and finding that the parachute failed to open, and the uncontrollable, headlong dive into the sea. He hoped that Gracie's second explanation was correct – a bullet through the heart or head and instant oblivion. It tormented him that he would never know the truth.

At length it occurred to him that he should write to Felix's parents. They would have been notified, of course. They must be listed as his next of kin, despite their estrangement. He wondered how Felix's mother, that unbending woman with the ice-blue eyes whom he had encountered once at the end of 1940, was coping with the news. There was another son, of course, the elder brother to whom Felix always referred in satirical tones as Brother Anthony. Presumably, Merry thought bitterly, as long as the inheritance was secure Lady

Malpas would not be too distressed by the death of the son she seemed only to despise. Nevertheless, he felt he ought to write. He drew a pad towards him and wrote,

> *Dear Lord and Lady Malpas,*
> *I should like to express my sincere condolences on the death of your son Edward. I am sure that you will have heard from his commanding officer that he was a brave man, a brilliant pilot and a respected leader. He was, in short, a hero. I should like to add that he was a man of great personal courage and integrity and a loyal and dearly loved friend. He will be deeply missed.*

Let them make what they like out of that, he thought. I have done him as much justice as I am able.

He thought, too, of writing to Harriet Forsyth, the old friend with whom Felix had had an abortive affair when he was still trying to live a 'normal' life, but he had long ago lost the address Felix had given him when he was in the hospital and he had no idea how to contact her.

The next morning he sought another interview with George Black.

'I want you to let me go, George.'

'Let you go where, old man?' his CO enquired.

'Back to my regiment. They're out in North Africa at the moment. I want to go back and fight.'

'You mean,' Black said dryly, 'you want to go back and die.'

'Yes, probably,' Merry agreed.

Black leaned forward and clasped his hands on the desk. 'Merry, I know how you're feeling. We've never talked about it, but I know what Felix meant to you. But what good is it to him if you go and throw your life away?'

'Whatever I do isn't going to make any difference to him,' Merry replied. 'And isn't it supposed to be a noble thing, to sacrifice one's life in the line of duty?'

'Perhaps,' Black agreed. 'But has it occurred to you that your duty may lie in quite a different direction?'

'Meaning?'

'You're not a fighting soldier, Merry. I can't see you being a great success as a tank commander, or whatever it is you've set your mind on. On the other hand, you have a talent none of those chaps possess. I don't have to tell you what your concerts have meant to men on the front line. I get the letters from their commanding officers, telling me how much you and your company have done to improve morale, but you've seen it for yourself at first hand. That's where your duty lies.'

Merry shook his head. 'I can't do it any more, George. I can't go out there and play the piano while other men, boys straight out of school, are getting killed or suffering horrendous injuries. I was sick to the heart of it before I came home, and now . . . I just haven't got the guts to face it again. You've got to let me go, George!'

Black sat back and considered him for a moment. 'As I recall, your last medical board classified you as unfit for active service,' he commented at length.

'But I'm much better now!' Merry insisted. 'I haven't had an asthma attack for over a year.'

'That's because you've been in a hot, dry climate.'

'Exactly. And that's what I want to go back to. Look,' Merry was pleading now, 'at least get me another board. If they say I'm fit, then let me go. If not . . .' He let the sentence fade into silence.

Black sighed. 'OK, if that's what you want. But it may take some time. Meanwhile, I want you to go back to talent-scouting for me. Agreed?'

'If you insist,' Merry said reluctantly.

A few days later Merry received a telephone call.

'Merry? It's Harry – Harriet Forsyth.'

'Harriet!' Taken by surprise he couldn't think what to say. 'How are you?' he added lamely.

'Merry, I've just heard the news about Felix. I'm so sorry! Look, I'm in London. Can we meet?'

'I have to go down to Kent this evening. In fact, I'm busy most nights. Would lunch be any good?'

'Yes, lunch would be fine. Tomorrow?'

They agreed to meet at Brown's Hotel in Albemarle Street and Merry put the phone down with a surge of contrary emotions. Over the last day or two he had reached a precarious equilibrium, in that he felt he was no longer liable to burst into tears at any moment, but the thought of meeting Harriet again threatened to disturb that. He had not seen her since the summer of 1939, when she had been Felix's mistress and he had been forced to watch hopelessly as their relationship followed the apparently inevitable path to marriage. They had spoken on the telephone once, after Felix had been shot down the first time, and he had despised her for running out on him when she saw the terrible damage the flames had done to his face. Then he recalled how jealous he had been, and how afraid, when he heard that Felix was seeing her again, until Felix had convinced him that his fears were groundless. Since then, Felix had told him how she had agreed to pose as his girlfriend to free him from the unwanted attentions of the fellow officers who were determined to see him paired off with someone. He had felt more kindly towards her after that and had sometimes wondered whether, in spite of everything, she was still in love with Felix.

He arrived at the hotel in good time and waited in the bar. She was there very soon after him, coming towards him in a smart, dark grey suit with a close-fitting waist and a perky little hat. They shook hands and she said, 'I wish there was something helpful I could say. But there's nothing that's any use in a situation like this, is there?'

'No,' he agreed. 'Words can't alter anything.'

'You must be completely desolated,' she went on.

'Yes,' he agreed. He had made up his mind that he was not going to adopt the 'chin-up, grin and bear it' attitude that seemed to be expected of him. 'Can I get you a drink?'

He ordered the White Lady she requested and a pink gin for himself and they moved over to sit in a quiet corner. He said, 'How did you find out?'

'About Felix? From my mother. I've been away for a while, taking photographs, and when I got back I telephoned her and she told me. We're neighbours of the family, you know. Our lands "march together" in the quaint old phrase. That's how Felix – Ned – and I knew each other.'

'You must find it difficult,' Merry said, 'having known him in both . . . incarnations, as it were.' Surprisingly, he was finding it a comfort to talk.

'Sometimes,' she agreed. 'But only when I talk to his family, or mine. I've got used to thinking of him as Felix over the years.'

'They still don't know how he spent those years before the war?'

'No. They don't even know that we still see each other – saw each other. Oh God! I can't . . . I can't bear to talk about him in the past tense.'

Merry looked at her with a sudden gentleness. 'You were very fond of him, weren't you.'

She raised her large, grey eyes, full of tears, and nodded. 'I used to think I was in love with him. Right from when we were both in our teens, I always dreamed that one day we'd be married. Of course, then I had no idea . . . no idea how wrong that would be for him.'

'But later,' he murmured. 'After the business at Cambridge. You must have known then.'

'He said he wanted to put all that behind him, and I wanted to believe him. But I think I always knew really that it wasn't going to work. I can never forgive myself for running out on him when he was in hospital, but in the long run it was for the best, wasn't it? You were what he really needed. You made him very happy, you do know that, don't you? Happier than he'd ever been, I think.'

Merry reached for his drink. 'It was mutual,' he said, his eyes on his glass.

The waiter was hovering near by with menus. They ordered lunch and then Merry said, 'Do you know how his parents have taken the news?'

'Mother says Lady Malpas is behaving as if nothing has happened. Of course, Lord Malpas is out of the country. There isn't going to be a memorial service or anything. Apparently the local people are up in arms about it, but no one dares say anything.'

'That woman must be made of ice!' Merry said.

'I think,' Harriet said slowly, 'I think she can't let herself feel anything. She adored Felix, you know. But she really believes that what he did was utterly degenerate and I'm afraid that the local rector has reinforced that opinion. She's a very religious woman.'

'If that's what religion does to people, then I'm glad I'm an atheist,' Merry said grimly.

They went into the dining room and while they waited to be served Merry said, 'What was he like – Felix – when he was young?'

Harry smiled for the first time. 'Oh, you can imagine it, I'm sure. Very charming, very dashing, very brave. He's a marvellous horseman, you know – I mean he was. When we rode to hounds he was always right up there with the leaders, jumping the biggest fences, even when he was quite young. It was more than his little mare could manage and he had so many falls his father bought him a big hunter. It was far too big for him really but it jumped like a stag and he'd put it over anything.'

Merry narrowed his eyes, trying to imagine the boy he had never known. He had never visualised the elegant, sophisticated Felix as the squire's son riding to hounds on his big horse, but now the idea was presented to him he could see how that boy segued easily into the daring pilot in his Spitfire.

Harriet went on. 'Of course, when you got to know him you saw that there was another side to him completely. Something much more sensitive, less self-confident than he seemed at first. But I don't have to tell you that.'

Merry met her eyes and bestowed one of his increasingly rare smiles. 'I think perhaps we two are the only people in the world to have seen that side of him.'

She reached across the table and laid her hand fleetingly on his own. 'I'm glad you see it like that. I was so afraid that you resented me.'

'I used to,' Merry agreed frankly. 'But now – well, we've got an awful lot in common, haven't we?'

The meal arrived and over it he asked about her career. She told him that she was now a fully accredited war photographer and had just returned from a mission to photograph naval ships and personnel at the base in Scapa Flow.

'But what I really want to do is go to North Africa and take some pictures of the real fighting,' she exclaimed. 'They won't let me get near the front line, just because I'm a woman.'

'Quite right, too,' Merry said. 'I've been there, in the desert, and believe me it's no place for a woman.'

She sat back and looked at him. 'Guy Merryweather, you disappoint me! I didn't expect you to have those entrenched masculine attitudes.'

He caught her eye and found himself grinning sheepishly. 'I suppose it is a bit out of character, isn't it?'

Merry passed the following weeks in a curiously schizoid state of mind. Outwardly he went about the business of reviewing performances and choosing new artistes to be added to the Central Pool. The only indication that there was anything wrong lay in the fact that he was much readier to accept the lavish hospitality of the officers' mess whenever it was offered, and many of his judgements were made through a delicate alcoholic haze. Inwardly he was in a state of suspended animation, waiting for the medical board that would release him to seek out the final oblivion that was all he desired.

He met Rose a couple of times. Since she was rehearsing during the day and he was always at work in the evenings it had to be on a Sunday, and they went walking in Hyde Park in the late summer sunshine. At first she tried to get him to talk about Felix, but after that one lunchtime meeting with Harriet he had closed the lid on the turbulent casket of memories and hopes and regrets that he had briefly allowed to escape and he dared not open it again. That night he had cried himself to sleep and he was not going to risk a repetition.

On the occasion of their second meeting Rose told him that the new show was now ready and they had instructions to leave for a tour the next morning. As usual, she had no prior knowledge of where they would be going but she promised that she would write to him as soon as she could. When they said goodbye she put her arms round him and hugged him.

'I do wish I didn't have to go, Merry! I hate to leave you like this.'

He smiled at her gently. 'Don't worry. I'll be OK. It's just a matter of time.'

She drew back and looked at him. 'Yes, it is, isn't it? We get over things, eventually. I know that. You will too. We just have to be patient.'

He nodded and did not disillusion her.

It was mid-October before Merry received notification of the date and time of his medical examination. The weather had turned damp and there was a smell of autumn in the air, a dark smell like dahlias left too long in a vase, compounded of fallen leaves and the smoke of newly lit coal fires. For three nights before his board Merry abjured all alcohol and as a result slept worse. On the last night he woke from an uneasy doze at three in the morning with the familiar, though half-forgotten, sensation of his chest being bounded by iron hoops. He eased himself up in bed, begging under his breath, 'Oh, not tonight! Please, not now!' But he knew only too well that the anticipation of some important and emotionally stressful event could frequently trigger an asthma attack. Combined with the change in the weather it was almost inevitable.

He dragged himself out of bed and put the kettle on the gas ring by the fire. When it boiled he crouched over it with his head under a towel, inhaling the steam, which eased his breathing a little, but still every breath had to be won with a struggle. He prayed desperately that he would not have to call a doctor, or end up in hospital as he had before, and little by little the spasms eased until he was able to crawl back to bed and, propped up on his pillows, catch a brief hour or so of sleep.

When he reported for his examination the next day he was pale and his eyes were puffy and bloodshot. The doctor looked at his notes.

'Asthma, eh? When did you last have an attack?'

There was no point in lying. 'Last night. But prior to that I hadn't had one for over a year.'

The doctor took his stethoscope and listened to Merry's chest. Then he looked up and smiled. 'Sorry, old man. Your eagerness to get back into the action does you credit, but there's no way I can send you back to active duty with a chest like that.'

15

Richard shivered slightly. Summer was over and a cool breeze was slicing across the dark beach from the distant mountains. It seemed strange to be here alone, without the sense of a silent, tense group waiting in the sand dunes behind him. He squatted, minimising the chance of his silhouette being seen against the faint phosphorescence of the sea. Then he came abruptly alert. Out in the bay a green light flashed out the Morse letter B. He straightened up and replied in the same way with the torch he was carrying, and a few moments later he heard the soft rasp of the boat grounding. A dark figure clambered over the thwarts and came towards him.

'*D'où viens tu?*'

'*De la Gare de l'Est.*'

'*Bonsoir. Bienvenu.*'

'*Merci.*'

Richard extended his hand and it was taken in a firm grip.

'*Salut!* I'm Tom.'

'Ricardo. This way. Let me give you a hand with that.'

He took hold of the suitcase the new arrival was carrying. It was very heavy. A casual observer might have wondered why anyone should travel with such a load. He led Tom along the path to the villa, where Ginny was waiting. Inside, in the light, he introduced him and added, 'We're certainly glad to see you. Being without a radio operator makes our job almost impossible.'

'I can understand that,' Tom said. 'When do I get started?'

Richard grinned at him. He was very young, twenty years old perhaps, and his expression was eager and without the stress lines Richard had grown used to seeing on the faces of his associates. *You'll learn!* he thought. Aloud he said, 'Give yourself a chance! Tomorrow we'll get you to Marseilles. Pat's waiting for you. He'll show you where you can operate from. But for God's sake be careful. The Germans are operating radio detection cars quite openly, with permission from the Vichy government, but they are also infiltrating their secret police in large numbers now.'

'Don't worry,' the young man replied. 'I've been well briefed. By the way . . .' He reached into an inner pocket. 'I've got mail for you.'

'For me?' Richard queried. Since leaving England in June he had been incommunicado and he had not expected any contact except through official sources.

Tom grinned. 'I think someone in the FANYs sweet-talked Jimmy Langley into letting me bring a letter.'

Richard opened the envelope. 'It's from my wife,' he said. Somehow the phrase had an unreal ring. He had had no opportunity to get used to thinking of himself as a married man. He excused himself and retired to the far side of the room to read.

My darling,

I don't know if this letter will get to you but Jimmy has promised to do his best. I know I probably shouldn't do this but it's been such a long time. Of course, you must destroy this letter as soon as you've read it, but I know I don't need to tell you that.

*I'm not going to go on about what I've been doing or
anything trivial like that. I just want you to know that I'm
all right, and that I love you and miss you terribly. I long
for the day when you come home so we can be together
again. I've got such plans for us, my darling, such wonderful
plans!*

    Take care of yourself – and come home soon.
    With all my love,
    Priss

Richard took out his lighter and carefully set fire to the corner
of the paper. He carried it into the kitchen, dropped it into the
sink, crumbled the ashes and washed them down the drain. He
felt curiously detached, as if the letter came from a stranger –
or perhaps a casual acquaintance. When he returned to the
living room Ginny and Tom looked at him sympathetically, as
if they expected him to have been upset by the letter.

Ginny said, 'Is everything all right?'

'Yes, fine,' he replied and left it at that.

Over a glass of wine they learned that Tom was an Australian
with a French mother, which accounted for his perfect command of the language. He had been recruited by Room 900 and
given a crash course as a radio operator, but Richard felt grave
misgivings about the extent of his training and his ability to
survive for long under cover. Nevertheless, he reminded himself, at least for the time being they had radio contact with
London. It was urgently needed as the number of escapers being
concealed at various safe houses had once again risen almost
beyond the capacity of the line's supporters to care for them.

Within days of Tom's arrival Richard received a message from
O'Leary telling him that a further pick-up by *Tarana* was due

on 5 October. He was working at the Lion d'Or again and he and Ginny had become familiar figures to the folk who lived around Canet Plage, but he was uneasy. Now that the summer crowds had departed the beach was deserted most of the time, but lately he and Ginny had both noticed a pair of men with binoculars strolling along the edge of the sea or sitting in the dunes. They appeared to be birdwatchers but their presence in the vicinity of the villa was disturbing. For this reason he sent Ginny back to Marseilles to suggest to O'Leary that they change the site of the next rendezvous and to give him the map coordinates of the new beach for Tom to transmit to London.

By the night of the 5th the villa was once again packed with men. As usual O'Leary had come with one group to take charge of the actual embarkation and by 1.30 all the men had been conducted by a back route among the dunes to the new rendezvous point. As the agreed time approached Richard began to flash the Morse signal – the letter V this time – but there was no response. At 2.30 they gave up and led the disappointed men back to the villa.

By the following evening the mood in the villa was edgy and fractious. Thirty men cooped up in four small rooms, with little to do and no access to fresh air and exercise, was an explosive situation. To add to everyone's discomfort, one of the lavatories had developed a blockage and the other seemed in danger of going the same way.

The arrangement with the ship was always that if she did not show up on the first night they should expect her on the next, so once again they trailed silently through the dunes to the pick-up point. Once again Richard sent out the signal. Tensely, aware of O'Leary at his shoulder, he stared out into the darkness. There was no moon and the night was over-cast. It was impossible to make out the horizon and only a faint phosphorescence marked the lines of breakers as they rolled up the sand. No answering light flickered in the blackness.

'Try them again,' O'Leary breathed.

Richard swallowed, his mouth dry. Behind him he could hear the men stirring and whispering. If the villa was being watched, it would not be hard for their pursuers to locate them. He raised the torch and flashed the signal again. Still there was no response.

He looked at O'Leary. 'Better give up and get the men back under cover.'

'Wait!' the other man whispered sharply. Above the hiss of the surf they heard the sound of oars and the outline of a small boat appeared just offshore. O'Leary advanced to the water's edge and gave the first part of the password in a hoarse whisper.

'Où sont les fraises?'

The answer should have been *'Dans le jus'* but instead there was a stream of derisive obscenities.

'It's a bloody fishing boat!' O'Leary muttered.

They waited until the boat had disappeared into the night and then, disconsolately, they all trooped back to the villa. When the men had been herded back inside Richard remained at the door with O'Leary.

'Pas de bateau que du beurre au cul!' O'Leary exclaimed in a furious undertone. It was the first time Richard had heard him descend to vulgarity of that kind and it was a measure of his fury and frustration.

'What do we do now?' he asked.

O'Leary shrugged wearily. 'God knows! If *Tarana*'s on her way back to Gib it will be days before we can get a message through to her. She maintains radio silence all the time she's at sea. We can't get this many men out over the mountains in one go, and we can't keep them here indefinitely either.'

'If we don't do something some of them will try to make a break for it on their own,' Richard said. 'I've heard mutterings already.'

'I know,' O'Leary agreed. 'That's the last thing we want. They'd be picked up, inevitably, and that would endanger the whole organisation.' He was silent for a moment, then he said, 'I'm going back to Marseilles. I'll get Tom to radio London and see if they can authorise Sunday in Gib to contact *Tarana* and send her back. Can you and Ginny cope here until I get back?'

'We'll have to,' Richard said, but the prospect was daunting.

The next days were some of the most unpleasant he could remember. Both lavatories had now ceased to function and they were forced to resort to using buckets borrowed from the Hôtel du Tennis and then burying the contents after dark in the sand dunes. Food was also a problem. Madame Chouquette at the hotel did what she could and Richard made visits to a number of black market outlets in Perpignan, but he could never risk buying in any quantity in case it aroused suspicion. He also called on his fellow musicians in the trio to assist, and Xavier appeared the following day with a ham from his aunt's farm and a sack of apples, which were a welcome addition to a diet that consisted mainly of bread and sausage.

The mood among the men became increasingly restless and despondent. On the fourth morning Richard was confronted by three airmen, lead by Squadron Leader 'Scotty' Mactavish.

'Listen, we've had a discussion and we've decided it will be best if we go it alone. This ship of yours obviously isn't coming and the longer we hang about here, the bigger the chance of someone smelling a rat and shopping us to the authorities. We'll leave tonight.'

It took Richard half an hour of earnest persuasion to make them accept that their chances of escape under their own steam were virtually zero, and then he succeeded only in getting them to agree to hang on for another three days. Each evening he had to leave to perform at the hotel, and he was glad that Val Williams had come in from Monaco with a group and had stayed to help. He would have been worried about leaving Ginny to cope on her own. It needed only one or two of the fugitives to be seen outside the villa to confirm the suspicions of whoever was watching and bring the Gestapo down on them.

On the third day O'Leary returned from Marseilles with good news. Room 900 had got on to Donald Darling, code-named Sunday, and he had broken radio silence to contact the ship and tell her to turn round and come back. The bad news was that by then *Tarana* was less than a hundred and forty miles from Gibraltar and it would take another two days for her to return. By then, the men would have been cooped up in the villa for a week. For forty-eight hours they sweated it out in the fetid atmosphere of the overcrowded rooms, but O'Leary's return had brought a kind of calm. Richard had admired him for a long time, but in those two days he was more than ever impressed by his quiet, authoritative manner. He never raised his voice, never seemed to lose his air of confidence, and the men instinctively obeyed him.

On the 11th they all trudged down to the beach again, and again there was no response to their signal.

'Right, that's it!' Mactavish said, as soon as they were back in the villa. 'I'm off. I'd rather take my chances in the fresh air than spend another day cooped up in this hellhole! Who's coming with me?'

To Richard's dismay half the men in the room surged forward, with a swelling murmur of agreement. It seemed that they were going to have a full-scale mutiny.

O'Leary stepped between Mactavish and the door. 'I can't allow you to do that, I'm afraid,' he said. His voice was still quiet but there was something in its tone that stopped the Scot in his tracks. 'If you walk out of here, and these others follow you, one of you will certainly be picked up before nightfall. Which of you is absolutely certain that you could remain silent in the face of what the Gestapo will do to find out where you have been hiding, and who has sheltered you?' There was an uneasy silence. O'Leary went on. 'I can assure you that the ship is on its way. A little more patience and every one of you will soon be safe in Gibraltar. Do you really want to jeopardise that – for all of us?' He held Mactavish's eyes and after a moment the Scot turned away.

'OK. I'll give it one more day.'

The next night it seemed as if O'Leary's reassurances had been only empty promises. From 1.30 until 3 a.m. they crouched in the dunes, waiting and straining their eyes for the answer to their signals. Then, just as they were about to give up, Richard saw something away to the north.

'Look! There!' he whispered urgently to O'Leary.

Out to sea and some four hundred yards or so from where they crouched a light was flashing the letter V. Richard threw caution to the wind and ran along the beach in that direction, fearful that the boat's crew would give up and go away before he could return their signal. It was with enormous relief that he saw the dinghy loom up out of the darkness and heard the answer to his whispered challenge.

'*Où sont les fraises?*'

'*Dans le jus!*'

As one of the crew scrambled ashore Richard hissed, 'Where the hell have you been? We waited two nights last week and last night.'

'Where have *we* been?' came the reply. 'We were here last week. There was no sign of you.'

'You're on the wrong beach!' Richard exclaimed.

'Then the bloody charts must be wrong,' said the other man.

By this time O'Leary had come up with the first group of escapers and there was no time to argue further. In tense silence they helped the men into the boat and watched them disappear on the dark water. It was half an hour before all had been safely dispatched, and Richard suddenly felt totally exhausted. It had been a week of constant tension and anxiety, with no chance of respite and very little sleep.

When they reached the villa O'Leary said, 'I want you and Ginny to clear out of here at once. It's too dangerous to go on using this place. Go back to Monte Carlo, Richard, and keep your head down. I'll get in touch with you via the teashop when we've had a chance to make new plans.'

They spent the rest of the night clearing up and removing the evidence of their 'guests' and then, as soon as the curfew was lifted, O'Leary and Val Williams left for the station. It was agreed that Richard and Ginny would follow shortly afterwards. When they were alone Ginny looked round the villa and said, with a wry smile, 'You know, I shall miss playing house here.'

Richard smiled in return. 'So shall I, although I can do without any more weeks like last week.' Then he added, 'It would have been nice if it could have been a real holiday, wouldn't it?'

'It sometimes felt like it, in the early days especially,' she said.

He moved closer to her, impelled by a sudden feeling of tenderness and an awareness, perhaps, of opportunities lost. 'We'll still see each other, won't we?'

'I expect so. But things are getting more difficult.' Her face was shadowed. 'Although I'm married to a Frenchman I'm still technically a British subject. If the Germans take over I may have to leave.'

'Will your husband go with you?'

She shook her head. 'He's a very patriotic man. He feels it is his duty to stay here and do whatever he can.'

He said, 'I've never met your husband. I wish I had.'

She gave him a small smile. 'I've never met your wife. Perhaps I will if I come to England.'

He felt a sudden wrenching sense of dislocation between the memory of Priscilla, which seemed almost ephemeral, and the living, breathing woman beside him. He reached out and put his arm around her.

'Oh, Ginny . . .'

For a brief moment his lips found hers, then she drew away from him. 'No, don't spoil it. Things have been so good between us. I don't want to have to look back with any regrets.'

He sighed and let her go and shortly afterwards they wheeled their bicycles out on to the track and set out for the station.

16

On the last day of rehearsal for the new show Rose waited until most of the company had left and then laid her hand on Monty Prince's sleeve.

'Can you spare a couple of minutes? There's something I want to show you.'

'What sort of something?'

'I know we agreed when I took on this job that I wasn't going to dance myself, but I've been working up a little number – a solo – and I wondered if we could include it. If you think it's good enough, that is.'

'What kind of a number?' Monty looked doubtful. 'Not ballet, is it? Not for an ENSA audience. We don't want a repeat of that fiasco we had in Fairbourne.'

'Not straightforward ballet, Monty,' she explained. 'I'm not going to wear a tutu or *pointe* shoes. It's more of a speciality item – a sort of dance/drama. Let me at least show you what I've worked up – please!'

'Of course. I know anything you've choreographed will be worth watching. Let's have a look.' Monty smiled at her encouragingly but Rose could see that he still had doubts.

She went to the side of the stage and wound up the gramophone. Normally Miss Finnegan played for rehearsals and the full band for performances, but Rose had not wanted to involve anyone else in case she found that her technique was not up to the ideas she had in mind. Instead, she had chosen recordings of Vera Lynn singing her signature tune, 'We'll Meet Again', and the other great favourite, 'There'll Be Bluebirds over the White Cliffs of Dover'. The piece was inspired by the images she saw all around her every day – images of women carrying on the business of everyday living without their men, and in many cases doing the jobs the men had left behind them – and she had been working on it quietly whenever she could get the rehearsal room to herself. It combined ballet techniques with movements taken from ballroom dancing and told a simple story of a young woman returning to her empty home from a day's work in the factory. Tired and lonely, she takes the photograph of her missing sweetheart from the mantelpiece and dances with it. Then a telegram arrives. She opens it. It is from him. He is coming home on leave. Joyfully, she tidies the room and sets the table to welcome him home.

When he had watched the piece through Monty said, 'It's lovely, Rose, lovely. But I don't know how it'll go down with the troops.'

'Let me try it, Monty,' she begged. 'If they don't like it we can forget it – but let me try it once!'

'OK,' he agreed. 'We'll give it a go. But don't be disappointed if it turns out to be a bit above their heads.'

The next morning the company assembled in the church hall where they had been rehearsing with their bags packed, ready to leave. The costumes and props were already stowed in the big wicker hampers. All that was missing was the destination for which they were all bound. Monty reached into his pocket and took out the official envelope containing their sealed orders.

'Right, boys and girls. Let's see where we're off to. Anybody want to lay any bets?' He slit the envelope and studied the contents and Rose saw an expression of comic dismay spread across his crumpled features. 'Oh, blimey!'

'What?' demanded several voices. 'Where are we going?'

'The Orkney and Shetland islands.'

'Where?' squeaked May.

'That's Scotland, isn't it?' Peggy asked.

'Off Scotland,' Monty said. 'It's just about as far north as you can get and still be in Britain.'

'All right for some,' Peggy muttered. 'You'll be able to go home, Vi.'

'Don't be daft,' the other girl replied. 'I come from Glasgow.'

'Who are we going to perform to there?' one of the men demanded. 'There's nothing there but bleeding sheep.'

'Our first venue is an anti-aircraft battery outside some place called Stromness,' Monty said. 'After that, we get fresh instructions.'

'I don't get it,' exclaimed Ronnie Cowley. 'Why all the cloak-and-dagger business? Why should the Jerries be interested in the whereabouts of an ENSA troupe?'

'It's not us the government's trying to keep secret, you klutz,' one of the Wilson brothers said. 'It's things like the location of that ack-ack battery.'

'Why us?' Peggy demanded. 'Why can't they send a Scottish group?'

'Come on, be fair,' Ronnie said with a grin. 'These chaps deserve something better than bagpipes.'

'If you're trying to imply that that's all we Scots can do . . .' Violet began angrily.

'Now then, Vi,' Rose cut in. 'It was a joke. Ronnie didn't

mean anything by it. Come on, everyone. We've got our orders. It's no good arguing among ourselves.'

Miss Finnegan picked up the basket containing a very angry Claude de Pussy. 'Well, it looks as if we've got a long journey ahead of us. We'd better get going.'

Rose followed the others out with a sinking heart. She had only the vaguest idea of where the Orkney and Shetland islands were, but islands meant a sea crossing and she had not forgotten how terribly sick she had been going across the Channel on that first trip to France.

It was even worse than she had anticipated. It took them a day and a night on a succession of trains to reach Thurso and when they boarded the ferry at Scrabster a gale was blowing and the sea was a heaving mass of grey. By the time they disembarked at Stromness she had gone beyond wishing she were dead and had come to the conclusion that she probably was. But there was no time to recover. The equipment and the cases were loaded into a waiting truck and within minutes they were bumping and swaying along the narrow road and out to a windswept headland. Here a red-faced sergeant conducted them to the two Nissen huts that were to be their accommodation for the night.

Rose looked round at the primitive facilities and braced herself for an explosion. Previously, Miss Finnegan had always insisted on being accommodated in a private hotel, shunning the theatrical 'digs' the rest of them had endured. The old lady put Claude's carrying case down on the floor and straightened up, rubbing her back.

'Well, it's not the Ritz – and it's far from clean. But if we can find a broom I'm sure we can improve things. Come along, girls. Get unpacked. We've got a show to do tonight.'

Alice was in tears. 'I'm exhausted! How can we be expected to dance after that journey? I can't do it, Rose!'

Rose put her arm round her and looked at the other three. All were grey faced and bedraggled and she herself was shaking from the after-effects of the crossing. All she longed to do was lie down and pull a blanket over her head. But she knew it was up to her to give a lead.

'Yes you can, Alice,' she said firmly. 'Remember, Dr Theatre is a great healer. Once you get your costume and your make-up on, you'll feel differently. These boys have been stuck out here for God knows how long. They deserve a bit of light relief and it's up to us to give it to them.'

She had little confidence in her own words but they proved true nonetheless. After a hot meal in the mess they all felt better, and by the time the curtain went up on the makeshift stage and the audience began to stamp and whistle their appreciation they had forgotten their aching heads and weary limbs. Rose was more nervous than the others. For the first time since her accident in France she was going to go out on stage and perform and she was unsure what sort of reception she would get.

The opening dance numbers were well received, to the accompaniment of wolf-whistles and various ribald suggestions. When Rose went on, wearing a full-skirted dress and a headscarf, she sensed that the audience were expecting a comedy number. There were whistles and one or two, hastily suppressed, invitations to 'show us your legs, girl!', but then a sudden silence fell. She heard none of the rustles and scrapings that denoted an audience that was bored or out of sympathy with what they were watching, and when she finished the silence continued for a full ten seconds. Then the applause came, warm and heartfelt. Her dance had, magically, brought the men close for a few moments to the girls they had left behind and whom they saw only in their dreams.

From that night on Rose's solo was a regular part of the programme, but her euphoria at being able to perform again was tempered by the news that their next date was aboard a battleship that was lying in Scapa Flow, giving its crew a brief respite from the horrors of the North Atlantic convoys. Mercifully, the wind had eased when the tender came to pick them up from the dockside, but Rose was glad when they drew alongside the grey bulk of the warship. Immediately a new challenge presented itself. The only way up the sheer side of the vessel was via a flimsy rope ladder that had been lowered from the deck.

'I'm not climbing up that,' Peggy announced.

'Don't be silly,' Rose responded, shivering. 'We're in much better shape than Monty. If he can make it, so can you.'

They watched the little man haul himself laboriously up the ladder, followed by the other members of the band.

'After you, ladies,' Ronnie said.

Rose looked at the other girls. They gazed back at her dumbly. She scrambled across the rocking deck of the tender.

'Here you go, miss,' said the sailor who was holding on to the end of the ladder. 'Let me give you a hand.'

As she started the climb Rose understood why the signal giving them their orders had also stipulated, 'Female personnel should wear uniform trousers, not skirts.'

Strong hands helped her on to the deck and she turned to look at the other girls, relieved to see that they were all following. Then she saw a lone figure sitting upright in the stern of the tender.

'What about Miss Finnegan? She's our pianist, but she'll never make it up that ladder.'

The young officer who had greeted her smiled. 'Don't worry, miss. We've made other arrangements for her.'

A few minutes later Rose had the pleasure of seeing Miss Finnegan winched over the ship's rail in a bosun's chair, her regal composure unruffled and on her lap the travelling basket containing a loudly complaining Claude de Pussy.

As usual, once they were on board, the warm welcome and the vociferous appreciation of the audience made them forget the inconveniences. They were getting used to being the only women in a male-dominated world, but Rose never felt really comfortable as the focus of so many hungry eyes. It was, she thought, rather like being eaten alive.

Over the next six weeks the *Lighten Up!* company performed almost every night. There were several more visits to ships in the vast harbour and then they worked their way around the islands, visiting remote outposts of the defensive shield that had been thrown up around the country. They performed for the civilians, too; though the God-fearing islanders were less enthusiastic about Monty's jokes and the sight of four long-legged girls in scanty costumes than the troops. Nevertheless, they were treated with great hospitality, and on their rare nights off were entertained themselves with traditional music and dancing. Rose enjoyed these evenings, and became quite proficient at the eightsome reel.

From Orkney they moved on to the Shetland Isles. Autumn was well advanced by now and most of the time the islands were battered by westerly gales, which sent great waves crashing against the cliffs. Rose had never seen anywhere so wild and remote and she marvelled that people actually

chose to live there. She was not the only one. All four girls were
homesick. May was tearful, Peggy more foul tempered than
ever and Alice was so pale and thin that Rose worried about
her. Only Violet seemed to be enjoying herself, thriving on the
constant diet of male admiration. Rose spent a great deal of
time and energy calming rows and comforting tears, and some
nights it took all her powers of persuasion to get her four
charges ready to go onstage. She was immensely relieved when
the signal finally came that ordered them all to return to
London.

Merry swallowed the last mouthful of whisky in his glass and
reached for the bottle to replenish it. He had taken to drinking
whisky instead of gin because it produced a marginally less
painful hangover. He was surprised to find the bottle nearly
empty. Surely, he thought, it was only this morning he had
opened it. He tried to think back. He had not had that many
drinks today, had he? He could not remember having given
any to anyone else. He decided that it must have been the
previous day that he started on this bottle. One thing was clear.
He would have to see if he could wangle a fresh one out of the
Mess sergeant.

He finished his drink and looked at himself in the mirror.
His uniform was correct, his tie properly tied. At least it looked
as if he was in control. There would be more false notes than
there should be in tonight's performance, but with any luck
only the band and the singers would notice – and they were
getting used to it.

Once his request to be returned to active duty had been
turned down George Black had insisted that he begin preparing a new show, to tour army bases in Britain. In vain he
had protested that he could not raise the enthusiasm or the

energy required to hold together the volatile mix of amateurs and professionals that constituted any Stars in Battledress company. He had pleaded to be allowed to tour on his own, giving solo recitals as he had once before, but George had been adamant. He needed a new company licking into shape and Merry was the man for the job.

So Merry had hidden his grief and despair under a veneer of professional detachment. The members of the new company were all strangers to him and they had never known the man whose flair had inspired his last concert party to christen themselves 'The Merrymakers'. They saw him instead as another in the long line of faintly seedy also-rans who had never quite made it to the top of their profession, a type that was all too common in their experience. It had not surprised any of them when he came to rehearsals smelling of whisky, though they were more disturbed when he began arriving for performances slightly unsteady on his feet.

He had managed, somehow, to pull together a more or less acceptable show, at any rate by the rather variable standards of the day, though it had none of the zip and energy that he usually managed to infuse into his colleagues. It had passed muster with his senior officers – just – and he and his company had been sent out to tour the army barracks and garrison theatres, where men were glad of anything to relieve the tedium of training and waiting for the 'big push' that never seemed to materialise.

He had been in Catterick on the Sunday, 15 November, when Churchill had ordered all the church bells to be rung for the first time since the invasion scare of 1940, to celebrate the victory at El Alamein. He had put his head under the pillow and cursed them for adding to the jangling discomfort of his hangover. He had sat in an officers' mess somewhere to listen

to the prime minister's broadcast in which he told the nation
that this was 'not the end, not even the beginning of the end'
but was 'perhaps the end of the beginning'. It had meant
nothing to him. As far as he was concerned the end had
already come and he was nothing more than a ghostly reve-
nant, waiting for the blessed moment of release from all
temporal affairs.

He got up and pulled his tunic straight, glancing at his
watch. Curtain up in fifteen minutes. The cast would be
assembled, ready dressed and made up. He left all that these
days to the able sergeant who acted as his stage manager. All
he had to do now was walk across the parade ground to the
mess hut where they were to perform and take his place at the
piano. For a moment he thought he was not going to be able to
do it. He closed his eyes and Felix's handsome, scarred face
appeared as if permanently engraved on the inside of the lids.
His body ached for the familiar touch, with a physical pain,
and his throat contracted on a sob. He drew a long breath,
forced his eyes open and walked out of the door.

17

Richard was sitting in the Scottish Tearooms in Monte Carlo when Miss Eva came bustling over to his table.

'Have you heard the news? I've just been listening to the BBC. The Eighth Army have broken through at El Alamein. Rommel and his troops are retreating.'

'That's wonderful news!' Richard replied. 'Let's hope they can hang on to their gains this time.'

'Oh, they'll be all right now that Monty is in charge,' the elderly lady assured him. 'He's really licked them into shape. What is it they call themselves? Desert Mice?'

'Rats, I think,' Richard said with a grin.

Three days later he arrived for his usual afternoon tea to find Val Williams and the two Misses Trenchard in excited conversation.

'More good news!' Miss Eva told him. 'The Allies have landed in Algiers! That means they're just across the water! Isn't it wonderful?'

'Do they mean a major invasion, or just a small expeditionary force?'

'Oh, it's a full-scale invasion, all right,' Val said. 'Large forces of American and British troops, the news said.'

'How are the French reacting?' Richard asked. 'After all, that's French territory. Officially it's under Vichy control.'

'Admiral Darlan has ordered his troops not to resist,' Val told him. 'But it's bound to have the Vichy authorities here worried. With Allied forces just across the Med the Germans are not going to sit back and rely upon the Vichy government to protect their southern flank.'

'You think the Nazis will move into the unoccupied zone?'

'It's inevitable, I should say.'

'That's bad news,' Richard said. 'It's going to put Pat and the others in even greater danger.'

A few days later they heard that German troops had begun moving into the unoccupied zone and it was not long before they reached Marseilles. Over the next two weeks Monte Carlo buzzed with rumours of imminent invasion by either German or Allied forces. On the 23rd came the news that Admiral Darlan, the commander-in-chief of French forces in North Africa, had thrown in his lot with the Allies and then, on the 27th, the news that the crews of the French fleet moored in Toulon harbour had scuttled their ships rather than hand them over to the Germans.

The day after the news from Toulon a message arrived in the teashop summoning Richard to a meeting with O'Leary at an address in Toulouse. He found him at a dress shop belonging to a supporter of the line, a woman named Françoise Dissart.

'I've just had a message from Ian Garrow, smuggled out of the castle of Meauzeac by one of the guards,' O'Leary said. 'Apparently there is a rumour that he's going to be moved from there within the next month and sent to Germany, to Dachau.'

'Dachau!' Richard exclaimed. 'By all accounts that is an absolute hellhole.' The thought of the Scotsman, who had risked his own life to get so many Allied soldiers and airmen out of France, including Richard himself, immured in a Nazi concentration camp made him feel sick. He had been one of the founders of the escape line, refusing the chance to get out himself in order to stay and help others.

'Quite,' O'Leary agreed. 'So we must get him out before that happens. I've been in touch with London and they agree that we should take all reasonable risks to free him. The question is, how.'

'Do you have any ideas?' Richard asked.

'Not so far,' O'Leary confessed. 'Since the Nazis took over everything is much more difficult. The trains are searched more frequently, there are spot checks on papers everywhere, and people are too afraid of the secret police to help. Some of our safe houses are under surveillance, I'm almost sure. Already I have begun to close them down and disperse our people. That's why I've moved my headquarters to Toulouse.'

'What's Meauzeac like?' Richard asked.

'More or less impregnable,' O'Leary replied. 'I sent Francis Dammaerts to reconnoitre but he was arrested yesterday.'

'Arrested!' Richard exclaimed. 'Can we do anything for him?' He had met Dammaerts once or twice and knew that he was another who risked his life for the *réseau*.

'For the moment he will have to fend for himself,' O'Leary said grimly. 'Ian is our first priority. That's why I want you here. I need you to act as a postbox to pass messages while I go up to Bergerac to see what can be done. But one thing is clear. If we're going to get Ian out it will have to be by stealth and not by force.'

'Just a minute,' Richard said. 'I've had a thought. If we can get hold of a guard's uniform he might be able to walk out with the night shift when they leave. It's how we got Chantal out of prison in Lille. Do we have a contact who could smuggle a uniform in?'

'There's the guard who brought out Ian's message. He's in it strictly for the money, but we might be able to bribe him sufficiently. And I know a tailor, a Jew here in Toulouse, who would make the uniform. But it's going to take money. I've already sent a message to Ginny. Her husband is well off and they've been very generous in the past. She may be able to help.'

Ginny arrived later that afternoon, bringing with her a substantial sum. Richard saw that her usual cheerful optimism had disappeared. When they were alone for a minute he said, 'Things don't look good. You should get Pat to send you to England.'

She sighed. 'I know. But I can't bear the thought of leaving Gilles on his own here. And I feel as if I'm running out on the others.'

'It won't help anyone if you're interned,' Richard pointed out. 'In England you might be able to find a way to go on helping.'

'Oh, I shall do that, all right,' she said firmly. 'I'm not going to sit back and let these bastards get away with what they're doing.'

'Pat ought to go, too,' Richard said. 'He's in worse danger than any of us.'

'He won't, though,' Ginny said. 'He'll stick it out as long as he possibly can.'

As usual, Richard proposed to find himself work in the area, so that he could give a reason for being there if stopped and questioned. O'Leary was dubious.

'Now that the whole place is crawling with Gestapo there's a danger that someone might recognise you, or at least remember that your name was on the wanted list.'

'It's a remote possibility,' Richard said. 'I think it would be more dangerous to be caught in a spot check without an adequate cover story.'

'Well, at least keep away from places the Germans are likely to frequent,' O'Leary insisted. 'And don't use the name you were known by in Lille.'

The next morning, as soon as the curfew was lifted, O'Leary left for Bergerac and Richard set out on a trawl of the bars and cafés in one of the less salubrious areas of the city. To begin with he had no luck. The proprietors told him that trade was so bad that they could not afford to pay an entertainer. Eventually he came across a place that looked rather more prosperous than the rest and went inside. It did not take him long to realise that what appeared from outside to be an ordinary bar was in fact a brothel. The madame, a dryly sarcastic character with hard dark eyes, looked him up and down and called a seedy little man from a back room.

'Jacques plays the piano to entertain the clients while they wait. Let's hear you sing.'

He sang '*J'attendrai*', which always reminded him painfully of Chantal but seemed appropriate to the situation, and afterwards Madame Louise offered to employ him on the basis that he would be paid in kind, with the services of whichever girl he chose. He pointed out that he could not live on that and they finally struck a bargain whereby he would receive tips from the guests and a free meal, and as much as he wanted to drink.

Because of the curfew most of the establishment's trade was now done in the afternoon and Richard assumed that he would be free to return to the flat before dark. He was soon disillusioned, however. In the evening the brothel became the exclusive preserve of German officers. Richard could only hope and pray that none of them had ever been stationed in Lille. He had told Madame Louise that his name was Maurice and she had not asked to see his papers.

★　★　★

The next day O'Leary reappeared, looking exhausted but optimistic. The guard had agreed, for a considerable sum, to smuggle in the uniform and had provided a small scrap of material as a pattern. O'Leary had made a careful sketch of the buttons, badges and other insignia required and both the material and the sketches were already in the hands of the tailor, whose name was Ullmann. The situation was, however, even more urgent than they had realised. The guard had told O'Leary that big changes were expected in the prison routine very soon.

Before Richard left for the brothel they were joined by a young man who introduced himself as Fabian and O'Leary called a council of war.

'There's a farmer who lives about twenty miles from the prison,' he said. 'He's helped us before and he's prepared to do it again. He has a car and an allowance of fuel for agricultural purposes. He will be waiting in a clearing in the forest a short distance from the prison. I shall be covering the gate. You, Richard, and Fabian will cover the machine-gun towers at either side. If anything goes wrong our revolvers won't be much of a match for their automatic weapons but at least we might be able to create enough of a diversion to give Ian a chance to make a run for it. If he gets out all right I shall take him to the farmer and he will drive us back to the farm. Tom Groome will be there with his wireless set so we can let London know if we've been successful. You two will have to make your own way back to Toulouse. I'll contact you here once Ian is safe. Any questions?'

That night, when Richard stood up to sing his first group of songs after the change of clientele in the evening, there was a disturbance as a group comprising several German officers and a few civilians came noisily through the street door. As the group began to settle, Richard recognised one of the civilians and the song died in his throat. The man had his back to him but there was no mistaking that sandy head, that cocky, self-confidant stance. For a moment Richard panicked. Then he did the only thing he could think of. He turned away from the audience and doubled up in a simulated fit of violent coughing. There were a few derisive catcalls from the clients and the pianist demanded to know what the hell was the matter with him. He muttered an apology and stumbled towards the back of the bar.

Out of sight of the clients, he stood still, forcing himself to breathe deeply. The sight of Paul Cole, enjoying himself among his new German friends, filled him with a choking anger. This was the man who had betrayed the *réseau* in Lille, when Richard was working there. The man who was responsible for the arrest of the gentle Abbé Carpentier, who had assisted so many escaping airmen by forging documents for them, and of who could tell how many others. The man who was responsible for the arrest of Chantal, and her ultimate death. Richard knew that the sensible thing to do would be to slip away before he was recognised, but the thought of leaving Cole carousing and later, presumably, enjoying the services of one of the girls was sickening. For a few minutes he waited, formulating a plan. Then he moved to a doorway where he could see Michel, the barman, without being seen by those in the room beyond.

When Michel came near he drew his attention with a low whistle. The barman moved closer. 'What's wrong with you? I thought you were going to be sick out there.'

'I nearly was. There's a bloke out there who ran off with my girl a couple of months ago. The ginger-haired little swine. See him?'

'Oh yes. I know him. Very pally with our German clients.'

'So I see. Well, that's just typical. Listen, I want to get my own back, give him a bit of a shock. Just tip me the wink when he goes upstairs and tell me which girl he's with, will you?'

'Look here, we don't want a fight on the premises. It's more than my job's worth.'

'I'm not looking for a fight. I just want to embarrass him. If I can tell my girl what he gets up to she won't have any more to do with him. Come on, he's obviously a collaborator. He deserves a bit of a shock, doesn't he?'

The barman hesitated, then he nodded briefly. 'OK. I'll let you know when he goes up. But if there are any problems later, I didn't know what was going on. Understood?'

'Yes, of course,' Richard agreed. 'I'll keep you out of it.'

Twenty minutes later Michel sidled over to where Richard was waiting. 'He's gone up with Adèle. You know which room?'

Richard nodded. He felt bad about lying to the man but all that mattered to him at that moment was to revenge himself on Cole. And the girl deserved whatever was coming to her. He had noticed before that she was always more than willing to flirt with the German officers. He waited a few minutes longer and then walked silently up the stairs. The corridor was empty but from behind some of the doors came the sounds of heavy breathing and grunts of pleasure. From the bar below he could hear laughter and the tinkling of the piano. All the girls would be fully occupied and Madame would be in the bar, keeping an eye on everything. The other staff had gone home and he knew from experience that the back of the building would be deserted. Outside Adèle's room he listened intently, but all he could hear was a low groan, whether of pain or pleasure he could not tell. He reached through the false pocket in his trousers for the gun he always wore strapped to his thigh. Then he took a deep breath and flung open the door.

For an instant he was taken by surprise. He was aiming for the bed but it was empty. Then he saw them, by the window. Cole was standing, his trousers round his ankles. The girl was on her knees before him. Richard levelled the gun but the split-second hesitation had given Cole time to react. He flung the girl aside and dived for cover, grabbing for his jacket, discarded on a chaise longue, in which, Richard had no doubt, he kept a pistol. The trousers hobbling his ankles tripped him and he fell heavily. Richard swore and took aim again. His plan had been to take Cole prisoner and march him at gunpoint out of the back entrance. With the streets empty because of the curfew he had reckoned it would not be too difficult to take him back to the flat. Once there O'Leary could decide how to dispose of him. But now that the element of surprise had been lost it had become a duel to the death. Cole was scrabbling in his jacket pocket. Richard's fingers tightened on the trigger but this time it was the girl who forestalled him. With a hoarse scream of '*Assassin!*' she hurled herself at Richard, uncoiling like a spring from her position on the floor, and knocked up his arm. The shot went harmlessly into the ceiling but at the same instant Cole fired. The girl gave a choking cry and fell into Richard's arms.

Richard knew he had only seconds to escape, before the sound of the shots brought everyone running. Already, feet were hammering on the stairs and voices were shouting questions. He shook off the girl, who was clinging to his arm, and swung round to search for Cole. He had taken the opportunity her intervention had given him to take cover behind the chaise longue. Richard saw the muzzle-flash of the pistol and felt the wind of the bullet brush his cheek. He fired a last shot at Cole's legs, the only part of him that was visible, and was grimly satisfied to hear a scream of pain. Then he ran to the window and wrenched it open. There was a small balcony with a wrought-iron balustrade, and the window was not high off the ground. He vaulted the balustrade, hung for a second at the full stretch of his arms and let himself drop into the street. For once he was glad of the curfew and the blackout. Keeping close to the houses he began to run. As figures appeared on the balcony he reached the corner of an alleyway and swerved into it, running light footed, until he came to small square. From here, there was a choice of four roads. He took one at random and ran until a large doorway offered further concealment.

He stood panting, listening hard. The occupants of the brothel were unlikely to pursue him, since it would mean breaking the curfew. But their German clients would have no hesitation about summoning the police and probably their own forces as well. As if to confirm his thoughts, booted feet clattered on the cobbles of the square and orders were shouted. There was a brief hesitation and then the footsteps headed away, down one of the other roads.

He had scarcely drawn a breath of relief before he heard the sound of a vehicle approaching the square. An armoured car ground into sight, its searchlight scanning the area. Richard pressed himself back into the doorway as the light probed his street. A moment later the vehicle turned towards him. His first impulse was to run, hoping to reach the corner before the light picked him out. Then he realised it was hopeless. His back was against a massive wooden door and as he shrank back farther his hand encountered the cold metal of a ring-shaped handle. He turned it and with a click the door gave inwards. Richard pushed it open, stepped inside and closed it just as the sound of the armoured car reached the point where he had been standing.

Inside, it was even darker than out in the street, but he had the sense of being in a large space and his nose told him what it was. He was in a church. As his eyes adapted, he saw at some distance a faint red glow. Then he began to make out the silhouette of arched windows high above him against the starlit sky. For a moment he stood absolutely still, listening for any sound that would betray the presence of another person, but the silence was absolute except for the faint growl of the receding car. He groped his way forwards, finding the back of the last row of pews, and then feeling his way down the aisle to where the red lamp showed the presence of the reserved sacrament. Near the altar he almost bumped into a stand for votive candles. Fumbling along it he found a box of matches and lit one of the candles, shielding it with his hand so that no glimmer of light would show through the high windows. Exploring further he came to a door in the corner of the transept and beyond it a flight of stairs leading upwards. Obviously the way up to the tower. For a moment he was tempted but it occurred to him that up there he would have no way of escape if they came looking for him.

Moving on towards the back of the church, he came upon a heavy curtain. Behind it was a stack of spare chairs and a heap of hassocks. It was as good a hiding place as he was likely to find. He pulled the hassocks into a rough couch and sank down, realising for the first time that he was shaking. He had been a fool, he told himself bitterly. He had allowed his hatred of Cole to make him forget all his months of training, all his trade-craft, and expose himself and the *réseau* to danger. It occurred to him that the Nazis might not make too much effort to find a jealous lover who had taken revenge on a man they knew to be a traitor to his own kind. But if Cole had recognised him and told them who he was they would hunt him down without mercy.

Minutes passed and became hours. From time to time he heard the armoured cars circling the area and saw the reflection of their searchlights through the windows, but no one came into the church. Then, to his immense relief, he heard the air-raid warning sound. Moments later came the drone of planes and then the dull concussion of exploding bombs. *Good old RAF!* he thought. *Just in the nick of time!* It was a big raid, more than adequate to keep his pursuers off the streets, and before long the noise of the searching vehicles was replaced by the wail of ambulance sirens and fire engines. Richard burrowed deeper among the hassocks and reflected ironically that it would be just his luck if the church received a direct hit.

He must have dozed eventually, after the sound of the all-clear. When he came to, the first faint hint of the winter dawn was lighting the sky beyond the windows. He got up, stretching cramped limbs and running a hand through his hair. Soon the curfew would be lifted and he would have the chance to mingle with the early morning crowds. His throat was parched. Coming out from behind his curtain, he saw the font and, lifting the cover, found a small pool of water. Was it sacrilege, he wondered, to drink water from a font? If so, he felt it would be excusable, in the circumstances. The water tasted faintly metallic, but it relieved the worst pangs of thirst. He brushed himself down and prepared to venture out into the street.

He had almost reached the door when he heard the clang of a latch from the far end of the church, magnified by the echoing silence. There was no time to retreat behind the curtain so he did the first thing that came into his head. With a swift movement he reached the nearest pew and fell on his knees. Peering through his folded hands he saw a priest, in his black cassock, enter from a door to the left of the altar, genuflect and begin lighting the candles in the sanctuary. He did not look towards the back of the church and after a few minutes he disappeared the way he had come. Richard rose and turned once more towards the door, but at that moment it opened to admit an elderly lady in widow's black. He dropped to his knees again as she shuffled past him and took her place in one of the front pews. Behind her came two more women, then a middle-aged couple, then two men in working clothes, and Richard realised that they were about to hear early mass. He was wondering whether he could slip out without being noticed when the priest reappeared in his vestments and the service began. To leave now would draw unwanted attention so Richard stayed where he was. It struck him suddenly that he would be much less conspicuous leaving with the rest of the small congregation than on his own.

The service progressed. Richard was not familiar with the Catholic rite but he had attended enough Church of England communion services during his schooldays to know roughly what was going on. He stood and knelt with the rest, until the moment came when they lined up to receive the sacrament. He was not particularly religious but a deep-seated instinct told him that to join them in his present frame of mind would, truly, be sacrilege. The last communicant received the wafer and returned to his seat and the priest paused and gazed up the nave to where Richard sat. For a moment, over the distance, it seemed their eyes met. Then the priest turned back to the altar.

When the service was over Richard joined the rest of the congregation moving towards the street, but at the door the priest laid a detaining hand on his arm.

'You did not partake of the sacrament, my son. Are you in some kind of trouble?'

Richard met kindly dark eyes and for an instant was tempted to confide and ask for sanctuary. Then he ducked his head and muttered, 'I am not in a state of grace, Father.' Before the priest could question him further he hurried out into the daylight.

The streets were busy now with people hurrying to work and women with baskets on their arms, queuing already outside the bakers' shops. Richard walked briskly, keeping his head down and using every trick he had learned at Beaulieu to make sure he was not followed. The dressmaker's shop was quite close but he made a wide circuit before turning into the street. No one was loitering outside the house, and there was no sign of any of the warning signals they had agreed. Richard paused for a while, pretending to join a queue outside a butcher's shop. Then, satisfied that the house was not under surveillance, he let himself in through the side door and went up to the flat.

O'Leary looked up from his breakfast and rose. 'Richard? Something's happened. What's wrong?'

Richard leaned his back against the door. He was breathing as if he had just run a mile. 'Cole's on the loose. And my cover's blown.'

'Cole! *Merde!* Are you sure?'

'He came into the place where I'm working. He was with a whole lot of German officers, all drunk and very chummy.'

'They must have let him out of prison when they took over,' O'Leary said. 'I suppose it's not surprising. He can be very useful to them. What do you mean, about your cover being blown? Did he recognise you?'

As briefly as possible Richard recounted the events of the night. 'You don't have to tell me what a bloody fool I've been,' he concluded. 'I'm sorry, Pat.'

O'Leary moved to the window. 'You're sure you weren't followed?'

'As sure as I can be.'

'Then perhaps the damage is not too great. But the situation is very dangerous for you, *mon ami*. He knows you both by sight and by name. You must go back to England as soon as possible.'

'Not till we get Ian out,' Richard said firmly. 'He got me home in '40. I owe him for that.'

'We both owe him,' O'Leary said. 'He got me out of St Hippolyte the same year.'

'Then that's settled,' Richard said, setting his jaw. 'I'm not leaving until he's free.'

18

With Christmas approaching, Rose and the company of *Lighten Up!* were on the road again, their first venue an RAF base on the coast of Norfolk. The show went well and, as usual, Rose's number was well received. It was afterwards, when they were guests in the sergeants' mess, that the real excitement occurred.

'Ooh, look!' Violet squealed. 'Yanks!'

'Where?' demanded Peggy.

'Look, over there. They must be from the American airbase. Gosh, aren't they tall! They make our chaps look like pygmies.'

'Don't be silly, Vi,' Rose chided her, her patriotic instincts aroused. 'There's nothing wrong with our men.'

But she had to admit that the Americans were a good-looking bunch. They were all tanned and fit, somehow larger and more vital – or perhaps just less inhibited – than their British counterparts, and it was not long before they descended on Rose and her girls, intent on monopolising their attention. Rose found them too brash and forward but the other girls revelled in the situation. Before long, someone put a record on the gramophone and invited one of the girls to dance. Soon they were all on the floor, swept away in the arms of first one tall Yankee figure and then another. There was no gainsaying them, no room for shrinking violets.

It was all quite enjoyable, until someone suggested a gentle-man's excuse-me. Then chaos broke out. A man would no sooner get his arms around a girl than there would be a tap on his shoulder and another would take his place. To begin with the girls found it amusing, but the British airmen had been getting steadily more irritated at not being able to get a look-in. Rose did not see who started the fight, but suddenly the whole room erupted. She took shelter behind the bar and the other girls joined her, screaming. Chairs and tables were hurled aside, punches were thrown and bodies squirmed and wrestled on the floor. Within minutes officers of the RAF Regiment arrived, whistles blew and calm was restored, and Rose and her girls were escorted, with many apologies, back to their quarters.

They were scheduled to remain in the area for the rest of the week, since there were a number of bases within a few hours' travel. The next evening an extremely shamefaced young lieutenant arrived from the American base to apologise for the behaviour of his men and to invite the whole company, by way of recompense, to attend a pre-Christmas ball at the base the following Saturday evening. Rose was inclined to refuse but the other girls begged to be allowed to go and she knew that it was her duty to accompany them, if only in the role of chaperone.

At the base a huge hangar had been festooned with paper chains and tinsel and hung with great swags of holly and ivy, while an enormous Christmas tree dominated one corner. There was a twenty-piece band playing Glenn Miller numbers and a bar stocked with every imaginable drink. There were officers present and Rose was relieved to see that there were plenty of other women as well. Obviously a lot of them were local girls, but there were one or two older ladies, who she guessed were the wives of some of the senior RAF officers who had also been invited. This party looked like being rather more decorous than the last one.

Nevertheless, Rose still felt that she would have preferred to stay in her digs and read a good book. There was something threatening and predatory about the large number of young men looking for dancing partners, although their manners were perfect – so far, at least. When the dancing began she succeeded in avoiding the early invitations but when the other girls returned she was bombarded with questions and exhortations.

'Come on, Rose! What's the matter?'

'Why aren't you dancing? You're a brilliant ballroom dancer.'

'We're here to enjoy ourselves, aren't we? Let yourself go, Rose!'

She smiled and shook her head. 'I'm quite OK sitting here. I think I've really grown out of this sort of thing.'

'Oh, for goodness' sake!' exclaimed Peggy. 'Anybody would think you were forty! You're only young, Rose! What are you – twenty-four?'

'Almost. But I feel older. I expect it's looking after you kids!'

'Kids, indeed!' snorted Violet.

They were interrupted by Alice. 'Oh, look! Do look! Over there, by the bar.' They turned their eyes to the spot she indicated. 'Isn't he just dreamy?' Alice whispered.

The object of her admiration was a USAF lieutenant. At first Rose could see only the back of his head, dark auburn hair as glossy as the coat of a racehorse, and broad shoulders in the perfectly tailored uniform jacket. Then he turned and she had to admit that Alice was right. His golden skin was smooth over high cheekbones and a chin with a distinct dimple in the middle.

'I bet he's in the movies in civvy street,' Peggy said.

'He's gorgeous!' breathed May. 'If only he'd ask one of us to dance!'

'He's bound to be with someone,' Violet said. 'When they're that good looking they always are.'

The MC announced a foxtrot and half a dozen men bore down on Rose and her party. She got up quickly and moved away, heading for the Ladies, but when the other four had been carried off and the disappointed suitors had turned elsewhere she felt it safe to return to her seat. A moment later a voice above her said, 'Pardon me, ma'am, but might I have the honour of this dance?'

The accent was from the deep South and made her think of *Gone with the Wind*. She looked up, and found the handsome lieutenant standing beside her. His eyes were golden brown, thickly fringed with lashes a shade darker than his hair. It crossed her mind that he might have been cast in bronze and for a split second she caught herself wondering whether the rest of his body was the same colour. He was smiling, but there was a hint of diffidence in his manner and she realised suddenly that he was much younger than he looked from a distance. She smiled in return and rose to her feet.

She discovered very quickly that he was an excellent dancer. She had not had such a partner since she danced the tango with Felix at the Big House in Wimborne two Christmases earlier – not since she and Richard . . . She closed her mind quickly to the memory and concentrated on her partner.

He smiled down at her. 'May I know your name, ma'am?'

'It's Rose,' she said. 'Rose Taylor. What's yours?'

They danced three consecutive foxtrots and then Rose excused herself, and this time she really did go to the Ladies. When she came out of the cubicle Violet and Peggy and Alice were waiting for her.

'Well?' Violet demanded.

'Well what?' Rose countered, trying to pretend innocence. 'What's he like?'

'He's very charming.'

'Yes.' Peggy could always be relied upon for a caustic comment. 'And I bet he knows it too!'

'No, I don't think so,' Rose said. 'Actually, I think he's quite shy.'

'Shy!' exclaimed Peggy. 'I don't believe that.'

'Oh, Rose, you're so lucky!' Alice murmured. 'We're all so jealous!'

'I don't see why,' Rose said.

'For goodness' sake!' Violet said. 'This man looks like Clark Gable and dances like Fred Astaire. What more could a girl ask for?'

Rose found herself smiling in spite of herself. 'He is rather gorgeous, isn't he?'

'What's his name, Rose?' Alice asked.

'His name?' Rose drew a deep breath and forced herself to keep a straight face. 'His name is Beauregard Lafontaine.'

'It's what?' squeaked Peggy.

'It's not!' snorted Violet.

They both collapsed in giggles and Rose, in spite of all her efforts, joined them. 'It is! It is!' she gasped.

'I think it's lovely,' Alice said. '*So* romantic!'

'Is that what you have to call him?' Violet asked.

'No,' Rose replied, in control again now. 'He says his friends call him Beau.'

'Like Beau Brummel,' said Peggy. 'Or Beau Geste.'

'Oh, I loved that film!' Alice said dreamily. 'You are lucky, Rose!'

'Look,' Rose said firmly, 'it was just a couple of dances. I expect he's found someone else by now.'

But when she went out he was waiting for her and immediately swept her away for a quickstep, whirling her across the floor so deftly that she felt that her feet were hardly making contact with the ground. At the end of the next set of dances supper was announced and Beau led her through to an area of the hangar that had been curtained off. Here a sumptuous spread was laid out, the like of which Rose had not seen since the start of rationing – and not often before that. Huge pieces of ham gleamed pinkly under the lights and enormous turkeys exposed their pale breasts to the carving knife. There were great bowls of salad and mounds of rolls – even slabs of real butter. Then there were the cakes. Rose had never seen cakes like these, thick with chocolate or cream and frosted with icing. There was even ice cream, and dishes of exotic fruits, pineapples and peaches, which Rose could recall seeing only in tins. As Beau led her along the table she had to resist the urge to pile her plate with everything in reach. He, however, seemed to have no such inhibitions and insisted on loading her plate with various delicacies, including little black fruits that she thought were grapes but which, when bitten into, turned out to have a powerful and rather bitter flavour. She found out later that they were olives.

As soon as they had finished eating he insisted on going back to the dance floor, though she protested that she had eaten far too much to be able to walk, let alone dance. After a couple of slow waltzes she recovered, however, and they danced more or less non-stop for the next hour. Eventually, she begged for a rest and a breath of fresh air and they went outside.

He said, 'You sure are the best dancer I've ever met in my life.'

'You're pretty nifty on your feet yourself,' she returned. 'Not many men dance like you.'

'Aw . . .' He grinned sheepishly. 'I guess I've always wanted to be Fred Astaire. I saw one of his films when I was a kid and I thought he was just fantastic. I still like to watch them and imagine it's me up there on the screen.'

'Did you ever think of trying to get into movies?' she asked.

'Who, me?' The idea seemed to come as a surprise to him. 'I wouldn't know how to start. Anyway, I'm here now. I guess there isn't going to be much chance of a movie career or anything else for a while.'

'You're a pilot, aren't you?' Rose said. 'Do you fly one of those big bombers?'

'Sure do!'

Rose shivered slightly. She had watched the huge planes taking off and forming up in great waves before heading out to sea – heading for German cities where women and children were experiencing the same terror that she had known during the Blitz in London. She knew that when the news bulletins reported raids on cities like Cologne or Danzig most people reacted by saying 'Serves them right. They're getting a taste of their own medicine!' But she remembered what Coventry had looked like and could only feel pity for the German people.

He sensed her reaction and said quietly, 'I know how you feel. I don't like what I'm doing, either. But I guess we don't have any choice in the matter.'

'No,' she agreed. 'I guess we don't.'

He changed the subject by asking her how she had got into ENSA and she told him about her earlier career as a dancer, but found herself skating over the intervening time when she had worked on the land. She did not mention Matthew – or Richard.

As they went back inside the MC announced the last waltz and Beau led Rose back on to the dance floor. Until now he had held her close enough for her to sense his movements but never less than correctly. Now, as they drifted along, he drew her closer and she felt his cheek against her hair. She found she liked the smell of his skin, the feel of his arm around her, the way their bodies moved in unison. Sensations awoke within her that she had repressed for almost two years.

When the dance ended he took her arm and escorted her back to the battered old ENSA bus that had brought them to the base. A short distance from it he stopped and took her hands. 'Rose, can I see you again?'

She had been anticipating that and preparing all sorts of excuses. 'I'm afraid it's not going to be possible, Beau. We have to move on tomorrow. We have one more date, near St Albans, then we're back in London, and I don't know where I shall be sent after that.'

'Will you be in London for a while?'

'Possibly. I really don't know.'

'Do you have an address there? Could I write you?'

She hesitated. The she found herself dictating her address in Lambeth. He wrote it down carefully.

'Do you have a telephone?'

'No, I'm afraid not.'

'If I can get some leave, may I call on you?'

'If you like. But do write first, or send a telegram. I might not be there.'

'I'll do that,' he promised. He took her hands again. 'I've really enjoyed tonight. I can't think when I've enjoyed an evening so much.'

'Yes, I've enjoyed it too,' she agreed.

He bent his head and kissed her on the cheek. 'I sure hope we'll be able to meet again, Rose.' Then he led her to the bus and saw her safely on board.

19

With Pat O'Leary and Ginny and the new man, Fabian, Richard spent the day following his confrontation with Cole hanging around the flat in a ferment of impatience and anxiety. Ullmann, the tailor, had promised the prison officer's uniform in forty-eight hours. It was impossible to do it in less. First thing the next morning, O'Leary collected the finished garments and took the train to Bergerac. Ginny went with him, leaving Richard to travel separately with Fabian. They were to rendezvous at a certain café close to the station.

When they arrived, they found Ginny and Tom Groome waiting for them. O'Leary had gone on ahead to contact the guard. He returned after an hour looking grimmer than Richard had ever seen him.

'It's a disaster!' he said. 'All our plans have gone for nothing. Now that Germany has occupied the whole country the French army is to be disbanded and the guarding of the prisoners at Meauzeac is to be taken over by civilian prison officers. All the uniforms will be different.'

'When does this happen?' Richard asked.

'Tonight.'

'Then our man won't be there after today?'

'Yes. He's keeping his job. It's just the uniform that is changing. But he says Ian is to be moved within the next four or five days, perhaps sooner.'

'Can we get a new uniform made in time?' Ginny asked.

'Who knows? They could decide to move Ian tomorrow, for all we know.'

'Isn't it worth a try?'

O'Leary considered. 'There is one positive point. The new guards are being drawn from prisons all round the area. That means they won't know each other, so they are less likely to notice a stranger walking out with them. If we could get the new uniform . . .' He got up. 'I'll go back to Toulouse and see Ullmann. It may be possible. Ginny can come with me. The rest of you had better go to the farm and wait. Tom knows where it is.'

They passed a tense twenty-four hours. The next day Ginny returned alone.

'Well?' Richard asked eagerly.

She shook her head doubtfully. 'It's touch and go. Ullmann hasn't got any of the right fabric. He's trying a colleague to see if he can produce some. If he can, Ullmann will try to get it ready, but he doesn't make any promises.'

None of them slept well that night, although they knew that if everything went according to plan they would get precious little sleep the next. The next morning O'Leary returned triumphant.

'God knows how they managed it, but the uniform is ready – braid, badges, the lot! They sewed all night, Ullmann and his wife. I've delivered it to our guard, with the first half of the money. Now all we can do is hope he carries out his part of the bargain.'

At midnight O'Leary, Richard and Fabian piled into the farmer's battered old car and drove through the narrow, twisting country lanes to the clearing in the forest. It was a risky business, but the farmer assured them that he had seen no German patrols or roadblocks in the area and they reached their destination without incident. The winter night was bitter and it was still dark when they moved off through the trees towards the castle, but it was not hard to locate the building, since its walls were brilliantly floodlit. Meauzeac stood on a small hill, separated from where they were by a steep-sided ravine, which was bridged at the point where the main gate opened by a causeway leading to the road. This causeway was fenced on each side by a triple row of barbed wire, and at its end were the two towers that O'Leary had mentioned in his briefing.

Fabian took up position within range of the nearest tower while O'Leary concealed himself in a ditch close to the road. Richard made his way farther along the slope to a point where he could see the guard manning the machine gun at the top of the other tower. He took out his revolver and sighted along it at the dark silhouette, which stood out clearly against the floodlit walls. He had discovered at Arisaig that he was a good shot, but he was at the extreme limit of his range. With luck he might be able to take out the gunner before he did too much damage, but it would require a very steady aim. He wriggled into a position where he could rest his arms on a fallen tree trunk and waited. In the cold air he was beginning to shiver. He put his gun in his pocket and clasped his hands under his armpits. It would not help if his fingers were too numb to pull the trigger.

As the first signs of dawn showed beyond the mountains he became aware of a noise from behind him. A truck was approaching along the road. It took him a moment to realise that this was the day shift arriving for duty. The vehicle stopped just out of sight and a moment later he saw the men tramping across the bridge. A postern gate in the great door was opened and they vanished inside. Silence fell. The minutes ticked by. Then the gate opened again and he heard voices. In a moment a stream of men in the same uniform appeared. They were talking and laughing among themselves, calling out goodnights to the guards in the towers, stamping their feet against the cold. He strained his eyes for a familiar figure. The first men had reached the far side of the bridge now and were climbing into the truck. Then he saw Ian. He was a head taller than the rest, though he walked with his shoulders slumped. Richard levelled his revolver and held his breath. The tall figure passed across the bridge and disappeared. The gate was closed. The engine of the truck fired and he heard it reversing. Then the noise faded into the distance.

For a moment Richard remained still, straining his ears for the sound of a challenge. Then he holstered his revolver and scrambled to his feet. By the time he reached the road it was empty and silent. He flitted across and headed for the clearing. A few paces away from it his way was blocked by a shadowy figure, but it was only Fabian keeping guard.

Suddenly, the silence was rent by the whining rattle of the old car's starter motor. It went on, whirring and churning, for what seemed an impossibly long time, but the engine failed to fire. Richard and Fabian exchanged agonised looks. The noise must be audible for miles in the quiet of the winter dawn. Again the motor whirred and again the engine remained dead. Richard started forward but, as he did so, the large figure of the farmer climbed ponderously out of the driving seat and went imperturbably to the front of the car. He cranked the starting handle once or twice and the engine burst into life. They watched as the car, with two figures in the back seat, bounced away through the trees.

'Is Ian in there with Pat?' Richard asked.

'Yes. When he reached the truck he just turned aside and pretended to pee. Then, while the rest were climbing aboard, he simply walked into the trees.'

'How did he look?'

'Very weak, but he's incredibly calm. Such courage!'

'I know,' said Richard. 'Well, he's out, thank God! Now all we have to do is get him home.'

They had to walk back to the village. By the time they reached the houses the curfew was over and people were going about their daily business. Dressed in the inconspicuous blue jacket and trousers of the French peasant, they joined the queue for a local bus and were soon back in Bergerac. From there they took the train to Toulouse and made their way to the flat above the dress shop. Ginny joined them shortly afterwards.

'Pat and Ian are safe at the farm. Tom radioed London to let them know that the first stage had been successful,' she said, 'but Ian is so weak they decided to stay where they are for the time being to give him a chance to rest. Pat will contact us here when he needs us.'

The following day dragged by without news, but at about midday on the day after they were taken by surprise to see two figures approaching the shop, one slight, the other tall and apparently the worse for drink, supporting himself on his companion's shoulder. There were footsteps on the stairs and then O'Leary staggered in and lowered Garrow into a chair. Richard was horrified to see that the big man he remembered had been reduced to a living skeleton.

The indomitable spirit, however, was undimmed. Garrow looked around the room and exclaimed, 'Richard! What are you doing here? I heard rumours the Gestapo had picked you up last year.'

'Inaccurate ones, fortunately,' Richard said, shaking hands. 'It's good to see you, Ian.' Then he caught the glimmer of a smile on O'Leary's face and realised that they had both spoken in English. He lifted his shoulders in a small shrug of surrender and Garrow said, 'Hang on. Have I put my foot in it?'

O'Leary said quietly, 'Don't worry, *mon ami*. We all realised a long time ago that Ricardo is not Italian. Besides, you gave yourself away the other day, Richard, when you said that Ian had got you out of France in 1940.'

'So I did!' Richard said. 'It's a good job you're not the Gestapo!' He passed the incident off lightly, but it worried him that he could have made such an elementary mistake, even in the company of someone as trustworthy as O'Leary.

While Ginny ministered to Garrow, O'Leary explained what had happened.

'At dawn yesterday morning a German patrol came to the farm, asking if the farmer had seen anyone lurking around his outbuildings. He managed to fob them off and they didn't search the house, thank God, but he insisted that we should leave immediately. We had to make our way across country because the roads were swarming with German patrols. It was hard going, especially for Ian. He's in a bad way. Apparently they've been kept on a starvation diet for months.'

'What happened to Tom?' Richard asked.

'He'd already gone back to his usual base, with his radio set. I hope to God he got there safely.'

'So, what now?' Richard asked.

'Ian will have to hide up here until he's fit to travel,' O'Leary said. 'With the Germans in occupation the beaches are sealed off, so there's no chance of a pick-up by sea. He will have to go over the mountains, so we will need to get his strength up.' He looked at Richard. 'And you, *mon ami*. You too must go, and soon. Now that Cole is active again it would be crazy for you to remain in France.'

'I'll wait until Ian is ready,' Richard said.

O'Leary shook his head. 'No, I want you to go at once, before the passes are blocked by snow. I need you to take Ginny. She could be interned at any moment and I don't want to send her on her own. I'm sure you see the sense of that.'

Unwillingly, Richard had to admit that he did.

The next day he and Ginny left for Marseilles, where Richard spent a night at the Rodocanachis' flat while Ginny went to make her farewells to her husband. He found Fanny Rodocanachi looking even more frail than on his earlier visits.

When he was alone with the doctor he said, 'You should both leave France, you know. You have done enough, more than enough.'

The doctor sighed and shook his head, smiling sadly. 'Pat has tried to persuade me of that, too. But it is impossible. Fanny is sick. She could never withstand the journey. I must remain here with her.'

Richard and Ginny were to travel to Perpignan under their usual guise of a pair of lovers heading for their secret love nest. Here, later that day, they were joined by O'Leary himself. He reported that Garrow was making good progress, under the care of Françoise Dissart, and should be able to travel in a few weeks. He had left him in order to escort them personally on the last stage of their journey.

The next morning a taxi took them up into the mountains to the village where they were to meet their guide. It was not the huge, piratical-looking Florentino, who had escorted Richard on his first crossing, but a small, lean man who spoke little and then in an incomprehensible patois.

O'Leary walked the first part of the way with them. At the top of a rise he stopped and held out his hand to Ginny. 'I must turn back here. I need to get back to Ian. *Bonne chance, ma chère!*'

Ginny threw her arms round his neck. 'Take care, Pat! We can't afford to lose you!'

He detached himself, smiling gently. 'None of us is indispensable, you know. But I hope we shall meet again, either in England or perhaps here, when the war is over.' He turned to Richard and offered his hand. 'Many thanks, *mon brave*, for all your help. Tell them at Room 900 that we shall continue for as long as possible to send back your airmen.'

'But for how long can that go on?' Richard asked, clasping his hand. 'Pat, you should come out with Ian! You said yourself that the line is under suspicion. It is only a matter of time.'

'But in that time we may yet save several lives,' O'Leary said quietly. 'Who knows how many? We cannot abandon the people who have come to rely on us. Now, you must go. Take care. Until we meet again!'

Richard abandoned his ingrained English reserve and embraced him in the French fashion. O'Leary kissed him on both cheeks, kissed Ginny in the same manner and turned away. They watched him going back down the slope until a fold in the landscape hid him from sight.

For Richard the rest of the journey had an eerie sense of déjà vu. He even recognised certain features of the landscape as they climbed higher into the mountains. At least, this time, his stomach was not playing up, but even so it was a long, hard slog. The guide led them at a relentlessly rapid pace and Richard, watching Ginny's slim but apparently indefatigable legs striding out ahead of him, felt a renewed surge of admiration.

This time, there was no encounter with the Spanish Frontier guards and they were able to take the train to Barcelona. By the following evening they were in Gibraltar.

Here they had to part company. Richard received orders that he was to return on a plane leaving the next day. Ginny would have to wait a little longer. He went to her hotel room to tell her the news.

She put her hands on his shoulders and looked into his eyes. 'We'll meet again, won't we?'

'Of course,' he said. 'In England. Here's my address in London.' He scribbled the address of Priscilla's flat on a scrap of paper and gave it to her. Then he added, 'What will you do?'

'I'm not sure. I won't be giving up the fight, you can be sure of that.'

He smiled. 'I can't imagine you ever giving up.'

She tilted her head. 'Perhaps you could put in a good word for me. I don't know who you work for, but maybe they could do with some extra help.'

He shook his head. 'I don't think they take women.'

'More fools them, then!' Ginny said.

'I agree. From what I've seen, you girls can often be worth half a dozen men.'

She kissed him lightly on the cheek. 'We've had some fun, haven't we?'

'We certainly have. It's a pity you're married.'

'It's a pity we both are!'

He kissed her properly then and she responded warmly. But after a few seconds she drew back.

'No, Richard. We're not going to give way, after all this time. We'd only feel awful about it afterwards. Let's just stay good friends.'

He sighed and let her go. 'You're right, of course – but it's a shame.'

'You'll get over it,' she told him. 'Tomorrow you'll be back with your wife.'

When Richard got stiffly out of the plane in the twilight of an English December evening he saw that a car was waiting for him on the tarmac, but he did not immediately recognise the trimly uniformed driver who stood to attention by the open door. Only when she saluted and said, 'Welcome home, sir!' did he realise who it was.

'Priss! Darling, what on earth are you doing here?'

She abandoned her formal attitude and threw herself into his arms. 'Oh, darling, darling! It's so good to see you! Welcome back!'

He held her tightly, aware of the half-forgotten response of his body to her slight, vital form. 'Sweetheart! It's wonderful to be back with you! How are you?'

'I'm fine!' She drew back a little and looked at him. 'And you? Are you all right?'

'Yes. I'm OK. Tired and stiff, but OK.'

The aircrew were making their way past them, casting amused looks in their direction. Richard said, 'What are you doing here? You're not a driver.'

She laughed. 'I know. But Jimmy tipped me the wink that you were on your way back and I knew they'd send a FANY driver to collect you, so I found out who it was and bribed her to swap with me.' She kissed him and then drew back. 'Come along. Let's go home, so we can say hello properly!'

20

The day after their return to London the whole company of *Lighten up!* was instructed to assemble in the main theatre bar at Drury Lane, where they were addressed by Bob Ricardo, the head of the variety section.

'I expect you'd all like to go home for Christmas,' he began, and there were hopeful murmurs from the company. 'But I'm afraid that isn't going to be possible,' he went on. The announcement was greeted with sighs of disappointment but no one raised an objection. They had not really expected to get leave at this time of year. 'The boys in the forces need all the cheering up we can give them at this time,' Bob went on. 'So I'm afraid you've all been booked to entertain units in Essex between Christmas and New Year. But after that, I promise you, you will get some leave.'

When the meeting was over, Bob called Rose over to him. 'Mr Dean wants a word with you in his office.'

'Mr Dean!' Rose said, dismayed. Basil Dean was one of the leading impresarios in London and had been in charge of ENSA since its inception. He rarely had direct dealings with humble members of a touring concert party. 'What have I done?'

'Nothing to worry about,' Bob reassured her. 'Just pop along and see him and he'll explain everything.'

Basil Dean looked up from a mound of paperwork and frowned at her.

'I'm Rose Taylor,' she explained hesitantly. 'Mr Ricardo said you wanted to see me.'

Dean smiled. 'Ah, you're Rose! Come in and sit down. It's all right. Don't look so nervous.'

When she was seated he went on, 'I didn't announce myself, but I was out front during the show in St Albans. I was very impressed with the dancing. And especially with your little solo. Am I right in thinking that you choreographed that yourself?'

'Yes, Mr Dean,' she answered breathlessly.

'And all the other dances in the show too?'

'Yes, Mr Dean.'

'How would you like to choreograph the numbers for a much larger troupe?'

'Me? I don't know!' Rose was desperately trying to catch up with a situation that was developing in a most unexpected way. 'How much larger?'

'Probably twelve dancers in the chorus and a couple of soloists. I'm putting together a much bigger company to tour some of the main venues. I need someone to arrange the dances and look after the girls. I think you would do it very well. What do you say?'

'It would mean leaving Monty . . . Mr Prince's company?'

'Yes, I'm afraid so. But you must think about your own career. Of course, I should want you to do a solo yourself – two perhaps. It would be a shame to waste talent like yours.'

Rose swallowed. Her throat had suddenly gone dry. She knew that this was her great opportunity, a chance that would probably never come again, but she was terrified. Then she suddenly remembered the resolution she had made back in the summer, when she was down in Wimborne. If she was going to be a spinster, she wasn't going to end up as an embittered old woman with no interests in life. She was going to make a career for herself.

'Thank you very much, Mr Dean,' she said. 'If you think I'm up to it, I'd like that very much.'

'Good,' Dean responded. 'I want you to start auditioning dancers straight away. Clifford Wallace is producing, so he'll fill in all the details for you. Report to me tomorrow morning and I'll introduce you to him.'

Rose approached Monty Prince rather hesitantly with her news but his response, as usual, was generous.

'Well done, girl! You deserve a step up the ladder. I always knew you had it in you.'

Two days later she returned to the flat to find Beau sitting on the doorstep. He rose to his feet as she approached and greeted her with the warm, slow smile she remembered from that first evening.

'They told me at the pub across the road that you were home,' he said. 'I'm sure glad I caught up with you.'

'You should have sent a wire,' she said, flustered by his sudden appearance. 'If my job hadn't changed I'd be somewhere in Essex by now.'

'Essex?' he queried. 'Where's that?'

She laughed. 'You make it sound like the far side of the moon! Come on up. I'll make us some tea.'

As she led him upstairs she was uncomfortably aware of how small and dingy the flat must appear, and how run down and scruffy the neighbourhood. Did he realise, she wondered, that he had come to one of the poorest areas of London, or did he assume that the whole city was like this?

'I'm afraid this isn't quite what you were expecting,' she said, taking him into the sitting room.

'How do you mean?' he asked.

'Well, I expect you have a beautiful home in America,' she said.

He looked around the room. 'Well, I guess it's larger,' he said. 'But then, we have a lot more space. This is kind of . . . cosy.'

'It's not very cosy at the moment,' Rose said. 'I'll light the fire. It'll soon warm up.'

He insisted on lighting the fire for her and she turned away, automatically heading for the kitchen to put the kettle on, and then turned back. 'Do you drink tea? Or you could go across the road and bring back some beer.'

'Do you have any coffee?'

'No, I'm sorry, I haven't.'

'Then tea will be just fine.'

He followed her into the kitchen and asked, 'Is this home, or is this just somewhere to stay when you're in London?'

'It's where I grew up,' she told him. 'It's my mother's flat, but she's moved down to the country to avoid the Blitz.' She set out cups and saucers and asked, 'Where do you live, in the States?'

'Virginia,' he said. 'Madison County.'

'I bet your family have a cotton plantation,' she said.

He frowned. 'No, they have a farm – a dairy farm. What makes you think we grow cotton?'

'A dairy farm?' she said. 'Oh well, at least that's something I know a bit about.'

'How's that?' he asked. 'Guess there aren't many cattle round these parts.'

'No,' she agreed, laughing. 'Not many cows in Lambeth! But I have worked on a dairy farm, all the same.'

Over tea and toast, on which he quite innocently used up her entire week's ration of butter, she explained about her

time as a Land Girl. But she still found herself skating over
her relationship with Matthew and her reasons for moving to
Shropshire. While they talked, half her mind was occupied
with the state of her larder. There was one egg left from her
ration and she had been planning to boil it for her supper,
but there was no way she could make it stretch to a meal for
two.

She was greatly relieved when he said, 'Well, little lady.
Time to get your glad rags on. I'm taking you out dancing.'

When she had changed he asked, 'Where do you want to
go? I heard there's a place called the Café de Paris that's
supposed to be good.'

Rose shuddered. 'No, we can't go there. It used to be very
popular, because people thought that being below ground
level it was safe from the bombs. But one night a huge bomb
came right through the ceiling and killed the bandleader and
over thirty of the dancers.'

So they went to the Lyceum instead and danced the night
away to Geraldo and his orchestra. As the evening drew to a
close Rose began to worry about where Beau was intending to
spend the night but it turned out that he had already found
himself a room in a hotel.

He insisted on taking her home in a taxi and as they crossed
the river he said, 'How long will you be in London?'

'I don't know,' she replied. 'If I get some leave I'll go down
to see my mother and sister in Dorset. But I'll have to be here
for a week or two, rehearsing this new show.'

'Maybe I can come up again and we could go dancing
again?' he asked.

She smiled. 'I'd like that.'

He got out of the taxi and took her right to her door, then
removed his cap and bent to kiss her, very gently, on the lips.

She went to bed humming 'Chattanooga Choo-choo' and feeling happier than she had done for a very long time.

Merry was neither surprised nor disappointed to learn that he and his company could not expect any time off over Christmas. In fact, it was a relief. The prospect of spending the so-called festive season alone, with nothing to distract him from his memories, was too terrible to contemplate. As it was, there were plenty of bibulous mess dinners to get him through to the beginning of each evening's performance. Better still, as he was moving on each day, he could always wheedle a new bottle of Scotch out of the mess officer, so that he had sufficient to induce the requisite degree of numbness that would allow him to sleep. He had given up trying to kid himself that he was making a bottle last longer than twenty-four hours.

Even so, he began to be aware over the Christmas period that he could not go on much longer in this manner. He felt that he was being pursued by shadowy figures, the ghosts of Felix and Rose and Richard and his own dead father. It was useless to remind himself that two of these people were still alive and could not, therefore, be ghosts. They continued to stand in the corner of his room, just beyond the edge of his peripheral vision, watching him with pity but also with shame. When he played the piano they stood behind his shoulder and cringed every time he played a wrong note. He wanted to apologise for letting them down so badly, but whenever he tried they vanished.

He survived Christmas itself and the days immediately following but the catastrophe came on New Year's Eve.

He managed to get through the first part of the programme that night without incident, but then the tenor came on to do his turn. He had a good voice but his choice of songs leaned heavily towards the sentimental ballads that were so popular at the time. Usually Merry was able to switch off, playing the accompaniment without taking in the words, but on this night of all nights the singer had chosen 'These Foolish Things'.

He got through the first verse all right. It was the next one that undid him, with its reference to 'a tinkling piano in the next apartment, The stumbling words that told you what my heart meant, And still the ghost of you clings . . .'

The singer stopped abruptly as the piano accompaniment ceased on a discordant crash. There were some boos and jeers from the audience, but Merry was only dimly aware of them. His head was on the keyboard and his whole body was racked with uncontrollable sobs. It was a moment before he felt hands gripping his arms, pulling him to his feet, and heard voices muttering words of encouragement and reproof. Still sobbing, supported on either side by two members of the band, he allowed himself to be led out of the room.

21

Two days later Merry sat opposite George Black in his office in Grosvenor Street. He had not had a drink for thirty-six hours and his hands were shaking, while the blinding headache of the previous day had dulled to a steady throb that no amount of aspirin seemed to touch. His eyes felt as if they were full of sand and his insides gave him the impression that he had been gutted and the space filled up with icy water.

Black looked at him and shook his head sadly. 'Oh dear, oh dear, Merry. What are we going to do with you?'

Merry started to shake his head in response, winced and shrugged instead.

'Look here,' said Black, 'I'd like to send you to see one of the army's trick cyclists.'

Merry raised his eyes and forced himself to focus on his senior officer's face. 'A psychiatrist? Oh no, George! Please, not that! I couldn't stand that.'

'You need help, old chap,' Black said earnestly. 'I don't know what to do for you. I can't send you back to work like this.'

'But not that!' Merry insisted again. 'I couldn't bear to be sent to one of those special hospitals for men with shell shock, or whatever they call it these days. It would finish me, George. I'd never come out again. Besides, what could I tell a psychiatrist? I could never talk about what really matters.'

'I don't suppose it would be anything they haven't heard before,' Black pointed out. 'These chaps are used to dealing with all sorts of cases, you know.'

'All the same,' Merry said, 'he – whoever it was – would have to report what I'd told him. And you know what that would mean, George. I don't have to go into details. It means I'd be cashiered for . . . I don't know, what do they call it? Moral turpitude? Conduct unbecoming? Perhaps that wouldn't matter. I've pretty well finished myself as far as the army is concerned anyway. But it would sully *his* reputation, too. He's a hero now. I want him to be remembered like that. Whatever you do with me, George, wherever you send me, I swear I won't talk to anyone about why I'm in this state.'

Black looked at him in silence for a long moment. Then he said, 'OK. You tell me what I'm supposed to do. Let you drink yourself to death? And ruin the reputation of SIB in the process?' Merry hung his head and after a pause Black went on gently, 'Do you really think you're doing justice to his memory the way you're going on now? Is this the way Felix would want you to remember him?'

Slowly Merry looked up. 'All right. Give me a chance to get myself straight, George. Give me a couple of weeks' leave and let me see if I can pull myself together.'

Black regarded him shrewdly. 'Where would you go? Is there someone who'll keep an eye on you? I'm not sending you off to brood on your own for two weeks.' Merry shook his head silently and Black went on, 'What about those people who looked after you when you came out of hospital that time? Down in Devon, wasn't it?'

'Dorset,' Merry said. Until now he had rejected all thought of returning to the Willises but suddenly they seemed to offer the only possibility of escape. 'I suppose I could ask,' he murmured doubtfully. 'But it's not fair to expect them to take me in, in this condition.'

'Then you'll have to do something about it, won't you?' Black said. 'You've got to get off the booze, Merry. That's a condition of me going along with this idea. I'll write you off for three weeks' sick leave. You have to promise me that you'll go teetotal for the whole of that time. If you can come back at the end of that time and look me in the eye and swear that you haven't touched a drop I'll send you back to work. Otherwise, it's the trick cyclist.'

Merry regarded him despairingly. 'You don't give me much choice, do you?'

'And you'll go and stay with these friends down in Dorset?'

'Yes, if they'll have me.'

Black pushed the phone across to him. 'Ring them now. No time like the present.'

Wearily Merry picked up the phone and asked for the Willises' number. After a short wait Enid Willis's warm West Country tones came down the line.

'Hello, Enid? It's Guy Merryweather.'

'Merry! How lovely to hear you! How are you?'

'Not too good, I'm afraid. I . . . . I've been ill. That's why I'm ringing. I was wondering if I could come down and stay for a few days.'

'My dear, of course you can! You know you're always welcome. I am sorry to hear you've been poorly again. Is it that wretched old chest of yours playing up again?'

'Well, partly that,' Merry lied. 'But don't worry. I'm not infectious or anything.'

'Well, you come along down as soon as you can, my dear,' Mrs Willis said. 'When shall we expect you?'

Merry hesitated and looked across at Black. 'Today?' Black nodded. 'Today, as long as I can get a train.'

Merry reached Wimborne that evening and Jack Willis picked him up from the station. His first evening at the Willises' was torture. The craving for a drink was almost sending him crazy and the tremor in his hands was worse than ever, and in addition he had to endure their sympathetic condolences on the death of Felix. Mrs Taylor and Bet came over from their new cottage and the three women fussed round him as they had done when he was recuperating from pneumonia, but whereas he had found their concern touching before, now it maddened him almost beyond endurance.

Worse was to come, for the next day Bet's two boys, Billy and Sam, came to visit. They had obviously been warned that Uncle Merry was not well and they had to be quiet and considerate, but they were bursting to show him the bicycles that their mother and grandmother had somehow acquired for them for Christmas. They were not new, of course. Such things were more or less unobtainable these days, but they had been bought from another family whose boys had outgrown them and lovingly refurbished by Jack Willis. Merry did his best to seem enthusiastic and to be patient as they demonstrated their expertise in the saddle by riding around the orchard, but the effort left him shaking and covered in a cold sweat.

It was the following afternoon, when he was sitting crouched over the fire in a vain effort to get warm, that he heard voices in the hall. The door opened and Rose came in. For a moment their eyes met and then she crossed the room and dropped on her knees by his chair.

'Oh, Merry! Why didn't you tell me things were this bad?'

He shrugged evasively. 'I don't know what you're talking about.'

'Yes you do,' she said. 'Mum wired me and told me you were ill, but it's not that, is it? What can I do to help?'

Merry turned his head away. 'No one can help. It's no good, Rose! I just can't manage without him. I know it sounds feeble, when hundreds of other people are having to cope with losing husbands and sons and brothers and friends. I know we're all supposed to be able to grin and bear it, carry on regardless, stiff upper lip and all those ghastly catchphrases – but I can't do it. I can't bear the thought that I'll never see him again!'

'Oh, Merry, love!' She put her arms around him and he buried his face in her shoulder. 'Poor love, poor old Merry!' she crooned, stroking his hair. When he lifted his head his face was wet and she got out her handkerchief and gently mopped his cheeks.

'Look at me,' he muttered. 'I'm a wreck. I'm ashamed of myself. I can't even play the piano any more. Look.' He held out his hands so that she could see how they shook.

She took them in her own and held them tightly. 'It will get better, Merry. I know that's hard to believe now, but I know what I'm talking about.'

'I promised George Black I'd lay off the drink for three whole weeks,' Merry muttered. 'But I can't do it, Rose.'

'Yes you can,' she said firmly. 'Listen. I've never talked about this, but I do know what it's like. You remember my father was in the first war? He died when I was only twelve and Mum thinks I don't remember much, but I do. He couldn't forget the trenches. He used to wake up at night, screaming. Then he started to drink, to try to forget. I can still remember him coming home smelling of whisky and shouting at Mum, and knocking things over. Then, one day, he decided to quit. I don't know why. Perhaps Mum threatened to leave him and take us with her. I don't know. But he made up his mind he wasn't going to touch another drop. His hands used to shake like this. When he felt really bad he used to ask me to sit on his lap, and he'd put his arms round me and I could feel his whole body shaking.'

'Weren't you frightened?'

'No. He was my dad. I knew he'd never hurt me. I just wanted to help him. But it passed, Merry. That's the point! After a few days the shaking got less and eventually he was back to being his old self. He never got over the war, I don't mean that. But at least he didn't drink any more – and I don't think he had the nightmares any more either.' She gazed intently up into his face. 'Time does heal, Merry. You think you can't bear something, but then time passes and in the end you find you can live with it. Believe me. I know!'

He looked down at her. 'Poor Rose. You've had your bad times, I know that. But you've always been braver. You never cracked up like me.'

'Maybe it was because I was sent off to that ghastly farm,' Rose said, with a small smile. 'I was so busy just surviving, I didn't have time to feel sorry for myself.'

'I wanted them to let me go back to active service, you know,' Merry said. 'They wouldn't let me because of my chest. I might have been all right at the front.'

'You might have been killed, too,' Rose said, 'and that would have been a terrible, terrible waste.' Then she added quietly, 'You've got your own battle front right here, Merry. Don't surrender!'

He held her gaze for a moment and squeezed her hands. 'I'll try not to – if you'll help me.'

★ ★ ★

For the next two weeks Rose was his constant companion. She explained that her mother's telegram had come at an opportune moment. They had just finished auditioning the dancers for the new show and she had been able to go to Clifford Wallace and remind him that she had been promised some leave before they started rehearsals.

Every morning they went walking, tramping for miles through the frosty beech woods and along the country paths. And while they walked, they talked. To begin with Rose talked mainly, telling him anecdotes from her experiences touring with Monty Prince and his company and describing her excitement at the challenge of choreographing the new show.

'And the director has given me two solo spots! I'm sticking with the one I worked up for Monty's show, but the other one's going to be much lighter – a tap dance to some Fred Astaire numbers. I wish I could show you, but I haven't got the music with me.'

At first, she did not mention Beau, and when she did it was only in passing. He had come up to London once more between Christmas and New Year and taken her dancing again, and as before it had been a very enjoyable evening. But she was still unable to make up her mind whether it was simply the pleasure of being taken out and the sheer joy of dancing with a good partner or whether it was Beau himself who made her feel so happy.

In the afternoons, as the winter darkness drew in, they sat in the Willises' kitchen or the sitting room of the Taylors' cottage and read or talked or listened to the wireless. They listened to *Hi, Gang!* with Bebe Daniels and Ben Lyon, and *Garrison Theatre* and, of course, *ITMA*, and once they were surprised, though not altogether pleased, to hear their old colleagues

Isabel St Clair and Franklyn Bell singing with George Mel-
achrino and his orchestra.

One afternoon, when they were at the cottage, Rose asked
her mother whether she had heard any more news of Barbara
Willis's impending marriage.

'Her chap's been posted to an aircraft carrier in the Mediterranean,' Mrs Taylor said, 'so there's no chance of a
wedding at the moment. If you ask me it will be for the best
if . . . well, if something happens to make her change her
mind.'

'What do you mean?' Rose asked.

'Well, a Canadian!' her mother returned. 'Just think of her
poor mother. If she marries him and goes off to Canada after
the war Enid'll never see her, or her grandchildren. Oh, she
puts a brave face on it but it'll break her heart if it happens.'

Rose was very quiet for some time after that. She told herself
that the possibility of marrying Beau had never even come into
her head – but if it ever did arise it would break her own
mother's heart if she went off to live in Virginia.

As the days passed Merry found that he was no longer
irritated by the solicitude of his hosts. Instead he found himself
soothed by the quiet domestic routine of these two matriarchal
households. Little by little, as Rose had promised, the head-
aches and cold sweats and tremors of withdrawal eased and he
stopped watching the clock, wondering whether he could get
through the rest of the day without a drink. It helped, of
course, that alcohol did not play a regular part in the lives of
either family, although Jack Willis did suggest once or twice
early on that he might like to go down to the pub for a beer.
That stopped after a day or two and Merry guessed that Rose
had probably dropped a hint to Jack. He still ached, mentally
and sometimes physically as well, for Felix's presence, but he

began to find small pleasures in the crisp, frosty air of the early morning, the warmth of the open fire in the living room of the cottage, light music on the wireless. He was even pleased to discover that Billy, whom he and Felix had taught to play chess on a previous visit, had developed a passion for the game and could now give him a good match.

One thing that surprised and disturbed him slightly was the discovery that Bet was now working for Matthew Armitage. He raised the point with Rose on one of their morning walks. 'Do you mind?'

Rose frowned and shook her head. 'Why should I? No – that's not being honest. I did to start with. But Matt's a good man. He deserved better than he got from me. I'm glad there's someone to look after him a bit. He needs it.'

'I've often wondered,' Merry said, 'if Richard hadn't turned up that night, would you have married Matt?'

'Oh yes, I expect so,' Rose agreed. 'After all, I had said I would.'

'Do you ever look back now and think that it might have been best that way?'

Rose walked on a few paces in silence before answering. 'Sometimes. I can imagine it would have been quite nice, looking after the farm, being . . . settled. But I don't think it would have been right, really. I mean, I was fond of Matt, but I wasn't in love with him. I can see that now.'

'You don't think it would have worked out?'

'Oh, I expect we'd have rubbed along all right. But it would have meant I never went back to the stage, and I think I would have regretted that sooner or later. It's better this way. I really enjoy what I'm doing.'

'I'm glad,' Merry said. 'It's good that someone has finally recognised how talented you are.'

She smiled at him. 'Thank you kindly, sir,' she said. Then she added, 'It's a pity we work for rival outfits, isn't it? It would be nice if we could do a show together.'

'I wouldn't call us rival outfits exactly,' Merry demurred.

'Oh!' She laughed. 'You should hear what they say at ENSA HQ about Army Welfare!'

'What do they say?'

'Oh, you know. There was a lot of bad feeling apparently when the Army Welfare people decided that they could provide all the entertainment for their own people and they didn't need ENSA muscling in, thank you very much. Of course, they've changed their minds about that now, but a lot of ENSA people still think we're given all the third-rate dates and sent off on wild-goose chases wherever possible.'

'Do you think that's true?' Merry asked.

'I don't know. It is true that we quite often arrive in places and find that no one has told them we're coming.'

'Well, that happens to us, too,' Merry told her. 'I think it's more a matter of lack of organisation than deliberate malice.'

'All the same,' she said, 'it is a pity we can't work together, isn't it?'

'Yes,' he agreed, looking at her affectionately. 'I should enjoy that.'

'I don't suppose it would be any good me enlisting in the ATS and hoping to get transferred to Stars in Battledress, is it?' she suggested, half seriously.

'I'm afraid we don't have women,' he said.

'What, no women at all?'

'No, not at the moment anyway.'

'Why not?'

'Well, you can't send women into a battle zone, can you?'

'I don't see why not. Women have to put up with their cities being blitzed. That's pretty much the same as being in a battle zone.'

'At least we're not sending them there deliberately. Anyway, it's not up to me to make policy, thank God. It would be nice to have girls, but the powers that be say no, so that's that.'

'That's a bit tough on the chaps, isn't it? I mean, I should have thought that a bit of glamour was what they wanted.'

'Oh, you'd be surprised how many chaps there are who are just itching to dress up as women,' Merry told her. 'And very attractive girls they make, too, some of them. I have actually seen a whole sergeants' mess dancing with the "ladies" of the chorus after a show.'

Rose looked at him. 'Oh! Isn't that a bit . . .' She stopped and blushed. 'I don't mean to criticise . . . Oh, you know what I'm trying to say.'

Merry met her eyes gravely. 'Yes, don't worry, I understand. But it's not what it sounds like. As you say, these men are desperate for a bit of glamour – even if they know it's ersatz.'

'Oh well.' She sighed. 'It was just a thought. Perhaps we can get together after the war. Maybe we could have our own company, like Monty and Dolly.'

He looked down at her and smiled, the first time he had really smiled for months. 'Maybe we could.' It struck him suddenly that it was the first time, too, that he had ever contemplated a future 'after the war'.

The next day they found themselves reminiscing about their days with the Follies and that led, naturally, to mention of Richard – and of Felix.

'I always wanted to ask,' Merry said. 'Did you and Richard have any kind of . . . understanding before the war?'

She shook her head. 'No. That was the trouble, really. He did ask me, once, quite early in the summer, but I told him to wait. I said it was too soon and he'd probably change his mind. I thought I wasn't good enough for him, you see, and if he tied himself up with me in the end he'd come to regret it. Well, I was right, wasn't I? Priscilla's much more the sort of wife he needs. I mean, she's well educated, well spoken. She probably understands the kind of music he really likes much better than I do. And with her money and her connections it's obviously going to be better for his career.'

'Do you think that's why he married her?' Merry asked.

She shrugged. 'How do I know? I didn't think he even knew her very well. He certainly kept very quiet about it.'

'You don't think it's possible that they met up again by chance after . . . after that New Year's Eve?'

She looked at him. 'I suppose they could have done. It's a bit of a coincidence, though, isn't it?'

'Then perhaps he had kept in touch – or kept her address – and he just married her on the rebound,' Merry said. 'I'm convinced he came back for you, Rose, in the first place.'

'Are you?' She was silent for a moment. 'I don't know. Why didn't he write when he was a prisoner? Why hasn't he answered my letter? He must have had the second one I wrote. Anyway . . .' She heaved a long sigh. '. . . it's all water under the bridge now, isn't it?'

They walked on in silence for a while. Then Rose said, 'Can I ask you something?'

'Yes, that's only fair.'

'Why was Felix pretending to be someone else? I mean, the other way round. Why was the Honourable Edward Mountjoy pretending to be Felix? Was it just because he wanted to go on the stage?'

'No,' Merry answered quietly. 'There was more to it than that. He fell out with his family. There was an . . . incident, while he was up at Cambridge. They felt he had disgraced them. I imagine you can guess what I'm talking about. They quite literally cut him off without a shilling and turned him out of the house.'

'How awful! Poor Felix! But they must be terribly proud of him now.'

'I wouldn't know. He never had any contact with them after that.'

Rose stopped in her tracks and looked at him. 'Do you mean to tell me they didn't go and see him after he had that terrible crash?'

'Not so much as a letter.'

'Oh, that's terrible! How can anyone treat their own child like that?'

'I don't know,' Merry said helplessly. 'It beats me.'

'And everything he did – winning the DFC and everything. That didn't make any difference?'

'Apparently not.'

'Poor Felix! Well, I hope they feel really guilty now that he's . . .' She trailed into silence.

'Now that he's dead,' Merry finished for her.

They walked on and she slid her hand under his arm. 'You loved him very much, didn't you?'

'Yes,' he said, 'very much.'

He took hold of her hand, felt that it was cold and thrust it and his into the pocket of his greatcoat. She said, 'I used to think he would marry Lady Harriet.'

'Yes, so did he,' Merry agreed.

'It wouldn't have worked, would it?'

'Oh, I dare say they'd have rubbed along, in the same way as you and Matt.'

'What happened to stop them?'

'The war – and Felix's crash. She couldn't cope with the state he was in.'

'So she let him down too?'

'You could say that, yes.'

She pressed his arm against her side. 'It's a good job he had you.' Then, after a pause, 'You made him very happy, Merry. You do know that, don't you?'

'We made each other very happy,' he said.

That evening, listening to *Forces' Favourites* on the wireless. Merry found himself recalling a conversation he had had with Felix during those last magical days on Malta. He suddenly realised that it was the first time he had actually allowed himself to think about their time together and he was terrified by the notion that his memories of Felix might fade beyond recall if he did not actively try to keep them alive. That night in bed he set himself the task of remembering every detail of their relationship, right from the day he had first set eyes on Felix when he had walked onstage to audition for Monty Prince.

He had known from the beginning that he was in love and he remembered how he had tried to probe below the man-about-town façade to find the real Felix, divining from the outset that there was a communion there that Felix sought strenuously to deny. He recalled the many rebuffs, the seemingly casual cruelties, which had only strengthened his conviction that Felix was drawn to him as powerfully as he was to Felix. Then had come the painstaking detective work and its final culmination in his discovery of Felix's true identity and the story of his fall from grace.

He remembered vividly their first physical contact, not many weeks after Felix had joined the company. Felix had come into the dressing room on a windy April morning, clasping his hand over one eye and swearing under his breath.

'The wind's blown sand in my eye and it hurts like hell!'

Merry had guided him to a chair and ordered, 'Let me have a look.' Once, long ago, when his father had insisted on him joining the Scouts, he had done a course in first aid and he vaguely recalled instructions on how to deal with this problem. He could remember, after all this time, the electric thrill he had felt as he took Felix's face between his hands and gently forced open the lids of the affected eye. It was bloodshot and weeping copiously, but he could see in the corner the offending grain of sand. Remembering what he had been told about the best method of removing a 'foreign body' from the eye he said, 'Hold still a minute,' and, bending, had delicately inserted the tip of his tongue between the eyelids. He tasted the saltiness of tears, felt the gritty sand between his teeth and heard Felix's sharp intake of breath, but his patient had neither flinched nor struggled. The whole procedure had such a strong erotic impact that Merry found himself constrained to turn away and busy himself at the washbasin, rinsing out a face flannel in cold water.

'Well,' Felix had remarked after a moment, in a rather strange tone, 'that's certainly a novel method, but it seems to have worked. Thanks.'

Merry had turned back and handed him the flannel. 'Don't mention it.'

He had since wondered what would have happened if, instead of turning away, he had kissed Felix then. They might have had two more years together. Once, recalling the incident much later, he had remarked upon the state of arousal that had caused him such temporary embarrassment and Felix had laughed. 'Why do you think I spent the next ten minutes sitting with a towel over my lap?'

Thinking of it now, he found himself smiling and realised that for the first time he had remembered Felix with pleasure instead of with anguish. He turned over and fell instantly asleep.

Rose had to go back to London before the end of Merry's leave and he found himself anticipating her departure with dread. He had come to value their morning walks as a way back to sanity, and he was worried, too, that without her to watch over him he might yield to the temptation to start drinking again. On her last morning they set out as always but she seemed unusually quiet.

After a little she tucked her hand into his arm and said, 'I'll miss our walks.'

'So shall I,' he agreed. Then he added, 'I don't know how to thank you, Rose. I don't know how I'd have got through these last two weeks without you. I think you may have, quite literally, saved my life.'

'Well, what are friends for?' she replied, smiling. Then she said, 'You remember we were talking about after the war the other day?'

'Yes, I remember.'

'We are going to win this war, aren't we, Merry? Now that we've got the Jerries on the run in North Africa?'

'It's hard to see that we can fail, now the Americans are mobilised,' he said. 'But it could be a long, hard slog yet and all sorts of things can go wrong. I wouldn't count any chickens yet.'

'I'm not sure about that,' she said thoughtfully. 'I think we have to have some idea where we're going, or else the war will suddenly be over and we shall all be cast adrift, not knowing what to do with ourselves.'

'I suppose you're right,' Merry said absently.

'You know what we were saying, about having our own company? Were you serious?'

The question brought him back to the present with a jolt. It had not occurred to him that Rose was making serious plans based on that notion. 'I don't know,' he said hesitantly. 'I suppose it could be fun – me in charge of the music, you doing the dancing. Yes, it could work out very well.'

She was looking up at him, with those huge violet eyes. 'Merry, I don't like to think of you being on your own again.'

The sudden change of tack puzzled him. 'I'll manage, somehow,' he said, but it did not sound convincing even in his own ears.

'I was thinking,' she went on, 'we're both lonely people. I missed my chance with Richard, and there will never be anyone I feel the same about. And you've lost Felix. But if we're going to work together one day . . .' She trailed off, then started again. 'What I'm trying to say, Merry, is – wouldn't it be a good idea if we got married?'

He stopped dead and stared down at her. 'Married? You and me?'

'Yes.' She gripped his hand and looked back at him intently. 'I know it wouldn't be a proper marriage. I mean, not what most people mean by marriage. I understand that you wouldn't want to . . . to sleep together or anything like that. But quite honestly I don't think that sort of thing matters very much to me. But we do like each other, don't we? And we would be company for each other. And if we're going to work together and travel around together, it would be so much easier. And we'd grow old together and look after each other. That's what terrifies me, Merry. The thought of growing old and being all alone. What do you think?'

She was breathless and her face was flushed. Something tugged at Merry's heart but he shook his head.

'Rose, dear, dear Rose. Thank you! Thank you from the bottom of my heart. But it won't do. I can't do that to you. It's very sweet of you to offer, but it wouldn't be fair.'

'But I like the idea of being married to you!' she cried.

'And I can see how pleasant it would be to be married to you,' he responded. 'But it wouldn't last, Rose. You say that you'll never want to have a proper, sexual relationship with a man. But you're still young, and you're very pretty. One day, perhaps next week, you'll meet someone and be completely bowled over and then you'll want a real marriage. And children. Don't you want children?'

'I don't know,' she answered hesitantly. 'I used to think I did. But now I'm not sure. I'm not even sure I want a "proper" husband. I want to go on doing what I'm doing now, and if I married I'd have to give that up, wouldn't I?'

'Not necessarily. You might marry someone in the profession.'

'But that's why I want to marry you!' she exclaimed.

He shook his head, tenderly. 'No, you don't really. You're feeling sorry for me and perhaps a bit lonely yourself but that's no basis for a marriage. And I couldn't promise even to be faithful to you, according to my lights. At present I feel like you, as if I shall never want another physical relationship with anyone. But I know myself. I'm not naturally celibate. You knew what was going on when we were down in Fairbourne – the casual pick-ups. How would you feel if that started up again?'

She frowned at him. 'I don't know. I suppose it wouldn't matter.'

'Yes, it would,' he said. 'It would matter to you, and it would matter to me.' He took both her hands and bent his head to kiss the warm skin above the top of her glove. 'I shall always be grateful for the offer, Rose, and immensely flattered. But please can we go on being just very good friends? Believe me, it will be the best thing for both of us.'

She sighed and then leaned up and kissed his cheek. 'If that's what you want, Merry. Just promise me that if things get bad again you'll come and find me – wherever I am, whatever we're both doing. I can't bear to think of you suffering on your own.'

'I promise,' he said.

At the end of his leave Merry once more faced George Black across the desk in his office.

'Well?' Black said, scrutinising him closely.

'I'm all right,' Merry said. 'I kept my promise, George. I haven't touched a drop since New Year.'

Black got up and came round the desk, holding out his hand. 'Congratulations, old man! Well done. I knew you wouldn't let me down.'

Merry gripped his hand firmly and looked him in the eye. 'I'm sorry about what happened before.'

'Forget it,' said Black. He returned to his seat. 'So, are you ready to go back to work?'

'Yes,' Merry said, 'but I want you to help me, George. I want you to send me back to North Africa.' Black looked doubtful and Merry went on, 'If you send me out on the road again here with another company I shan't be able to resist temptation. You must be able to see that. Out in the desert it will be different.'

'Well,' Black conceded, 'you may have a point there. And there's certainly room for another company with the Eighth Army.'

'Not a company!' Merry said quickly. 'I don't want the responsibility of running a company. I don't want to be responsible for other people's lives. Give me a truck and a piano and I'll take music right up to the front line, where it's really needed. I want to be up there, where the action is.'

'Where you can get yourself killed, you mean,' Black said sourly.

'No,' Merry returned. 'Not any more. I'll take my chances, like anyone else. If there's a shell out there with my name on it, fair enough. I have to do this, George. They won't let me fight with the others – and perhaps they're right. But at least I can share the risk with them!'

His commanding officer looked at him for a long moment in silence. Then he said, 'OK. If that's what you want.'

Merry drew a deep breath. 'That's what I want.'

22

Richard and Priscilla spent Christmas with his parents, who were still living with his aunt in Didsbury. Once again, he was grateful for her ability to chat with all three of them and the way she seemed to fit so easily and tactfully into the family setting. At the same time, he had to admit to a sensation akin to jealousy, because she seemed so much more at ease with them than he felt. It was hard to be natural when he had to be constantly on his guard in case he let slip some hint of what he had been doing over the last six months. He told himself it was natural that his mother should be curious, but her questions drove him to distraction.

It was a relief to return to London on the day after Boxing Day, but he rapidly discovered that the festivities were far from over. They were invited to spend New Year's Eve at a party given by Sir Lionel and Lady Vance. He had planned to take Priscilla out for a quiet, romantic dinner to celebrate the anniversary of his proposal of marriage, but she was adamant that they could not refuse her guardians' invitation.

'They'd be so hurt if we didn't go! And anyway, there will be lots of people there that I want you to meet.'

The guests at the party were the usual mixture of foreign diplomats, high-ranking staff officers and an eclectic combination of people from all branches of the arts. Among them was a young Hungarian pianist by the name of Zoltan Onescu, who had huge, soulful dark eyes in a very thin face and an expression that reminded Richard of an unhappy blood-hound. He was obviously one of Priscilla's discoveries and followed her around the room with a look of abject adoration. Richard took an instant dislike to him.

Among the other guests were two young men in civilian clothes, one tall and thin, the other shorter and rather chubby. Richard thought at first that they might be foreigners, since all the Englishmen under forty were in uniform of one kind of another, but when Priscilla introduced them he found he was mistaken.

'Richard, this is Jeremy Stone and this is Craig Wishart. Jeremy's a poet and Craig writes novels.'

Richard shook hands and asked, rather too pointedly, 'Is writing a reserved occupation now, then?'

'Civil service, old boy,' said the taller of the two, and winked meaningfully. 'Hush-hush, you know.'

Richard wondered whether they were in intelligence or maybe some other clandestine organisation and asked no more. Then later, as he was standing with a small group of Priscilla's friends, half listening to a conversation that did not really interest him, he heard their voices behind him.

'Of course,' said Jeremy, the tall one, 'if we'd had any sense at all we'd have buggered off to the States right at the start instead of hanging on here to be blitzed into kingdom come.'

'Like dear old Wystan and Christopher,' agreed his tubby companion.

'Or Ben Britten and Peter,' added Jeremy. 'At least then we could have got on with our proper work without interruption. This is no place for anyone with any artistic talent or sensitivity.'

Richard had a sudden mental image of Dr Rodocanachi and his frail, indomitable wife, valiantly keeping up the appearances of civilised living with a flat full of escaping airmen and the threat of imprisonment and torture an ever-present reality. He pictured Pat O'Leary, or whatever his real name was, slipping from safe house to safe house as the Gestapo closed in on his trail, and Chantal, hobbling out of the prison gates on her mutilated feet.

He swung round and confronted the two men. 'Perhaps it would be a good idea if you buggered off now and left the air of this country a bit cleaner for the rest of us! Or maybe you'd find that your artistic sensibilities would be better appreciated by the Nazis!'

He had expected them to look angry, or perhaps ashamed. Instead they gazed back at him with pitying amusement. He pushed past them and marched out of the room.

Priscilla found him standing on the landing, leaning on the balcony rail at the head of the stairs.

'That was a bit uncalled for, darling.'

'Was it?' he returned woodenly.

She slipped her hand under his arm. 'Not everyone is as brave as you, you know.'

'It isn't about me!' he exploded. 'For God's sake, if you knew what some people are doing . . .' He broke off. He couldn't even tell his wife about the images he carried in his brain.

'Never mind,' she said soothingly. 'Come back in. There's someone who's very keen to meet you.'

He let her lead him back into the big reception room and over to an older man with hair greying at the temples, whom he felt he should recognise but could not place.

Priscilla said, 'Darling, this is Reginald Harrison, who works for the BBC. Reggie, this is my husband, Richard.'

The other man frowned at him for a minute and then his face cleared. 'Got it! I knew we'd met somewhere. You were singing with a concert party before the war. Where was it, Eastbourne?'

'Fairbourne,' Richard corrected. 'Of course, I remember now. You gave me your card.'

'You never contacted me.'

'Well, the war intervened, unfortunately.'

Harrison looked him up and down. 'So, what are you doing these days? I mean, I can see you're in the army. What outfit are you with?'

'I'm with something called Inter-Services Liaison,' Richard said. The lie slipped glibly off his tongue these days.

'Oh yes? Based in London?'

'Not all the time. I travel a good deal.'

'But he's going to be in the London area for a while now,' Priscilla put in.

Richard glanced at her with a frown. It was likely that he would remain in England for a while, but there was no way of knowing exactly where he would be based.

'Still singing?' Harrison asked.

'Off and on,' Richard said.

'I'm glad to hear it. Can't let a fine voice like yours go to waste.'

At that point the inevitable happened. Lady Vance clapped her hands for attention and announced that some of the guests would entertain the company, if they would all care to move next door to the music room.

Zoltan Onescu was the first to perform. He played Liszt, with great flair and attack. Richard had to admire his technique but he found the performance unsympathetic. Was he biased, he wondered, or was it just that he did not particularly care for Liszt? In any case, he reflected, he would rather listen to Merry playing Beethoven any day.

When the Hungarian had finished Lady Vance turned to Richard and asked him to sing. It was useless to say that he didn't have any music with him, since Priscilla had made a point soon after their wedding of buying all the sheet music of his core repertoire and depositing it in her guardians' music room in anticipation of such eventualities. He selected the aria *'Largo al factotum'* from *The Barber of Seville*. Zoltan accompanied him, but he was far too assertive for that function, forcing the pace and never once looking at Richard for direction. The performance seemed to please the audience, however, and there were requests for an encore. Richard gave them 'Old Man River' and then retired with relief to get himself a drink.

He had been thoroughly debriefed immediately after his return from France and then given three weeks' leave, which was normal for any agent returning from the field. He anticipated that, once the Christmas and New Year festivities were over, he would be able to relax and enjoy a much-needed rest. Within days, however, he found he was getting bored. Priscilla had had to return to her duties as a staff officer with the FANY and he was left alone in the flat with very little to do. As had happened on his last return from abroad, he found it very hard to shake off the sense of leading a double life and the habits of living under constant threat of discovery. Strolling down Oxford Street he caught himself glancing at the reflections in the shop windows to make sure that he was not being followed. If he took a taxi he had to restrain himself from altering his destination halfway through the ride and then doubling back in a different cab. On his first night home Priscilla had gently removed the revolver he had placed under his pillow in case of a dawn raid, murmuring, 'You're not going to need that here, darling.'

Once, early on, he had a vivid dream, not quite a night-mare but sufficiently disturbing to make him cry out in his sleep. He woke to find Priscilla leaning over him, stroking his hair.

'It's all right, my love. You're at home. You're quite safe.'

He blinked up at her, gripped by a sudden fear. 'Was I talking in my sleep?'

'Just a bit.'

'What language was I speaking?'

She chuckled. 'Double Dutch, I should think. I couldn't make out a word. Go back to sleep.'

He was still worried. The recollection came to him of Jack Duval's remark about the services of Madame Lulu, whose job it was to find out whether agents talked in their sleep. He had never enjoyed that lady's favours but he had wondered at the time whether Priscilla might have been persuaded that it was her patriotic duty to perform the same function.

'Do I often talk in my sleep?' he pursued.

'No, not really. You mumble sometimes.'

'But you can't make out what I'm saying?'

'No.' She put her arm round him. 'It's all right, darling, you haven't given away any secrets. And even if you had, I wouldn't tell anyone, you know that.'

'I didn't mean it like that,' he murmured, drawing her closer. 'I was just afraid that I might call out in English.' He caught himself. 'I mean, I don't make a habit of sharing a bed, but people have been known to drop off on trains or a room might be bugged . . .'

'Well, you needn't worry. It would have to be a very clever spy to make anything out of what I've heard,' she said drowsily. 'Can we get back to sleep now?'

★ ★ ★

Two days into the new year Richard was sitting over the newspaper and wondering what to do with himself all day when the telephone rang. It was Harrison.

'I wondered if we could have lunch together. Are you free today, by any chance?'

Richard said he was and they agreed to meet at the BBC Club in Langham Place. As he walked in, Richard thought that a few years earlier he would have given a great deal for an invitation to meet a producer here. Now, it all seemed irrelevant. They chatted pleasantly enough over lunch, largely about Richard's training in Italy and mutual acquaintances in the music world. Then Harrison said, 'So, what are your plans for the future?'

'I really don't know,' Richard replied. 'It's difficult to make plans, under present circumstances.'

'I can see that, from the point of view of a serving soldier,' Harrison agreed. 'But all the same, you have to recognise the fact that once the war is over there is going to be a hell of a scramble for jobs, in all walks of life – not least in the arts. There are a lot of people who are making very big reputations for themselves in ENSA and other such organisations and they are all going to be looking for employment when they eventually get demobilised. You can't afford to be left behind.'

'What would you suggest?' Richard asked.

'How about taking one or two freelance engagements with us?'

'Sing for the BBC?'

'Why not? We could record your contributions at a weekend or some time when you're off duty. We're already doing that with other service personnel. How about it?'

Richard's heart was beating rapidly. This, surely, was the break he had waited for for so long. 'I'd like that very much. But I'll have to clear it with my CO first.'

'Naturally. But I can't imagine that there will be any difficulty there. As I say, we already use servicemen from various other units. It's good public relations for them and good for morale all round.'

When he left Harrison Richard walked down to Baker Street, to the headquarters of the 'Inter-Services Liaison Bureau'. He had to wait for half an hour before Maurice Buckmaster was free, but once in the senior officer's room he was greeted warmly.

'Richard! I thought you were on leave? Don't tell me you're tired of the fleshpots already!'

'As a matter of fact, I am getting bored,' Richard said. 'But that isn't what I wanted to talk about. I wanted your advice.'

'Well, you're welcome to it, for what it's worth. Fire away.'

Richard outlined his conversation with Harrison. 'It's a wonderful opportunity for me, personally,' he concluded. 'It could make all the difference to my career after the war if I can establish a bit of a reputation now. But I wondered how SOE would view it.'

Buckmaster sat back and sucked his teeth thoughtfully. After a moment he shook his head regretfully. 'I'm sorry, Richard. I can see the importance of it from your point of view but I'm afraid it's not on. If you hadn't used your singing career as a cover in France it would be different, but we know that you're on the Gestapo's wanted list.'

'But they only know me as Ricardo Benedetti, a cabaret artiste,' Richard protested, 'not as an opera singer.'

'Wasn't it part of your cover that you were a singer with an opera company in Belgium?' Buckmaster said. 'And didn't you sing opera for that Italian liaison officer in Marseilles – with German officers as part of the audience?'

'That's true, I did,' Richard agreed.

'We know that the Gestapo monitor all BBC broadcasts,' Buckmaster went on. 'If there was any chance that someone over there might have recognised your voice you could never use that cover again. And we may need you to, one day. Besides that, there are the other people who have been associated with Ricardo Benedetti. It isn't going to help them if he turns out to be Captain Richard Stevens of the British army.'

Richard sighed deeply. 'I suppose you're right. I'll just have to tell Harrison that it's not on.'

'If you like,' his CO offered, 'I'll draft a letter to him, saying that it's not department policy to allow our officers to accept other engagements. That'll make it clear that you haven't had any choice in the matter. At least that should stop him from holding it against you in the future.'

With that Richard had to be satisfied, but when Priscilla got home that evening she immediately said, 'Well? Haven't you got anything to tell me?'

'To tell you?' he queried. Then, 'You knew Harrison was going to invite me to lunch.'

'Darling, I've been working on him for weeks! How did it go?'

'What do you mean, you've been working on him for weeks? You mean he only offered me work as a favour to you!'

'No! Don't be silly! The BBC doesn't work like that. He offered you something because he thinks you've got a beautiful voice and a great future.'

'So, what did you mean when you said you'd been working on him?'

'Just making sure that he came to the party, and then making sure that he didn't forget to contact you. You have to make connections, darling! That's how you get on in this world. You have to put yourself in front of people and make sure they notice you.'

'Well, you could have saved yourself the trouble,' he said bitterly. 'I'm not going to do it.'

'What do you mean you're not? It's a wonderful opportunity.' She came closer and put her hands on his arms. 'Darling, I know it's only one or two freelance engagements at the moment but you can't afford to turn it down. There's no knowing what it might lead to. You mustn't be too proud.'

He shook her hands off and turned away. 'It's not a question of pride. I'm not allowed to do it. I've checked with Baker Street and they say it's not on.'

'Not on? Why ever not?'

'Security reasons.'

'Oh, what rubbish! How can it be a breach of security for you to sing on the wireless? That's just typical of those old fuddy-duddies at the War Office.' She moved away, taking off her uniform tunic. 'Don't worry, love. Uncle Lionel knows Sir Charles Hambro. I'll get him to have a word and sort things out.'

'Who's Hambro?' Richard asked.

She looked at him in surprise. 'Your boss, sweetheart. Didn't you even know his name? Well, no, I suppose you wouldn't.'

'You shouldn't either,' Richard said, shocked at the breach of security. 'As far as I'm concerned, he's always referred to as CD. And for God's sake don't tell your guardian to go trying to pull strings for me. It'll start all sorts of alarm bells ringing and I'll probably end up being sent to serve as an intelligence officer on the Faroe Islands or something for the rest of the war.'

Her face puckered. 'But darling, we can't let this chance go! I'm working so hard to see that you have a proper career to come back to. You must see how important it is.'

He put his arms round her, sighing. 'Love, I wish I could do it. Of course I do. It's the best chance I've ever had. But they're right. I can't explain why, but it would jeopardise all sorts of things if I became too well known. I'm sorry. I know you're disappointed and I do appreciate what you're trying to do but you know what sort of outfit I'm mixed up with. We've just got to be patient until the war's over.'

'To hell with the war!' she exclaimed passionately. 'I'm fed up with everything having to be subordinated to the bloody war effort!' She turned away and threw her tunic on to a chair. 'Oh well, that's that, then. I was expecting to go out and celebrate tonight, but I suppose we might as well stay in after all.'

'We've been out practically every evening as it is,' he said. 'It might be nice to have a quiet evening in by ourselves.'

She looked at him for a moment. Then she shrugged. 'OK. If that's what you want.'

He ended by taking her to dinner at the Savoy, though it worried him that the accumulated pay, which had made his bank account look so healthy on his return, was rapidly disappearing.

A couple of days before the end of his leave Richard had a phone call from Ginny, to say that she had finally reached London and was staying with friends. He mentioned her arrival to Priscilla, who insisted on asking her to dinner. He was glad to see her again, and to note that she seemed to have recovered, both physically and mentally, from the privations of the long trek across the Pyrenees. Nevertheless, it was not a successful evening. Priscilla was the perfect hostess and had managed to conjure all sorts of delicacies out of the black market for the enjoyment of her guest, but there were too many things that neither he nor Ginny could speak of in front of her, and Richard felt that she sensed their constraint and misinterpreted it. He kept remembering the evenings they had spent in the villa at Canet Plage, sitting over a bottle of Fitou by the light of an oil lamp after he returned from singing at the Lion d'Or. They had always retired eventually to separate beds but in some strange way it had felt more like a marriage than his present life with Priscilla.

When Ginny had gone Priscilla remarked, 'I suppose you two had a bit of a fling while you were . . . wherever it is you've been.'

'No!' Richard exclaimed, almost more shocked by her even tone than by the implication. 'For goodness' sake, Priss! I wouldn't be unfaithful to you.'

She came close and looked up into his face. 'I wouldn't blame you, you know. I mean, it's a long time – for a man – to be celibate.'

He said stiffly, 'We're not all creatures of instinct, you know. Men have morals as well as women.'

She put her arms round his neck and laughed. 'Oh, darling, you are sweet!'

She kissed him and he let himself be seduced, but her apparently casual attitude worried him more than he cared to admit to himself. If she was prepared to be so easygoing towards him, did that mean that she might apply the same standards to her own conduct? He tried to banish the thought but it lurked at the back of his mind.

In a brief moment alone with Ginny, while Priscilla had gone to the kitchen to fetch the next course, he asked her what she planned to do now. She frowned and said unhappily, 'I wish I knew! I keep putting out feelers, but no one seems to be interested. I just don't know who to contact. There must be a job for me somewhere – and I don't mean helping out in a munitions factory!'

At the end of his leave Richard was sent back to Beaulieu as a Conducting Officer, which was what he had anticipated. He was glad to be back at work but found bad news waiting for him. Jack Duval, his radio operator during his first assignment, had ceased to transmit and the assumption was that he had been arrested by the Gestapo. There was other news that gave him food for thought, too. He was surprised to find that SOE had begun training women agents, the first of whom were passing through Beaulieu at the time. There was a great deal of disapproval of this move in some quarters and the women were given a pretty hard time, but Richard had seen at first hand how valuable they could be in the field. The discovery, coming on top of his conversation with Ginny, gave him a difficult decision. He knew that it was exactly what Ginny was looking for and that she would be ideally suited to the work, but to recommend her would be to expose her to terrible risks. *She's done enough*, he told himself, *risked her life too often already. And there's her husband to think of, back in France.*

A few weeks later Ginny telephoned again and asked him to meet her. This time he arranged a rendezvous at a small club in Ebury Street, a place that was popular with members of the various clandestine organisations that flourished in London but not somewhere where he was likely to run into any of Priscilla's friends. He saw at once that something was wrong. Her face was pale and her usually exuberant manner

completely eclipsed. He bought them both a drink and led her
to a quiet corner table.

'What's happened, Ginny?'

'It's Gilles,' she said, her voice thick with tears. 'I had a
message from Jimmy Langley asking me to go and see him.
They've heard from Marseilles that Gilles was arrested a
month ago. He was held for a while and then . . .' She broke
off.

'Then what, Ginny?' he prompted.

'They shot him. The bastards shot him! Those swine! God
alone knows what they did to him before they killed him!'

He reached across the table and gripped her hands. 'Oh
God, Ginny, I'm so sorry! I wish there was something I could
say – or do.'

'Get me back to France,' she said fiercely. 'Richard, I've got
to do something! I shall go mad if I stay here, thinking of what
happened to Gilles and what might be happening to Pat and
all the others. I've got to do something practical. I've got to get
back at those bastards somehow.'

As it happened, two days later Beaulieu received a visit from
SOE's Director of Training and Operations, Major General
Colin Gubbins. He was a spare, energetic man with a neat
moustache and sharp eyes with a humorous twinkle in them.
Richard had never had much contact with him but he had
always liked what he had seen of him. Seizing the opportunity,
he asked for a private interview and told him about Ginny.
Soon afterwards she telephoned again to say that she had had
'a very interesting conversation with a rather strange man in
the Northumberland Hotel'.

'Yes, I know who you mean,' he replied, 'and it will give you
the result you are looking for. But for God's sake, Ginny, think
long and hard before you make any decision.'

Not long afterwards he heard from a colleague that a girl who passed under the name of Eloise had started initial training at Wanborough and had wished to be remembered to him, with the message 'don't forget our little villa by the sea'.

In the middle of March he got a note from Jimmy Langley asking him to call at his flat in St James's Street when he was next in London. So on his next free evening he made his way there. Langley was there with Airey Neave as usual, waiting for any message from Room 900 to say that a signal had been received from one of their agents in the field. Both were looking unusually sober and worn.

'I thought you would want to know,' Langley said. 'Pat was arrested on the third in Toulouse.'

'Oh God!' Richard sank into a chair and passed his hand over his face. 'I knew it had to happen. I begged him to come out with me – or at least with Ian.'

'Ian tried to persuade him, too,' Neave said, 'but he was determined to carry on as long as he could.'

'How did it happen?' Richard asked.

'It seems he was betrayed by a character known as Roger le Blanc, who posed as a sympathiser and actually brought several men down from Paris to prove his bona fides. He arranged a meeting at a café with Pat and Ullmann, the tailor, and the Gestapo were waiting for them.'

'How do you know all this?' Richard asked. 'Through Tom Groome?'

'I'm afraid not,' Neave said. 'Tom didn't come up on the air for several weeks and when he came back the security checks were missing from his messages. We suspect he's been taken and is being forced to transmit under duress.'

'Not Tom, too!' Richard groaned. 'So how did you find out?'

'Another man, who's code name is Fabian, was arrested at the same time. He managed to escape by jumping through the train window when they were being taken to Paris and got to Switzerland.'

'Fabian?' Richard said. 'I know him. He was with us when we got Ian out of Meauzeac. I'm glad he's all right, at least. But what about Pat? Is there nothing we can do?'

'We've got people keeping their eyes and ears open, of course,' Langley said. 'But he seems to have disappeared from view. The likelihood is that he's been sent straight to Germany, to one of their concentration camps.'

Richard shook his head miserably. 'Poor Pat! If only we could have got him to see sense.' Then he looked up. 'I'll tell you one thing, though. If anyone alive can stand up to the Nazis and come through it's him.'

'Well, we must just hope and pray that he can hold out until we're able to liberate the camps,' Langley said. 'But I'm afraid that's not going to happen for a long time yet.'

'At least it looks as if things are beginning to go our way at last,' Richard said. 'We've got Rommel on the run. It can only be a matter of time before we drive the Huns out of Africa. Then, surely, the next step must be to invade southern France.'

'Maybe,' Langley agreed. 'But my money's on an invasion of Italy. The Italian army has proved a much softer target than the Germans. If we can roll them up like we did in Tunisia we'll be on Hitler's doorstep by next spring.'

'Well, let's hope for Pat's sake that you're right,' Richard said. He paused and then added, 'That name always seems so inappropriate. I've never met anyone so unconvincing as an Irishman.'

Langley smiled. 'It was his choice. But I don't suppose it's the name he's using wherever he is now.'

Richard went home with a heavy heart. He knew that he had been exceptionally lucky in escaping from France three times and felt an obscure guilt at the thought of the lengthening list of those who had remained behind to be captured – Jack Duval, Pat, Tom Groome, Ginny's husband Gilles. He suspected that it would not be long before he would be required to go back himself. He dreaded the thought but at the same time felt a thrill of excitement. This soft living, dividing his time between the pleasant surroundings of Beaulieu and the music and arts scene in London, was beginning to pall.

The Germans had resumed their bombing raids on London earlier in the year and Richard had just reached home when the air-raid warning sounded. He found Priscilla waiting anxiously for him.

'I'm so glad you're back. I was afraid you might get caught in the raid and have to spend the night in a shelter.'

'Do you want to go down to the shelter now?' he asked.

She shook her head and shivered. 'I loathe those places. The smell, the crowds, children crying . . . I'd much rather stay here and take my chances.'

He put his arms round her. 'All right. We'll stay here. This block of flats has been lucky so far. Let's hope it stays that way.'

She nestled against him and murmured, 'Anyway, I want to talk to you about something special.' Then, drawing away with a brightening tone, 'Let's have a drink, shall we?'

He mixed a dry martini for them both and they settled down side by side on the settee. In the distance they could hear the dull thunder of explosions and the sharper crack of anti-aircraft fire.

'What did you want to talk about?' he asked.

She smiled. 'I've got some wonderful news for you – for both of us.'

It occurred to him that she was going to have a child and in that split second a myriad of different emotions chased each other through his mind, the only one of which he fully grasped was the idea that this was not the right time.

Priscilla went on, 'You remember the woman I introduced you to last week at Aunt Eleanor's soirée? Mary Glasgow?'

'Vaguely.'

'Oh, really, darling!' She gave him a little shake. 'You must try to remember people like that. She's the chairman of CEMA.'

'Which is? Remind me.'

'Richard! Honestly, sometimes I think you just pretend to be vague to annoy me.'

He looked at her. He was tired and half his thoughts were still on what had happened to Pat O'Leary. 'No, I don't, my sweet. It's just that I do have other things on my mind.'

'Well,' she said mysteriously, 'you can forget all that now.'

'What?'

'CEMA, since you seem to have forgotten, is the Council for the Encouragement of Music and the Arts. They've been doing wonderful work since the outbreak of war trying to keep the arts alive in this country. In fact, they've been so successful that many more people have had access to performances of classical music or opera and ballet than ever did before the war.'

'Oh, I know who you mean now,' Richard said. 'They're the people behind Myra Hess's concerts at the National Gallery.'

'That's right. But they do a lot more than that. They've been sending people out all over the country to give concerts and recitals – and the wonderful news is, Mary Glasgow wants you to work for them!'

She smiled at him triumphantly. He blinked back at her. 'Darling, you know I can't do that. The people I work for wouldn't let me do a few broadcasts for the BBC. They certainly aren't going to let me go trekking round the country giving recitals.'

'But that's the whole point!' she exclaimed. 'You wouldn't have to work for them any more. Mary's convinced that she can pull the right strings to get you seconded to CEMA for the duration.'

'Seconded?' He stared at her in disbelief. Then he began to laugh. 'Darling, don't be silly! You know the kind of thing I'm involved in. Oh, all right, I know you don't know any of the details and I can't tell you about them. But you know I'm involved in some pretty hush-hush activities. Do you really imagine my superiors are going to let me go, to go gallivanting around the country?'

She looked offended. 'I don't see why not. You're not going to suddenly go blurting out everything you know to your audiences. I can't imagine what you could tell anyone that's so secret, anyway.'

He sat back, drawing away from her. 'It isn't a question of what I might tell people,' he said quietly. 'But I have certain training, certain areas of expertise, that can be useful to the war effort – and I wouldn't be allowed to waste that, even if I wanted to.'

'You're telling me you don't want to? That you'd rather be playing soldiers than doing what *really* matters, the thing you're better at than almost anyone else? Is killing people really more important to you than singing wonderful music?'

'You know it isn't, Priscilla,' he said. 'You know I hate the war as much as you do – perhaps more, because I've seen it at closer quarters than you have. But the fact is, we are at war with one of the cruellest, most hateful and pitiless regimes the world has ever seen. If we don't beat them, then no one will ever be able to sit peacefully and listen to music without fear or guilt in this country again.'

She got up and flounced over to the cocktail cabinet to refill her glass. 'Oh, that's just dramatic nonsense, Richard. I don't believe it really makes a ha'p'orth of difference to most people who's running the country when it comes to things like music or painting.'

'Don't you?' Richard said. His voice was still very quiet but it had taken on a hard edge. 'Well, I for one couldn't sing for the people who have done some of the things I know have been done in the last year or two. And I have no intention of leaving it to other people to face the dangers and the hardships of stopping them, while I spend the time pursuing my own career.'

'It's not a question of pursuing your career!' she flung back at him. 'It's a question of priorities.'

'Exactly,' he replied. 'And my priority at present is to do everything I can to defeat the Nazis.'

'I don't understand you!' she stormed at him, her eyes full of tears. 'I've spent months planning and scheming so that you can be doing the things that you really want to do. And so that you don't have to keep going away to God knows where for months on end. So we can be together! Don't you want that?'

'Of course I do.' He crossed the room and tried to take her in his arms but she turned away from him petulantly. 'Darling, I do appreciate what you're trying to do. I only wish this wretched war would end so that I could stay here with you and start singing properly again. But until it does I have to do my bit. You must understand that.'

She looked round at him, her face streaked with tears. 'Oh, go to hell!' Before he could say any more she pushed past him and went into the bedroom, slamming the door behind her.

* * *

Richard slept in the spare room that night, and when he got up to return to Beaulieu in the morning Priscilla's door remained firmly shut. Back in Hampshire he tried to immerse himself in his work but in every quiet moment his brain kept fretting over the dual images of Pat O'Leary in the hands of the Gestapo and Priscilla's angry, tear-stained face. At first he felt angry with her for not understanding how trivial her ambitions for him seemed in the face of the sufferings he knew others were undergoing. Then he came to a more reasonable frame of mind and realised that her principal concern was for his own safety and that he should be grateful for that. He resolved that next time he was able to get up to town he would make it up to her.

It was some time before the opportunity arose. On 20 April Winston Churchill announced that from now on church bells might be rung again for services, since the threat of invasion was past. Soon after that, the news bulletins announced that the Allied armies were within twenty miles of the city of Tunis and Rommel was evacuating his troops from North Africa.

The next day Richard received a summons to meet Major General Gubbins in his office at Baker Street. The appointment was for 10 a.m. so he decided to go up the night before and take Priscilla out to dinner. As he turned his key in the door he was surprised to hear the sound of a piano. He paused in the hallway and listened. The pianist was playing Liszt. A few steps brought him to the half-open door of the sitting room. Zoltan Onescu was seated at the piano and Priscilla was standing beside him, a cocktail in one hand and the other resting intimately on the back of the pianist's neck.

She caught sight of Richard out of the corner of her eye and immediately put down the glass and came towards him. 'Darling! How lovely! I wasn't expecting you.'

'So I see,' he remarked, but she did not seem to register the irony in his tone. She put her arm round his neck and kissed him.

'You remember Zoltan, don't you?'

The young Hungarian had turned away from the piano and was glowering at him as if he were an audience member who had crassly interrupted in the middle of a recital. He could smell scented hair oil and had the impression that Priscilla's hand had left a smear of it on the back of his neck. He said brusquely, 'Of course.' Then, looking at his wife, 'I thought we might go out for dinner.'

'Lovely!' she exclaimed. 'We can take Zoltan with us. You'd like that, Zoltan, wouldn't you?'

It was not a pleasant evening. Richard took them to an Italian restaurant in Soho where the food was pleasant, within the constraints imposed by rationing, but reasonably priced. He was damned if he was treating this Hungarian hanger-on to the Savoy, or one of Priscilla's other expensive watering holes. Onescu spent the whole time being elaborately gallant to Priscilla, as if Richard's presence was completely irrelevant. Priscilla chattered away in her usual easy manner but tonight Richard found his teeth set on edge by her social finesse. It was the same whether she was talking to his parents or to this lecherous little central European. It was entirely superficial, a skill she had been brought up to, like royalty. He, in response, became increasingly monosyllabic in his replies.

After the meal he succeeded in getting rid of Onescu and as soon as they were alone in a taxi Priscilla said, 'You're very gloomy tonight, my sweet. What's wrong? Problems at work?'

He had spent a large part of the previous night engaged in one of those mock interrogations, which he hated almost more in the role of interrogator than he had when he had suffered it as the victim. He knew that they were an essential part of an agent's training but they always left him feeling guilty and in some way touched by the contagion of the brutality they were mimicking. The previous night had been particularly distressing, as it had ended with the subject of the questioning, a young man of great courage but as highly strung as a racehorse, breaking down in tears and swearing at them all as sadists who took a malignant pleasure in what they were doing. Richard had not got to bed until 4 a.m. He was tired and tense and it maddened him that she could ask her question as if he had merely been spending a normal day in an office somewhere.

'It's nothing to do with that,' he said irritably. 'If you must know, I resent having to spend my meagre salary entertaining your boyfriends.'

'My what?' she said. Then, to his surprise, she laughed. 'Oh, darling, you're jealous! How sweet!'

'It is not *sweet*!' he snapped. 'And I don't think it's funny.'

She said, in a different tone of voice, 'You're not seriously accusing me of having an affair with Zoltan, are you?'

'You certainly looked pretty intimate when I arrived this evening.'

'I don't know what you're talking about.'

'You had your hand round the back of his neck.'

'Oh, that!' She laughed again. 'That didn't mean anything. It was just . . . just a little pat. The way you might pat a dog, or a child.' He said nothing and she went on. 'Darling, I feel sorry for Zoltan. He's a brilliant pianist and he's had such a hard time, having to flee his own country and everything. And now he lives in a miserable little bedsit with no piano. That's why I invited him to come and play ours. He's got a recital in a few days and he really needs to practise. I was just trying to make him feel . . . well, that someone cared about him.'

'And I suppose it's escaped your notice that he's dying to get his hands on you. I've never seen such naked lust in anyone's eyes before.'

'Oh, you shouldn't pay much attention to that. He's Hungarian – and he's an artist. You have to make allowances for the artistic temperament.'

'I'm supposed to be an artist too, when I get the chance,' he said angrily. 'No one makes allowances for my temperament.'

She slid across the seat and tucked her hand under his arm. 'But, sweetheart, that's what I love about you. You're so down to earth and sensible. It's such a change from all these highly strung, sensitive types.'

For once he refused to be seduced by her physical closeness. 'If that means I'm supposed to stand by and smile while you lavish your care and attention on every stray dog who comes sniffing around you, you can forget it.'

She drew away again and said coldly, 'Don't you think you're making a mountain out of a molehill, rather?'

He was silent for a moment, then he said with a sigh, 'I suppose you're right. I'm sorry. I'm tired and I just wanted to spend a nice quiet evening with you and make up, after what happened last time I was home.'

She responded at once. 'Oh, darling, I'm sorry. I didn't think. I just wasn't expecting you, and I'd promised to take Zoltan out to eat, just to make sure he got a square meal. I couldn't very well turn round and tell him the invitation was off, could I?'

'No, I suppose not,' he said wearily, and put his arm round her.

She nestled against him. 'Well, you've got me all to yourself for the rest of the night. Will that do?'

'It'll have to,' he said.

As soon as they got back to the flat Priscilla led him to the bedroom and started to make love to him, but he was too much on edge to respond with his usual ardour and it was clear that she found it unsatisfactory. Afterwards he wanted only to go to sleep but Priscilla snuggled up to him and said, 'Darling, I've had a wonderful idea.'

'Mmm?'

'I think we should forget all about trying to establish your reputation with the musical establishment until after the war.'

'Good idea. Night-night.'

'No, listen a minute.' She propped herself on her elbow and looked down at him. 'I must tell you this before we go to sleep. There won't be time in the morning. I've been thinking about all those people who have suddenly discovered opera and ballet and classical music because of the war – through organisations like CEMA and because Sadler's Wells and people like that have had to move out to the provinces.' He was drifting off to sleep. She shook his shoulder impatiently. 'Do listen! When the war is over we can't let that just fizzle out. So I think we should start our own touring opera company. There! What do you think?'

He opened his eyes unwillingly. 'Five people singing all the roles and nothing but a couple of chairs for scenery?'

'No! Not like that at all. A proper company, with scenery and costumes and the best young singers available. I've got the money to fund it and I know lots of up-and-coming musicians and designers and choreographers who'd be only too happy to work for a company like that. We could revolutionise the whole concept of touring. And you would sing all the leading baritone roles. Don't you think it's a marvellous idea?'

'So I get to sing the leads in the company my wife has bought for me,' he said heavily. 'Priss, you can't buy success. You ought to have learned that by now.'

She flounced over on to her other side. 'Oh, don't be so stupid! It wouldn't be like that at all.'

After a moment he reached across and put his arm round her. 'I'm sorry. I didn't mean to be such a killjoy. But can we talk about it again when I'm not so tired?'

In the morning, while he was dressing, she said, 'You know what you said last night . . .'

'Please, don't let's start all that again,' he begged.

'No, it's something else. You said something about not spending your hard-earned salary.'

'Ah.' He paused in the act of tying his tie. 'Yes, since you mention it, I did want to say something.' He turned to look at her. 'I don't want to sound mean, Priss, but we are going to have to draw our horns in a bit. I just can't afford to keep up with the sort of expensive lifestyle you're used to. If it wasn't for the fact that I had quite an accumulation of back pay owing to me I'd have been skint long ago.'

'But, sweetheart, why didn't you say so?' she demanded. 'If you'd said you were short I would have picked up the bill last night.'

He turned away, feeling the same unreasonable anger rising in his throat as he had felt the previous night. 'I don't want you to pay for me. There are enough people around already who think I married you for your money. I don't want to give them any more ammunition.'

'Did you?' she flashed back. 'Did you marry me for my money?'

'Would we be having this conversation if I had?' he snapped.

'Then why won't you let me help out? It's ridiculous to say we can't go out and enjoy ourselves when I can easily afford to pay for both of us.'

'Can't you see?' he exclaimed desperately. 'I don't want to live off my wife.'

She was silent for a moment. Then she said sadly, 'Perhaps you should never have married me, then.'

He turned to take her in his arms but she slipped past him and went to the kitchen. By the time he was ready breakfast was on the table. He went and took her hands.

'Darling, I didn't mean to hurt your feelings.'

'I know,' she replied, and kissed him. 'Eat your breakfast. You'll be late. Will you be back tonight?'

'I'm afraid not. I'm due back on duty at six.'

As he was about to leave she came to him with an envelope in her hand. She put her arm round his neck and tucked the envelope into his pocket.

'Don't open it now. Wait until later. 'Bye, darling.'

He kissed her and went down to hail a taxi. In the back of the cab he opened the envelope. It contained a cheque for £500 – more than his captain's pay for a whole year. For a moment he sat and stared at it blankly. Then he folded it up and pushed it back into his pocket.

Major General Gubbins kept him waiting only a few minutes and got down to business without spending time on preliminaries.

'We're setting up a new section,' he said, 'under Douglas Dodds-Parker, to operate from North Africa. Its brief will be to conduct operations into southern Europe and it will be designated AMF – code name Massingham. One of its early tasks will be to help in the interrogation of Italian POWs, with a view to investigating the possibility of turning them and sending them back as double agents. Your fluency in Italian will obviously be of great service there, and perhaps later in other ways if Allied landings are made on Italian territory. I'd like to transfer you to Massingham, with immediate effect. How do you feel about that?'

'I'd be very happy,' Richard said, without hesitation. 'When do I leave?'

23

The colonel lowered his field glasses and glared at the young captain standing beside him. 'Where does that blithering idiot think he is?' he demanded.

Below them, on the tortuous road that wound up towards the mountain pass they now held, after a day of bitter fighting, a single vehicle was raising a plume of dust as it headed for their position. The captain, realising that the question must be rhetorical but feeling that some response was required just the same, murmured, 'I really couldn't say, sir.'

'Wandering around in a soft-skinned vehicle, as if he's on a day out from Aldershot! Doesn't he realise that there could be enemy snipers on those hills?' the colonel enquired. 'Who is it, anyway?'

'There's no way of knowing, sir,' his companion replied, 'but I've sent out a patrol to intercept him.' He pointed. 'There they go now.'

Two armoured cars had appeared round the shoulder of the hill. The two officers watched as they closed with the approaching vehicle, which stopped a few yards from them. They saw a soldier get out of one of the armoured cars and go over to speak to the newcomer and then, after a brief exchange, return to his own vehicle. The armoured cars turned round and fell in, one ahead and one to the rear, and the little convoy headed back towards the wadi where the tanks were leaguered.

'Well, we'd better go down and see what he wants,' the colonel grunted, leading the way down the steep rear slope of the hill.

By the time the two officers reached the encampment the convoy had arrived. The strange vehicle was now shown to be an unarmed truck with a canvas hood, painted in desert camouflage but bearing no regimental insignia. A tall, slim man in corduroy trousers, a khaki shirt and an officer's cap was climbing stiffly out. Reaching the ground as the colonel came up to him he came to attention and saluted.

'Lieutenant Merryweather, Army Welfare, sir.'

'Army Welfare!' exclaimed the senior officer. 'What the hell do you want? We're in the middle of a battle here.'

'Yes, I know, sir,' Merry replied. 'I've been watching it from the hill back there for most of the day. It seems to have quietened down for the night so I thought perhaps your men could do with a bit of entertainment.'

'Good God!' the captain burst out, forgetting his deferential manner. 'It's the phantom pianist!'

Merry permitted himself a small smile. 'I gather that is what they call me in some quarters.'

'The what?' demanded the colonel.

'The phantom pianist, sir. You must have heard the rumours. He turns up wherever the fighting is thickest and plays the piano.'

'Is that you?' The colonel fixed Merry with a look of incredulity. 'I've heard the rumours, of course, but I'd assumed that you were a myth – like the Angels of Mons.'

Merry's eyes glinted with amusement. 'I wish I were that potent! No, not a myth, just a wandering minstrel. You won't mind if I play for the men after they've eaten?'

'Good Lord no!' The colonel dropped his fierce tone and extended his hand. 'Good to meet you. Welcome to the Eleventh Hussars.' As they shook hands he added, 'You do realise that until this morning that road was mined? And the Jerries are just the other side of the hill?'

'Yes, I do realise,' Merry agreed calmly. 'But I watched your chaps sweeping the road first thing – and I think Jerry has had enough for today, don't you? Maybe he'll appreciate a bit of music too.'

The colonel grinned and looked suddenly ten years younger. 'You'll do! Phil, take our guest over to the mess, will you? I expect he could do with a drink.' He nodded to Merry. 'I must get on, but we'll talk again later.'

When the evening meal of tinned bully beef and hard biscuits had been consumed Merry drove his truck into the centre of the clear space in the middle of the circle of tanks. There, with the help of a couple of volunteers, he folded back the canvas awning and manhandled the old upright piano from the position it occupied while travelling, anchored against the back of the driver's cabin, to the edge of the tailboard. Then he lit a couple of oil lamps, produced a set of small spanners and set about tuning the instrument. It had occurred to him, while he was waiting in London for George Black to organise transport to Egypt for him, that this would be a very useful skill. So he had persuaded Black to send him on a crash course with an elderly gentleman who was responsible for tuning the pianos for several of London's major concert halls. The techniques he had learned had proved invaluable over the last weeks.

By the time he had finished men had started to gather in the open space around the vehicle. In little groups, they settled on the rocky ground, leaning on their packs for support, talking quietly among themselves. In the sudden desert darkness cigarette ends glowed like fireflies and a full moon rose clear of the mountains. There was a small stir to one side as stretcher-bearers carried two patients from the first aid tent and set them down, and they were followed by a group of walking wounded, some with arms in slings, others hopping on crutches or with bandaged heads. Folded blankets were laid on the ground and the newcomers were made as comfortable as possible.

Looking across the space, Merry saw the colonel and two other officers moving through the crowd. Afraid that the colonel intended to make some kind of introductory speech, he settled himself on the piano stool and began to play the first thing that came into his head. Unsurprisingly, it was the Moonlight Sonata. Usually he began with popular music of some kind, but tonight there was a magic in the atmosphere that required something more profound. His ears attuned, as always, to the reaction of his audience, he heard the murmur of conversation die away, allowing the music to spread like ripples across a pond until it was swallowed up in the silence of the desert. He played the sonata in its entirety and for the duration of the whole piece there was scarcely a stir among his audience. When he finished the last notes were allowed to die away before a kind of collective sigh swept across the assembled company and the applause started.

After a short break he changed the mood, though not the subject, with Glenn Miller's 'Moonlight Serenade' and followed that with 'A Nightingale Sang in Berkeley Square' and 'Smoke Gets in Your Eyes'. Then he turned and spoke to his audience for the first time.

'Any requests?'

There was no shortage and he played until Phil, the young captain, climbed up on to the truck and murmured, 'Colonel says he'd like to listen all night but he thinks it's time the men got some shut-eye.'

As the crowd was dispersing Merry became aware of a young soldier standing by the tailboard. In the moonlight his face was chalk white and under his open shirt his chest was swathed in bloodstained bandages.

'Excuse me, sir,' he said diffidently, 'I just wanted to say thanks. My best mate was killed this morning. You helped me through a bad patch.'

Merry had to swallow hard before replying. 'I'm sorry about your friend. I wish there was more I could do, but I'm glad if the music helped.'

The young man nodded silently and then, with a murmured 'Goodnight, sir', turned away and headed back towards the Red Cross tent.

The colonel came over. 'Wonderful performance, Merryweather! Tremendous morale booster. The men had a pretty bloody time of it today. This has taken their minds off it. Care for a nightcap?'

Merry shook his head. 'No thanks, Colonel. It's been a long evening. If you don't mind I'll just turn in.'

As the camp settled down for the night Merry spread his sleeping bag on the rough bunk he had had constructed along one side of the truck, pulled off his boots and crawled in. The canvas awning was still folded back and he lay with his hands behind his head, gazing up into a sky so dense with stars that it scarcely seemed dark. He wondered dreamily whether the Germans, encamped somewhere on the far side of the ridge, had heard the notes of the piano hanging in the still, clear air, and, if so, what they had made of it. He thought of the young soldier who had lost his friend and felt a stab of pain, as if from an old wound that he had learned not to aggravate. Then he thought of the silence that had settled over the troops when he began to play and allowed the memory to soothe him. It was not a new phenomenon in his experience, but an effect that he had seen repeated over and over again in the past weeks.

He had reached Tripoli in the middle of February, arriving by air this time after an uneventful flight via Gibraltar. He was grateful that he had not had to endure the long cruise out to Cairo via the Cape, since he was convinced that he could not have withstood the temptation to drink during weeks on board ship. For the first weeks after his return to duty he had abjured alcohol altogether. Then, in the desert heat, he had found he could permit himself an occasional beer without danger, but so far he had avoided all situations where he might be tempted into an extended drinking session.

On arrival he had reported to a Colonel Nigel Patrick, who was in charge of entertainments for the whole Middle Eastern Command. He had heard of him before the war as an actor and was glad to be dealing with a fellow professional, but he found him in a somewhat irascible mood, complaining that Army Welfare resented his interference and did not keep him fully informed about the activities of SIB units. Merry presented a letter from George Black outlining his mission, but Patrick had at first refused to countenance the idea of sending him out to the front line on his own and had tried to persuade him to take charge of a concert party. Merry had remained adamant, insisting that that was not what he had been sent to Africa to do, and eventually Patrick had given way. There had then been a further delay, while a spare vehicle was found and a piano commandeered. They had wanted to give him a driver, but again he had refused, determined to stick to his resolution to be responsible for no one but himself. Finally, he had been allowed to set off in a convoy taking supplies and reinforcements to the 8th Army, who were then engaged in beating off a fierce counter-attack from Rommel's panzers in the area of Medenine.

Once in the battle zone he was able to deduce from troop movements and casual conversation with other officers where the various units were stationed, and early one morning he had slipped away from the base camp and headed across country towards the sound of the guns. His first sight of the battlefield had been sickening. Burnt-out tanks and armoured cars littered the desert and among them lay the bodies of the dead, mainly German but with a number of corpses whose tattered uniforms bore the insignia of regiments of the British 7th Armoured Division. It was clear that all attempts to collect or bury the dead had been abandoned, and already the vultures were at work.

He had found the 1st Royal Tank Regiment leaguered in a shallow depression and had been greeted with incredulity by a young major who looked scarcely old enough to be out of school. His face was soot-blackened and his tunic stained with blood and he gazed at Merry as if he were a creature from another planet.

'You've come to do what? For God's sake, man, this is the front line. We've been fighting all day.'

'Yes, I know. But I've just come from HQ and the word is that the enemy is retiring all along this sector,' Merry said quietly. 'The fighting's over for the time being.'

'Yes, but the men are exhausted. The last thing they're in the mood for is a bloody concert!'

'Perhaps you're right. But you won't mind if I just park up somewhere and play? They don't have to listen if they don't want to.'

'Oh, do what you like!' the other officer said, turning away. Then, looking round at him, 'As long as you realise that the Jerries could counter-attack at any minute.'

So Merry had driven his truck to a corner of the encampment, not far from the first aid post, eaten a spartan meal from the provisions he carried with him and begun to play. Within minutes faces appeared round the flap on the first aid tent, staring at him in stunned surprise. Then two or three men came out and wandered over to the truck. A few others rose from the shadow of a tank, mess tins in hand, and joined them. By the time he was halfway through 'Serenade in Blue' a crowd of men were sitting on the sand around him.

From then on he had followed the tanks as they advanced until they reached the Mareth Line, the fortified line that divided Libya from Tunisia. It was an exhausting and risky existence, grinding and bouncing across the desert, often in imminent danger of overrunning the front line and finding himself in the middle of a German panzer unit. On several occasions shells landed uncomfortably close to the truck and once he had to abandon it and throw himself into the shelter of a derelict tank to escape the attentions of a Stuka dive-bomber. It occurred to him only afterwards that the instinct of self-preservation had been stronger than the desire for oblivion, which he thought he had been seeking. Often, by the time he found an encampment where his services might be appreciated, he was almost too weary to play, but he invariably found that once he started he forgot his aching limbs. In the same way, he found that the scepticism and on occasions downright hostility that greeted his arrival rapidly dissipated once the music began. Before long his reputation had spread and he had become, as the young captain had said, a kind of mythological figure – the Phantom Pianist.

*   *   *

Merry woke to the sound of tank engines starting up and the immediate fear that this was going to be a repeat of the retreat from Gazala. He sat up and peered out of the truck, and was reassured to see that the tanks were preparing to move out in good order. Phil, the captain, jogged over to him as he was pulling on his boots.

'We're advancing, but we're leaving the medics and a small protective force here, if you want to hang on. Once we've cleared the next sector you can come up and join us.'

'OK,' Merry agreed. 'I'll do that.'

By the time he had eaten breakfast the sound of gunfire had started up on the far side of the ridge and before long the first field ambulance arrived. Merry hastened over to help unload the stretchers. A tank had received a direct hit and caught fire. Three of the crew had been severely burned. The thought flashed through Merry's mind – *More guinea pigs for Archibald McIndoe!*

As the ambulance prepared to leave he said to the driver, 'Can I be any use out there?'

The driver hesitated, then said, 'We can always use another stretcher-bearer – if you want to take the risk.'

Merry climbed in beside him. 'Count me in.'

For the rest of the day he combed the battlefield, picking up wounded and dying men and transferring them back to the first aid post in the wadi, until he was as dust covered and blood spattered as any of the combatants. By nightfall another mile or two of road had been won from the enemy, a few more hilltop strongpoints wiped out, and the base camp was moved forward to another valley. Exhausted and filthy, Merry made use of what primitive ablutions were available and shared another frugal meal with the men. Then he climbed into the truck and played until he could not keep his eyes open any longer.

From that day on he was adopted as a kind of regimental mascot by the 11th Hussars and travelled with them as they forced their way through the Gabes Gap and on northwards, now in hot pursuit of the fleeing German army, towards Tunis. On 7 May B squadron of the Hussars led other units of the 7th Armoured Division into the streets of the city, to be greeted by the French inhabitants with wine and flowers. Among their ranks was a battered truck containing a piano. On the 12th, Merry witnessed a remarkable scene as the last German troops came in to surrender outside the town of Enfideville. Two battalions of the Queen's Royal Regiment were drawn up to hold the road and an area had been cordoned off for the surrendering troops to dump their equipment. All morning RAF bombers had kept up their attacks on the German lines, but as the 3 p.m. deadline approached the battlefield fell quiet. Senior officers from both the British and American armies arrived to take the surrender and the lines of dispirited men in field grey began to file past. Suddenly, the quiet was disrupted by the sound of an approaching shell and all the top brass dived ignominiously for cover. The shell passed harmlessly along the line of the front. Subsequent investigation by an expeditionary party discovered that it was a desperate plea for help from a German artillery unit marooned beyond a minefield and wanting to surrender.

The subsequent days passed in a daze of euphoria. The victorious troops were entertained and made much of by the local inhabitants, and after months in the desert the men encamped along the coast were able to swim and relax on the beaches or stroll along the palm-fringed promenades. One day, Merry, returning from a visit to a hospitable French family, was intrigued by the sound of a military band. He turned down a side road towards the beach and was greeted by an amazing sight. On the sand an impromptu football match was in progress between members of two British regiments, while others lazed on the sand or splashed happily in the water. Meanwhile, in a roped-off enclosure on the promenade, a German band in full uniform was playing 'Roll Out the Barrel' and other popular favourites for their entertainment. Merry parked the truck and got out to sit on a bench near by. Suddenly he found himself laughing. The spectacle seemed so ludicrous, so totally unlikely after everything they had been through. It was the first time he had laughed out loud since the news of Felix's death, and once he started he could not stop. Hysteria gripped him and he laughed until he was exhausted. Several men near by glanced at him curiously and then returned to their occupations. After the long months of danger and privation it was not unusual to see men behaving oddly.

The 11th Hussars were encamped near the ruins of Leptis Magna, and there they were visited by the colonel-in-chief, none other than His Majesty King George VI. Merry, hovering on the margins of the parade to watch, found himself called forward and, much to his embarrassment, presented.

'This is the man we call the Phantom Pianist, sir,' the colonel explained. 'Some regiments have a piper to lead them into battle. We have our own pianist to play us to sleep after it.'

'You've been with the regiment all the way through?' HM enquired.

'Not quite, sir. I joined up with them at the Mareth Line. Before that I was sort of freelance.'

'And you brought a piano all the way? Where did you start?'

'Tripoli, sir.'

'Remarkable!' said the King.

The atmosphere of euphoria was short lived, however. Men who had fought their way across North Africa, many of whom had not seen their families for more than a year, had been promised that after victory they would get home leave. Soon, rumours began to circulate that they were not to be sent home after all but to be prepared for a new campaign in southern Europe. Training began for seaborne landings. Many of the troops became sullen and gloomy and there were murmurs of mutiny in some quarters. General Montgomery toured the various camps in an attempt to raise morale and a general order went out that every effort should be made to keep the men entertained. It was decided to stage a lavish concert party in the George Metaxas Theatre in Tunis and Merry found himself drafted in to act as musical director.

Somewhat to his own surprise he discovered that he was not averse to returning to the familiar task. Over the weeks of living and working with the Hussars he had lost his taste for solitude, almost without realising it. He scoured the camps for latent talent and found it, as always, in abundance. Within a week or two they were ready to open with a variety performance that filled the theatre night after night.

They were not alone, however. Troopships in the harbour began disgorging buses painted with the letters ENSA. Some of the biggest names in show business had been mobilised to entertain the victorious armies. At vast open-air concerts in the desert Marlene Dietrich sang 'Falling in Love Again', Gracie Fields sang 'Sally', George Formby sang 'Leaning on a Lamppost' and 'When I'm Cleaning Windows'. Tommy

Trinder, Jack Benny and Bob Hope told jokes and Elsie and Doris Waters performed their Gert and Daisy sketches.

One morning Merry was not best pleased to receive a signal from Colonel Patrick informing him that a major musical show, which was now in Tripoli, would be arriving in Tunis the following week and would require the use of the Metaxas Theatre. Orders were orders, however, and he set about restructuring his company into smaller units to tour some of the camps. When the new company arrived he showed the producer around the theatre, had a brief chat with the new MD and was about to leave when a woman's voice hailed him excitedly.

'Merry! Merry, wait!'

He swung round. Rose was standing on the stage, one hand shading her eyes against the glare of the footlights, the other eagerly waving.

'Rose!' He bounded up the gangplank that had been laid across the orchestra pit and caught her in his arms. 'Rose! How wonderful! I had no idea you were in North Africa.'

She drew back, laughing up at him. 'Well, I wrote to you. But I thought you were still in Cairo.' Becoming serious, she scanned his face. 'How are you, Merry? It's ages since I heard from you. Are you all right?'

'Yes,' he said quietly. 'I really believe I am. Not . . . not like I was a year ago. Not happy, like that. But all right.'

'I'm so glad,' she murmured. 'I've been so worried about you. Why haven't you written?'

'Because for a long time I couldn't have posted the letters even if I did write. But I wrote you a long letter a few weeks back, soon after we got here.'

She shook her head. 'I suppose by the time your letter got back to England I was already on my way here. But anyway, it doesn't matter. You're all right, and here we both are. Isn't it lovely?'

'Yes,' he agreed, looking at her fondly, 'it is lovely. But what are you doing here? Is this the show you told me about back in Wimborne, the one you were asked to choreograph?'

'Yes,' she said with a laugh, 'it's still the same one, with a few new acts and new routines. We toured it all round England and up into Scotland to start with and then we were told we were going overseas. 'Course, nobody knew where. The rumour was we were headed for India or Burma. I was glad when it turned out to be North Africa. I kept hoping I'd run into you but no one seemed to have heard anything about you.'

'Well, I've been keeping myself to myself,' he said. 'At least until we got here. Then I was given the job of putting a show on in this theatre.'

'And we've come and pushed you out. Are you very cross?'

'Not very. I've given up being cross with anything the army decides to do. Listen, are you busy or can we go and have lunch somewhere?'

She looked around. 'There really isn't much I can do at the moment, until the stage crew finish unloading the scenery and putting it up. Lunch would be lovely.'

He took her to a little French restaurant on the seafront and they sat drinking Algerian wine and looking out over the sparkling waters.

Rose heaved a sigh. 'It's hard to believe there's a war on sometimes, isn't it?'

'Just now it is,' he agreed. 'You should have been here a month or so back.'

She looked at him. 'You've been in the thick of it, haven't you. What have you been doing, exactly?'

He gave a brief résumé, without dwelling on the gorier details, and when he had finished she studied his face for a minute and then said, 'It sounds awful, but it was what you needed, wasn't it?'

He nodded. 'Yes, I suppose it was.'

Rose said, 'You haven't had any of my letters, then?'

'A couple caught up with me in Tripoli, but that was back in March.'

'So you haven't heard about Reg.'

'Reg?'

'Bet's husband.'

'No. Heard what?' Merry asked, with sudden misgiving.

'He was killed, just before I left England.'

'Oh, no! Where? Over here?'

Rose shook her head. 'Scotland. Apparently they were on some sort of training exercise in the mountains. Reg's truck went off the road in thick fog and fell over a precipice. They said he was killed instantly.'

'Oh God!' Merry murmured. 'Poor Bet! How is she coping?'

'Well, you know Bet,' Rose answered. 'She's never been one for showing her feelings. She just went very quiet and sort of buttoned up, if you know what I mean. Of course, that was immediately after it happened. I felt terrible about leaving her but we'd already got our embarkation orders.'

'Have you heard from her?'

'Oh, yes. She writes, and so does Mum, of course. Mum says she seems to be OK.' Rose paused for a moment and then added, 'You know, the funny thing is, I think Bet would have found it easier if he'd been killed in battle somewhere. She kept saying "he never even saw a Jerry".'

'I suppose,' Merry said thoughtfully, 'it would help if she

could think of him as a hero. It must seem a very . . . I don't know, a very pointless sort of death.'

'I think that's exactly how she feels,' Rose agreed.

Merry said, 'Will she be all right financially?'

'She'll have her widow's pension, of course – and Mum has hers so for the moment they're all right. Then there's Bet's job up at the farm. And of course there's the shop. At the moment it's closed down but I've told them I've no further interest in it so if they want to sell up and take what they can get, that's up to them.'

'How about the boys?' Merry asked. 'It must have been a terrible blow to them.'

'They were upset, of course,' Rose said, 'but . . .' She hesitated and then went on, 'It's an awful thing to say but quite honestly I don't think they really miss him. I mean, they've hardly seen him for four years and that's a lifetime for little kids. Sam was only five when the war started. And when Reg did come back there were always rows. He was just the stranger who came home occasionally and tried to order them about. Does that sound terrible?'

'It's sad,' Merry said, 'but I suppose it must be happening to thousands of families.'

'The truth is,' Rose confided, 'I can't help feeling that in the end it might all be for the best. Oh, I know that sounds heartless and terribly cruel to poor Reg, but I don't know what would have happened if he'd come home at the end of the war and insisted on them all moving back to town. The boys would have hated it, and Bet wasn't keen either. I think there would have been endless rows.'

'Well, perhaps you're right,' Merry said. 'But all the same, it'll be lonely for Bet if anything happens to your mother.'

'She's got the boys,' Rose pointed out. She smiled suddenly.

'I'll tell you who they do miss – you. They keep asking when Uncle Merry's coming home.'

'I'm surprised, after last time I was there,' Merry remarked. 'I can't have been much fun.'

'Well, they understood why. They miss Felix, too. We all do.'

A waiter brought their meal and Merry, feeling a change of subject was required, said, 'What's happened to your American admirer? Do you still hear from him?'

Rose smiled. 'Beau? Oh yes, he writes when he can. Quite often, actually.'

'So you went on seeing him.'

'He came and took me out a few times when we were rehearsing but I couldn't see him often once we started the tour, of course. But we did have quite a good time on my embarkation leave.'

'Have you taken him to meet your family?'

'No.' Rose met his eyes squarely. 'Why should I?'

'It's not serious, then.'

'No.' She was very firm. 'It's just a bit of fun. We both like dancing, that's all.'

Merry put his head on one side and raised an eyebrow quizzically but she refused to be drawn any further.

A few evenings later Merry was able to make a space in his own schedule of engagements to go and see Rose's show at the Metaxas Theatre. He had to admit that it had a polish and glamour that it was impossible to achieve with the limited resources at his disposal. Afterwards he went backstage to congratulate her.

'The dance routines are breathtaking, Rose! Absolutely superb!'

'Oh, you're biased,' she said, smiling and blushing.

'No. Well, yes, of course I am. But it's the truth. And your solos are delightful. Many congratulations. I always knew you had talent, but I didn't realise you were this good!'

'Oh well.' She gave him a look that was half teasing, half serious. 'We shall be all right together, then, when we set up our own company after the war.'

'You're still thinking about that?'

'Well, why not?'

He looked at her and contemplated the idea seriously for the first time. He had to admit that it had its attractions. He took her hand and squeezed it.

'Well, why not indeed. But there's a lot of water to go under the bridge before then. We'll see.'

Some of the cast passed them and called out friendly goodnights to Rose. She answered cheerfully and Merry suddenly realised how much she had changed over the last year.

'You're really enjoying yourself, aren't you?' he said.

She looked at him, a small frown of anxiety between her brows. 'It seems dreadful to admit it, but yes, I am. Is that terribly selfish of me?'

'No, of course not. You've had your share of bad times, God knows. Make the most of the good ones.'

She smiled. 'I am doing. To be honest with you, Merry, I'm having the time of my life. I mean, look at me! I'm in charge of twelve dancers and Clifford lets me have carte blanche to do whatever I want. And I'm seeing places I never even dreamed of going to.' She broke off and put her hand on his sleeve. 'I just wish I could make you as happy as I am.'

He smiled at her and sighed inwardly, wondering whether he would ever get over Felix as completely as she appeared to have got over Richard. 'Don't worry about me, Rose. It does me good just to see you so happy. You go ahead and enjoy yourself.'

All through June the intensive training and re-equipping of the armies for a seaborne landing went on. At the beginning of July rumours began to circulate that the next offensive was about to begin. On 10 July the first Allied landings took place on the island of Sicily. In spite of all the intensive planning for a massive airborne assault a sudden change in the weather meant that the paratroopers were blown off course, many of them coming down in the sea, and German resistance was far stiffer than anticipated. Days of bitter fighting ensued before the Allied beachhead was securely established. As soon as it was, and the first convoys of supplies and reinforcements began to come ashore, among the vehicles rolling off the landing craft was the same battered lorry containing a piano and driven by a tall, deeply tanned lieutenant.

24

Richard passed through the gates in the high fence with a sinking heart. Ahead he could see the tents and the prefabricated huts of the prison compound, already quivering in the desert heat. Heading for the hut where interrogations took place he passed between wired-off cages, in which prisoners of different ranks and nationalities paced like animals. How many days, weeks, months was he condemned to spend in this hellhole? he wondered.

Suddenly he became aware of a face staring at him from the other side of the wire. A small man in the uniform of a captain in the Italian army was gripping the wire with both hands, his expression one of comic perplexity. It took a moment for Richard to recognise him. He was no longer the rotund figure he remembered from Marseilles but the dark eyes were still bright.

'*Capitano Parigi! Come sta?*'

'*Sta bene. E lei?*'

'*Non c'è male.*' He continued in Italian, 'I'd like to say I'm pleased to see you, but under the circumstances . . .'

The little man raised his hands and shrugged. '*Che sera, sera.*' He lowered his voice. 'But you. What are you doing here, my friend – like this?'

Richard moved closer and adopted the same conspiratorial tone. 'I'll explain later.' Then he turned to the military policeman who was accompanying him and said in English, 'I want to interrogate this man at once. Have him brought to my office.'

In the interrogation hut Richard took off his tunic and flopped into the chair behind his desk. A ceiling fan churned the heavy air above his head without creating a perceptible breeze and already the room was stifling. His secretary, a girl in ATS uniform, came in with the usual pile of buff folders and said cheerily, 'Good morning, Captain.'

'Is it, Mary?' he asked ruefully.

'Come along, sir, cheer up,' she chided him. 'It might never happen.'

'That's exactly it, Mary,' he said. 'I'm afraid it never will.'

She shook her head at him. 'I'll get you a nice cool drink.'

A 'nice, cool drink' was Mary's answer to every problem – the desert equivalent of a nice cup of tea. Richard sighed. He had been based at Cap Matifou, outside Algiers, for almost a month, and his sole occupation had been the interrogation of Italian POWs in search of potential secret agents. He had interviewed men who fervently affirmed their devotion to Mussolini and the Fascist creed, men who declared themselves to be communists, men who shrugged and maintained that they had no political affiliations whatever and wished only to be left to get on with their lives in peace. These last were by far the majority. But not one of them had seemed to have the slightest inclination or aptitude for clandestine activities. And Richard was bored, bored, *bored.*

Heavy boots approached along the corridor and the MP presented himself at the door. 'The prisoner you sent for, sir.'

Richard thanked him and he stamped, turned about and marched himself out of the door. Richard rose and went round his desk, extending his hand. '*Capitano*, please. Come and sit down.'

The little Italian stared at him. 'It is you, isn't it? I'm not mistaken. Ricardo Benedetti? The young opera singer I met in Marseilles? You gave a recital for me and my friends at the Hôtel Louvre et Paix. What are you doing here, masquerading as a British captain?'

Richard smiled as he resumed his seat. He was beginning to enjoy himself. 'I'm afraid, signor, that I have deceived you. My name is Richard Stevens, and I am English.'

'But your perfect Italian,' Parigi exclaimed, 'and your voice! No Englishman sings Verdi like that!'

'Well, here's one who does,' Richard said. 'But part of what I told you was true. I did train in Milan.'

'Ah!' said the Italian. 'That explains it – in part, at least. But then,' he frowned, clearly trying to reassess their two previous encounters, 'when we first met, you were an English officer, even then?'

'No. That first time I was an ordinary English private soldier trying to get home after Dunkirk.'

'And the second time?'

'Then I was on a mission for my government.'

'A spy?'

'No. I was not looking for information. I was trying to set up a network to help other British servicemen to get back to England.'

'And I gave you a pass to get into the occupied zone!' Parigi said, and burst into laughter. 'What effrontery!' He sobered and then added, 'And the young woman who sang with you. Was she a British agent too?'

'No, she was French. But she worked for one of the escape lines.'

'And did you find her again, when you came back that time?'

'Yes,' Richard said quietly, 'I found her.'

'But?' Parigi looked at him perceptively. 'What happened? She had found someone else?'

'No. She died. She was betrayed to the Germans.'

'They shot her?'

'No. But the treatment she received at their hands killed her.'

Parigi spat. 'Filthy Nazis! If you only knew how I hate them!'

'And the Fascists in your own country?'

'They are just as bad. Dragging us into this war. I tell you, I am glad that we have lost here in Africa. Mussolini cannot survive much longer. The sooner we get rid of him the better.'

'I'm delighted to hear you say that,' Richard murmured. He was beginning to wonder whether he might have found, in this unlikely little man, the potential agent he was looking for. But, on the other hand, Parigi was so open, so patently good natured, Richard doubted whether he had the capacity to deceive.

Parigi leaned across the desk. 'So, tell me, you are still singing?'

'Oh, from time to time. I don't get much chance to practise.'

'You must not let that voice go to waste! I tell you, as *répétiteur* at Bologna Opera I have heard many great voices but very few like yours.'

'I'm flattered, signor,' Richard said, flushing with pleasure. 'That is indeed a compliment.' He pulled a folder towards him. 'Forgive me, but I think we are both forgetting that I am supposed to be interrogating you, not the other way about. You will not mind if I ask a few questions? Tell me, how do you come to be here?'

Parigi shrugged. 'When the Germans took over the whole of France the German/Italian liaison committee in Marseilles was wound up and I was posted to Tunis. When your army moved in I was rounded up with the rest.'

Richard asked a few more routine questions and then looked across the desk at Parigi.

'You have told me you would like to see Mussolini deposed. Would you consider working to that end?'

'Working for you, you mean?'

'For my government.'

'I should relish the chance!' Parigi's eyes flashed. 'Tell me what I can do.'

'That isn't up to me,' Richard said. 'What I can do is send you back to my superiors in London. If they think you are suitable you will be given the appropriate training. But I must warn you, it could be very dangerous.'

Parigi rose to his feet. 'I have sat quietly and let these monsters have their own way for too long. Now it is time for me to show that I, too, can be a fighter. Send me! I swear you will not regret it.'

Richard got up in his turn. 'Very well. It may be a few days before you hear anything further. I need hardly tell you that it is vital that you give no hint of this conversation to your fellow prisoners.'

'I am not such a fool,' Parigi assured him.

Richard extended his hand. 'I wish, most sincerely, that we were not on opposite sides.'

Parigi smiled. 'It will not always be so. Have patience. When the war is over we shall meet again as friends.' He hesitated and then added, 'Will your people invade my country?'

'I'm not in a position to know what our future strategy is,' Richard replied evasively.

'If they do, Mussolini will be deposed and the new government will sue for peace,' Parigi said with conviction. 'There is no appetite in Italy for war with the British.'

'I hope you're right,' Richard said. 'I should hate to think of cities like Rome and Florence suffering as Berlin and Dresden have suffered.'

Parigi shuddered. 'Let us not even think of it!'

Richard went to the door. 'Is there anything you need?'

'Some soap perhaps? And toothpaste.'

'I'll see you are given some. That's all I can do for the moment.' He called the guard. 'You can return the captain to the compound now.'

Parigi turned in the doorway. 'And remember, when this is all over you are going to come to Bologna and sing for me. I shall look for you.'

'I should like to do that, very much,' Richard said, but at that moment he could not visualise circumstances under which it would be possible.

That evening Richard was sitting in the bar of the hotel that had been requisitioned as the officers' mess when he received a message that his boss, Douglas Dodds-Parker, wanted to see him at once. There was a thick buff folder on the senior man's desk, which Richard recognised as his personal record.

Dodds-Parker offered him a drink and then said with a smile, 'I hear you've been making a nuisance of yourself.'

'Me?' Richard responded. 'In what way?'

'Complaining of boredom and wanting to get back to something more active.'

'Oh, that!' Richard said, with relief. 'Yes, I have passed comments to that effect.'

'Well,' Dodds-Parker went on, 'I think we may have just the thing for you.'

'Really?' Richard sat forward. His common sense told him that what he was about to be offered would be far more dangerous than what he was doing now, but anything was better than the daily grind of interrogation after interrogation.

'It won't come as a surprise to you to learn that there is likely to be an invasion of Italy some time in the near future. From the reports of interrogations carried out by yourself and others, and from other sources that I won't go into, it seems clear that there are already groups of disaffected men there who have gone into hiding in the mountains. Some of these have already formed themselves into partisan bands and are carrying out subversive activities, but we don't know to what extent. We need first-hand information about these groups. We need to know what sort of numbers are involved, whether they have arms or other equipment, where they are located and who the leaders are. If we find that there are enough of them to make it worth our while, and that there are leaders who we can rely on, we may consider dropping arms and ammunition and possibly personnel to assist with organisation and training. And the only way of reliably obtaining that information is to send someone over there to make contact with them. It seems to me that you are ideally suited to the job.' He paused and looked at Richard. 'Well, what do you say?'

'It's a big country,' Richard said. 'Where do I start?'

'Good man!' said Dodds-Parker. He spread a map of Italy on the desk. 'According to our information there is at least one group active in the Piedmont area, quite close to the French border, and others in the Apennines between Bologna and Livorno. This cover story of yours, as a cabaret entertainer, this would stand up in Italy?'

'I don't see why it shouldn't.'

'You're confident that you can pass as an Italian.'

'Yes. Particularly after speaking Italian all day for the last month.'

'Good. The plan I would like to suggest is this. We will put you ashore in the Viareggio area from one of our "Q" ships. You would need to find a job there, a temporary one, which would give you a chance to get to know people, see if you can pick up any whispers about partisan activity. Does that sound feasible?'

Richard thought. 'There shouldn't be any difficulty getting a job singing in a bar or a club somewhere. After that – well, the Italians are not noted for being tight lipped. Whether I shall actually be able to meet any of these partisans is a matter of luck, really.'

'Quite,' agreed Dodds-Parker. 'Anyway, once you've found out as much as you feel you are going to in that area, I suggest you move north along the coast to Genoa and from there west towards San Remo and the French border, keeping your ears open all the way and hoping to make contact with other groups in the mountains there.'

'And how do I get all this information back to base?' Richard asked. 'Will I have radio contact?'

Dodds-Parker shook his head. 'I'm afraid not. We considered sending a wireless operator with you, but it was felt that that would greatly increase your chances of detection. For the same reason it was decided not to lumber you with a set of your own.'

Richard considered this information with mixed feelings. Certainly he had no wish to lug around one of the cumbersome suitcases he had seen radio operators carrying in France. For a man carrying one of those any random search brought the threat of instant discovery, quite apart from the danger of being picked up by an enemy detector van in the act of transmitting. On the other hand, the prospect of being marooned in enemy territory without any communication with base and no contacts with possible helpers in an underground resistance movement was unnerving.

'So, how do I get the information back?' he asked.

'You memorise as much as possible and report to me on your return.'

'And how do I get back?'

'I gather you have contacts in Monte Carlo.'

'Yes, if they are still there. I can't see any reason why they shouldn't be.'

'Is there somewhere you would suggest as a safe place for a rendezvous?'

'Yes. The Scottish Tearooms. They are owned by a pair of maiden ladies, the Misses Trenchard. They're a wonderful pair and have been very helpful to escaping airmen and POWs.'

'Right. You will be given a date on which someone will meet you there. He will have a ship standing offshore. If you are not there, he will return at the same time for the next two days. That date will be one week before the full moon. If you fail to make the rendezvous then the ship will come back two weeks later – in other words one week after the full moon – and as before your contact will wait for you in the same place on three successive days.'

'And if I can't make it then, either?'

'Then it will be a question of either hiding out until the Allied invasion reaches you or making your way back into France and contacting one of our agents there.'

'And how long do I have to achieve all this?' Richard asked.

'We are now at the beginning of June. London wants the information by the middle of August. So, less than three months. Say ten weeks?'

Ten weeks, on his own, in enemy territory. Richard felt his stomach turn over at the prospect. But he had wanted a change from the work he was doing, had found himself craving excitement as an addict craves tobacco. He could not refuse now.

'Right,' he said. 'When do I leave?'

The fishing boat lay hove-to on the dark swell under a slit of moon, while her crew, without the need for orders, silently lowered a rubber dinghy. Richard stood straining his eyes towards the land a few hundred yards distant. He was experiencing a strong sense of déjà vu. This was the third time he had made one of these night landings. The difference this time was that there would be no friendly reception committee to meet him and direct him to a safe house. He was about to land, not in occupied territory where the inhabitants might reasonably be expected to be on his side, passively if not actively, but on enemy ground, whose occupants would probably be quite likely to turn him over to the authorities.

A tall, broad-shouldered man in a fisherman's jersey swung himself out of the wheelhouse and came over to him.

'They're ready for you.' He looked Richard over and grinned. 'I can see you've done this before.'

Richard had taken off his trousers and tied them around his neck. 'Once or twice,' he agreed.

The other man held out his hand. 'Good luck, Richard.'

'Thanks, Gerry.' Richard shook his hand. 'Don't forget our date in Monte.'

'Don't worry. I'll be there.'

Earlier that evening they had leaned, side by side, over a chart spread out on the table in the tiny cabin.

'We're going to put you ashore here,' his companion said, stabbing the map with his forefinger. 'A few miles south of Viareggio, near the estuary of the River Arno. The area seems to be more or less uninhabited and our aerial reconnaissance boys report that the beach doesn't appear to have been mined.'

'What's this?' Richard asked, indicating a large blue area just inland.

Gerald Holdsworth peered at a name on the map. 'Torre del Lago Puccini. Wasn't he the opera chappy?'

'Giacomo Puccini,' Richard said. 'Yes, he wrote operas. Now I come to think of it I remember reading that he lived somewhere in this area. Very keen on wildfowling, I believe. That's why he bought the house by the lake.'

Holdsworth looked at him as if seeing him in a new light. 'Opera buff, are you?'

'Just a bit,' Richard agreed.

Now he turned to lower himself down into the dinghy, where two sailors in dark clothes and with blackened faces were waiting. Someone handed down his suitcase and the sailors dipped their oars. As the little boat glided through the water Richard told himself that the coincidence of the location was a good omen. Phrases of music ran through his mind – one of the great arias that made him wish he were a tenor rather than a baritone, '*Nessun dorma!*', 'None shall sleep'. It seemed appropriate at that moment. Then he remembered the triumphant conclusion, '*A l'alba vincero!*', 'With the dawn I shall conquer'. He decided that it was a good enough watchword to see him through the next few hours.

Ten minutes later he was scrambling ashore and his last contact with his own people was pulling away into the darkness. He stood still at the edge of the waves for a few long minutes, listening and looking around him. His eyes were already adapted to the night and he could make out the outlines of the coast. There appeared to be no sign of movement and his straining ears picked up nothing but the suck and hiss of the waves breaking behind him. He walked up the beach, praying that intelligence had been right about the mines, and then paused by a flat-topped rock to put on his trousers and shoes.

The beach ended in low sand dunes, on which grew tufts of marram grass and low, prickly plants that caught at his ankles. Beyond the dunes was a flat area of rough scrubland that melded into the outskirts of a forest of small pines. Richard took a bearing from the stars and walked cautiously into the trees. He knew from the maps he had studied that if he kept walking east he would eventually reach the main road that followed the coast up to Viareggio. But before that he had to cross the railway. He came upon it in a shallow cutting and lay flat at the top of the bank, listening and watching, until he was sure that there was no patrol near by. Then he scrambled down and crossed the lines as quickly as possible, keenly aware that he was exposed to the view of any watcher. On the far side he paused, listening again, but there was no sound except for the chirruping of frogs from some marshy area near by. He pressed on, following a narrow track between the trees. He was on top of the road before he realised it. He heard the sound of engines and dropped flat on the ground while a convoy of lorries with carefully shielded headlights passed across his line of vision.

When they had passed he moved back into the trees and sat down with his back against the trunk of one. His watch told him that he had a couple of hours before dawn. He settled himself as comfortably as possible to wait. To be seen wandering along the road during the hours of darkness would be to invite arrest.

He must have dozed for a while, for he came to at the sound of voices and feet tramping along the road. Instantly alert, he strained his ears to catch what was being said. After a few seconds he relaxed. There were only two men and they were discussing something to do with cattle. Farm labourers, on their way to work in the fields. He waited until their steps faded and then opened his case and took out a bar of chocolate and a bottle of mineral water – Italian chocolate and Italian mineral water, provided by the back-up team at base. Having made a frugal breakfast, he left the shelter of the trees and looked up and down the road. It was deserted. He climbed up the bank and set off in the direction of Viareggio.

Before long he heard vehicles behind him. It was a convoy of army trucks and he let them pass, simply waving cheerily to the leading driver, at the same time automatically noting the type of vehicle and the regimental insignia and other markings and storing them away in his memory. The next vehicle to approach was a private car and as it neared he saw that the driver was a priest. He raised his hand, begging a lift in the recognised Italian manner. He was wearing the special shoes with the lift in the sole that made him limp and he had no intention of walking any farther than necessary. To his relief, the car drew up a little ahead of him.

'Where are you going, my son?' the priest asked, as Richard leaned down to the window.

'Viareggio, Father, if possible,' he replied.

'Get in.'

'And what takes you to Viareggio?' the priest asked, as they drove on. 'Do you have family there?'

'I am looking for work,' Richard explained. 'I am a singer. I had an engagement in Lucca but it came to an end. Now I am going to try Viareggio.'

'Why are you not in the army?'

'I was, but I was wounded and discharged. So now I have to earn a living somehow, but times are hard.'

'For all of us,' the priest agreed.

'I would ask you if you can recommend anywhere,' Richard said, 'but I don't suppose you frequent those sorts of places.'

'That rather depends on exactly what sort of entertainment you provide,' the priest returned. 'I am very fond of good music. You might try the Grand Hotel Europa. I know they used to have a cabaret before the war.'

Richard thanked him and the priest dropped him opposite the hotel, which was an imposing red-stone building on the elegant promenade. It was still early, so Richard went into a small café-bar that was obviously frequented by people who worked locally, and ordered coffee and a roll. After a little he found an opportunity to engage the proprietor in conversation and explained that he was a stranger to the town and in search of work and a place to stay. By the time he left he had been recommended to the house of a widow a few streets away, who took in paying guests, and a bar by the harbour which was known to employ musicians from time to time. The widow was delighted to let an empty room and charmed by her good-looking and well-spoken young visitor. By 10 a.m. Richard had washed and shaved and was ready to go in search of employment.

This turned out to be surprisingly easy. There was a dearth of young male entertainers, with all those of military age away fighting, and in a country where the love of music was bred in the bone a good-looking young man with a magnificent voice was bound to attract custom. By the end of the day he had arranged an early evening spot at the hotel, followed by later appearances at the club by the harbour. The clientele at the two places was very different and he felt that this gave him the maximum opportunity for making useful contacts.

He was glad to see that Viareggio had maintained its air of sophistication, in spite of the war, and the Grand Hotel Europa had a select and loyal clientele. The customers were mainly respectable professional people, doctors, lawyers and businessmen, who brought their wives and families for an evening out. There was also usually a good sprinkling of army and naval officers, both Italian and German, which meant that he had to be particularly circumspect, but that was no novelty. He quickly established himself as a popular favourite with his repertoire of light operatic arias and traditional ballads.

The habitués of the Club Il Pirata were a very different lot, mainly sailors or fishermen or those who worked around the waterfront, together with their girlfriends and the occasional prostitute. Richard varied his repertoire accordingly.

He made a habit of drinking in the bar at both the hotel and the club after he had finished performing, and it was not hard to strike up a conversation with the customers. There was a natural curiosity about his sudden appearance in their midst and the fact that he was not in uniform, which he was very ready to satisfy. He had added a rider to his story. At the end of it he would say, 'It's just as well the army threw me out. I should have made a terrible soldier. I'm not a fighter – that is unless I can see something worth fighting for.'

The tone was jocular but his eyes tried to convey a different message, an invitation for his interlocutor either to affirm his loyalty to Il Duce or to hint that he, too, would not wish to sacrifice his life for the current regime. The bait was never taken, however. Either his companions were too circumspect to allow any suggestion of disloyalty to pass their lips or they were simply not interested. Richard breakfasted every day at the café where he had stopped on the first morning and took his lunch at a small restaurant patronised by businessmen in the more prosperous part of the town, but none of his conversations looked like yielding any useful hints. If there was an underground movement in Viareggio he could not see how he was going to make contact with it. In frustration, he began to take risks. One lunchtime, in the restaurant, he pretended to have drunk too much and made several belligerently indiscreet remarks about Mussolini and the Fascists, until the proprietor came to his table and hissed, 'Shut up, you fool! Do you want to get us all thrown into jail?' But his charade seemed to have had no other effect.

He was beginning to think that he would have to find some excuse for travelling up into the mountainous region behind the coast when the breakthrough occurred. It came about in a most unexpected way. One evening at the hotel he noticed among the guests a family he had seen there two days earlier. The father was a distinguished-looking man with strongly marked features and hair greying at the temples, the mother a typical Italian signora, in that what had once obviously been a voluptuous figure had ripened into a comfortable and well-corseted plumpness. With them was a girl of about twenty or so who was obviously their daughter but who had the misfortune to inherit her father's powerful nose and jaw rather than her mother's softer features, and so might be described as handsome, even striking, but never pretty. Richard remembered having seen the father once or twice on his own, lunching in the restaurant. That night, however, it was the daughter who caught his attention, not because he felt particularly drawn to her but because she was quite plainly attracted by him. Indeed, he had never received more obvious invitations from the eyes of an apparently respectable girl.

When, at the end of his last number, a waiter came over with an invitation for him to join the family at their table he went with considerable hesitation, knowing how protective Italian fathers were of their unmarried daughters and worried that he was about to be warned off. He was courteously received, however, and offered a glass of wine. The father introduced himself as Alfredo Mancinelli and his wife as Giovanna. The daughter's name was Antonia. The conversation took its usual course and he concluded with his usual half-joking comment about his lack of enthusiasm for fighting. For once, this remark provoked a response.

'But you would fight if necessary in a good cause?'

'Oh yes, signor! I hope I am not a coward.'

'And what would you see as a good cause?'

Richard thought carefully. This man could equally well be preparing to denounce him as a traitor as attempting to recruit him into a subversive organisation. Or perhaps it was merely a philosophical speculation.

'I would fight,' he said, 'for freedom – or for love.'

'Ah-ha!' The older man laughed. 'A true romantic! What a pity you are a baritone. You are temperamentally much suited to the tenor roles – more a Cavaradossi than a Scarpia, no?'

Richard laughed in turn and the conversation moved to opera in general and then to other neutral topics. Signor Mancinelli, he learned, was a lawyer with a practice in the town and an ardent music lover. His daughter was a nurse in a hospital in Castelnuovo, on the other side of the mountains. She was home for a week's holiday. Richard would have found the company pleasant, except that he was still unnerved by the flirtatious looks she cast in his direction.

The next day a note was waiting for him when he arrived at the hotel, inviting him to take luncheon with the family on Sunday. In the interim he went over and over the previous conversation, trying to decide whether there was anything in it to suggest that he might be on the right track at last. It seemed more likely that Mancinelli was simply playing the indulgent father to a daughter who had obviously taken a fancy to this itinerant musician.

Lunch was enjoyable but provided no further clues. After the meal, Signora Mancinelli suggested that they should take a stroll and they joined the other local families parading gently up and down the promenade. Richard had seen many of these *passegiatas* before and knew their purpose. They were to allow the unmarried young people of both sexes a chance to view each other and perhaps effect introductions. To be seen walking with a young lady and her parents was tantamount to an announcement of an engagement. Inevitably, the signor and signora walked ahead, leaving him to escort Antonia.

As they strolled along Richard racked his brain for a way of hinting that he was not available. A wife formed no part of his cover story and he was about to invent a jealous girlfriend when Tonia remarked, 'I wish you could meet my brother, Armando.'

'You have a brother? I suppose he is away with the army.'

'No, not with the army.'

'The navy, perhaps? Or the air force?'

'No. He would not fight in this war. Like you, he did not see it as a just cause.'

'So, where is he?'

'He went away.'

'That's what I should have done, instead of letting myself be conscripted. If only I had known where to go . . .'

'It would be good if you could meet him. You have much in common, I think.'

'I should like that very much,' Richard said, and for a moment their eyes met.

She changed the subject after that and soon her parents turned back towards home and he was politely dismissed. But the next day Alfredo Mancinelli appeared at the restaurant at lunchtime and invited Richard to join him. After the meal they strolled down to the seafront again.

'I have been thinking about what you said on the first evening we met,' Mancinelli remarked. 'I believe Tonia told you that we have a son who feels much as you do.'

Richard knew that the moment had come for him to make a move that would commit him, for good or evil.

'I admire him for having the courage to leave home rather than be conscripted to fight in a cause he does not believe in,' he said. 'I wish that I had had the courage to do that.'

'Your wound was not entirely . . . accidental, then,' Mancinelli queried with a sideways glance.

'Not exactly,' Richard said, with a significant hesitation. 'Perhaps providential would be a better description.'

They walked in silence for a while and then Mancinelli continued, 'You travel a good deal, looking for work?'

'Yes, indeed. My profession takes me all over the country.'

'You could perhaps carry a letter with you to an address in Bologna, say? A letter I would give you. One that could not be entrusted to the usual channels.'

'I should be very happy to be employed in that way,' Richard said. He paused and looked his companion in the eye. 'In fact, it would not be the first time I had carried sensitive messages.'

Mancinelli scrutinised him for a moment and then nodded. 'Well, I will bear it in mind.'

After a moment Richard added, 'But what I should really like is to be of greater use than simply acting as a messenger. I wonder . . . I wonder if your son, Armando, might know of someone who could use my services.'

'That might be difficult,' Mancinelli said. 'As Tonia told you, he is not here at present.'

That evening the hall porter at the hotel handed Richard a note. 'For you, from the Signorina Mancinelli.' He rolled his eyes expressively. '*Che bella bambina!*'

Richard produced what he hoped was a suitably gratified smirk and thanked him. The note invited him to meet her the next morning, by the bandstand on the promenade.

Tonia was waiting for him as arranged and when he arrived suggested they should walk together. After a little she said, 'You wanted to meet my brother.'

'Yes, very much.'

'Why should he want to meet you?'

After a moment's hesitation Richard said, 'I might be able to be of use to him.'

She looked at him challengingly. 'Why should I trust you?'

He said quietly, 'Put it this way. If you take me to see your brother I think I can convince him that I am genuine. If he's not satisfied – well, I am alone and I imagine he has friends with him. I shall be at their mercy. He can dispose of me as he wishes.'

Tonia continued to stare at him for a long moment. Then she said, 'Come.'

A short distance up a side road a small car was parked. They got in and Tonia headed out of town. As they drove she said, 'If anyone stops us you are Dr Emanuelle Fioretto and we are going to attend a difficult confinement in the village of Isola Santa. Look in the glovebox. You will find identity papers for Dr Fioretto.'

Richard found the papers. There was a suitably indistinct photograph of a dark-haired young man who might just be himself. He put the papers in his pocket and looked at Antonia with a new respect. 'You have done this sort of thing before.'

She shrugged. 'Perhaps.'

He settled back in his seat. 'Just as long as I'm not actually required to assist at this confinement!'

They drove north, following the coastline, until they reached Pietrasanta. Then Antonia turned the car inland, following a river valley towards the mountains, which rose in a steep, tree-clad scarp, slashed here and there by the white scars of marble quarries. At Ruosina they made an abrupt turn away from the river and began to climb in a series of hairpin bends, through forests of sweet chestnut and beech lightened by the pale plumes of acacia. The roadside verges were vivid with valerian and poppies and for a while Richard was able to calm his nerves in contemplation of the spectacular beauty of his surroundings. Just as it seemed they had climbed almost to the level of the craggy summits the road plunged into a long tunnel, where the car's headlights showed up walls of spectral grey. As suddenly, they were out in the sunlight again, descending through a narrow defile between precipitous cliffs.

'*Ecco!*' Antonia exclaimed. 'This is what we call the Garfagnana.'

'Garfagnana?' he repeated.

'It is a valley between the Alpi Apuane and the Apennines. Once it was an important pilgrimage route from Switzerland and France to Rome. Now . . .' She lifted her shoulders. 'It is a forgotten area. The people here are very poor. But it is beautiful. You will see, soon.'

'And this is where you work?'

'Castelnuovo, yes. It is just below us now. It is the main town of the area.'

At length the road levelled out and the walls of the defile fell back to reveal glimpses of the valley. Richard saw a broken landscape of sharp hills and ridges, falling away to a winding river. Most of it was thickly wooded, with the occasional patch of pastureland or the silver of olive groves, and every hilltop seemed to be crowned with a cluster of grey stone houses, sheltering beneath the protection of a ruined castle.

Ahead of them he saw the outskirts of the town, but before they reached it Antonia swung the car to the right, into a narrow, unmade track, and they began to climb again. Here, the banks on either side were dotted with the pink spikes of orchids. Eventually they came to a bridge over a stream and beside it a ruined cottage, and Tonia stopped the car.

'Now we walk. I hope your leg will stand up to a climb.'

'I'll manage,' he told her.

They trudged upwards for some twenty minutes, until they reached another ruined building. As they rounded the corner of it two men with caps pulled low over their eyes and scarves wound about their faces appeared from behind a wall and Richard felt the muzzle of a pistol cold against his neck. A voice said. 'Keep quiet and you will come to no harm.'

With an effort of will he forced himself to remain passive as a sack of some kind was slipped over his head. He was prodded forwards, stumbling on the uneven ground, propelled and supported by hands gripping his arms. He had known from the start that he was putting himself into the hands of Tonia and her brother – if he existed. Now he must trust that he had not misjudged the situation. His feet rang on cobbles and he smelt the farmyard odours of dung and hay. He heard a door open, stumbled down two steps and sensed the change from sunlight to a dim interior. Then the sack was removed and he found himself in a large, stone-flagged room with a low, beamed ceiling. In the centre of the room was a rough wooden table at which a man was sitting. Two others stood behind him like guards. All three wore balaclava helmets that left only their eyes and mouths exposed.

The seated man said, 'Tell me why I should let you leave this place alive.'

'Because we are fighting on the same side,' Richard said. 'Because I can be very useful to you.'

'Prove it.'

'May I take off my jacket?'

The man looked beyond him at his escort. 'Has he been searched?'

'No, *Capitano*.'

'Idiot! Do it now.'

Richard raised his hands as the man behind him began to rifle through his pockets. 'You will find a revolver strapped to my thigh, inside my right trouser pocket.'

A hand plunged into his pocket and retrieved the .32 Colt that he always carried when working undercover. The searching hands felt down one leg and then the other.

'That's all, *Capitano*.'

'Good.' The leader nodded. 'You were wise to declare that gun, my friend. We might have got quite the wrong impression. Now, you can remove your jacket if you wish.'

Richard stripped off the jacket, turned it inside out and, with a sharp tug, pulled out one of the shoulder pads. He laid it on the table. 'Do you have a knife?'

'Yes.'

'Cut the stitching there.'

The man produced a penknife and did as Richard had indicated. Then he turned the little pouch formed by the shoulder pad upside down and shook it. Out fell Richard's military identification discs and a small document in English, German and Italian identifying him as a British officer and as such entitled to the protection of the Geneva Convention on prisoners of war.

The Italian picked up each item and studied it carefully. Then he raised his eyes to Richard.

'You are a British officer?'

'Yes.'

'Why are you here?'

'Our intelligence reports suggest that there are partisan groups hiding out in the mountains who are engaging in subversive activities. I have been sent to assess the validity of these reports and to estimate the numbers involved, the armaments available, the extent of the sabotage and other acts being carried out. Above all, to ascertain whether, in the event of an Allied invasion, these groups would be prepared to assist the Allied war effort.'

The dark eyes behind the balaclava were studying him intently. 'And if your report proves favourable – what then?'

'Final decisions are not up to me, of course. But I understand that, if my superiors are satisfied that the effort would be cost effective, suitable groups would receive parachute drops of supplies.'

'Arms and ammunition?'

'Yes, certainly – provided I can convince my people that they are going to be used to assist the Allied advance.'

'Automatic weapons? Explosives?'

'Presumably. Also, we might drop British liaison officers to help with training and radio operators to keep in touch with our bases, so you can let them know what you need most. They would also transmit intelligence reports. We would want to know about troop movements, artillery positions, locations of airfields and HQs and so on.'

There was a pause. Then the Italian rose to his feet and in the same movement stripped off the balaclava. Coming round the table he extended his hand to Richard.

'Welcome to the Fiamme Verde, Captain.'

Richard's first reaction was a shock of recognition. Here were the Roman nose and the determined jaw that robbed Antonia of the appellation 'beautiful', together with the intelligent dark eyes and the thick, black hair that made her attractive. In this male version the result was a man of striking good looks. His second thought was surprise at his youth. From the quiet authority of his bearing he had expected someone considerably more mature but he was possibly even younger than Richard himself.

From behind him, Antonia said, 'Ricardo, this is my brother Armando.'

'I had already guessed that,' Richard said, taking the outstretched hand with a grin. 'You and your sister are remarkably alike, signor.'

'So we have often been told,' responded the other. 'But, Tonia, this man is not Ricardo. He is,' he glanced at the identity document on the table, 'Captain Richard Stevens of the British army.'

'No!' Richard said quickly. 'That information must not go

beyond this room. I am Ricardo Benedetti, a singer – and that is what you must call me.'

'*Capito*,' agreed Armando. 'You can rely on us. I must apologise for your rather rude reception, but you understand we have to be careful. You were not manhandled in any way, I hope.'

'Your men were the soul of courtesy,' Richard assured him. 'I should have been very worried if you had let me arrive here without taking such precautions.' He looked at the items on the table. 'Do you mind if I take those back now?'

'Of course.' Armando handed him his gun and slipped the identity discs back into the open shoulder pad.

Antonia took it from him. 'This will need stitching up. I will see to it for you. I have needle and thread here in my bag.'

She sat at the end of the table and Armando turned to one of the young lieutenants, who had now also unmasked. 'Silvano, bring some wine. We have something to celebrate.' He indicated a chair. 'Please, Ricardo, sit. There are many things we need to discuss.'

As they settled themselves round the table Armando asked, 'This invasion. When will it take place?'

'I'm not privy to that kind of information,' Richard said. 'All I can tell you is that preparations were being made when I left North Africa for large-scale landings somewhere. I don't know where, or when, except that the authorities want my report by the middle of August. I would guess they intend to invade before the summer is out.'

Silvano set a jug of wine and glasses before them. Armando raised his glass. 'To the British and the Americans! May they come soon and drive these *fascisti* and their Nazi masters out of our country!'

The toast was drunk with enthusiasm and then they settled to the real business of the occasion.

'How many of you are there here?' Richard asked.

'Nine at present. But more come every week, as they learn about our existence.'

'Do you have arms?'

'Some. Not enough. Five of the men are deserters from the army. They brought their rifles with them and I have a pistol. The others have shotguns. But if we are to be any use we must have machine guns and explosives.'

'Understood,' Richard agreed. 'Are there any other groups like yours in the area?'

Armando nodded. 'Not far from here, at Alpe Sant Antonio, there is a group of Garibaldini. They are the communists. We Fiamme Verde, the Green Flames, are Christian Democrats who cannot tolerate the Fascists on both religious and political grounds. We and the Garibaldini have completely different philosophies but we are united in one thing – in the desire to get rid of Mussolini and the Nazis.'

'Do you cooperate?' Richard enquired.

'Sometimes. Theoretically, we all come under the orders of the Committee of National Liberation.'

'Who are they?'

'Each major city has a committee, formed by an alliance of various underground groups. There are the SAP, the Squadre d'Azione Patriotica, and the GAP, the Gruppo d'Azione Patriotica, and so on. Our father – mine and Antonia's – is a member of the committee in Viareggio. That is why he was anxious to recruit you.'

'He wants me to take a letter to Bologna.'

'Yes. That is the control centre for our operations.'

'Could I meet these people?'

'Of course. My father will give you a letter of introduction to a lawyer in Bologna. He will put you in touch with the committee.'

Silvano and another young man came in bearing plates containing olives and bread and a few slices of ham. As they set them on the table, Antonia produced, from her nurse's bag, a round cheese wrapped in sacking.

Armando unwrapped it with a gasp of delight. 'Tonia! A whole Pecorino! I haven't seen a cheese like this for weeks. Where did you get it?'

His sister smiled. 'A present from a farmer whose wife I helped through a difficult confinement. I have been saving it for you.'

As they sat down to eat Richard asked, 'Are food supplies a problem?'

'Frankly, yes,' Armando replied. 'The local people are suspicious of us. They have been told by the authorities that we are bandits who will steal their food and murder them in their beds. And anyway, they are starving themselves. Already they are living on bread made from ground-up chestnuts, with last year's dried tomatoes and the occasional egg.'

'And you? How do you manage?'

'We live on what we can shoot or trap – rabbits, mainly. And sometimes we can buy bread, or chestnut flour. God knows what we shall do when winter comes.'

Over the meal Richard probed for further information and they discussed possible future action. It became clear to him that he was dealing with men who were brave and idealistic but who lacked the training and basic equipment to allow them to survive, let alone cause the enemy any serious problems. Nevertheless, he was impressed by Armando's intelligence and his commitment and concluded that, if there were others like him, it would be well worthwhile to encourage and supply them.

All through the meal Antonia had sat next to one of Armando's young lieutenants and when they finally rose to leave she brought him over.

'Ricardo, I want you to meet my fiancé, Gianni.'

Richard shook hands with the young man and congratulated them both. He turned to Armando.

'I don't know if we shall meet again and I can't promise that any of the things you ask for will be forthcoming in the immediate future. All I can do is report to my superiors. But I wish you all the very best of luck.'

In the car on the way back to Viareggio he said, 'You didn't tell me you were engaged.'

She cast him a sideways look. 'I know. I'm sorry. You must have thought I was very bold and forward.'

'Well,' he agreed, 'you did make me a bit nervous.'

She laughed. 'But it was necessary, you see. I had to give my father an excuse to invite you to lunch. People had to have a reason for seeing us together.'

'Of course,' he agreed. 'I can see that now.'

She glanced at him again, half amused, half apologetic. 'I hope you are not too disappointed.'

He hesitated and then said, gallantly, 'I might have been, very disappointed indeed, but for one thing. You see, I am a married man.'

'You are married? But of course! I should have realised that. You are too good looking to be single. Your wife is English? But there – I must not ask questions. Better not to know.'

'Yes, better that way,' Richard agreed.

★   ★   ★

Over the next day or two Richard let it be known at the hotel and in the bar that his mother had written to him from Bologna to say that his father was ill and he should return home as soon as possible. At the end of the week he packed his bag, said goodbye to his landlady and paid a last call on the Mancinellis.

Antonia kissed him on both cheeks and said, 'Take care, *caro mio*. I shall pray for you.'

He returned the kiss, chastely. 'You are the one who needs to be careful. I don't know if I'll be back, but I hope I may be. *Arrivederci, cara.*'

Signor Mancinelli handed him a letter. 'This is addressed to a friend of mine, a fellow lawyer. It is couched in terms that would seem quite innocent to anyone else, but he will understand why I have sent you to him. You are a brave man. God go with you.'

Signor Mancinelli's letter opened many doors. Richard was found work, singing in a bar owned by another member of the underground, and plunged into the complex political entanglements that underpinned the resistance. He met members of the GAP and the SAP and sundry other splinter organisations with a variety of political and religious affiliations. It became obvious very quickly that the communists were the most numerous and the best organised, but it disturbed him to reflect that any assistance rendered to them by the Allies might place them in a strong position to take power when the war finally came to an end. He took comfort in the thought that such decisions were not in his province. He could only report what he found and let others weigh up the best course of action and its possible consequences.

It was while he was in Bologna that the news came through of the Allied invasion of Sicily and Richard was heartened by the secret jubilation that greeted it among his new associates. Rumours were rife that the Allies would be in Rome before Christmas and the war would be over soon after. Richard was beset by pleas for Allied support, so that the partisans could do their share before it was too late.

From Bologna he was passed on to another group, farther north in the hills above Parma. Then he was off again, travelling west and south through the mountains towards Genoa, meeting small bands of dissidents hiding out in the remote valleys. Sometimes he travelled by car, driven by local priests or doctors. More often he went on foot or on mule-back. After several months of more or less sedentary occupa-tion he found the going hard to begin with. He quickly abandoned the special shoe with the lift that exaggerated his limp, and as the weeks passed he felt his muscles harden and his lungs grow accustomed to the thin mountain air. He loved the mountains – the spare beauty of the upland pastures with the snow-covered peaks beyond, clear against a sky of unbroken blue; and the deep, shady forests of beech and chestnut with their tumbling streams. He developed a great admiration for the idealistic young men who had chosen to abandon their homes rather than fight for a regime they despised, but he was increasingly worried by their circum-stances. Some of the villages he visited were supportive but many were suspicious or afraid. Without help, he wondered whether the little bands of partisans would survive very long.

He was staying in a tiny village high up in the Piedmont when the news came through that Mussolini had fallen and been replaced by King Victor Emanuel as Chief of the Armed Forces and Marshal Badoglio as prime minister. The rejoicing of the villagers was unanimous and that night there was a huge party and they all got very drunk.

Three days before his first scheduled rendezvous with Gerald Holdsworth and his 'Q' ship Richard slipped unhindered across the frontier and presented himself at the Scottish Tearooms in Monte Carlo. The Misses Trenchard were amazed and overjoyed to see him but could give him no news of Pat O'Leary. They were able to tell him that Dr Rodocanachi had been arrested but no one knew where he had been taken. Richard had arrived feeling triumphant and optimistic but the thought of that upright and unselfish man in the hands of the Gestapo reduced him to a turbulent mixture of rage and despair.

On the appointed day a tall, well-built man in casual clothes entered the teashop and ordered a pot of Earl Grey tea and scones, with the proviso that they must be made to the original Scots recipe. His order was brought to the table by a new, part-time waiter with a slight limp. When the customer departed he left a tip and folded into it was a note: '*1 a.m. The South Jetty*'. By dawn next morning Richard was on his way back to Algiers.

25

Rose gazed from the hotel window across the skyscape of domes and minarets and shook her head incredulously. Cairo! Never in her life had she imagined that her career might take her to such an exotic destination. Tunis had been thrilling enough. '*It's just like being on the set of* Casablanca!' she had written to her mother. '*I keep expecting Humphrey Bogart to walk into the hotel and say "Of all the gin joints in all the world . . ."*' Cairo left her speechless. She was fascinated by its cosmopolitan atmosphere and the vivid contrasts between the Western sophistication of the hotels and clubs and the teeming streets and markets that seemed to have changed little since biblical times. They had been in the city for two weeks and she and the girls had been taken to see all the great sights. To be completely honest, she had been just a little disappointed in the pyramids. Once you got over marvelling at the sheer size there wasn't much else to see. And she was distressed by the poverty and squalor that prevailed once you got away from the places frequented by Westerners. But, as she kept reminding herself, it was something to tell Bet's two boys about when she got home.

After Tunis they had all thought that the next move would be back to England. Instead, they had been shipped to Cairo, where several new acts were to join them, and Rose had been told to devise a whole set of new routines for the dancers. That evening they were due to open at the Opera House with a completely new show. It was a challenge she was happy to accept. The only cloud on her horizon was a nagging worry about how things were going at home.

At the reception desk she was handed a package of letters. She carried them into the lounge and opened them eagerly. The first was from her mother. Rose scanned it quickly, anxious for some reassurance, but there were only platitudes and the usual village gossip. Barbara Willis had married her Canadian and Enid Willis was putting a brave face on things; someone's son had been home on leave; another's had been killed when his destroyer was sunk in the North Atlantic. No hint of how Bet was coping with her husband's death.

Rose felt guilty because she had had so little time to comfort Bet after Reg had been killed and when she left for North Africa her sister had still appeared numbed by the shock of his death. Now she could not make out from her letters what her state of mind was. Admittedly, Bet had never been a great correspondent but these days her letters were shorter and less informative than ever. She was 'fine'. The boys were 'OK'. Billy had joined the village cricket team, which was now composed of young boys and old men. Sam's guinea pig had had babies. There was no mention of Reg, or of how she was feeling. Rose's questions met with no response. *They're hiding something*, Rose thought. *It's hit Bet harder than they make out and they are not telling me because they don't want me to worry.*

She turned to the rest of her mail. There was a letter from her old friend Sally Castle, who was still working at the Windmill Theatre, full of racy anecdotes that would have amused Rose if she had not had other things on her mind. The letter that worried her even more than the one from her mother was the one she opened last. It bore the postal insignia of the USAF.

My darling Rose,

I can't tell you how much I miss my best girl! We had such happy times together and I can't wait for the day when we shall be together for good. I've written my folks back home about you and they can't wait to meet you. I keep imagining the day when I take you back to Virginia. I know they're all going to love you and all my pals will be green with envy.

There was a good deal more in the same vein, interspersed with snippets of news about life on the airbase. There was very little about the missions he flew over Germany but she was not surprised by that. They would not have got past the censor anyway. It was not the first letter like this Beau had written, and it worried her profoundly. Nothing had ever been said about the future while she was in London and the relationship had never gone beyond the exchange of a few fairly chaste kisses, but it was clear that he had taken it for granted that it was to be permanent. She liked him very much and while they were together she had begun to think that she might be falling in love with him. But marriage would mean going to live in America. How could she possibly inflict on her own mother the distress she had seen Enid Willis suffering? And what sort of life could she expect? She was pretty sure Beau would not want her to go on with her career, even if that were possible. At the same time, she felt she could not write and disillusion him, when he was risking his life with every mission he flew. How could she live with herself if she wrote and told him that he was mistaken about their relationship and then he went and got himself killed?

Rose folded the letter and pushed the problem to the back of her mind. There were more pressing matters to deal with. Today, of all days, with the show opening that night, two of the girls had gone down with what the soldiers called 'gippy tummy' and others, more sophisticated, referred to as 'Tutankhamun's revenge'. And then there was Alice, who had hardly stopped crying since they were posted away from Tunis and the young private she had fallen in love with there. With a sigh, Rose picked up her hat and set off for the Opera House.

Richard strolled into Shepeard's Bar and looked about him. There were several groups of officers sitting around, chatting and drinking, but no one he recognised. He ordered a beer and reflected despondently that there would be some advantage in belonging to a regular regiment instead of operating as he did with a unit whose members were largely unknown to each other. He had been in Cairo for three weeks and, as usual after a few days of inactivity, he was bored. Where had it come from, he wondered, this addiction to excitement? He was supposed to be resting and enjoying himself but he was beginning to suspect that he had forgotten how.

He had tried to persuade his superiors to send him straight back to Italy, to rejoin the partisans, but he was kept at HQ, writing reports. Once he had been squeezed dry of every drop of information he was dispatched to Cairo and told to 'take it easy'. So it was that he found himself kicking his heels in Shepeard's Bar while important events were taking place in the country he regarded as his second home. On 3 September the Allies had made their first landing on the Italian mainland and on the 8th General Eisenhower had announced over the radio that the Italians had surrendered. Jubilation was short lived, however, as the Germans made it clear that they had no intention of allowing the collapse of their former ally to provide the British and American armies with an easy passage to their own back door.

On the 10th the German army occupied Rome and other major cities and disarmed the Italian forces. Now, if ever, Richard repeated to himself feverishly, the partisans could play a crucial role, if only they were given the means.

He had other reasons for wanting to immerse himself in the business of the war. Mail had been awaiting him on his return. There were the usual letters from his mother, and from Priscilla, describing concerts and plays she had attended and useful contacts she had made in pursuance of their future plans. There had also been one from Victor, who had once acted as his Conducting Officer and more recently had been best man at his wedding. On that occasion he had so charmed Priscilla's aunt that he had become one of Lady Vance's regular circle of guests. Now he wrote.

I don't know if I should be writing this letter at all, but I feel it is better you should hear this from a friend than that it should come to you by way of casual gossip. It seems that your wife has been spending a great deal of time with the young Hungarian pianist, Zoltan Onescu. They are seen about together constantly at parties and concerts and I have heard that Onescu has moved into your wife's flat. Of course, this may mean no more than that she has given him the use of a spare room as an alternative to the rather miserable lodging he was occupying, but understandably it has given rise to a good deal of talk. Perhaps you know all about this already. If so, I apologise for intruding into your affairs. I beg you to accept that I am writing purely out of friendship for you and concern for your reputation.

Richard had brooded over that letter off and on for three weeks and he still could not decide how he felt. While he could not say that he viewed the situation dispassionately, the emotions it engendered were sadness and regret, rather than anger or jealousy. He found that he did not seriously doubt that the implications of Victor's letter were correct. If Onescu had moved into the flat, then it was almost certain that he and Priscilla were having an affair. He recalled her casual assumption that he, Richard, had been sleeping with Ginny on his last assignment and her amusement at his outraged rejection of the idea. The question was not was his wife being unfaithful, but what did he feel about it. Did he actually care?

He thought back over their marriage. It was two years since he had met Priscilla again, just over one since their wedding, and in all that time they had never spent more than a few weeks together. It was not surprising that she had felt the need to seek other companionship. He thought of all the plans they had made, but even at the time they had always felt like *her* plans and he recognised a lingering resentment that his life was being taken over. On the other hand, what a fool he would be to throw away all the opportunities she was creating for him. When the war was finally over and he was free to take up their life together, would a passing fling with a lonely refugee really matter so very much? He knew from experience that when they were apart he found it hard to remember the effect Priscilla had upon him, but once they were together again his feelings would change. He would be mad to destroy all that with an angry letter, accusing her of infidelity. Better to wait and let matters take their course.

His thoughts were interrupted by someone calling his name and, turning, he saw a young flying officer with whom he had become friendly heading in his direction.

'Hello, Tim. What are you having?'

'Can't stop now, old boy. Got to catch up with a rather pretty WAAF before she leaves the office. Glad I spotted you, though.

Some of the lads and I are going to see the new show at the Opera House this evening. Tommy Trinder's in it and they say there are some gorgeous girls in the chorus. Fancy joining us?'

Richard had tended to steer clear of the ubiquitous concert parties, partly because he had the 'professional's' distaste for anything that smacked of the amateur and partly because he was afraid they would bring back too many memories of his one season with the Follies. He told himself, however, that he could hardly complain about being bored if he was not prepared to make some effort to entertain himself. So he said, 'Yes, why not? Thanks, I'd like that.'

'See you at the Opera House about seven fifteen, then? Must dash. Cheers!'

Richard returned to the officers' club on the Sharia Hod el-Laban, where he had a room, to shower and change. He was just finishing an early dinner when an orderly came over to his table with a piece of paper.

'Excuse me, Captain Stevens. Signal for you, sir.'

Richard read, '*Return HQ immediately. Dodds-Parker.*'

He scribbled a note to Tim explaining that he would not, after all, be attending the performance at the Opera House and ran upstairs to pack. At the airfield he found that a Dakota of Transport Command was due to leave for Algiers within the hour and cadged a lift with the crew. First thing the next morning he presented himself at Dodds-Parker's office.

'That was quick,' his CO remarked. 'Still eager, then.'

'Rather! I was bored to the back teeth lounging around in Cairo.'

Dodds-Parker smiled. 'Well, you'll be delighted to hear that it's been decided to drop several agents as British liaison officers to some of the groups you made contact with. You will be one of them. Who would you like to be dropped to?'

'Armando's band, in the Garfagnana,' Richard said without hesitation. Then, in a different tone, 'Did you say *dropped*?'

The senior officer nodded. 'Since the invasion the Germans have tightened up security on all the beaches and they've been extensively mined. The chances of putting you ashore successfully again are minimal. You'll be dropped by parachute, along with a radio operator. As soon as you have established contact and found a suitable dropping zone we can start to send in supplies and arms.'

Richard hesitated. 'I . . . I've never done any parachute training.'

'No, so I see from your file,' Dodds-Parker agreed briskly. 'Also, it's a long time since you did your basic training in the use of explosives and general sabotage techniques. I'm sending you on a refresher course at our base at Club des Pins. Then you'll be transferred to our new HQ at Monopoli for parachute training. This will be a very different operation from what you've been used to. For a start, you won't be undercover. You'll be dropped in uniform, with official sanction. Right?'

'Right,' Richard agreed faintly.

'Oh, one more thing. Your promotion's come through. As from today you're a major. Congratulations.'

Merry was running a concert party in Syracuse when the signal came through ordering him to report to a Major Philip Slessor in Naples. Slessor's office was in a hotel that had been requisitioned for the duration when the city fell to the Allies on 30 September. German resistance had been tenacious, the city had suffered a severe battering and there had been considerable looting before the Nazis finally left, but nothing could destroy the beauty of the bay and the view from the major's window was breathtaking.

Merry saluted. 'Lieutenant Merryweather reporting for duty, sir.'

Slessor looked up. 'Ah-ha! The Phantom Pianist! I've been looking forward to meeting you.'

'I'm trying to live that down,' Merry said, mildly embarrassed.

'Nonsense!' said Slessor. 'That's the sort of myth that does wonders for morale. Anyway, welcome to Naples!' He rose and offered his hand. 'Now, I've got a couple of bits of news for you. First of all, you've been promoted. You can put your captain's pips up forthwith.'

'Promoted?' Merry exclaimed. 'I'd no idea that was on the cards.'

'Ah well, wait and see what comes with it. I don't know if you're aware of it, but I'm in charge of all army entertainments for this theatre of operations. You've been appointed my 2i/c.'

'Second-in-command – for the whole of Italy?' Merry gazed at him. 'I wouldn't know where to begin.'

'Don't worry about that,' said Slessor. 'I can find you plenty to do. As I understand it, you've had experience running all sorts of shows and made a bloody good job of them, too. George Black has every faith in you, and so have I.'

Bless you, George! Merry thought. Aloud he said, 'Look, I don't want to sound ungrateful, but I'd hate to be stuck behind a desk. I really feel my place is up there with the chaps in the front line.'

'I can appreciate that,' Slessor said. 'Don't worry. I won't keep you tied down here indefinitely. As we advance I shall need someone up at the sharp end to look after things. Meanwhile, we've got a big job to do here. ENSA are sending out some big names and we've got to coordinate their efforts with SIB. I want to put on some really first-rate shows and I need you to help with the musical side.'

'Music?' Merry said, relieved. 'Oh yes, I can do that all right.'

'Splendid! OK. You need to get yourself sorted out after the journey. See my secretary on the way out. She's organised a room for you in a little hotel round the corner. Get settled in and we'll start work in the morning.'

Standing on the balcony of his hotel room and looking out over the bay, Merry interrogated his inner feelings for the first time in months. He was no longer, he realised, acutely miserable. The desire for oblivion had departed somewhere back in the desert, leaving a kind of numb endurance. Since then there had been moments when he had actually felt pleasure. And now, with the promotion and the new challenges ahead of him, there was satisfaction and a thrill of excitement. Could he actually regard himself as happy? The answer came at once. Not *happy*. Happiness had departed for ever with the loss of Felix. He had never known such joy as he had experienced with him, and he would never know it again. But he had won through to a kind of contentment. He could take pleasure in his work and to a limited extent in the company of others. He could even trust himself with the occasional drink. It was enough. It would have to do. It was as good as – better than – he had ever expected.

The following morning Merry woke to the sound of cheering in the street below his window. Hurrying downstairs he encountered the signora, who flung her arms around his neck and kissed him enthusiastically on both cheeks. He had made an effort to learn some Italian during his time in Sicily but her ecstatic torrent of language was quite unintelligible to him. Fortunately her son, a boy of about twelve, was with her.

'She say – my mama say – we friends now.'

'I hope so,' Merry agreed, still mystified.

'No,' the boy said, 'British, Yanks, Italianos – like this!' He clasped his two hands together. 'Fight together!'

Merry gaped at him. 'You mean Italy is going to fight with us against the Germans?'

'*Si, signor!*'

On his way to the office Merry was accosted and embraced by complete strangers, while small boys raised triumphant fingers in imitation of Winston Churchill's famous V-sign. When he reached his destination Philip Slessor was able to confirm the rumours. That morning Italy had declared war on Germany and would fight alongside the Allies.

'Though how far they'll be trusted, after the poor showing they made in Africa, is another question,' he added dryly. 'Anyway, that's not our problem and we've got enough to occupy us, God knows. Pull up a chair and let's get to work.'

There was certainly plenty to do. Already Slessor had a list of names of celebrities who were scheduled to come out from England and at the same time a troopship was heading for Alexandria to take on board a contingent of ENSA performers destined for Naples.

'All these people have got to be accommodated and we have to find performance venues and work out touring schedules for them,' Slessor said. 'It's not going to be easy. From what I hear travelling is pretty hazardous all along the sector. It's been an unusually wet autumn and the army is bogged down along the Volturno river. All the roads are full of shell holes and axle deep in mud and the bloody Huns have blown every bridge and culvert. Moving people about is going to be a nightmare. Never mind, we'll deal with each case as it arises. Meanwhile, our job here is to convince everyone that everything is wonderful and the war will be over by Christmas – or soon after. And that particularly applies to our new-found allies! Now, on that subject, I've got a project in mind that I'd like you to make your special pigeon. We have an ace up our sleeves. Guess who is due here just before Christmas.'

'No idea,' Merry said. 'The King?'

'Better than that, from our point of view. The Master!'

'The Master? You mean Noël Coward?'

'I mean Noël Coward. He's in Gibraltar at the moment. Then he's going on to Malta and he's due here on December the nineteenth.'

'Terrific!'

'Have you ever worked with him?'

'No such luck. But I've seen all his shows and I'm a great admirer. Although,' Merry paused for thought, 'I'm not sure how he'll go down with the average Tommy.'

'All that camp sophistication, you mean? Don't worry. I've seen him working a hall full of really hard-bitten types. He had them eating out of his hand within five minutes. Now, what I have in mind is this. The Opera House is still pretty well intact. I want to stage a really spectacular show when Noël is here. The first half will be a showcase for the very best SIB can produce – as lavish as we can make it. Then Noël will take the second half on his own. We'll invite all the top brass and all the local dignitaries. I want to really impress them with what SIB can do. What do you think?'

'Sounds wonderful. What do you want me to do?'

'For a start, I want you to scout out all the best acts among the local units. Most of them have got their own concert parties. You were with Seventh Armoured in the desert, weren't you? They're here now, so you'll probably know some chaps already. We need to get a band together. And then I need a really top-notch musical director. That's your job.'

'MD?' Merry said. The tiny spark of excitement that he had felt yesterday ignited into a steady flame. 'Really? I'm very flattered.'

'I'm going to leave the whole project in your hands,' Slessor said. 'Get a programme together for the first half and then come to me and we'll see what you need in the way of logistic support. I want a big chorus, plenty of really rousing numbers, lots of glamour. OK?'

'I'll do the best I can,' Merry promised.

'Right. I've organised an office for you along the corridor and a secretary. Jenny will show you where. I'll let you get on with things.'

Merry got to his feet. 'Oh, one thing – that shipload of ENSA people that's supposed to be on its way. Can I use some of them?'

'No,' Slessor said, surprisingly. 'I want this to be an exclusively army project. I'll deal with the ENSA contingent.'

'I was just thinking about girls,' Merry said. 'You said you wanted glamour.'

'See what talent you can find among the ATS and the WAAFs,' suggested Slessor.

From then on Merry found his days fully occupied, leaving him no time for introspection. In the evenings, he formed the habit of dining at the officers' club that had been set up in another of the city's leading hotels. Here he found his reputation had preceded him. There was a piano in the lounge and it was not long before he was besieged by requests to play after dinner. He was glad of the opportunity to keep in practice, though he found that in that atmosphere the less demanding light popular music went down better than the classics.

One evening he was amusing himself with a medley of popular songs. He had just embarked on 'As Time Goes By', the melody that had been on everyone's lips since the release of the film *Casablanca*, when a voice from behind him said, 'Play it, Sam!'

In spite of the assumed American accent he thought he recognised the voice and when the man began to sing he knew he was right. The style was new to him but there was no mistaking that velvety baritone. So when, at the end of the song, a hand was dropped on his shoulder and he looked up to see Richard smiling down at him, he felt no sense of shock. He got up, ignoring the calls of 'Encore!', and held out his hand. 'Good to see you, Richard! Where have you sprung from?'

'Oh, just passing through,' Richard said, shaking hands. 'I heard you were in town so I thought I'd drop by.'

'How are you? You're looking well.'

'Oh yes, I'm pretty fit, thanks. So are you if . . .' His eyes swept over Merry. '. . . if a little on the thin side.'

'Oh well.' Merry brushed the comment aside. 'That's army life for you. Look, I think this calls for a drink, don't you?'

'Several, I should think,' Richard agreed.

They walked towards the bar and it was Merry's turn to look Richard up and down. 'Well, well. You've come up in the world since we last met. You were plain Private Stevens, if I remember rightly. And now you're a major! Congratulations.'

'And you've got a DSO,' Richard commented, returning his gaze. 'Congratulations to you, too.'

'Oh, that was all a mistake,' Merry said.

'Oh yeah?' Richard returned with a sceptical grin.

Merry ordered the drinks and went on, 'By the way, I read about your marriage in the paper. Congratulations on that, too. How is Priscilla?'

'Well, as far as I know,' Richard returned. 'I haven't been home for several months, like most of us.'

'Tell me,' Merry said, 'how did that come about? I never realised when you were in the Follies that you were anything but casual acquaintances.'

'Nor were we,' Richard replied. 'I hardly knew Priss then. We just happened to run into each other in London in the summer of '41 and we were married about a year later – as you know.'

'Well, I can understand why,' Merry said. 'You obviously have a great deal in common. Your musical and aesthetic tastes were always on a higher plane than the rest of us.'

'Bollocks!' said Richard crisply. He grinned at Merry. 'You are the most consummate musician I know.'

The drinks arrived and they moved over to sit at a table.

'So, what are you up to these days?' Merry asked.

'Oh, this and that,' Richard responded vaguely. 'I'm with an outfit called Inter-Services Liaison. Pretty boring, really.'

Merry looked at him appraisingly. He was deeply tanned and the slim youth he remembered had filled out into a muscular, broad-shouldered man. 'You don't look as if you spend much time behind a desk,' he remarked.

'Oh well, I get to travel about quite a bit,' Richard said. 'How about you? I hear you did great things in the desert.'

'I played my piano,' Merry said flatly. 'There's nothing remarkable about that.'

'Except when there are shells falling all round you,' Richard commented drily. 'So what are you doing in Naples?'

Merry outlined his current occupation and then an idea occurred to him. 'Are you likely to be in Naples for a while?'

Richard shook his head. ' 'Fraid not. I'm expecting to leave at any time. Why?'

Merry explained about the big show he was planning. 'I'd love to have you on the bill. Give the whole thing a touch of class! No chance you could get back here for that?'

Richard sighed and shook his head again. 'I'm afraid it's most unlikely. Once I leave here there's no knowing when I'll be back – if at all. Pity! I'd really like to do it. It would be like old times.'

'Well, bear it in mind – just in case,' Merry told him.

Then came the moment he had been dreading. Richard said suddenly, 'I haven't asked after Felix. How is he?' He looked at Merry's face and his tone changed. 'You are still in touch, aren't you?'

Merry kept his eyes on his glass. 'Felix was killed more than a year ago. His plane was shot down in the Med, somewhere between here and Malta.'

Richard reached across the table and touched Merry's sleeve. 'Oh God, Merry, I'm so sorry. What a tactless fool I am! I had no idea.'

'No reason why you should have,' Merry said.

'You must be terribly cut up about it,' Richard murmured. 'I mean, I know . . . I think I know how much he meant to you.'

Merry kept his eyes down. Richard and Rose were the only people in the world he trusted with that knowledge. Others might guess at his relationship with Felix but he would never do anything to confirm their suspicions. He had never actually discussed it with Richard. It was something he had intuited during the course of their last meeting, on that fateful New Year's Eve.

He said, 'Yes, it hit me pretty hard at the time. But I'm over the worst now.'

'I wish I'd been around,' Richard said. 'Not that I could have done anything but . . . I'd like to have lent support, if I could.'

'Thanks.' Merry looked up and smiled at him. 'I would have been glad to have you there – but that's the way it goes.'

An orderly threaded his way through the tables and bent over Richard.

'Excuse me, sir. There's a man outside who asked me to give you a message. He says your transport's waiting.'

Richard looked up sharply. 'Now? Right. Tell him I'll be with him immediately.' He finished his drink and said apologetically, 'Look, I'm terribly sorry to rush off at this juncture. I've been waiting for this for several days now and I've just got to go. Sorry!'

Merry said reassuringly, 'Don't worry about it. I know how things are. The army calls and we have to jump to it. You can't help it.'

They both rose and Richard held out his hand and took Merry's in a long clasp. 'Take care, old man! Good luck with the show. I wish . . . I *wish* I could be in it.'

'So do I,' Merry replied. 'You take care, too. I don't know where you're off to, and I won't ask – but somehow I don't think it's a desk job. Look after yourself.'

'And you.' Richard pressed his hand and then turned away and walked briskly across the room to the door.

Merry sat down and took a sip of his drink. Then he jumped up and hurried after the departing figure. Richard was not in the lobby and when Merry reached the main door it was just in time to see a jeep disappearing into the darkness.

'Damn!' he exclaimed aloud. 'I still haven't got an address for him!'

26

R ose gripped the rail of the troopship and tried to keep her
eyes fixed on the horizon, which was difficult since at
times it seemed to be above her head and at others it disappeared completely behind an advancing mound of foam-
flecked water. When they left Alexandria the weather had been
pleasantly warm, with just a refreshing easterly breeze. Now,
on the other side of the Mediterranean and approaching
Naples, the sun was still shining but the breeze had turned
into a brisk wind that had chopped the sea into white-crested
waves and sent the ship, and the rest of the convoy, bucking
and rearing like a herd of demented horses.

'And I thought the Mediterranean was always calm!' Rose
said out loud.

Beside her, Alice hung farther over the rail and groaned for
the twentieth time, 'I wish I was dead! Oh God, let me die!'

Rose put her arm round the girl's shoulders. 'Hang on, love.
We'll be in port soon. You'll be OK as soon as you get your
feet on dry land.'

They both started violently as there was a sudden blast on
the ship's siren and a voice boomed over the tannoy, 'Action
stations! Action stations!'

'Oh no!' Alice moaned. 'Not another drill!'

Rose had seen something, far above them to the north,
like a small flock of silver arrows, heading fast in their

direction. She gripped Alice's arm and pulled her away from the rail.

'Come on, love. We'd better go to our boat station.'

In what had once been the first-class lounge of the converted liner they found the rest of the company assembling. Rose looked around her. All the faces were familiar now. Some of them had been with the company since they sailed from England; some of the girls she had known even longer, as they had been with her in Monty's concert party. Others had joined more recently, when the show was revamped in Cairo, but of these two faces belonged even farther back in her past. She had been amazed – and not entirely delighted – to discover that among the new acts were the singing duet Franklyn Bell and Isabel St Clair, now firmly established as stars after numerous broadcasts.

A steward was passing out life-jackets and Rose had just finished putting hers on when the ship juddered under their feet as the anti-aircraft guns mounted in the bows opened up. At the same time, the guns of the rest of the convoy and their escorting destroyers went into action. Above the roar Rose heard another noise, a high-pitched howl that came closer and then passed just above their heads. A second later the bottles behind the bar shuddered and the deck under their feet vibrated with the force of two nearby explosions. Rose did not have to ask what was happening. She had huddled in enough air-raid shelters to recognise the sound of a bomb dropping.

She looked around the group again. Frank was swallowing a long draught from a hip flask. *Typical!* Rose thought. Isabel stood at his side, pale but silent. Rose turned her attention to the girls in her charge and did a rapid head count. Seven, eight, nine and herself and Alice made eleven. One missing! Who was it? Violet! Trust Violet! Rose knew where she would be. She would be with Jimmy Clarkson, the trumpet player from the band, whose assembly point was in the restaurant, aft of their position. She would have to be found and brought to the right place. Rose looked at the others. Some of the girls were crying. Alice had slumped down by a table and had her head in her arms. Peggy was smoking silently, aloof from the others. Rose made a decision. Peggy was moody, but she could usually be relied on to act with common sense.

'Peg, you look after the others. Make sure everyone stays together. I'm going to find Violet.'

Without waiting for a reply Rose set off aft towards the restaurant. The noise of the guns and the howl of dive-bombers was now unceasing. Rose felt as if she were trapped in the middle of a drum kit being pounded by a demented percussionist. The deck continued to tilt and rock under her feet, sending her sliding into bulkheads and tables. Someone yelled at her to get back to her boat station but she ignored him. She found Violet, as she expected, clinging to Jimmy.

'Violet, you're supposed to be with our party!' she shouted over the din. 'Get back there now!'

'But I want to stay with Jimmy!' the girl protested desperately.

'You can't!' Rose told her. 'You have to be where you're supposed to be otherwise . . .' She had been about to say 'Otherwise there might not be room for you in the boat,' but she realised that that would only spread panic. 'Otherwise you could be in trouble,' she finished. Then, to Jimmy, 'You ought to know better. Didn't you realise we'd be looking for her?'

She gave Violet a shove in the right direction and followed her towards the door. She had almost reached it when there was a thud and the ship shuddered as if it had run into a brick wall. Almost immediately, the deck beneath her feet began to tilt and she lost her balance and only saved herself from sliding into the wall by grabbing the legs of a table. Bottles and glasses crashed off the bar and shattered around her. After a breathless moment the ship seemed to right herself and Rose was able to scramble to her feet. Around her, others were hauling themselves out from under tables and chairs, their shouts and screams adding to the din. Rose called out to Violet, but she had disappeared amid the chaos.

A siren began to sound and over the loudspeakers came a voice. 'Abandon ship! Abandon ship!'

With a sickening lurch of panic Rose remembered the warnings they had been given at boat drill. If the boats had to be lowered, anyone not in the right place would be left behind. She screamed again to Violet and found Jimmy beside her.

'She's gone!' he yelled. 'I saw her go out the door.'

Rose started towards the door and he grabbed her arm. 'Stay here. You'll be safer here.'

She shook him off. 'I must get back to the others.'

Out on deck she realised for the first time how acute the danger was. The ship had keeled over so far that the rail on the port side, where she was, was almost touching the waves. By good luck, a line had been rigged along the superstructure to give extra handholds in the rough weather, and by clinging to this she was able to slide and scramble along the tilting deck. As she did so, she kept searching the waves as they broke against the side, terrified that she might see the body of Violet bobbing among them.

All along the deck groups of passengers were being marshalled into the lifeboats, which hung from their davits only feet above the water. Already, one or two were full and had been lowered. Panting, soaked by spray and deafened by the continual roar of aircraft and the noise of the guns, Rose struggled onwards until she reached the spot where her company was to embark. It was only then that she realised that the davits hung empty and, looking over the side, she saw the boat pulling away.

A figure clambered to its feet and waved frantically. 'Rose! Rose!' The voice came to her faintly through the din and she saw that it was Violet. *Thank God, she made it!* she thought, in an oddly detached moment. They had seen her, she reasoned. Now they would come back for her. But the distant figure was pulled down on to the thwarts and the boat continued on its way.

Rose turned and gazed around her, wild eyed. All along the deck, boats were being lowered. Soon they would all be gone. She began to struggle back the way she had come. As she approached the first boat she saw it jerk and begin its descent. She waved wildly and screamed, 'Wait! Wait for me! Please!' But her voice was carried away on the wind and the boat splashed down into the sea.

Then, as she passed the companionway leading up to the bridge, her arm was seized and a voice yelled, 'Where the hell have you been!'

She found herself looking into the face of a young officer she had danced with in the mess the night before. She began to explain but he shook his head.

'Never mind that. This way!'

She was half pulled, half carried towards the stern, where a last boat was filling up with members of the crew. In a confusion of shouts she was bundled aboard and a moment later they were bobbing and pitching on the waves as the men pulled on their oars.

The young lieutenant who had saved her called out, 'Don't worry. There are plenty of other ships around. We shall be picked up very quickly.'

Rose twisted in her seat and saw that they were heading for a destroyer, which had altered course towards them. Within minutes they were being helped up a steep companionway on to the deck, where they were greeted with blankets and cups of scalding, sweet tea. Rose turned to her saviour.

'Thank you. I think you saved my life.'

'Oh, rot!' he said with a grin. 'We'd never leave a pretty girl like you to drown.'

'The rest of my girls . . .' Rose said. 'They were in another boat. I need to find out if they're all right.'

'Rose! Rose!' Violet was running along the deck to meet her and as they embraced she sobbed, 'Oh, Rose, we thought you were a goner! And it was all my fault. I'm so sorry!'

'It doesn't matter,' Rose said. 'You're safe. That's all that matters. Are the others all right?'

She found them all huddled together farther along the deck. When she had checked that they were all present and unhurt she turned to look out to sea and saw Isabel St Clair standing by the rail. She was staring across the water to where the troopship lay, her port rail almost touching the water. Rose went to her and put an arm round her shoulders.

'Where's Frank?'

'I don't know,' was the toneless reply. 'They insisted on taking all the women first. I begged them to let Frank come with me but they wouldn't.'

'Don't worry. I'm sure they will have got him off safely.'

'I can't see him,' Isabel said, with a deadly calm. 'He isn't here and I can't see any more boats.'

'He's probably been picked up by another ship,' Rose consoled her. 'Look, there are three others, all taking people on board. Frank will be on one of them.'

Isabel looked at her, her eyes dull. At that moment there was a sound from the assembled women on the deck, a kind of universal moan, and looking back they saw the troopship turn turtle, settle and then disappear beneath the waves.

Isabel shook off Rose's arm and moved away and Rose found Peggy beside her. 'It wasn't her who begged them to let him come with us. It was him. He tried to make out it was because she was frightened, but he was the one who was shitting himself with panic.'

By luck, Merry was in his office when the message came through. He hurried along the passage to find Philip Slessor.

'I've just had a signal. The troopship bringing those ENSA people from Alexandria has been dive-bombed and sunk.'

'Christ Almighty! Many casualties?'

'I don't know yet. The signal just says survivors have been picked up and are heading for port.'

'You'd better get down there and try to get a list of names. Signal Cairo and see if you can find out who was supposed to be on board. Then get the survivors looked after.'

'Right.'

By the time Merry reached the docks the first ships of the convoy were entering the harbour. For the next couple of hours he and the sergeant who had been assigned to him as an assistant were kept busy listing names and dispatching the shaken survivors either to local hospitals or to the accommodation that had been prepared for them. Mercifully, there seemed to be few injuries. Suddenly, in the queue of strained and unfamiliar faces, he found himself looking into one he knew.

'Frank! Good lord! I didn't know you were on the ship.'

Bell peered at him, apparently uncertain who he was. Then he said, 'Good grief! It's Guy Merryweather, isn't it? What are you doing here?'

'Looking after your welfare at the moment,' Merry said. 'Are you all right?'

'Yes, as it happens. No thanks to the navy. It was bloody chaos on that ship!'

Merry had already heard others praising the calm and orderly manner in which the evacuation had been handled and he knew Frank of old, so he ignored the remark.

'Which company are you with?'

'Starlight Revue. Listen, have you seen my wife? They wouldn't let me stay with her. Poor kid was terrified but they insisted on dragging her off into a different boat – all this women-and-children-first rubbish. Do you know where she is?'

'Not at the moment,' Merry said, 'but I'm sure she'll be here somewhere. If you just go and wait with that party over there some transport will be here shortly to take you to your accommodation.'

'Wait!' Bell exclaimed. 'Haven't we done enough sitting about in open boats, without having to hang around here? I need a stiff drink and a hot bath.'

'I'm sure you're not the only one,' Merry murmured. 'There's a NAAFI counter over there. You can get a hot drink if you want one. Now, I must get on. Excuse me.'

Having cleared the queue at his own checkpoint Merry set off along the dock to where another ship had tied up. Over the heads of the crowd he spotted a familiar figure and felt a surge of delight.

'Rose!' he yelled. 'Rose, over here!'

She heard his voice and turned to battle her way through the crowd towards him.

'Merry! Merry, darling, how lovely!' She threw her arms round him and kissed his cheek.

He kissed her in return and gently disengaged himself. 'Are you OK? I had no idea you were on that ship.'

'I'm fine. We were very lucky. All the girls are OK, give or take a few bruises. What are you doing here?'

'I'm based here now – second-in-command for Stars in Battledress for the whole of Italy!'

'My word, that does sound grand!' She laughed.

'Look,' he said, 'I've got to get on. I'm responsible for seeing all you people have a bed for the night. Who are you with?'

'Starlight Revue.'

'With Frank Bell?'

'Yes. Is he here?'

'Large as life and twice as nasty. Hasn't stopped complaining. Have you seen Isabel?'

'Yes, she's over there. See?'

'Thank God for that!'

He directed Rose towards the group waiting for transport to their hotel and promised to come and see her when he had finished work.

It was late in the day before he was able to get away and he found her sitting in the lounge of the Pensione Buonavista with Isabel and Frank.

'Thank God you've turned up at last,' Frank snapped. 'The conditions in this place are appalling. One bathroom between God knows how many and no hot water at all. You can't expect professionals like us to put up with this.'

Merry looked at him. He had never liked him, even when they were both part of the Follies company. He had always been big-headed and Merry could see that fortuitous fame, which the war and a few lucky breaks in wireless programmes had brought him, had done nothing to reduce his sense of his own importance.

'I might point out,' he said coldly, 'that until a few weeks ago this city was occupied by German troops, who made a point of wrecking as much of it as they could manage before they were forced to withdraw. Quite honestly, you're lucky to have a roof over your heads. It's been a real logistical problem finding beds for all you people. And I can't promise you that you'll be as well off once you start touring.'

'Why?' Frank demanded. 'Where are you sending us?'

'I don't have your precise schedule to hand at the moment,' Merry told him, 'but obviously we'll be moving you up as close to the front as we dare. I should warn you, conditions are not very good. The terrain had been fought over for days and the weather has been appalling. You'll have to be prepared for a degree of hardship.'

'Well, that's only to be expected,' Rose said firmly. 'We haven't come here for a holiday, have we?'

'No, of course not,' Isabel agreed softly. 'I'm sure it'll be nothing compared with what our boys are having to put up with.'

Frank looked as if he was about to complain and then thought better of it. Instead he remarked, 'Never thought you'd end up as a kind of glorified nanny, Merry.'

'How do you mean?' Merry asked.

'Well, you're with Army Welfare, aren't you? Running round, finding people billets and so on.'

'He is not a glorified nanny!' Rose exclaimed indignantly. 'He's second-in-command for this whole area.'

'It's still Army Welfare, though, isn't it?' Frank said. 'Seems a terrible waste of your talents, old boy. You should have stayed out of the forces and joined ENSA like us.'

'Oh, I get to do a bit of entertaining from time to time,' Merry said. He caught Rose's eye and winked.

Rose, however, was not going to leave matters like that. 'You don't understand, Frank. Merry's with Stars in Battledress. It's the army's equivalent of ENSA. He puts on some fantastic shows – and he went all through North Africa with the Desert Rats, entertaining them right up at the front. *And* he's won a DSO! So don't try to patronise him.'

'All right! All right!' Frank mumbled. 'Keep your hair on. No offence meant, Merry, old boy.'

'So what are you actually doing here in Naples?' Isabel asked.

Merry told them about the gala performance he was preparing for a few weeks ahead. Then, rising to leave, he added, 'I'll be up tomorrow to go over your performance schedule with the director.'

'Look here, old chap,' Frank said, 'this gala performance. Couldn't you do with a few real professionals to fill out the bill – a bit of real star quality, don't you know?'

Merry paused and gave him one of his rare grins. 'Sorry, Frank. This is an exclusively army bash. And as for star quality – we've got Noël Coward playing the second half.'

27

Richard sat with his legs hanging through the gaping hole in the floor of the Halifax, below him a void of dark, rushing air. The dispatcher hooked up the line that would open his parachute and gave it a tug.

'There we are, sir. All secure.'

Richard nodded and tried to smile but his teeth were chattering so hard that he dared not part his lips. *It's not as if you haven't done it before!* he told himself. *It's always been all right, so stop worrying.* It was no good. The thought of casting himself into that dreadful void filled him with terror.

He had got through the parachute training at the airfield near Monopoli somehow, but it had been touch and go. One of the worst moments had been when he stood at the top of a rickety tower, where a contraption of ropes and weights was supposed to simulate the speed of a parachute descent. He had suddenly remembered a day when, at the age of twelve, he had stood for ten long minutes on the top diving board at the swimming pool and willed himself to jump and in the end had retreated, humiliated, by way of the ladder. The sergeant in charge at the top of the tower had given him a cheerful grin.

'Don't worry, sir. It's a piece of cake. Just remember to keep your feet together and roll with the impact.' He put a hand on his arm and drew him forward to the edge of the platform. 'I wouldn't look down, if I was you, sir. Just act like you was stepping off the kerb.' And then a hand in the middle of his back had propelled him gently but firmly forward and he was hanging in midair. The impact had been less painful than he expected and he had even remembered to relax his knees and roll. Before walking away he had paused to look up to the top of the tower and exchange a cheery thumbs-up with the sergeant.

After that had come the first drop from a plane, a lumbering Italian S82 bomber. He had stood in the open doorway, closed his eyes and flung himself out. There had been a terrifying few seconds as he tumbled over and over in the slipstream, then a sudden jerk and an amazing sensation of serenity as he floated earthwards. *I can do this!* he had said to himself. *And if it's the only way I can get back to Armando and the others I bloody well will!*

Now he was not so sure of himself. For a start, he was not dropping in sunlight over a level airfield but in the dark of the moon over unknown mountainous terrain. Since there was no radio contact with any of the partisans it had been impossible to warn Armando of his arrival, so there would be no flares lit to mark the dropping zone. All he could do was point out Armando's valley on the map and hope that the pilot would be able to find it.

He looked across the open hatch at his companion. Macdonald was the son of a Scots father and an Italian mother and had volunteered to drop with him as his radio operator. He was a sergeant in the Black Watch, a couple of years younger than Richard, built like a whippet. When they first met he had been dressed in full Highland uniform, including kilt, and Richard had looked him over and remarked, 'Are you going to drop dressed like that?'

Macdonald had grinned. 'And risk getting my balls frost-bitten, sir? No, I think I'll put some trousers on.'

'That's a relief,' Richard responded. 'I wouldn't want to cause mass hysteria among the female population.'

From that moment on they had been good friends.

'What do people call you?' Richard had asked.

'Name's Nicholas, sir. My mates just call me Mac.'

Now his face was inscrutable. Richard could not tell whether he was suffering the same debilitating terror, but if he was he concealed it well.

He saw the dispatcher tense as the pilot's voice crackled in his earphones. Then he bent and shouted in Richard's ear. 'Pilot reckons he's over the spot, as near as he can tell, sir. He's coming in for his run now.'

The plane banked, levelled out and Richard heard the engines being throttled back. The dispatcher crouched beside him. Above their heads the light turned from red to green.

'Good luck, sir!'

A firm push in the middle of his back ejected him into space. There was the usual split second of terror as he was certain that his parachute had failed to open, then the jerk that cracked his head back on his neck and the sudden quiet. He looked around him. On either side mountain peaks reared up, and below was the deep cleft of a valley. He could see the faint reflection of starlight on water, showing the course of a river, but there were no lights, no sign of habitation. He struggled to remember the contours of the Garfagnana, but there was nothing he could recognise. He twisted his head, trying to see above him to pick out Mac's parachute, but the canopy of his own blocked his view. For a while he appeared to be descending quite slowly. Then, as the ground drew closer, it seemed to be rushing up towards him. He could make out trees clothing the side of the valley, a narrow strip of open ground beside the river. None of it looked familiar. For a moment he was terrified that he was going to come down in the trees. He had heard too many tales of parachutists being caught up in the branches and unable to free themselves so that they hung there, helpless, until they died of exposure or starvation.

Then, quite suddenly, the trees were rushing past him and the open field was under his feet. He struck the ground, rolled, got up and was dragged several feet by his 'chute before he managed to get it under control. He freed himself from the harness and flung himself on the billowing silk, pummelling it into submission. Then he straightened up and looked around him. The night was still and silent. There was no sign of Macdonald. He whistled softly, a prearranged signal. No answer came. He began to walk back down the valley. After a few paces, to his immense relief, a figure appeared from the direction of the river. He whistled again and received an answer. They met and gripped each other's arms in greeting and relief.

'You all right?'

'Wet! Dropped in the bloody river! Otherwise OK.'

It took them a few more minutes to locate the radio set and the pack containing their kit, which had been dropped separately. Then they looked around them again.

'Is this the right place, sir?' Mac asked.

'I honestly don't know,' Richard admitted. 'It doesn't look right at the moment. But if we follow the river downstream we should come to a village sooner or later.'

Close by, they came upon a beaten track, leading downstream, but they had gone only a few yards when they heard voices coming towards them. Richard jerked his head sideways and they stepped off the track into the sheltering darkness beneath the trees. The voices came closer and Richard was relieved to hear that they were speaking Italian.

'They can't be far away. I saw them come down somewhere around here.'

The speaker was an elderly man and in the faint light Richard could make out that he was carrying a shotgun. He decided it was time for one of those risky gambles that always had to be taken sooner or later. He put his mouth close to Macdonald's ear and breathed, 'Cover me!' Then he stepped out on to the track in front of the two men and said, in Italian, '*Buona sera, amici.* I think it is me you are looking for.'

The two men stopped short and stared at him. Then the elder said hoarsely, '*Tedesco?*'

'*No, Inglese.*'

'*Inglese? Ciao, amico! Benvenuto!*' The old man dropped his gun and spread his arms and Richard submitted to a whiskery embrace. 'My name is Luigi,' the old man went on, 'and this is my son, Carlo. But where is the other one? We saw two parachutes.'

Richard called Mac out of the undergrowth and he greeted the two strangers in fluent and accentless Italian.

'*Eh, come si chiamo?*' Luigi demanded.

'*Mi chiamo Nicco.*'

Within minutes they had been relieved of their burdens and were heading down the track towards Luigi's farmhouse. As they went Richard questioned the old man as to their whereabouts and discovered that they had, in fact, been dropped into the right valley but considerably farther upstream than the village of Sassi, above which Armando was encamped. Luigi assured him, however, that it was not a problem. Tomorrow his grandson would guide them there. For tonight they must rest in his house.

Back at the farm Carlo's wife, Julia, was up and had the fire going in the range. While they ate potato soup and black bread, washed down with potent draughts of grappa, Richard attempted to field a constant barrage of questions. Why were they here? And why alone? Were they the advance guard of a full invasion? When would the rest of the British troops arrive?

'Tell them to come soon!' Luigi said. 'We want these filthy Germans driven out. They are taking our young men and forcing them to work in labour camps. And they take reprisals against the villagers because of the partisans in the mountains.'

That night he insisted that Richard and Mac share his bed, maintaining that he would not sleep again and would be quite comfortable by the fire in the kitchen. As they settled, rather self-consciously, the Scot murmured, 'Goodnight, sir.'

'Goodnight, Nicco,' Richard responded, smiling into the darkness.

The next morning the radio set was loaded on to the back of a mule and they set off, guided by Carlo's son Andrea. The track wound up and down through the forest of sweet chestnut trees but the atmosphere was very different from Richard's last visit. There were no flowers now and they walked on a carpet of fallen leaves, made mushy by the heavy rains. From time to time they saw women and children bent low among the trees, scavenging for the last fallen chestnuts. They looked up, but made no attempt to speak.

By mid-afternoon they were approaching Sassi. Richard felt uncomfortably exposed in his British army uniform. He called a halt while he studied the surrounding area through his field glasses. He had been assured by Luigi that there were no German patrols operating in the area at present, and his observations convinced him that the only people in sight were local peasants going about their normal business. Just the same, he decided to play safe and give the village a wide berth.

They scrambled up through an untended vineyard until they reached the track along which Antonia had brought him on his first visit. At the ruined cottage where she had left the car he turned to Andrea.

'There's no need for you to come any farther. Here.' He opened his pack and took out a bar of NAAFI chocolate. 'This is for you. But remember, you must not tell anyone that you have seen us. Otherwise it could mean big trouble for you and your family.'

The boy took the chocolate with shining eyes and nodded. 'I understand. You can trust me, *Capitano*.'

They unloaded their gear from the mule and watched until the boy and the animal had disappeared down the track. Then Richard led Nick up the path beside the cottage. As they approached the barn he turned back to his companion.

'Watch out here. There should be a couple of sentries on duty.' He called out. '*Olà, amici!* It's me, Ricardo. Don't shoot!'

There was a brief silence and then the slight figure of Silvano appeared, carrying a shotgun. Richard took off his cap.

'*Ciao*, Silvano. Remember me?'

The young man stared for a moment and then threw his arms wide in a gesture of welcome. 'Capitano Ricardo! You've come back! Welcome!'

Richard and Nick were conducted the remaining distance to the farmhouse and Richard was amused to discover how much shorter it seemed than when he had stumbled over it blind-folded. As they entered the yard he noticed several men whom he did not recognise, who jumped to their feet at the sight of him and his companion. In response to Silvano's shouts the door of the farmhouse was flung open and Armando appeared. For a moment he stood stock still, staring. Then he burst out, 'Ricardo! Is it really you? Welcome! Welcome back!' He strode across and embraced him. 'I never thought we should meet again.'

'But here I am, you see,' Richard responded, hugging him in return. Then he turned to introduce Nick.

Once the greetings and explanations were over and Richard had enquired after Antonia and the Mancinellis they settled down round the long, scrubbed table in the low-ceilinged room with glasses of wine. Once again, the first question was, 'When will the Allies be here?'

Richard said soberly, 'It isn't going to be soon, Armando. The Germans are making a very determined stand. Just before I left I heard that our forces have broken through on the Volturno but we're having to fight every step of the way. And now winter is coming things are going to get worse, not better. But that's why we're here. From now on, we've got to make things as uncomfortable as possible for the Huns. The more of a nuisance we can be, the more of Hitler's forces we can pin down here in the mountains, the fewer there are to face our troops.'

'And there will be equipment? Supplies of ammunition and arms?'

'Yes, that's our first job – to organise a drop of supplies.'

Armando's face split into a broad grin. 'So, at last we fight side by side! And we have something worth fighting for. Yes?'

'Yes,' Richard agreed. 'Yes, we do!'

Armando raised his glass. 'To victory!'

When the toast had been drunk Richard said, 'So, how are things here? There seem to be more of you than on my last visit.'

Armando nodded, his eyes gleaming. 'Yes, we are thirty now. You know what happened when the armistice was signed and the Germans moved in? They started to round up our troops and march them off to prison camps. Many of them deserted and took to the hills and some have found their way here. And now the Germans are conscripting young men of military age to work in their labour camps, so even more are going into hiding. Soon there will be hundreds of us.'

'Do you have weapons for all these men?' Richard asked.

'Not enough, but more than we had when you were here last. Some of the soldiers had kept hold of their rifles. With the reinforcements we decided to attack the police post at Molazzana. We knew there were modern rifles there. We captured ten. Then, with those, we ambushed a small German patrol. From them, we obtained two Sten guns and some more rifles. So, you see,' he grinned triumphantly, 'we have not been idle while you were away.'

'You certainly haven't,' Richard agreed warmly. 'Bravo! How about relations with the locals? Any improvement there?'

'Oh yes. Since our government's decision to come in with the Allies they have realised that we are all on the same side. Several of the local towns have formed their own committees to support our activities. Trassilico, for example, and Vergemoli, to the south of us, and Molazzana just below us. They let us have what food they can spare. But when winter sets in things will be desperate just the same. Many of our men don't have warm clothing or proper boots. We urgently need supplies, Ricardo.'

'They will come,' Richard assured him. 'But we have to find a suitable area, where the stuff can be dropped without ending up somewhere inaccessible.'

* * *

It took several frustrating days to find a place, in the broken and densely wooded countryside. Eventually they chose a spot high up on the flank of Mount Pania Secco, where the trees gave way to rock and scrub, and Richard encoded a message for Nick to transmit. The answer came back the next day. There would be a supply drop, but exactly when a plane would be available HQ at Monopoli could not say.

The supply drop came at the beginning of November. Already there had been snow on the high ground and Richard and the others had a long, freezing wait before they heard the plane coming in low over the mountain peaks between them and the sea. Bonfires had been set to mark the area and a cheer went up as the first parachutes came floating down. There followed a period of hectic activity, as the containers were collected and loaded on to mules and the parachute silk committed to the fires. Some of the men wanted to keep it, to give to wives and girlfriends, until Richard pointed out that the possession of even a scrap of it could mark the owner out as a traitor to the occupying regime.

Back at the farmhouse the containers were opened. Rifles and ammunition, grenades, plastic explosive and another precious Sten gun were laid out on the table. Another container held thick woollen sweaters, socks and boots, and a third was packed with tinned meat and hard-tack biscuits and chocolate. One remained. Silvano threw it open and his face fell, in an expression of comic consternation.

'What is it, Silvano?' Armando asked.

'Tea!' was the reply. 'Packets and packets of tea!'

After the tension of the evening the look of outrage on his face reduced Richard to helpless laughter. 'Oh, I'm sorry!' he gasped. 'I'm afraid you have to understand. It's taken as a universal truth in England that if you are in a really tight spot what you need more than anything else is a good strong cup of tea!'

'Why couldn't they send coffee?' Silvano demanded. 'Or bread? Something useful?'

The problem was solved by Sasha, a big Russian ex-POW. He knew that there were prisoners from various parts of eastern Europe in the labour camp outside Gallicano. The following night, he and three others made their way down the mountain and managed to contact some of them through the wire. They returned triumphant, having exchanged most of the tea for loaves of black bread.

As the weeks passed Richard settled in and began to enjoy himself. There was danger, undoubtedly, but at least he did not have to play a double role and the open risks he ran were infinitely preferable to the daily fear of the Gestapo's hand on his shoulder. He liked the easy camaraderie of the partisans and his friendship with Armando deepened by the day. He discovered that, like his father, Armando had a passion for opera and sometimes, in their lighter moments, they would sing through their favourite works together. With the new equipment they became bolder and the tally of successful operations grew. The group derailed a train carrying reinforcements to the front, blew up an anti-aircraft emplacement and ambushed a convoy taking supplies to an artillery post. They were pinpricks, Richard knew, but the point was that all through the Apennines similar attacks were being carried out and the Germans could not afford to ignore them. Every partisan band kept a number of German troops pinned down as guards on roads and bridges or garrisons for power stations and other vital services. And eventually, if they could make themselves enough of an irritant, troops might have to be withdrawn from the front line to flush them out. It was cat-and-mouse, with Armando and his men as the mice. It was up to them to keep gnawing away at the German resources. Richard had been told, firmly, before he left Algiers that he was not supposed to play an active part in operations. 'You are there to train and give advice,' Dodds-Parker had said. 'Leave the fighting to the Italians.' He ignored the order.

Richard sat at the long table in the farmhouse kitchen, encoding a message for Nick to send on his next scheduled radio transmission. He groaned as he worked. It was always a laborious process but at present he had so much information to relay that it had become a chore that kept him from more urgent work. As well as the sabotage activities, he had set up a network of informers, many of them women, in the local villages. Other reports came from nurses recruited by Antonia from the hospital at Castelnuovo. In this way, he had accumulated extensive intelligence about German troop movements, locations of supply dumps and arms depots and other matters useful to the Allies as they advanced. His problem was that it was so detailed that it was almost impossible to encapsulate it in a coded message. What he really needed, he thought, was a chance to talk to Major MacIntosh, his CO at Monopoli, face to face.

Voices in the yard made him look up. Armando was in earnest conversation with a boy of about sixteen or seventeen. A moment later he came in, looking thoughtful.

'Problems?' Richard asked.

The Italian seated himself at the table. 'No, not problems. Just a rumour and some information. That boy out there, Claudio – you saw him? – comes from Castiglione, on the other side of the River Serchio. He says the Germans are moving a lot of troops and equipment along the road over the pass from the north. Reinforcements, presumably. One convoy every morning, according to the boy.'

'Hmm.' Richard looked at his map. 'As far as we know there's no one operating over there. Perhaps we should cross the river and give the Huns a bit of a shake-up.'

'My idea precisely!' Armando agreed, grinning. 'But that brings me to the rumour.'

'What's that?'

'Claudio says they've been hearing stories about a small band of partisans in the mountains on the far side of the river, led by an English "milord".'

'An English milord?' Richard repeated.

Armando laughed. 'I shouldn't pay too much attention to that. To the peasants round here all Englishmen are "milords". It goes back to the days of the Grand Tour, when the only Englishmen ever seen in these parts were wealthy aristocrats.'

'Well, it could be that another British liaison officer has been dropped over there,' Richard said, 'but if that's the case I haven't been informed. Alternatively, it could be a British POW. Either way, I should try to make contact and see if we can cooperate.'

'Maybe we could combine the two,' Armando suggested. 'If we take a force over there to ambush one of the convoys some of us could go up into the mountains afterwards and see what we can find.'

'Sounds feasible,' Richard agreed. 'Anyway, let's concentrate on that convoy for now. See here,' he pointed to the map, 'where the road crosses the river just south of Castiglione? That looks like a likely place. We might be able to blow the bridge.'

Nick came down from the upper room where he operated the radio.

'Message for you, *padrone*.' Since they spoke Italian all the time he had adopted that form of address and Richard found he preferred it to the more formal 'sir'.

It took Richard some time to decode the message. Then he looked across at Armando. 'Damn!'

'What's wrong?'

'Base want me back. They're sending a plane to pick me up.'

Armando looked aghast. 'What for?'

'Debriefing. They've got a point. There's a lot of information I need to pass on that can't be sent by radio.'

'When?'

'Night of December the seventeenth.'

'But you will come back, won't you?'

Richard smiled at him. 'You can count on that. If they try to keep me I'll go AWOL and get back here, if I have to walk! But if they're sending a plane we need to find a suitable landing ground.'

'The only possible place is down in the valley, somewhere near the river,' Armando said. 'But it's risky. There are too many German roadblocks all along the main road.'

'We'll scout the area when we go across to Castiglione,' Richard said. 'The sooner the better.'

By evening their plans were laid and Armando called for volunteers. There was no shortage and he and Richard picked two dozen of their best men and instructed them to be ready to leave at first light the next morning. Nick pleaded to be allowed to come too, but Richard refused.

'I can't afford to risk you, Nick. We have to have radio contact with base. If anything goes wrong we may need to ask for a wounded man to be evacuated. Sorry, but you'll have to stay here.'

Soon after dawn they were on their way. They crossed the road leading to Viareggio, by which Richard had first entered the valley, and skirted the outlying suburbs of Castelnuovo. The next obstacle was the crossing of the Serchio. At Ponte-cosi they had to take the chance of being challenged as they crossed the bridge. Richard sent the men over in twos and threes and, since they were all dressed indistinguishably from the local peasants, they were allowed to pass without question. Richard, too, had discarded his uniform, although it meant that he might be shot as a spy if captured. He and Armando were leading the mules laden with explosives and detonators, hidden under bales of hay, and they had a tense few minutes as they passed the blockhouse where the sentry was warming his hands over a brazier, but he barely glanced up.

Late in the afternoon they paused in the ruins of a derelict farmhouse to eat the rations they had brought with them. By evening they were climbing again, with Castiglione on the scarp above them. Claudio had come with them as a guide and as the light began to fail he stopped in a clearing and pointed to a rocky bluff near by.

'From there you can see the road, and the bridge over the river,' he said.

Leaving the rest of the men and the mules in the clearing, Richard and Armando climbed the bluff and lay on their stomachs to study the terrain below through their field glasses.

'As we expected,' Richard murmured, 'there are guards on the bridge. Blockhouses at either end, and a regular patrol. If we're going to lay charges it will have to be from underneath.'

'The river is in spate,' Armando demurred. 'You'll never be able to stand against it.'

Richard studied the bridge and the river below it again. 'There's no chance on this side. The bank drops straight into the water. But on the far side it's less steep and there are a few bushes growing out of the rock. It might be possible to climb along there and get underneath the bridge. Can we get to the other side, without using this bridge?'

A brief consultation with Claudio produced the information that there was a ford a few kilometres back, in a small village.

'Right,' Richard said. 'I'll take four men with me to help carry the explosives and go back to the village. You go on down to the bridge and deploy the rest of the men along the road on this side of the river. If all goes well and we blow the bridge when the first vehicles are on it, the rest of the convoy will be a sitting target. If we don't manage to set the charges you will just have to cause as much damage as possible. Try to disable one of the trucks so that it blocks the road. But don't hang around too long.'

Armando gave him a taut smile. 'Don't worry. As soon as there's any sign of organised retaliation we shall just melt away into the forest, as usual. We have done this before, you know.'

'Sorry,' Richard said with a wry smile.

'I'm worried about you, though,' Armando said. 'You don't know how treacherous the current can be in these rivers – and how cold the water is.'

'I've no intention of going into the river, if I can help it,' Richard assured him. 'But if I have to I'll make sure I'm securely roped to someone else. Don't wait around for me. We'll rendezvous at the farmhouse where we rested. If I haven't shown up an hour after the attack is over, go on back. I'll find my own way. OK?'

He chose four men who were strong and reliable, among them the Russian, Sasha, and Gianni, Antonia's fiancé. Then he shook hands with Armando and set off back along the track, led by Claudio. When they came to the outskirts of the village they left the boy with the mule and divided the explosives between them. The houses were dark and silent and they moved in single file, keeping to the soft ground at the edge of the track. The ford, as Claudio had predicted, was unguarded, but just as they reached the other side a dog began to bark in a nearby house and a window was thrown open, while a hoarse voice demanded to know who was there.

'*Amici!*' Richard called back, softly. 'Go back to bed.'

There was a brief hesitation and then the window was slammed shut. Whether they were active sympathisers or not, the local people had no wish to get on the wrong side of the guerrilla groups operating in the surrounding country-side. Richard silently thanked God that there were no tele-phones in these villages, so no danger that the occupant of the house might alert the authorities, and gestured to his compa-nions to move on.

On the far side of the river they found a track leading back towards the bridge and followed it until they were within a hundred yards. Crouching in the bushes, Richard reassessed the situation. He could see the head and shoulders of a sentry patrolling the bridge and glanced at his watch to check how often he passed. Close beneath him, the river rushed by in its steep, rocky bed. Armando had been right. After the wet autumn, the current was fast and deep, but at least the noise of the water would cover any sounds he might make. He turned his attention to the bank. Even on this side it dropped almost sheer into the water, but the rock was cracked and in the fissures a few shrubs and small trees had managed to take root. He turned and whispered instructions to his companions.

Two of them were dispatched with a Sten gun to the road above them, to watch the sentries and give covering fire if necessary. Sasha and Gianni followed Richard as he inched cautiously forward, clinging to the bushes for support. They managed to get to within ten yards of the bridge but at that point the rock dropped smooth and bare into the water. Richard turned back and put his lips close to Sasha's ear.

'I'll have to try and wade the last bit. You and Gianni hang on to the rope in case I lose my footing.'

Reluctantly, he took off his boots and then removed his trousers and underpants. The night air was cold and he shivered as the wind touched his bare flesh, but he knew that when he came out of the water he would need the dry clothes to put on. He replaced his boots and tied the end of a coil of rope, which Sasha had carried on one shoulder, securely round his waist. Meanwhile, Gianni had transferred all the necessary equipment into one pack. Richard heaved it on to his shoulders and reflected that if he did lose his footing the weight of it would drag him under immediately.

'Belay that rope securely round that tree trunk,' he whispered, and Sasha answered, 'Don't you worry about that, *padrone*. We won't let you go. Good luck!'

Slowly Richard let himself down into the icy water. The current dragged at his legs and within a minute they were numb with cold. He was relieved to find that he touched bottom when the water was only up to the top of his thighs. Clinging to every tiny projection on the rocky bank he clawed his way forward until he was directly below the bridge. Here he was able to wedge himself against one of the piers that supported it while he swivelled the rucksack containing the explosives round to the front and fumbled open the straps. In the darkness he had to work by touch but his fingers were numb and he was shivering so violently that he was afraid of dropping essential bits of equipment into the river. Groping in front of him, he made out the rough stonework of the pier and managed to strap the package of plastic explosive to it. Above his head he heard the footsteps of the sentry passing on his beat. It seemed to take for ever to fix the detonator. He could not use a time pencil to detonate the explosive since he did not know precisely when the convoy would pass. Instead, he must unroll a length of wire to attach to a manual detonator on the riverbank. He had to wait until the sentry had passed by again before he dared to begin the struggle back downstream to where his two companions were waiting. He had a sudden vision of himself being arrested and dragged off for interrogation, naked from the waist down. It was not a comforting thought.

Eventually he heard the man pass and eased himself away from the solid stones he had been clinging to. The current was with him this time but his feet and legs were so numb that he could not feel the stones under his feet and he was encumbered by having to unroll the detonator wire. The journey back seemed farther than the way out and he began to realise that if he did not get out of the water soon he was going to pass out. Grimly, he forced his unfeeling limbs forward, slipping and stumbling, until suddenly his legs went from under him and he floundered forward, half swimming. The rope jerked tight about his waist and a second later strong hands grasped him and hauled him up the bank. He lay only half conscious while Gianni chafed his legs with the scarf he had been wearing round his face and Sasha pulled off his wet jacket and replaced it with his own. It was some time before he was able to sit up and put his clothes back on and take a long swig of grappa from Gianni's flask Then they scrambled back towards the road, where the other two were waiting for them, concealed in a clump of bushes, unrolling the detonator wire as they went.

Richard attached the wires to the detonator and muttered, 'Right! We're ready for them.'

'Now what?' Gianni whispered.

'Now we wait,' Richard replied. He looked at his watch. 'It'll soon be dawn.'

After a while he realised that he was beginning to shiver again. He needed to move around and keep the blood circulating. He whispered to the others, 'I'm going for a slash. Need to get my legs moving again, anyway.'

He crept back into the forest a short distance and then, feeling he was far enough from the road, stopped in a small clearing and began some energetic exercises. When he could feel the blood tingling in his toes again he relieved himself and then began to make his way cautiously back. Suddenly a sound behind him made him swing round. His assailant was on him before he had time to see who it was and he reacted with the instincts that had been imbued in him during his training at Arisaig. The blow that had been aimed for the back of his head caught him on the shoulder and then they were grappling at close quarters. Richard quickly realised that his opponent, though fit and wiry, was not accustomed to unarmed combat. He pretended to relax, then, feeling the other man's grip slacken, he threw him off and kicked out, catching him as he intended in the groin.

The man doubled up with a single, gasped expletive. 'Shit!' The word, and the voice, were both unmistakably English.

Richard had pulled out his revolver and reversed it, raising his arm to club his attacker on the back of the neck. The word froze him in mid-action. With his free hand he reached into his pocket for a torch and shone the beam on to the man's face. He was wearing a woollen cap, pulled low over his brow, and a scarf that covered his nose and mouth, so that only his eyes were visible.

'Who the hell are you?' Richard demanded, and the other, his eyes on the gun, panted, 'Don't shoot! I'm British!'

Richard reached down and yanked the scarf away and pulled the cap off. Pale hair gleamed in the light of his torch. He caught his breath.

'Good God! How the hell did you get here?'

28

Merry looked at the pile of papers in his in-tray and sighed deeply. The last few weeks had flown by in a flurry of administrative decisions and solutions to problems, both large and petty. The company of Starlight Revue had been dispatched to tour just behind the front line and it had given Merry a few moments of malicious pleasure to think of the conditions Franklyn Bell was now having to endure. He was less happy at the thought of Rose having to put up with the same inconveniences, but he knew that she was well able to cope. The other companies and solo performers who had arrived at around the same time had also been sent off, some to tour hospitals and rest camps, others to the battle zones.

In between making these arrangements he had been busy choosing and rehearsing the various acts for the gala performance and putting together an orchestra. He had found a designer and negotiated for the loan of costumes from the Opera House. He had discovered, to his relief, that his sergeant, Johnny Pemberton, had been a stage manager in civilian life and could be left to deal with such technical matters as scenery construction and lighting design. Electricians, carpenters and painters had been forthcoming from the many trades and skills represented in the army units stationed in the area. Invitations had gone out to every senior officer and civic dignitary and he had heard on the grapevine that there was hot competition to be included on the guest list. Nevertheless, the main body of the theatre would be filled with the rank and file, soldiers back for a temporary respite from the front. Bit by bit the whole thing had come together. Now it was 18 December and there were only two days to go before the big night. This afternoon there would be a full technical runthrough; the next afternoon the dress rehearsal for all those in the first half. By the time that was finished their guest of honour would have landed and been received by Philip Slessor, and Merry had the job of helping to entertain him for the evening. By then, barring accidents, everything should be ready. Merry felt a quiver of pleasurable anticipation at the thought.

But this morning he had to get through his paperwork. With another sigh he reached for the first document and forced himself to concentrate. Almost immediately, he was distracted by a disturbance in the outer office. His secretary was a formidable young WAAF corporal called Jean, and he could hear her voice, raised in remonstrance.

'I'm sorry, but you can't go in there! Captain Merryweather is very busy!'

Merry rose and strode across to fling open the door. 'What's going on in here?'

For a split second he saw a frozen tableau. Jean was holding on to the sleeve of a ruffianly-looking character who was dressed in what might once have been battledress, though it was now so grimy and tattered that it was impossible to tell which army it had belonged to, let alone which service. On his head was a woollen cap, pulled low over the ears, and round his neck a grubby white scarf made of what was obviously parachute silk. Because Jean was pulling his sleeve he had turned away, so that Merry saw only the back of his head, but at the sound of Merry's voice he turned and pulled off the cap, his face breaking into a smile.

'Hello, Merry.'

Merry felt the floor tilt beneath his feet. He stepped back and put his hand on the door jamb to steady himself. From what seemed a long way off he heard himself say, 'You'd better come in.'

His visitor passed him into the inner office and Merry shut the door and leaned against it, afraid that if he moved away from its support he would fall down. A large lump, like a bubble of gas, seemed to be rising from his chest and threatening to choke him.

'You're supposed to be dead!' he said hoarsely.

Felix had stopped smiling. He came to where Merry stood and took him by the shoulders. 'I know. And I'm so sorry. *So sorry!* I would have moved heaven and earth to let you know I was still alive, but there was no way – no way.'

'But how . . . where . . .?' Merry mumbled.

Felix shook his head. 'I'll tell you later. It's too long, too complicated for now. Oh, Merry, don't look at me like that, *please*! I can't bear it.'

He pulled Merry away from the door and wrapped his arms round him. For a moment Merry hung in his grasp, feeling that his legs were about to give way. Then, slowly, he regained control over his muscles and lifted his arms to fold Felix to him.

'Tell me you're real!' he whispered. 'Tell me you're not a ghost, and I'm not going mad.'

'I'm real,' Felix answered softly. 'It's all right. Everything's going to be all right.'

Merry held him, his eyes closed, feeling at some half-conscious level how thin he was, nothing but bone and hard muscle, and how musty and unwashed he smelt; but beneath all that, how familiar, how exactly, wonderfully known.

A tap at the door made them break apart and Jean's voice called, 'Is everything all right, Captain Merryweather?'

Merry took a deep breath and forced himself to call back evenly, 'Yes, it's all right, Jean. Everything's fine.'

Felix said, 'She thinks I've come to assassinate you.'

'Probably,' Merry agreed. 'You look the part.'

They gazed at each other. Felix said, 'Captain, eh?'

Merry nodded. 'Mmm.' Then the bubble that had been rising in his throat burst and suddenly his cheeks were wet with tears.

Felix caught him in his arms again. 'Oh, don't! Don't! Poor old chap, you're shaking like a leaf. I ought to have let you know I was coming instead of barging in like this.'

'Oh no!' Merry gasped. 'That would have been much worse.' He drew back a little and looked at Felix again. 'But I don't understand. Where have you been all this time?'

Felix took a breath. 'OK. In a nutshell, I've been with the partisans up in the mountains.'

'But why?' Merry persisted. 'Whose idea was that?'

For a moment Felix looked puzzled. Then his eyes widened. 'You think it was deliberate – that I was sent there on purpose. Oh, Merry! You can't believe that! If I'd known, if I'd had the faintest inkling of what was going to happen, I would have found some way of letting you know. I mean, to hell with national security and the Official Secrets Act! I would never have let you suffer all this time. You must believe that.'

'Then what happened?' Merry asked. 'You were shot down in the sea. They couldn't even find the wreckage of your plane.'

'I'm not surprised. I was way off course when I baled out. I was picked up by an Italian destroyer and made a POW. They took me into port and put me on a train north, but I managed to escape. I hid with a local farmer and eventually joined up with a group of partisans. I was with them until yesterday. That's it, basically. I'll tell you all the details later.'

'You'll have to,' Merry said. 'I haven't taken half of it in.'

Felix looked round the room. 'You'd better sit down before you fall down,' he remarked, and led Merry to a chair. Then he crouched beside him and looked up into his face.

'I really have given you a terrible shock, haven't I? But you are pleased to see me, aren't you?'

'Pleased!' Merry gasped. 'Oh, Felix!' He leaned down and hugged him again.

Felix drew back and looked at him tenderly. 'How have you been, Merry? Have you been OK?'

'Yes, sort of. No. No, not really. I've managed, somehow.' He shook his head. 'Oh no. I've been so lonely, so bereft! I thought I'd died inside.'

'And I've missed you,' Felix answered, 'and worried about you. I've lost count of the nights I lay awake, wondering where you were and what you were doing. It was bad for me but at least I had the hope that one day I'd get back and find you. I can't bear to think what it's been like for you.'

Merry looked down at him and a shaft of pure joy broke through the numbness that had gripped him. 'It doesn't matter any more. You're here, that's all that matters.' He took him in properly for the first time. His face was streaked with grime and there was a couple of days' growth of stubble on his chin, in a curious patchwork effect produced by the skin grafts. His hair, normally so immaculately groomed, was matted and dull.

Something close to hysteria bubbled within Merry. 'Felix, you're filthy. What on earth have you been doing?'

Felix grinned. 'Not washing very much. The facilities for ablutions are not very good in the mountains.'

They laughed and kissed for the first time, and then Felix said, 'Can't we go somewhere else – somewhere a bit more private?'

'Of course,' Merry said. 'I've got a room in a hotel round the corner. We can go there.'

'Can you get away?'

Merry glanced at the pile of papers on his desk. 'Of course I can. To hell with that lot! Someone else can deal with it.'

He got up, shakily, and started across the room to fetch his cap from its hook. Then he stopped and turned back.

'I'm afraid if I take my eyes off you, you might disappear.'

Felix squeezed his arm. 'Don't worry. I'm not going anywhere.' He looked around the office. 'I must say, you've done very well. You seem to be the big cheese round here.'

'Not exactly,' Merry said. 'Just a small Gorgonzola.'

He led the way to the door. Jean looked up from her desk, wide eyed with curiosity. Merry choked back the hysterical laughter that still threatened to overwhelm him and said blithely, 'Jean, this disreputable-looking character is actually Flight Lieutenant – sorry, Squadron Leader – the Hon. Edward Mountjoy. He'll probably be in and out quite a bit from now on, so let him pass next time.'

The girl goggled. 'Very good, sir.'

'Now,' Merry went on, 'I'm taking the rest of the day off. If anyone wants me tell them I'm down with a bad attack of gippy tummy – or whatever the local term is – and refer them to Sergeant Pemberton.'

'But what about the technical rehearsal?' Jean began, but her boss was already on his way to the door.

'Tell Johnny to handle it.'

They reached the courtyard and got into Merry's jeep, but once there he sat motionless, gazing at Felix in disbelief, until Felix said gently, 'Let's go, shall we?'

As he started the engine questions were beginning to form in Merry's mind. 'How did you get here?'

'Ah,' said Felix. 'You can thank Richard for that.'

'Richard? Richard who?'

'Richard Stevens, of course.'

'*Our* Richard?'

'Our Richard, exactly.'

'What on earth has he got to do with all this?'

'You may well ask!' Felix remarked. '*Our* Richard, as you call him, is playing with some very rough people indeed. I warn you, never get into a fight with him. He bloody nearly killed me!'

'Richard did? Why? What the hell were you fighting about?'

'Oh, it was all a misunderstanding. He thought I was a Jerry and I thought he was. But it's thanks to him I'm here now. I'll tell you the full story later.'

They stopped outside the hotel and Merry led Felix inside. Hearing their voices, Signora Lucia bustled out of the back regions and threw up her hands in dismay at the sight of Felix. Merry introduced him and explained that he was a dear friend who had been presumed dead but had now, miraculously, reappeared. The signora threw her arms around Felix and kissed him on both cheeks, declaring that any friend of the *capitano*'s was welcome. Merry had improved his grasp of the language considerably in the past weeks and had been happy to show it off in front of Felix, until he heard the effortless and idiomatic Italian in which he replied to the signora's outburst. A sudden thought struck him.

'Felix, when did you last eat?'

Felix shrugged. 'Can't remember. Yesterday some time.'

'You must be ravenous! Signora Lucia, is there any chance you could find some lunch for the two of us?'

Of course she could, and it would be sent up to Merry's room – '*Subito! Subito!*'

He led Felix up the stairs. 'Your Italian is better than mine.'

'It should be. I've spoken nothing else for the last fifteen months.'

When the bedroom door had closed behind them they moved together and held each other in a long embrace, until Felix detached himself and said regretfully, 'I hadn't realised until I caught sight of myself in that mirror on the stairs how disgustingly filthy I am. Is there any chance of a bath, do you think?'

Merry smiled and moved across to open a door on the far side of the room.

'Your own bathroom!' Felix exclaimed. 'My word, you are doing well for yourself!'

'And there's even hot water,' Merry said, turning on the taps. 'Usually,' he added doubtfully, as the plumbing rattled and coughed. Luckily, after some more hissing and choking, hot water began issuing from the tap and Felix stripped off his dirty clothes and dropped them in a pile on the floor.

'Can I borrow your razor?'

'Of course. I'll put a new blade in for you.'

He found shaving soap and a sponge and an unused toothbrush and laid them out on the edge of the bath. Felix stepped in and lowered himself with a shudder of delight.

'Hot water! I can't remember the last time I had a hot bath in a proper bathroom.'

There was a tap on the outer door and Merry opened it to

the landlady's son bearing a tray on which were a bottle of Asti Spumante, in an ice bucket, two glasses and a dish of olives.

'From my mama,' the boy said. 'On the house – to celebrate. She say, lunch come soon.'

Merry thanked him, tipped him in the usual currency of NAAFI chocolate and took the tray into the bathroom.

Felix was shaving. 'Bubbly! Just the ticket!'

'From the signora, to celebrate your return to the living,' Merry said, thumbing off the cork.

He poured two glasses and knelt by the bath. Felix rinsed his face and took one.

'What shall we drink to?' Merry asked.

'To us, and the future. We're going to win this war, Merry, and we're both going to bloody well survive!'

'To us and the future,' Merry repeated, and had to swallow the lump in his throat before he could drink. Then Felix leaned over and kissed him and his mouth tasted of wine.

After a few minutes Felix took up the sponge and began to wash. A line of dirty scum appeared around the edge of the bath. Merry took off his tunic and rolled up his sleeves, then took the sponge from him and scrubbed his back, and after that found a bottle of shampoo and set to work on his hair.

He had just finished the job when there was another tap at the door. This time the boy was carrying a larger tray, on which were piled a loaf of bread, some sliced mortadella sausage, a goat's cheese and a dish of sliced tomatoes, gleaming with olive oil and sprinkled with basil, together with another bottle of wine – red, this time. For those days of shortage and rationing it was a feast. Merry tipped the boy again, and carried the tray to a table by the window.

'Food!' he called.

Felix came out of the bathroom, naked except for a towel round his waist, his hair still damp and tousled.

'Lunch is here,' Merry repeated.

Felix glanced at the tray. 'Later,' he said.

'I thought you were hungry.'

'So I am – ravenous,' Felix agreed, discarding the towel. 'But right now food is not at the top of my list of priorities.'

Merry looked at him and then moved swiftly to turn the key in the lock. At the same time Felix closed the shutters, so that the room was plunged into an amber dusk. On his way from the door Merry was unbuttoning his shirt and the rest of his clothes came off in the same dreamlike trance that had gripped him ever since Felix first appeared. Then they were both in bed and he gasped at the sweet shock of flesh on flesh. Usually, in their lovemaking, it was Merry who took the lead, but today he found himself gently pressed back upon the pillows while Felix leaned over him, his eyes bright and moist. He understood that on this occasion he was to be indulged and gave himself up to a pleasure that was sometimes so acute that it was akin to pain. It had been a long time, for both of them, and it was not in Merry's nature to receive without giving in return, so soon they both lay panting, temporarily exhausted. Merry, coming back to full consciousness, felt the weight of Felix's body sprawled across his own, felt his pounding heartbeat slowly steady, felt his still-damp hair against his cheek and raised a hand to caress it.

'I can't believe this is happening,' he whispered. 'It's too wonderful. It's like a miracle.'

Felix lifted his head and smiled down at him. 'At least you know now I'm not a ghost.'

'Yes, I think you've proved that to my satisfaction. Mind you, I might need further convincing, later.'

'I expect that could be arranged.'

Felix's stomach rumbled loudly and they both laughed.

'I'd forgotten!' Merry said. 'You haven't eaten. Stay there.'

He disentangled himself and slid out of bed. In a moment he was back, with the tray, and they sat up side by side to eat. Merry picked cautiously, making sure that Felix got the lion's share, and smiled as he wolfed down every scrap.

'Know what this reminds me of?' Felix said.

'What?'

'That first morning at Shoreham, when you brought me up breakfast in bed. Do you remember?'

'Of course I remember,' Merry said fondly. 'It was the happiest morning of my life – well, except perhaps today.' He paused and went on, 'Tell me the full story now. I still haven't really grasped what happened.'

'OK.' Felix mopped up the last of the olive oil with the remains of the bread, chewed, swallowed and sat back. 'Well, you know I was shot down.'

'Yes, but they couldn't find you. Your whole squadron looked for you, all that day and the next morning.'

'They couldn't find me,' Felix said, 'because I wasn't where I was supposed to be. It's the oldest story in the business. You break the rules, and you pay for it. I suppose I was tired, or just careless because I knew I was going on leave the next day. Anyway, we had a bit of a run-in with some Me 109s off Sicily . . .'

'Yes, I heard about that.'

'I'd hit one of them and he dived away, trailing glycol, and it was then I made my first big mistake. I followed him down, to make sure it wasn't just a ruse. They always tell you, never follow an enemy down. God knows, I've dinned that into the heads of enough young pilots to know better! But I wanted to make sure it was a genuine kill. And I was right, in a way. After a bit he levelled out and started to run for home. So I thought, no you don't, you crafty bugger, and I went in after him again. And that was where I forgot the second golden rule – "always watch out for the Hun in the sun". One of his mates must have been up above me and, of course, I'd lost my wingman long ago.' He stopped. 'Christ! I hope Len Harrison got back all right!'

'He did,' Merry assured him. 'He wrote me a very nice letter of condolence.'

'He did? Good old Len!'

'Go on.'

'Well, the first I knew was a blast of gunfire right along my starboard side. I wasn't touched, luckily, but the engine cut out. That was when I tried to radio base and discovered my radio was u/s. It was pretty clear that the kite was headed straight into the drink, so I opened the canopy, rolled her over and dropped out. 'Chute opened OK and my life-jacket inflated. Even the sea wasn't all that cold. It wouldn't have been a problem, except that chasing that 109 I'd gone a long way north of my original position and, of course, without a radio I couldn't pinpoint where I was for the air-sea rescue boys. I bobbed around for quite a long time and I could see our chaps looking for me, away to the south, but they never came near enough to spot me. It was starting to get late and I was beginning to feel pretty chilly. I actually thought I'd probably had it. Then I heard an engine and saw this destroyer heading towards me. It was Italian, of course, and I knew that meant I'd be taken prisoner, but by that time I didn't care. I waved and shouted and they lowered a boat and picked me up. I must say, they treated me pretty fairly – gave me dry clothes and a hot drink – but as soon as we got into port they handed me over to the military police and I spent the next few weeks in prison in some kind of castle, along with a lot of other POWs.'

He took a sip of wine, cleared his throat and went on.

'Eventually, they put us all in a train made up of cattle trucks, and sent us north. I don't know where we were headed – Germany, probably – but somewhere in the mountains north of Florence there was an almighty jolt and then the truck started swaying and finally collapsed on to its side. Apparently, some Garibaldini – that's the communist resistance – had decided to derail the train. I don't know if they knew what it was carrying. Anyway, you can imagine the chaos. I was lucky. I damaged my ankle in the crash but otherwise I was unhurt and the impact had sprung the doors open. It was the middle of the night and I saw that if I could get away before the guards recovered from the shock I might stand a chance, so I scrambled out and managed to cover about a hundred yards until I fell into a ditch. I couldn't walk very well, so I just stayed where I was and waited. It wasn't long before the guards had rounded up the rest of the prisoners and eventually another train arrived from the opposite direction and took them on board. By that time it was getting light so I waited until the train had gone and then headed for a farm I could see a short way off. That was when I realised that the damage to my ankle was a bit more than a sprain. Somehow, I managed to crawl and hop until I reached the farm and found a barn full of hay, so I thought I'd lie up there until nightfall and hope my ankle would get better. But I hadn't been there more than a few minutes before a man came in and called out in English, "British Tommy, I know you're there. Don't be afraid. I'm on your side." Well, there wasn't a lot of point in trying to pretend I wasn't there, so I came out. It turned out that the man was the farmer. His name was Alfredo and he and his wife, Maria, were rabidly anti-Fascist and prepared to do anything they could to assist the Allies. They took me in and got a doctor from the village to look at my ankle, which turned out to be broken, and they hid me all that winter.' He stopped and looked at Merry, his voice thickening. 'When all this is over, Merry, I must go back and thank them properly.'

'I'll come with you,' Merry promised. 'Go on, what happened next?'

'Of course, all I could think of was that I'd have been posted "missing, believed killed", and you wouldn't know otherwise. I was desperate to find some way of communicating with our side. I asked around to see if anyone knew if the partisans were in radio contact, but it seemed they were operating completely independently at that point. Then I thought of making my way to the coast and trying to steal a boat, but I don't know the first thing about boats so I'd probably have ended up either drowning or starving to death. The only other way was to try to walk to Switzerland, but of course there was no chance of that until my ankle healed. By then it was late in the year and Alfredo pointed out I wouldn't stand a chance of surviving in the mountains in winter, so that was that.' He looked at Merry. 'I did try, Merry – truly.'

Merry put his arm round him. 'I know you did.'

'Anyway,' Felix went on, 'by spring two other POWs had joined us. There was a Frenchman who'd been captured fighting for the Free French in North Africa and a Yankee pilot who'd been downed over the mountains. And we were hearing rumours about Allied successes in the desert. Everyone kept saying that we would invade Italy in a couple of months and when that happened Mussolini would fall and Italy would capitulate and then we could all go home. It didn't work out quite like that, but at the time it seemed best to stay where we were and wait for the army to come to us. Except that we were all getting a bit restless. We'd been helping out on the farm as much as possible to pay for our keep, but Alfredo really didn't need three of us, and we were beginning to feel pretty useless. So that's when we decided to join the partisans.' He paused and looked at Merry. 'I'm going on a bit, aren't I? I told you it was a long story.'

'That's all right,' Merry said. 'I want to hear. Go on.'

'Well, there isn't a lot more. We made our way up to a place where we'd been told there was a small group of partisans. Damn nearly got shot as spies, but we managed to convince them we were genuine and after that they made us feel very welcome. The leader was a man who called himself Bernardo, but I don't think that was his real name. I think he was the local landowner – an aristocrat of some sort – but I never found out for sure. We were based in his house, a beautiful villa on top of a hill. There were only about a dozen of us but we amused ourselves all summer holding up local police posts to steal weapons and then using them to ambush army patrols and so on. But when the Germans took over things changed. They sent a strong patrol of Brigata Nera, the Italians who had stayed loyal to the Nazis, to carry out a *rastrallamento*, an operation to round us up. Bernardo sent us all to hide out in a cave high up in the mountains but he stayed in the villa. I think he hoped to pass himself off as just another mildly eccentric farmer. The Brigata never found us, but when we came down again the villa had been burned to the ground. The villagers told us that the Fascists had rounded up all the men in the village and shot them. Bernardo had disappeared and we were never able to find out what had happened to him.' He paused again and drained his wineglass. '*Bastards!*'

'Quite,' Merry agreed.

'After that,' Felix went on, 'we felt we couldn't go on operating in the same area and expecting the locals to support us. We based ourselves in the cave and concentrated our efforts on the other side of the mountain, where there were fewer people. Then, about a week ago, we learned that the Germans were moving a lot of men and equipment along a road into the Garfagnana valley, which was about a day's march from where we were, so we thought we ought to go down and make a nuisance of ourselves. The plan was to ambush them as they crossed a bridge over the river. We crossed the pass and got down to the river by nightfall, and hid out in a disused watermill. Then, an hour or two before dawn, we started moving up to the road. We'd fanned out to cover a front of about a hundred yards and as I was creeping through the forest towards the road I suddenly saw this figure ahead of me, moving in the same direction. I knew he wasn't one of our lot. I decided I'd better strike first and ask questions later. I crept up behind him and was just going to dot him over the head with the butt of my revolver when he heard me. The next thing I knew I was fighting for my life. He was heavier than me and very strong, and believe me, what this chap didn't know about unarmed combat isn't worth knowing!'

'And this was *Richard*?' Merry exclaimed incredulously.

'*Our* Richard, as you call him. Nice, quiet, diffident, un-assuming Richard.'

'It's hard to believe. Did he hurt you?'

'He kicked me in the goolies and I collapsed, as one does. He drew a pistol and I thought my last moment had come, but I must have cried out in English because suddenly he shone a torch in my face.'

'It must have given him a terrible shock,' Merry commen-ted. 'I'd told him you were dead only a few weeks ago.'

'Gave us both a shock,' Felix agreed, with a grin. 'I couldn't believe my eyes when I realised who it was. But there wasn't time to chinwag at that point. I called my men in . . .'

'*Your* men?'

'I'd become a kind of de facto leader since Bernardo was taken. We had a quick conference and it turned out Richard was there on exactly the same mission, with a much larger and better-equipped group. What's more, he'd mined the bridge – though God knows how, the river was running really high. Anyway, we agreed to cooperate and a few minutes later the convoy arrived, as expected. I must say, it all went off like clockwork. Richard blew the bridge and the leading vehicles went into the ravine, so of course all the rest were stuck on the road on the far side, surrounded by Richard's men. With us firing from across the ravine into the head of the column they didn't stand a chance. It was like shooting fish in a barrel!'

'But the Germans must have fired back, surely?'

'Oh yes, once they got over the initial shock. But as soon as they looked like becoming a serious threat we did what all good guerrillas do and melted away into the forest. Richard sent his chaps off with a message to say he'd be along later and came back to the mill with me. You can imagine, it was quite a reunion, but even so we didn't have time to talk long. He told me he'd seen you in Naples and of course I immediately asked if there was any chance he could get a message out to let you know I was still alive. At which point he gave me a funny sort of smile and said, "I'll do better than that. I'll send you back to him, gift wrapped and with my compliments."'

'And so he did. God bless his soul!' Merry said fervently. 'But how?'

'You may well ask! He must have some pull in very high places, because he whistled up a plane to fly us both back. All he would say at the time was that I should meet him in the church at Sillico at midnight five nights from then. I was a bit worried about walking out on my chaps, but he pointed out that they'd be much better off joining up with the group he was working with, which was better equipped and was getting regular supply drops. So five days later we all trekked over to Sillico and Richard was there, as he promised, with a chap called Armando, the leader of this other group. Some of his men took charge of my lads and then Richard said, "Come on. Your carriage awaits," and off we went again farther down the valley until we came to a level stretch It was all very efficient. His people had fires ready to light to make a flare path and just as it started to get light we heard an aero engine. I couldn't believe my eyes when this extraordinary little plane appeared – enormously long wings and a tiny fuselage. The pilot told me later it was a German job, a Fiesler Storch. And the next thing I know we're both crammed into the rear cockpit and three men are hanging on to the tail while the pilot runs the engine up for take-off. I don't mind telling you, I thought we'd never make it, but we did. We must have missed the top of the next ridge by inches. Then it was up, up and away and within an hour or so we were touching down at the airfield just up the road.'

'What an incredible story!' Merry said. 'I can see why you didn't want to embark on it straight away.'

'Other things on my mind at that point,' Felix said with a smile.

'So what, exactly, is Richard up to?' Merry pursued. 'When I met him he said he was with something called Inter-Services Liaison but I thought at the time he didn't look as though he spent much time behind a desk.'

'The liaison bit is right,' Felix said. 'As far as I can make out he's acting as British liaison officer for this partisan group.

Dropped in by parachute to teach them how to blow up bridges and derail trains. All very cloak-and-dagger!'

'Who'd have thought it?' mused Merry. 'Mind you, with his fluent Italian I suppose something like this was always on the cards. Where is he now?'

Felix shrugged. 'Search me. I haven't seen him since we landed.'

'He didn't tell you where to contact him?'

'No. In fact he was very tight lipped about the whole operation.'

'So he's disappeared again?' Merry exclaimed with irritation. 'Who does he think he is, the Scarlet Pimpernel?'

'Something along those lines, I fancy,' agreed Felix, laughing.

A sudden thought struck Merry. 'Does anyone else know you're back, apart from me and Richard? I mean, have you reported in, officially?'

Felix shook his head. 'Not so far. When we landed Richard pointed out that if I went through the official channels I'd probably be handed over to intelligence, who would keep me for hours or even days and might even want to ship me straight back to England. Of course, that wasn't what I had in mind at all. So he told the pilot to taxi over to the far end of the field where I could hop out behind some huts. Frankly, I guess he wasn't supposed to have brought a passenger with him so he was quite glad to keep quiet about it. After a bit, an erk arrived with a truck and said, "I believe you want a lift into Naples, sir," so I hopped in the back of the truck and here I am.'

'Here you are,' Merry echoed, 'like a dream come true. Except I never let myself even dream of something like this.'

'Poor Merry,' Felix murmured, leaning against him. 'Has it really been hell?'

'Pretty much,' Merry agreed. 'For the first few months anyway. After that I suppose it was more like purgatory.' He laid his cheek against Felix's hair and wondered whether he would ever find the courage to confess to him what form his private hell had taken.

'How did you hear? That I was missing, I mean.'

'A telegram from Jumbo Gracie. I was at the house at Shoreham, waiting for you. It was my birthday and when the telegram arrived I thought it was from you, to tell me why you'd been held up.'

Felix raised his head and stared at Merry, horrified. 'It came on your birthday?'

'It made no difference what day it was.'

'What did you do?'

'I don't know. I've no recollection of the next few hours. Then I took the train to London. I had to talk to someone. Thank God, Rose was at the flat in Lambeth. She was back in town rehearsing a new show. She got me through the next twenty-four hours. Then I went back to work.'

'Best thing you could do, probably,' Felix said, relaxing against his shoulder again.

Merry was silent for a while, remembering. Then he said, 'I suppose we shall have to report your arrival to someone. I could take you to the hotel where the AOC has his head-quarters.'

Felix put the empty tray aside and slid down in the bed. 'I suppose so,' he agreed, smiling up at Merry. 'But not now. Later.'

Later – considerably later – they both slept, or at least Merry dozed, never quite losing consciousness of the warm presence beside him. When he opened his eyes finally Felix was fast asleep, lying on his side, the beautiful, unscarred left profile exposed to view. Merry remembered that, from his account of recent events, he had not slept for over twenty-four hours and let him sleep as long as he dared. He got up himself, washed and dressed and then collected Felix's filthy rags and took them downstairs for the hall porter to burn. Finally, late in the afternoon, he leaned over Felix and gently woke him. Felix yawned, stretched luxuriously and opened ineffably blue eyes, then reached up and embraced him.

It would have been very easy at that point to get back into bed. Instead, Merry said, 'I really think we ought to go and make your resurrection official. I'd hate you to be arrested as a deserter or something.'

'I suppose you're right.' Felix sat up and said suddenly, 'I've got nothing to wear. I can't put those dirty clothes on again.'

'You certainly can't,' Merry agreed. 'I've taken them to be burned. I don't think you were the only occupant, if you see what I mean.'

Felix grimaced. 'Sorry! Can I borrow something from you?'

Merry was taller than Felix but they were both slim. He found him some civilian trousers and a shirt and as he dressed said, 'You don't think Richard was right about them shipping you back to England, do you?'

'They'd better not try!' Felix said. 'Otherwise I will go AWOL.' Then, seeing Merry's face, he came and sat beside him, putting his arm round him. 'Look, there's bound to be someone I know at HQ and I can talk my way into or out of most things, you know that. Anyway, I reckon I'm due for some leave. After all, I was about to go on leave when I was shot down. I'll ask if I can take it here. I don't see how they can very well refuse. Is there any chance of you getting a few days off?'

'I don't know,' Merry murmured. 'Not for a day or two, anyway. I've got a big show at the Opera House the day after tomorrow. But after that, I can't see why not. Everything's organised for Christmas and I can't remember the last time I had leave . . . Anyway, it was nearly a year ago. I must be entitled to a holiday.'

'Great!' said Felix. 'We'll have a couple of weeks somewhere nice.'

Merry gazed at him with a kind of awe. 'You and me, on leave together?'

'Why not?'

'Why not?' Merry repeated. 'After all, I should be the last person on earth to deny that miracles do happen!'

In the jeep on the way to the headquarters of the Air Officer Commanding Felix said, 'Tell me about this big show you've got coming on.'

Merry told him and he whistled appreciatively. 'You really are moving in elevated circles, aren't you! Any chance of a ticket?'

Merry pursed his lips. 'I don't know. All the ordinary seats are sold out and I'm told that there has been blood on the carpet in the fight for invitations.' Then he caught Felix's eye and grinned. 'Of course you can come! I'll get you the best seat in the house, if I have to bump the GOC to fit you in. And, what's more, I shall require your assistance to entertain our guest of honour tomorrow night, and at the reception after the show.'

'Entertain him?' Felix said. '*Quis custodiet* . . . How do you entertain the supreme entertainer?'

Merry glanced at him and allowed himself a rare excursion into 'camp'. 'My dear, I don't think *you* would have the slightest difficulty.'

Felix chuckled. 'Then *I* shall require a chaperone.'

'Oh, you'll have one. Don't worry.'

As they entered the foyer of the hotel a man in the uniform of a squadron leader was coming down the stairs towards them. At the sight of Felix he stopped in his tracks and exclaimed, 'Ned Mountjoy, as I live and breathe!' He took the remaining steps in a couple of bounds and shook Felix enthusiastically by the hand. 'Ned, you old rascal, where the devil have you sprung from? We all thought you were dead.'

Laughing, Felix said, 'Hello, Peter. Sorry to disappoint you, but as the man said, the rumours of my death have been greatly exaggerated.' He turned to Merry. 'This is Peter Lloyd. We were together at North Weald during the Battle of Britain. Peter, this is Guy Merryweather, an old friend.'

Lloyd shook hands with Merry and then turned back to Felix. 'Where on earth have you been all this time? No, wait! The old man will want to hear all about this. No point in you saying it twice. Hang on a minute.'

He made a phone call and a few minutes later they were ushered into the office of the AOC himself. Here Felix repeated his story, though in somewhat less detail. When he had finished the AOC sat back in his chair and remarked, 'Well, I've heard some yarns in my time, but that one takes the biscuit! So, what do we do now? Does London know you're back?'

'No, sir.'

'We must signal them at once and get them to let your next of kin know. Are you married?'

'No, sir.'

'Your parents, then. They'll be overjoyed, I'm sure. Then I expect you'd like to get back home to see them.'

There was a brief pause. Then Felix said, 'Not really, sir. I haven't had much contact with my parents for several years. I've no particular reason for wanting to go home.' Then, as the two officers absorbed this information, he added, 'I would appreciate some leave, though. But I'd rather take it here, if that's OK.'

The AOC recovered himself. 'I don't see why not, but there aren't many recreational facilities here and the place is bursting at the seams. We could send you to Cairo for a couple of weeks. How would that suit?'

Felix glanced at Merry, who nodded imperceptibly. He had rather enjoyed his time in Cairo – the first time around, anyway.

'Yes, thank you, sir. Cairo would be fine.'

'Right. Well, I expect the intelligence boys will want to have a word with you first. You'd better hold yourself available for a day or two. Have you got anywhere to stay?'

Felix smiled. 'Yes, thank you, sir. Merry here has kindly said I can share with him for the time being.'

'Excellent! As I said, accommodation is at a premium. Good, well, that's settled, then. Time for a celebratory drink, I think. Oh!' He broke off and looked at Felix. 'We can't take you into the mess looking like that. Peter, any chance of finding something more suitable for him?'

'I'm sure we can manage something, sir,' Lloyd said.

Twenty minutes later Felix was back, wearing a uniform that more or less fitted and with his hair suitably trimmed, and they went down to the mess. Here they met three more officers who had known him at one time or another and Merry found himself relegated to the role of audience as Felix had to repeat his saga again. He didn't mind. It was enough to sit and watch as Felix held court, eyes bright, one elegant left hand illustrating his conversation with precise gestures, the right hand, functional but no longer beautiful, usually out of sight under the table. Listening to him, Merry thought, *You may not be able to conjure any more, my dear, but the old magic is still there and, by God, you can still hold an audience!*

It was a bibulous evening and Merry expended considerable energy resisting the invitations to 'drink up and have another'. Felix had no such inhibitions and by the time they left his steps were wayward and Merry had to take his arm to keep him on course as they walked to the jeep. Back at the hotel Felix put his arms round his neck and murmured, 'I'm too drunk to make love. Do you mind terribly?'

Merry held him close. 'No, of course I don't mind. You're here, that's all that matters.'

In the middle of the night Merry woke from a confused dream, in which Felix was performing the disappearing lady trick, except that it was Felix himself who entered the magic cabinet and disappeared. Still half asleep, he cried out, but instantly an arm came round him and Felix nuzzled the back of his neck and murmured, 'It's all right. I'm here. Everything's going to be all right.'

29

The following morning Merry dropped Felix off at Air Force HQ and then went back to his office and tried to concentrate on his job. Before settling at his desk, however, he went along to Philip Slessor's office and negotiated a fortnight's leave.

'Everything's in hand for the Christmas period,' he assured his superior. 'Starlight Revue is going into the Opera House immediately after the gala and every unit in the field will have a pantomime or a concert party or some other form of entertainment between Christmas and New Year.'

'Excellent,' said Slessor, beaming at him. 'And from what I hear the gala is going to be a great success. You thoroughly deserve a break. Where do you want to go?'

'I thought perhaps Cairo.'

'Yes, why not? I'll fix it.' Then, as Merry was about to leave, 'Has something happened, or are you just excited about tomorrow night?'

'Sorry?' Merry turned back, puzzled.

'Well, you're not quite your usual calm, sardonic self. In fact, you're lit up like a Christmas tree. If I didn't know you better I'd think you'd been at the bottle.'

Merry paused and then said quietly, 'Oh well, you know, sometimes life turns out not to be quite such a bitch as you thought.' He bestowed one of his rare smiles on his CO and went out.

The technical rehearsal had gone as well as could be expected, Pemberton informed him, which Merry took to mean that it had been virtually free of hitches. They started the dress rehearsal immediately after lunch and by early evening Merry was quietly triumphant. There was not one act that would have disgraced a professional stage and some were far better than many Merry had worked with before the war. Technically, Johnny Pemberton had done a brilliant job, adapting and making do with the scenery and lighting equipment that had survived the depredations of the Nazi withdrawal. There was only one problem, and that was the scenery change before the final chorus which was to bring the first half to a triumphant conclusion. They all wanted something really spectacular, but it was taking too long to get everything into position.

'We can't leave the audience sitting in the dark all that time,' Merry said, 'and if we put the lights up they'll all think it's the interval and start heading for the bar.'

'How about a musical interlude?' Pemberton suggested.

'Not time to rehearse anything extra with the orchestra,' Merry said, 'but I suppose I could do a piano medley – string a few popular songs together.'

This seemed the best solution, so they settled for that and the company was dismissed. Merry found Felix sitting quietly at the back of the stalls.

'Merry, it's going to be superb! You really have moved up a gear since Fairbourne. You're in your element here, it's obvious. I always knew you were wasted on us lot.'

'Oh no, not wasted!' Merry protested. 'Just think what good company I was in!'

As they changed, ready to go out and meet their celebrated guest, he asked Felix how the interrogation by intelligence had gone.

'Oh, pretty boring but no problems. Actually, they seemed more interested in what Richard was up to than in anything I could tell them about the partisans or the enemy. Confirms my suspicion that all these clandestine outfits spend more time snooping on each other than on the Germans.'

'Typical!' Merry agreed. 'Come on, we'll be late.'

Though neither of them would admit it they were both nervous about meeting the Great Man, but in the event it turned out to be a thoroughly enjoyable evening. Coward quickly put them at their ease and he was clearly enchanted by Felix, who, to Merry's secret amusement, seemed slightly abashed by his attentions. He enquired delicately about the origin of the scars on his face and, on being told about the crash and the subsequent work of Archie McIndoe, remarked with superb tact, 'He must be a very clever man. Not only is he obviously a great surgeon, but he has the eye of an artist to see that a slight irregularity is so much more interesting than bland symmetry – so much more piquant.'

Merry passed the next morning in a frantic effort to clear his desk before going on leave, with the subsidiary benefit of keeping his mind off the evening. After lunch he took their visiting star to the theatre and ran through the arrangements for his performance. Coward tried out the piano, had a word with Johnny Pemberton about the lighting and pronounced himself satisfied.

At 6.30 Merry drove Felix to the Opera House.

'Shall I come backstage with you?' Felix asked.

Merry shook his head. 'You go and have a drink in the bar. There's bound to be someone there you can natter to. It'll be a madhouse backstage and there's really nothing you can do. I'll see you afterwards.'

'OK.' Felix laid a hand on his arm. 'Stop worrying. It's going to be a huge success.'

'I hope so!'

'I know so! Break a leg, old chap!'

Merry smiled at the familiar theatrical formula and got out of the jeep. 'Thanks. See you at the reception.'

Once through the stage door he was immediately swept into the atmosphere of electric excitement. He decided he liked working with amateurs. Not that these people could be called amateurs in the pejorative sense. Most of them could hold their own on the professional stage and many would make their careers there after the war. But they had not had time to become blasé or to develop star temperaments or the petty rivalries that beset the professional theatre. Some of them were nervous, that was understandable, and he spent some time murmuring words of reassurance and repeating small pieces of advice, but by and large he was greeted everywhere with broad grins and jokes.

Just before the five-minute call he was standing in the orchestra room under the stage, waiting for his cue and listening to the musicians tuning up and the hum of a large, excited audience, when a corporal who was doubling as call boy came hurrying down the stairs.

'Excuse me, sir, but there's a Major Stevens up there. He asked me to give you this note urgently.'

Merry unfolded the paper and read, *'Sorry to leave this until the last minute, maestro, but if you can still fit me in I'm here. I haven't got my dots, but I'm sure you can play "Non piu andrai" and "White Christmas" from memory. Is there still room for me on the bill? Richard.'*

Merry pulled out a pencil, thought for a moment and then scribbled on the back of the note: *'You're on at number nine, the last item before the final chorus in the first half.*' Then he turned to the corporal. 'Give this to Major Stevens and then see Sergeant Pemberton and the MC and tell them there will be an extra item at number nine. The MC can liaise with the major about how to announce him. Got that?'

As the corporal departed Merry sensed the house lights dimming and the audience grew quiet. Then his cue light came on. He took a deep breath, squared his shoulders and went out. There was the usual rather perfunctory applause that greets the appearance of the conductor but Merry hardly heard it. He stepped on to the podium, glanced at the orchestra to check that everyone was ready and then stood for a second, savouring this magical moment when all was anticipation. Then he raised his baton and launched the musicians into the opening chorus.

The performance exceeded even his expectations. The comedians kept the house convulsed with laughter and never quite overstepped the mark, though some of them came close. The speciality acts, the conjurors and jugglers, accomplished their manoeuvres without mishap and were well received. The music was superb and the chorus performed like real troupers and was greeted with stamps and whistles of approval – especially the 'ladies'. Merry had quickly abandoned the idea of trying to establish a chorus line from among the willing but untrained girls in the women's services. They would be pretty and winsome, but would never cast off their inhibitions sufficiently to make themselves the glamorous sex objects Merry knew the audience of 'rude, licentious soldiery' would be crying out for. By contrast, the dozen good-looking young men he had recruited had no qualms about fluttering their false eyelashes and wiggling their befeathered bottoms, to the hysterical delight of their comrades in the stalls.

When the moment arrived for item number nine on the programme Merry held his breath. It would not have surprised him, even at this juncture, if Richard had failed to appear. However, the MC walked on to the stage and announced that there would be a surprise addition to the bill.

'At great expense,' he declared, 'and at considerable personal inconvenience to himself, the management has acquired the services of that wonderful baritone, Major Richard Stevens!'

Richard walked into the spotlight to applause that was polite but not particularly enthusiastic. His name was not familiar and he had no friends in the audience, apart from one, who leaned forward in his seat in the front row of the dress circle in delighted astonishment. He acknowledged the applause with a smile and announced, 'Ladies and gentlemen, *signori e signore*, I should like to sing for you an aria from Mozart's opera *The Marriage of Figaro*. Figaro is addressing a young man called Cherubino. Cherubino has just discovered sex and is making a nuisance of himself by falling in love with every woman in sight, but he has overstepped the mark by trying to seduce his employer's wife, the beautiful countess. Not surprisingly, the count decides he needs to be taught a lesson and so he tells him that he is sending him off to join the army. Figaro, who is glad to be rid of the little pest too, is enjoying himself by giving him an outline of the delights that await him as a serving soldier.'

There was an appreciative chuckle from the audience and Richard looked down into the orchestra pit, where Merry had moved from the podium to the piano. For a moment their eyes met and they were back in the little theatre at the end of the pier, with the twenty-two-year-old Richard making his first professional appearance and Merry grinning up encouragingly from the pit. Then Richard nodded and Merry played the first chords of '*Non piu andrai*'.

Richard sang the first stanza in English, so that the audience in the main body of the stalls could appreciate its relevance.

> *Say goodbye now to pastime and play, lad,*
> *Say goodbye to your airs and your graces.*
> *Here's an end to the life that was gay, lad,*
> *Here's an end to your games with the girls!*

Then he reverted to Italian and at the end of the aria it was the Italian section of the audience which cheered him to the echo with shouts of '*Bravo! Bravo!*'

Richard took his bow, smiling, and said, 'And now I'd like to finish with something you all know, and which is very appropriate to this time of year – though perhaps not to this particular place.'

At the first notes of 'White Christmas' there was a cheer from the English contingent. This had been the hit song of the previous year and had been played over and over again on the wireless as Christmas approached. Richard reverted to his new, cabaret style of singing and gave it a treatment of which Bing Crosby himself would have been proud, and by the end the audience were singing along with him. At the end the soldiers, determined not to be outdone by their Italian one-time enemies now turned allies, stamped and whistled and yelled for an encore. Richard caught Merry's eye again but in answer to his raised eyebrow he shook his head, bowed once more and walked off into the wings.

It was time for Merry's piano medley. He had given it a good deal of thought over the last couple of days and settled to play with deep feeling overlaid with a secret, tongue-in-cheek amusement. Only Felix, sitting in the circle among more gold braid than he had ever set eyes on in one place, understood the significance of the old Marie Lloyd musical hall song that opened the sequence.

> *The boy I love is up in the gallery,*
> *The boy I love is smiling down at me . . .*

But Felix's smile was replaced by a different expression when he recognised the second melody. It was the one Merry had fingered out from memory on the piano Felix had bought him, one evening two summers earlier, just before he left for North Africa. The song from Ivor Novello's *The Dancing Years* beginning 'My dearest dear'.

From there Merry segued into 'Smoke Gets in Your Eyes' and, the first time he had played it since the previous New Year's Eve, 'These Foolish Things'. Then, in what might be taken as a tribute to the artiste who was going to dominate the second half of the programme, 'I'll See You Again' and 'Somewhere I'll Find You'.

He finished with Vera Lynn's signature tune 'We'll Meet Again', which had the whole audience singing with him. It was a potent combination guaranteed to leave hardly a dry eye in the house, but for one man the effect was almost overwhelming. Up in the circle Felix was wrestling with his emotions and was vastly relieved when the curtain went up on the raucous final chorus and he was able to take out a handkerchief and blow his nose without attracting too much attention from his illustrious neighbours.

In the bar during the interval he sipped his drink and eavesdropped on the conversations around him. The comments were universally complimentary. 'Wonderful show! Really professional!' said a major general. 'Must say, you army people have come up trumps tonight,' agreed a group captain. 'Excellent public relations, Slessor. Our Italian friends are really enjoying it,' said the GOC. 'Congratulations!'

After all that, the second half might have been an anticlimax but Coward was not called 'The Master' for nothing. Watching the faces of the men on either side of him, Felix saw them relax into laughter at 'Mad Dogs and Englishmen'. Below him in the stalls were three rows of wounded soldiers. He had noticed one young lad in particular, who had obviously lost both hands. Unable to applaud, he stamped his feet and whistled his appreciation. When the show ended with an invitation to the audience to join in 'London Pride' the theatre was filled with full-throated song.

As soon as he could Felix pushed his way through the crowd to the pass door that led to the stage. The cast was there already, bubbling with excitement and raucous with the relief of tension, and Merry was standing in the middle of them, next to Coward. Trestle tables had been set up and a buffet was being laid out on them. Felix took possession of three glasses of wine and elbowed his way to where Merry was standing.

'Wonderful show, Merry! Many congratulations! The whole thing was absolutely superb. And you, sir,' he said to Coward, 'what a brilliant performance! You had them all absolutely enthralled.'

'Nice of you to say so,' Coward drawled in response. 'I must admit, after such a brilliant first half I really wondered if anyone would want to listen to me. Follow that, I said to myself, if you can!'

'And you did – effortlessly,' Merry said. 'It was a privilege to watch you.'

At that moment the great man was distracted by an autograph hunter at his elbow and Felix took the opportunity to whisper to Merry, 'You rat! That medley – you practically had me blubbing on the GOC's shoulder!'

Merry's lips twitched. 'Strange how potent cheap music is,' he said, quoting a line from Coward's play *Private Lives*.

Coward turned back from signing a programme and lifted an eyebrow. 'I seem to have heard that somewhere before.'

'Not that I regard that as cheap music,' Merry added diplomatically, 'any more than you do, I suspect.'

'Speaking of music that is definitely not cheap,' Coward pursued, 'what's happened to that remarkable young man with the beautiful baritone voice?'

'Richard!' Felix put in. 'Yes, where is he, Merry?'

'I'm afraid I don't know,' Merry said, with a tinge of exasperation. 'Apparently he left immediately after finishing his number.'

'You mean to say he's disappeared again?'

'Looks like it.'

'Oh, really!' Felix exclaimed. 'This is taking all that Scarlet Pimpernel stuff a bit too far!'

Several thousand feet above the Mediterranean, on his way to Algiers to give his superiors a first-hand briefing on the situation behind enemy lines, Richard settled back in his seat with a sigh of regret. He wished fervently that he had been able to stay on and talk to Merry after the show, and to make sure that Felix had found his way to him. It would have been good to see the two of them together again. But already, when he drove on to the airfield, the Dakota had been warming up for take-off. A few minutes more and he would have missed the flight altogether. Until the very last minute he had thought that it would be impossible to make the performance at all. Then his flight had been delayed by a couple of hours and he had managed to wangle the loan of a jeep. It had been a silly thing to do, really, a sudden impetuous decision that could have landed him in a lot of trouble. But he was glad he had done it, just the same.

He remembered the sensation of standing on the stage. It had felt good. Good to be singing in public again, in a real theatre. Good to hear the applause. Good, especially, to look down and see Merry in the pit. For a moment it had felt like being back with the Follies again. He had almost expected to find Felix waiting in the wings, in his top hat and scarlet-lined cape, and to see Rose clattering up from the dressing rooms in her tap shoes, her face vivid with make-up, her violet eyes shining in the stage lights. Oh, Rose, *Rose!*

He wondered how she was getting on, back there in Dorset with her farmer husband. Probably there were children by now – one, at least. He thought of Priscilla. Would they ever have children? Somehow he found it hard to imagine Priscilla as a mother. Anyway, if Victor was to be believed, Priscilla was shacked up with her Hungarian pianist and presumably no longer interested in her husband. It occurred to him that there would be mail waiting for him when he got back to Algiers.

Rose braced herself against the jolting of the bus on the potholed roads and wished her head did not ache so badly. For a month they had bounced and swayed their way from one end of the front line to the other and it had rained almost the whole time. They had played in marquees erected in the middle of fields reduced to a quagmire by tank tracks, to men whose faces were still streaked with the dirt of battle. They had played in unheated village schools and a town hall that had suffered damage from shelling, where the rainwater came through a hole in the roof and pooled in the centre of the stage. They had played in the temporary hospitals and clearing stations, where many of the men were apparently unwounded but were suffering from the condition that they termed 'bomb happy'. It was here that a boy of eighteen had wept in her arms and told her how much he missed his mother.

Now, at last, they were on their way back to Naples. They should have been there hours ago, but a temporary bridge had collapsed under the weight of tanks and troop carriers crossing it and they had had to take a roundabout route. Her feet were completely numb, her head throbbed with every bump in the road and she had run out of aspirin. Still, with any luck, when they got back there would be the chance of a hot bath and a proper bed. Then, tomorrow, they moved into the Opera House for the Christmas season and perhaps, finally, Frank would stop beefing about performing in conditions 'no self-respecting artiste should be expected to endure'.

She wondered how Merry's gala performance had gone. If they had arrived on schedule they would have been in time to see it. Poor Merry! Her heart still bled for him, but at least he seemed to be getting over the loss of Felix at last. She remembered him ashen faced and shaking the previous January and then pitifully thin but bronzed and at least able to smile in Tunis in the summer. A month ago, when they arrived in Naples, he had seemed almost his old self, except for a new air of authority and self-confidence. Yes, she decided, Merry would be all right. His talent had been appreciated and he was fully occupied. Work would be his saviour, as it had been hers.

The following morning they moved into the Opera House. 'Get in' days were always chaotic and Rose knew that she would not be able to get her girls onstage until the stage crew had finished putting up the scenery. She was sitting in the stalls when a familiar voice said, 'Ah, there you are!'

Looking round she saw Merry standing in the aisle. He beckoned and she slid out of her seat to join him.

'Merry, I'm so sorry I missed your show! We got held up. Everyone I've met has said it was absolutely wonderful.'

'It did go well,' he agreed. 'How are you?'

'Oh, tired. Thankful to be back in something like civilisation. It's terrible up there at the front. And you? How are you?'

'Never better!' Something about his tone and the light in his eyes set her wondering. Was it possible that he had met someone else? Or was it just the previous night's triumph?

Merry put his hand on her arm. 'Can you get away for a while? I've got a surprise for you.'

'A surprise? Yes, there's nothing for me to do here. Where is this surprise?'

'Upstairs in the circle bar. Come on.'

Rose followed him up to the bar, more and more convinced that he was about to introduce her to a new lover. She knew she ought to be glad for him but in spite of herself she was uneasy. She found it hard to imagine anyone worthy of taking Felix's place and wondered how she should behave.

At the door Merry turned to her. 'Ready?'

'Yes.'

He touched her arm. 'It's a really big surprise, so be prepared.'

Then he swung the door open and stood back. Rose saw a figure in air force blue. Then he turned and she thought her heart had stopped. For a crazy moment she thought Merry had found someone to dress up as Felix, for a joke. Then he came to her and took both her hands.

'Hello, Rose. It's lovely to see you again. Sorry if I'm a bit of a shock. I told Merry he ought to prepare you.'

'Felix?' she whispered. 'Is it really you? We all thought you were dead.'

After that there was a confusion of questions and answers, which carried them out of the bar and into a local restaurant, where Merry ordered lunch. She sat enthralled by Felix's story until the point came when he had to explain who had sent him back to Naples.

Rose moistened dry lips. 'Richard? You've seen Richard?'

'Yes. He seems to be working with some kind of clandestine operation, behind enemy lines.'

'Oh God! How was he?'

'Thriving. He's a major now.'

'Did he . . . did he ask about me at all?'

Felix took her hand. 'No, I'm afraid not. But we really didn't talk about our personal lives at all. There wasn't time.'

'I wonder how Priscilla . . . how his wife is.'

'He didn't mention her, either.'

'Where is he now?'

Merry and Felix exchanged glances. Merry said, 'We don't know. As a matter of fact, he did a surprise item in my show last night – just turned up out of the blue at the last moment. I didn't even get a chance to speak to him. And by the time the curtain came down he'd disappeared again.'

Rose gazed into his eyes. 'Richard was here, last night? And if we hadn't got held up on the way back I'd have seen him.'

Merry nodded and for a moment they were all silent. Then Rose said, 'Oh well. It's probably better that way. Water under the bridge, and all that.'

* * *

Merry and Felix celebrated New Year in Shepeard's Bar in Cairo, after ten days in which they had basked in the luxury of sunshine and good food and the absence of war, and above all in each other's company. Towards midnight, the noise in the bar grew so tumultuous and the room so hot that they retired to the veranda. Felix took out his cigarette case and offered it to Merry, who took one cigarette, put it between his lips and lit it, drew a long inward breath and then handed it back.

'You've become very abstemious in your old age,' Felix commented, drawing on the cigarette in his turn. 'I understand the need to give up smoking, in your case, but you seem to have cut down on the booze as well. You used to be able to knock it back with the best of us.'

'Ah well – old age, as you said,' Merry murmured. Then he added with sudden vehemence, 'God, I hate New Year's Eve!'

'Why?' Felix said, looking at him in some alarm. 'You've enjoyed this evening, haven't you?'

Merry smiled at him in the reflected light from the windows behind them. 'I didn't mean tonight. Tonight is wonderful. I was thinking of previous years.'

'Ah! You're remembering 1940, when Richard turned up at the Willises' and Matthew announced that Rose was engaged to him. Yes, that was awful.'

'And then there was '41, and that ghastly business with Tom Dyson,' Merry said slowly. 'And that was here – or very near here, anyway. Perhaps it was a mistake to come to Cairo after all.'

Felix said, 'Look, I've told you, you don't have to fret over that. It doesn't bother me that you had a one-night stand two years ago.'

'I wasn't thinking of that so much,' Merry replied. 'I was thinking of poor Tom. I really behaved very badly to him, you know, and a few weeks later he was dead.'

'He forced himself on you, remember,' Felix pointed out, 'not the other way about. You can't go on dwelling on it and blaming yourself.'

'I don't, normally. It's just tonight has brought it all back.'

They were silent for a moment and then Felix said, with his usual intuitive understanding, 'And last year? What happened last New Year's Eve? I know it wasn't another Tom Dyson, because you've already told me there hasn't been anyone else. So what was it?'

Merry reached for the cigarette and took another long drag. He had known deep down that sooner or later he would have to tell Felix what had happened the previous winter.

'It goes back before that,' he began. 'You remember I told you that twenty-four hours after I got the telegram saying you were missing I went back to work? Well, it wasn't quite as straightforward as that. I decided – well, I felt – that if you were dead I didn't want to go on living . . .'

They were standing side by side, leaning on the rail of the veranda. Felix moved closer and slid his arm through Merry's. 'Silly clot!' he murmured.

'I applied to be returned to my regiment,' Merry went on, 'for active duty. I thought I might as well get killed in a good cause. Of course, George didn't want to let me go but I persuaded him in the end to fix me up with a medical board. You won't believe this. I hadn't had an asthma attack for a year, and I haven't had one since, but the night before my board I had a really bad one.'

'Obviously your body was making sense, even if your head wasn't,' Felix commented.

'You can imagine the result. So I went back to George and he sent me off touring the country with a concert party.' Merry paused and drew a long breath and Felix silently passed him the cigarette. 'I suppose I made up my mind at some level that if I couldn't get myself killed fighting I might as well do it another way. It started with a couple of whiskies to help me sleep. Then it was a couple more to get me through the show each evening. Well, you know how it goes. I won't bore you with the details. Before long I was getting through a bottle a day, and even that wasn't enough.' Felix squeezed his arm gently. 'The funny thing is, I always managed to get through the performance somehow – until last New Year's Eve. I'd been drinking pretty steadily all day, but even so I think I'd have got through the show – if it hadn't been for that bloody idiot of a tenor choosing to sing "These Foolish Things". You know?' He half sang, softly, ' "A tinkling piano in the next apartment, The stumbling words that told you what my heart meant".'

Felix still said nothing but Merry heard him make a sound in his throat that might have been a stifled sob and the pressure on his arm had become vice-like. He went on, in a low voice, 'I broke down, Felix. Just gave way completely – sobbed like a child. They had to carry me out of the hall.'

He glanced sideways at Felix but his head was turned away and the hand on Merry's arm was trembling. He realised that it was up to him to finish the story.

'George wanted to send me to see a psychiatrist but I refused. After all, what could I possibly have said to an army trick cyclist about the reason for my drinking? In the end he gave me three weeks' leave and an ultimatum – dry out and come back ready for work, or it's an army psychiatric hospital.'

Felix had got himself under control now, though his voice was husky. 'What did you do?'

'I went to stay with the Willises.'

'Thank God for the Willises!'

'Yes, they were wonderful to me. But it was Rose who really saved me, you know.'

'Rose? How?'

'She was in town again, rehearsing another show. She took a couple of weeks off and came down to Dorset and we just walked and talked, and talked. They call psychiatry the talking cure, don't they? Well, Rose did me more good than any psychiatrist could have done.'

'What did you talk about?'

'Oh, you and me, her and Richard.' He paused. 'You know, she even offered to marry me.'

'Marry! You and Rose?'

Merry looked at him, a faint smile touching his lips. 'Bizarre, isn't it? Apparently, the way she saw it was that now Richard's married and she's burnt her boats with Matthew there's no likelihood of her finding anyone else. She understood, of course, that it could never be a proper marriage but she reckoned we could work together and we'd be a comfort to each other in our old age.'

'You turned her down, I hope.'

'I have to admit,' Merry's voice had taken on a teasing edge, 'the idea did have its attractions – coming home in the evening to find my dinner on the table and my slippers warming by the fire, you know?' Then, seriously again, 'Of course I turned her down. I mean, even if I could have made it work for me, which I couldn't have done for any length of time, it wouldn't have been fair on her. She's still young and pretty. She could meet a man tomorrow and fall in love and have a proper marriage and children. I pointed that out to her. But it was a turning point for me.'

'How so?'

'Well, for one thing she'd been dinning into me that I was letting you down badly. That the worst service I could do your memory was to let your death ruin my life. And then, I suppose, the knowledge that at least one very sweet person loved me enough to be prepared to spend the rest of her life with me . . . Anyway, I went back to London, told George I was cured and asked him to send me back out here – just me, on my own with a piano. I didn't want to be responsible for anyone else. So he did, thank God, and I went out into the desert, in time-honoured fashion, to seek my salvation.'

'And found it.'

'Up to a point.'

There was a silence. Then Felix said, 'Remind me to buy Rose a very nice present, will you?'

'I'll go halves with you,' Merry agreed.

'It's curious, isn't it?' Felix went on after a moment. 'Richard and Rose. She saved you for me, and he rescued me and sent me back to you. I wish we could do the same for them.'

Behind them there was a sudden eruption of cheers as midnight struck and then the sound of voices singing 'Auld Lang Syne'. Felix looked at Merry. 'Welcome to 1944, my dear. Let's hope it's better than '43.'

'It can't help being,' Merry said. 'You're here.'

'Who knows,' Felix added, 'next New Year we could be celebrating at home, in peace, and all this idiocy might be over.'

'Who knows?' Merry echoed. He looked past Felix to the windows of the bar. 'Do you want to go in and join the celebrations?'

Felix shook his head. 'Not really.' He straightened up, drawing Merry with him. 'Come on. Let's go home to bed.'

*   *   *

Richard celebrated New Year at the Club des Pins at Cap Matifou, outside Algiers. Next morning, he was nursing a hangover over a cup of black coffee when an orderly came over to him.

'Post for you, sir.'

Richard opened the large envelope in which his superiors had stored up the letters that had arrived for him while he was in Italy. There were several from his mother, two or three from his aunt, one from Victor and a few, surprisingly few, from Priscilla. He slit the envelope on the most recent.

Dear Richard,

This is an awful letter to have to write in the middle of a war. As usual, I have no idea where you are or what you are doing but I hope it will get to you. I think it's best for us both to know exactly where we stand. I want a divorce.

I hope that isn't too much of a shock to you. I think we both realise that our marriage has not turned out the way we expected it to. It's sad, because we didn't rush into it the way so many people are doing these days and we seemed to have so much in common and had such wonderful plans for the future. Perhaps if you had stayed in England and taken that job with the Council for the Encouragement of Music and the Arts, as I begged you to do, things would have been different. I thought we had the same priorities and values but it seems other things are more important to you. As it is, I have met someone else who, I now realise, is much closer in his attitudes and ambitions to me and with whom I want to spend the rest of my life.

'That slimy little Hungarian! I wish her joy of him!' Richard muttered as he turned the page.

His name is Jean-Claude and he is over here attached to General de Gaulle's staff, but in civilian life he is a film director. He has made me realise that rebuilding the arts in Britain after the war is simply not the top priority. What is going to be really important is creating a new basis for the arts in Europe, in the occupied countries and even in Germany itself once the Nazis have been overthrown. He wants me to marry him and go to live with him in Paris as soon as it is liberated.

I need to be free to marry as soon as possible, as Jean-Claude is convinced the war cannot last much longer, but he doesn't want to be cited as co-respondent because he feels it will cause trouble for him with de Gaulle. I've told him I am sure you will do the decent thing and let me divorce you. I'm sure you can persuade your superiors to let you come home on leave on compassionate grounds. After all, you've been away for simply ages. If not, my solicitor says a signed affidavit from a hotel manager or something similar would probably do.

Please write immediately and let me know what you intend to do.

Yours,
Priscilla

A s usual, the main characters in this book are fictional but many of the peripheral ones are real and many of the events actually happened. The 'O'Leary line' really existed and the exploits described here are a matter of historical record. I have merely taken the liberty of inserting the character of Richard into the action. 'Pat O'Leary' was the *nom de guerre* of Albert-Marie Guérisse, a Belgian doctor who offered his services to the British after the fall of his own country. He was eventually arrested by the Germans and sent to Dachau where he was tortured but survived until the camp was liberated. He received the George Cross and the DSO for his services and died in 1989. Ian Garrow was a captain in the Seaforth Highlanders who chose to stay in France to assist the escape line. He was arrested but later escaped and survived. Dr and Mrs Rodocanachi were Greeks who had taken French nationality. They sheltered many escaping servicemen in their flat in Marseilles, at great risk to themselves. Dr Rodocanachi was arrested and died in Buchenwald in February 1944. Jimmy Langley and Airey Neave were the officers in charge of MI9, whose brief it was to help in the rescue of allied servicemen. Neave, who was a lawyer by profession, went on to be one of the prosecutors at the Nuremberg trials. He entered Parliament and became Secretary of State for Northern Ireland. He died when his car was blown up by the INLA outside the Houses of Parliament in 1979. Douglas Dodds-Parker was in charge of SOE operations in North Africa. Captain George Black commanded the army's entertainments unit, Stars in Battledress, and Basil Dean was in charge of ENSA. The variety acts mentioned in Chapter 20 were all well-known performers in their day and Noël Coward really was in Naples at Christmas 1943.

Those wishing to learn more may like to consult the following:

Stars in Battledress – Pertwee, Bill. Charnwood Library 1993

The Greasepaint War – Hughes, John Craven. New English Library 1976

Showbiz Goes to War – Taylor, Eric. Robert Hale 1992

Safe Houses Are Dangerous – Long, Helen. William Kimber & Co 1985

Escape and Evasion – Dear, Ian. Cassell 2000

Saturday at MI9 – Neave, Airey. Hodder and Stoughton 1969

Six Faces of Courage – Foot, MRD. Eyre Methuen 1978

From Cloak to Dagger – Macintosh, Charles. William Kimber & Co 1982